William Hayley

The Life of John Milton

With Conjectures on the Origin of Paradise Lost

William Hayley

The Life of John Milton
With Conjectures on the Origin of Paradise Lost

ISBN/EAN: 9783337055639

Printed in Europe, USA, Canada, Australia, Japan

Cover: Foto ©Raphael Reischuk / pixelio.de

More available books at **www.hansebooks.com**

THE LIFE

OF

JOHN MILTON,

WITH CONJECTURES ON THE ORIGIN

OF

PARADISE LOST.

BY

WILLIAM HAYLEY, Esq.

BASIL: Printed and sold by JAMES DECKER.

STRASBURGH: Sold by F. G. LEVRAULT.

1799.

TO

THE ABBÉ DELILLE

THE VIRGIL OF FRANCE

THIS NEW EDITION

OF THE LIFE

OF THE BRITISH HOMER

IS INSCRIBED

BY THE EDITORS

P. J. OTTO, J. DECKER, F. G. LEVRAULT.

DEDICATION

TO THE

Rev. *JOSEPH WARTON*, D. D. &c.

MY PLEASANT AND RESPECTABLE FRIEND!

IN prefixing your name to this volume, I feel
and confeſs the double influence of an affectionate
and of an ambitious defire to honor you and
myfelf. Our loſt and lamented Friend GIBBON
has told us, I think very truly, in dedicating a
juvenile work to his Father, that there are but
two kinds of Dedications, which can do honor
either to the Patron or the Author—the firſt arifing from literary eſteem, the fecond from perfonal affection. If either of thefe two characteriſtics
may be fufficient to give propriety to a Dedication,
I have little to apprehend for the prefent, which
has certainly the advantage of uniting the two.

The kind and friendly manner in which you
commended the firſt edition of this Life might

I

alone have induced me to infcribe a more ample copy of it to that literary veteran, whofe applaufe is fo juftly dear to me. I have additional inducements in recollecting your animated and enlightened regard for the glory of M I L T O N.   It is pleafing to addrefs a fympathetic friend on a fubject that interefts the fancy and the heart. I remember, with peculiar gratification, the liberality and franknefs, with which you lamented to me the extreme feverity of the late Mr. Warton, in defcribing the controverfial writings of Milton. I honor the rare integrity of your mind, my candid friend, which took the part of injured genius and probity againft the prejudices of a brother, eminent as a fcholar, and entitled alfo, in many points of view, to your love and admiration.   I fympathize with you moft cordially in regretting the feverity to which I allude, fo little to be expected from the general temper of the critic, and from that affectionate fpirit, with which he had vindicated the poetry of Milton from the mifreprefentations of cold and callous aufterity. But Mr. Warton had fallen into a miftake, which has betrayed other well-difpofed minds into an unreafonable abhorrence of Milton's profe; I mean the miftake of regarding it as having a tendency to fubvert our exifting government. Can any man juftly think it has fuch a tendency, who recollects that no government, fimilar to that which the Revolution eftablifhed for England, exifted when Milton wrote. His impaffioned yet difinterefted ardor for reformation was excited by thofe grofs abufes of power, which that new fettlement of the ftate very happily corrected.

Your learned and good-natured brother, my dear friend, was not the only man of learning and good-nature, who indulged a prejudice, that to us appears very extravagant, to give it the gentleft appellation. A literary Paladine (if I may borrow from romance a title of diftinction to honor a very powerful hiftorian) even Gibbon himfelf, whom we both admired and loved for his literary and for his focial accomplifhments, furpaffed, I think, on this topic, the feverity of Mr. Warton, and held it hardly compatible with the duty of a good citizen to re-publifh, in the prefent times, the profe of Milton, as he apprehended it might be productive of public evil.

For my own part, although I fincerely refpected the highly cultivated mind that harboured this apprehenfion, yet the apprehenfion itfelf appeared to me fomewhat fimilar to the fear of Falftaff, when he fays, " I am afraid of this " gunpowder Percy, though he be dead." As the profe of Milton had a reference to the diftracted period in which it arofe, its arguments, if they could by any means be pointed againft our exifting government, are furely as incapable of inflicting a wound, as completely dead for all the purpofes of hiftility, as the noble Percy is reprefented, when he excites the ludicrous terror of Sir John : but while I prefume to defcribe the profe of Milton as inanimate in one point of view, let me have the juftice to add, that it frequently breathes fo warm a fpirit of genuine eloquence and philanthropy, that I am perfuaded the prophecy of its great author concerning it will be gradually accomplifhed ; its defects and its merits will be more temperately and juftly eftimated in a future age than they have hitherto been. The prejudices fo recently entertained againft it, by the two eminent writers I have mentioned, were entertained at a period when a very extraordinary panic poffeffed and overclouded many of the moft elevated and enlightened minds of this kingdom—a period when a retired ftudent could hardly amufe himfelf with perufing the nervous republican writers of the laft century, without being fufpected of framing deadly machinations againft the monarchs of the prefent day; and when the principles of a Jacobin were very blindly imputed to a truly Englifh writer of acknowledged genius, and of the pureft reputation, who is, perhaps, of all men living, the moft perfectly blamelefs in his fentiments of government, morality, and religion. But, happily for the credit of our national underftanding, and our national courage, the panic to which I allude has fpeedily paffed away, and a man of letters may now, I prefume, as fafely and irreproachably perufe or reprint the great republican writers of England, as he might tranflate or elucidate the political vifions of Plato a writer whom Milton paffionately admired, and to whom he bore, I think, in many points, a very ftriking refemblance. Perhaps they both poffeffed too large a portion of fancy and enthufiafm to make

good practical statesmen; the visionaries of public
virtue have seldom succeeded in the management
of dominion, and in politics it has long been a
prevailing creed to believe, that government is like
gold, and must not be fashioned for extensive use
without the alloy of corruption. But I mean not
to burden you, my lively friend, with political
reflections, or with a long dissertation on the great
mass of Milton's prose; you, whose studies are so
various and extensive, are sufficiently familiar
with those singular compositions; and I am not
a little gratified in the assurance that you think as
I do, both of their blemishes and their beauties,
and approve the use that I have made of them
in my endeavours to elucidate the life and character of their author. Much as we respected the
classical erudition and the taste of your lamented
brother, I am confident that we can neither of
us subscribe to the censure he has passed on the
Latin style of Milton, who, to my apprehension,
is often most admirably eloquent in that language,
and particularly so in the passage I have cited
from his character of Bradshaw; a character in
which I have known very acrimonious enemies

to the name of the man commended, very candidly acknowledge the eloquence of the eulogiſt.
Some rigorous idolaters of the unhappy race of
Stuart may yet cenſure me even for this diſpaſ-
ſionate revival of ſuch a character; but you, my
liberal friend to the freedom of literary diſcuſſion,
you will ſuggeſt to me, that the minds of our
countrymen in general aſpire to Roman magnanimity, in rendering juſtice to great qualities in
men, who were occaſionally the objects of public
deteſtation, and you join with me in admiring
that example of ſuch magnanimity, to which I
particularly allude. Nothing is more honorable
to ancient Rome, than her generoſity in allowing
a ſtatue of Hannibal to be raiſed, and admired
within the walls of the very city, which it was
the ambition of his life to diſtreſs and deſtroy.

In emulation of that ſpirit, which delights to
honor the excellencies of an illuſtrious antagoniſt,
I have endeavoured to preſerve in my own mind,
and to expreſs on every proper occaſion, my
unſhaken regard for the rare faculties and virtues
of a late extraordinary biographer, whom it has
been my lot to encounter continually as a very

bitter, and sometimes, I think, an insidious enemy to the great poet, whose memory I have fervently wished to rescue from indignity and detraction. The asperity of Johnson towords Milton has often struck the fond admirers of the poet in various points of view; in one moment it excites laughter, in another indignation; now it reminds us of the weapon of Goliah as described by Cowley;

" A sword so great, that it was only fit
" To cut off his great head that came with it;"

now it prompts us to exclaim, in the words of an angry Roman:

" Nec bellua tetrior ulla est
" Quam servi rabies in libera colla furentis."

I have felt, I confess, these different emotions of resentment in perusing the various sarcasms of the austere critic against the object of my poetical idolatry, but I have tried, and I hope with some success, to correct the animosity they must naturally excite, by turning to the more temperate works of that very copious and admirable writer, particularly to his exquifite paper in the Rambler (N° 54) on the deaths and afperity of literary men. It is hardly poffible, I think, to read the paper I have mentioned without lofing, for fome time at leaft, all fenfations of difpleafure towards the eloquent, the tender moralift, and reflecting, with a fort of friendly fatisfaction, that, as long as the language of England exifts, the name of J O H N S O N will remain, and deferve to remain,

Magnum & memorabile nomen.

As long as eloquence and morality are objects of public regard, we muft revere that great mental phyfician, who has given to us all, infirm mortals as the beft of us are, fuch admirable prefcriptions for the regimen of mind, and we fhould rather fpeak in forrow than in anger, when we are forced to recollect, that, like other phyficians, however able and perfect in theory, he failed to correct the infirmity of his own morbid fpirit. You, my dear Warton, whom an oppofite temperament has made a critic of a more airy and cheerful complexion, you are one of the beft

witneffes that I could poffibly produce, if I had
any occafion to prove that my ideas of Johnfon's
malevolent prejudices against Milton are not the
offsprings of a fancy equally prejudiced itfelf
against the great author, whofe prejudices I have
prefumed to oppofe; you, my dear friend, have
heard the harfh critic advance in converfation an
opinion against Milton, even more fevere than
the many detractive farcafms with which his life
of the great poet abounds; you have heard him
declaim against the admiration excited by the poetry of Milton, and affirm it to be nothing more
than the cant (to ufe his own favorite phrafe)
of affected fenfibility.

I have prefumed to fay, that Johnfon fometimes appears as an infidious enemy to the poet. Is
there not fome degree of infidious hoftility in his
introducing into his dictionary, under the article
Sonnet, the very fonnet of Milton, which an enemy would certainly chufe, who wifhed to reprefent Milton as a writer of verfes entitled to fcorn
and derifion? You will immediately recollect
that I allude to the fonnet which begins thus:

" A book was writ of late called Tetrachordon."

The fonnet is, in truth, contemptible enough, if we fuppofe that Milton intended it as a ferious compofition ; but I apprehend it was an idle *lufus poeticus*, and either meant as a ludicrous parody on fome other fonnet which has funk into oblivion, or merely written as a trifling paftime, to fhow that it is poffible to compofe a fonnet with words moft unfriendly to rhyme. However this may be, it was barbarous furely towards Milton (and, I might add, towards the poetry of England) to exhibit this unhappy little production, in fo confpicuous a manner, as a fpecimen of Englifh fonnets. Yet I perceive it is poffible to give a milder interpretation of Johnfon's defign in his difplay of this unfortunate fonnet; and as I moft fincerely wifh not to charge him with more malevolence towards Milton than he really exerted, I will obferve on this occafion, that as he had little, or rather no relifh for fonnets, which the ftern logician feems to have defpifed as perplexing trifles (*difficiles nugæ*) he might only mean to deter young poetical ftudents from a kind of verfe that he difliked, by leading them to remark, how the greateft of our poets had failed in this petty compofition. You, who perfectly know how much more inclined I am to praife than to cenfure, will give me full credit for my fincerity in faying, that I wifh to acquit Johnfon of malevolence in every article where my reafon will allow me to do fo. I have been under the painful neceffity of difplaying continually, in the following work, the various examples of his feverity to Milton. Nothing is more apt to excite our fpleen than a ftroke of injuftice againft an author whom we love and revere; but I fhould be forry to find myfelf infected by the acrimony which I was obliged to difplay, and I fhould be equally forry to run into an oppofite failing, and to indulge a fpirit of obloquy, like Mrs. Candor, in the School for Scandal, with all the grimaces of affected good nature. I have fpoken, therefore my own feelings, without bitternefs and without timidity. I cannot fay that I fpeak of Johnfon "*fine ira & ftudio*," as Tacitus faid of other great men (very differently great!) for, in truth, I feel towards the fame object thofe two oppofite fources of prejudice and partiality ; as a critical biographer of the poets he often excites my tranfient indignation; but as an eloquent teacher of morality he fills me with more lasting reverence and affection.

His lives of the poets will probably give birth, in this or the next century, to a work of literary retaliation. Whenever a poet arises with as large a portion of spleen towards the critical writers of past ages, as Johnson indulged towards the poets in his poetical biography, the literature of England will be enriched with " the Lives of the Critics," a work from which you, my dear Warton, will have little to apprehend; you, whose essay teaches, as the critical biographer very truly and liberally observed, " how the brow of criticism may be " smoothed, and how she may be enabled, with " all her severity, to attract and delight."

Yet to show how apt a writer of verses is to accuse a profest critic of severity, we may both recollect, that when I had occasion to speak of your entertaining and instructive Essay on Pope, I scrupled not to consider the main scope of it a little too severe; and in truth, my dear friend, I think so still; because it is the aim of that charming Essay to prove, that Pope possessed not thofe very high poetical talents, for which the world, though fufficiently inclined to difcover and magnify his defects, had allowed him credit. You confider him as the poet of reafon, and intimate that " he ftooped to truth, and moralized his fong," from a want of native powers to fupport a long flight in the higher province of fancy. To me, I confefs, his Rape of the Lock appears a fufficient proof that he poffeffed, in a fuperlative degree, the faculty in which you would reduce him to a fecondary rank; he chofe, indeed, in many of his productions, to be the poet of reafon rather than of fancy; but I apprehend his choice was influenced by an idea (I believe a miftaken idea) that moral fatire is the fpecies of poetry by which a poet of modern times may render the greateft fervice to mankind. But if in one article you have been not fo kind, as I could wifh, to the poet of morality, I rejoice in recollecting, that you are on the point of making him confiderable amends, and of fulfilling a prediction of mine, by removing from the pages of Pope a great portion of the lumber with which they were amply loaded by Warburton. You will foon, I truft, prove to the literary world, as you perfectly proved to me fome years ago, that the poet has fuffered not a little from the abfurdities of his arrogant annotator. It is hardly poffible for a man of letters, who affectionately venerates the name of Milton, and recollects fome expreffions of Warburton concerning his poetry and his moral character, to fpeak of that fupercilious prelate without catching fome portion of his own fcornful fpirit : you will immediately perceive that I allude to his having beftowed upon Milton the opprobrious title of a time-ferver*. Do you recollect, my dear learned critic, extenfive us your ftudies have been; do you recollect, in

* With what peculiar propriety Warburton applied this name to Milton, the reader will beft judge, who recollects the humorous Butler's very admirable character of a time-ferver, which contains the following paffage: " He is very zealous to fhow himfelf, upon all occafions, " a true member of the church for the time being, and " has not the leaft fcruple in his confcience againft the " doctrine and difcipline of it, as it ftands at prefent, " or fhall do hereafter, unfight unfeen; for he is refolved " to be always for the truth, which he believes is never " fo plainly demonftrated as in that character that fays " ' it is great, and prevails;' and in that fenfe only fit

the wide range of ancient and modern defamation,
a more unpardonable abufe of language? Milton,
a poet of the moft powerful, and, perhaps the
moft independent mind that was ever given to a
mere mortal, infulted with the appellation of a
time-ferver; and by whom? by Warburton, whofe
writings, and whofe fortune—but I will not copy
the contemptuous prelate in his favorite exercife
of reviling the literary characters, whofe opinions
were different from his own; his habit of indulging a contemptuous and dogmatical fpirit has already drawn upon his name and writings the natural punifhment of fuch verbal intemperance;
and the mitred follower of his fame and fortune,
who has lately endeavoured to prop his reputation by a tenderly partial, but a very imperfect
life of his precipitate and quarrelfome patron,
has rather leffened, perhaps, his own credit, than
increafed that of his mafter, by that affected cold-
nefs of contempt with which he defcribes, or

" to be adhered to by a prudent man, who will never
" be kinder to truth than fhe is to him; for fuffering is
" a very *evil effect*, and not likely to proceed from a
" *good caufe.*" Butler's Remains, vol. ii. p. 220.

rather

rather disfigures, the illustrious chastiser of Warbur-tonian insolence, the more accomplished critic, of whom you eminent scholars of Winton are very justly proud; I mean the eloquent and graceful Lowth.

But as I am not fond of literary strife, however dignified and distinguished the antagonists may be, I will hasten to extricate myself from this little group of contentious critics; for it must be matter of regret to every sincere votary of peace and benevolence to observe, that the field of literature is too frequently a field of cruelty, which almost realizes the hyperbolical expression of Lucan, and exhibits

"Plus quam civilia bella;"

where men, whose kindred studies should humanize their temper, and unite them in the ties of fraternal regard, are too apt to exert all their faculties in ferociously mangling each other; where we sometimes behold the friendship of years dissolved in a moment, and converted into furious hostility, which, though it does not endanger,

yet never fails to embitter life; and perhaps the
fource of fuch contention,

> . " teterrima belli
> " Caufa—"

inftead of being a fair and faithlefs Helen, is nothing more than a particle of grammar in a dead
language.   O that the fpleen-correcting powers of
mild and friendly ridicule could annihilate fuch
hoftilities!—Cannot you, my dear Warton, who
have the weight and authority of a pacific Neftor
in this tumultuous field, cannot you fuggeft effectual lenitives for the *genus irritabile fcriptorum.*
The celebrated Saxon painter Mengs has, I think,
given us all an admirable hint of this kind in
writing to an ingenious but petulant Frenchman,
who had provoked him by fpeaking contemp-
tuoufly of his learned and enthufiaftic friend Winkelman. Se io poffedeffi il talento di fcriver bene
(fays the modeft painter) vorrei efporre ragioni,
e fatti, e infegnar cofe utili fenza perdermi a con-
tradir veruno poiché mi fembra, the fi poffan fare
buoni libri fenza dire che il tale, o il tal foggetto
s' inganna; e finalmente fe ella mi può dimoftrare,

che la maldicenza fia cofa onefta, allora io con-
verrò che importa molto poco il modo, con cui
fi attacca la riputazione del proffimo: e aggiungo
che il farcafmo e l'infulto fono la peggior maniera
di mormorare, e di biafimare donde rifulta fempre
il maggior danno a chi lo ufa.—Opere di Mengs,
tomo primo, p. 243.

These admonitions are excellent, and want only
the good-example of the monitor to make them
complete; but Mengs, unfortunately, in his pro-
feffional writings, has fpoken of Reynolds in a
manner that grofsly violates his own doctrine; fo
difficult is it, my good Doctor, to find a pacific
preacher and his practice in perfect harmony
with each other.

To feeling and fervent fpirits there can hardly
be any provocation more apt to excite afperity
of language, than an infult offered to an object of
their efteem and veneration. In writing upon Milton, and thofe who, to my apprehenfion, have
infulted his name with contumelious feverity, I
may have been hurried beyond the bias of my
temper, which is, I truft, neither irafcible nor
cenforious; but I will imitate fome well meaning

catholic writers, and making you, my dear Warton, my inquifitor as well as my patron, I will
here very honeftly fay to you, " *Si quid dixerim*
" *contra fpiritum caritatis evangelicæ indictum*
" *volo.* "

Let me now haften to apologize to you, as I
think I ought, for fuch deficiencies as your nice
difcernment cannot fail to obferve in the work I
addrefs to you. You remember that Plutarch, the
amiable prince of ancient biographers, has very
juftly mentioned the advantage arifing to a writer from refiding in a city amply furnifhed with
books;—it is my lot, you know, to live in a
little fequeftered village, and I chufe to do fo for
the reafon which attached the good-natured Plutarch to his native Cheronæa, that it may not become lefs. Had it fuited me to devote much time
and labor to extenfive refearches in the public
and private libraries of London, it is poffible that
I might have difcovered fome latent anecdotes relating to Milton; yet after the patient inquiries
of the intelligent and indefatigable Dr. Birch, and
after the fignal difcovery of your more fuccefsful
brother, little novelty could be expected to reward

the toil of such investigation; and perhaps a writer too eager to make new discoveries on this beaten ground, might be hurried by such eagerness into the censurable temerity of Peck the antiquarian, who, in his memoirs of the great poet, has affixed the name of Milton to a portrait and a poem that do not belong to him.

Though my work has been executed in a retired village of England, my inquiries have extended far beyond the limits of our own country, by the aid of some intelligent and obliging friends, who had the kindness to search for me the great libraries of Paris and Rome, in the hope of discovering some neglected composition, or latent anecdote, that might be useful to a biographer of Milton. The success of these researches has not been equal to the kindness and the zeal of the intelligent inquirers; but an unexpected favor from a literary friend, who is known to me only by his writings, has enabled me to throw, perhaps, a new ray of light on that inviting subject of conjecture, the real origin of Milton's greatest performance.

In the diſſertation, which I have annexed to this life of the poet, you will find ſome account of an Italian drama on the inhabitants of Paradiſe, which, though it riſes not to the poetical ſpirit of Andreini, may have had ſome influence, I apprehend, on the fancy of Milton. You will alſo find, that I have followed your example, in recommending your old acquaintance Andreini to the notice of the public. He happened to engage my attention, when the health of my revered friend, Mr. Cowper, allowed him to be my gueſt; and, after our more ſerious morning ſtudies, it afforded us a pleaſant relaxation and amuſement to throw ſome parts of the *Adamo* into Engliſh, in a rapid yet metrical tranſlation. In this joint work, or rather paſtime, it would be needleſs, if it were poſſible, to diſtinguiſh the lines of the united tranſlators, as the verſion had no higher aim than to gratify the curioſity of the Engliſh reader, without aſpiring to praiſe. A very different character is due to that verſion of Milton's Latin poetry, which my excellent friend has finiſhed with ſuch care and felicity, that even from the ſeparate ſpecimens of it, with which this life is embellished, you, my dear Warton, and every delicate judge of poetry, will, I am confident, esteem it an absolute model of poetical translation. For the honor of Milton, and for that of his most worthy interpreter, I hope that the whole of this admirable performance may be soon imparted to the public, as I trust that returning health will happily restore its incomparable author to his suspended studies; an event that may affect the moral interest and the mental delight of all the world — for rarely, very rarely indeed, has heaven bestowed on any individual such an ample, such a variegated portion of true poetical genius, and never did it add greater purity of heart to that divine yet perilous talent, to guide and sanctify its exertion. Those who are best acquainted with the writings and the virtues of my inestimable friend, must be most fervent in their hopes, that in the course and the close of his poetical career he may resemble his great and favorite predecessors, Homer and Milton; their spirits were cheered and illuminated in the decline of life by a fresh portion of poetical power; and if in their latter productions they rose not to the full force and fplendor of their meridian glory, they yet enchanted mankind with the fweetnefs and ferenity of their defcending light.

Literature, which Cicero has fo eloquently defcribed as the friend of every period and condition of human exiftence, is peculiarly the friend of age; a truth of which you, my dear Warton, are a very lively illuftration—you, who at a feafon of life when unlettered mortals generally murmur againft the world, are miniftering to its inftruction and its pleafure by continuing to write with temper, vivacity, and grace.

That you may long retain and difplay this happy affemblage of endowments, fo rare in a critical veteran, is the cordial wifh of many, and particularly the wifh of your very fincere and affectionate friend,

W. H.

Eartham, October 29. 1795.

THE
LIFE
OF
MILTON.

LIFE

of

MILTON.

THE LIFE OF MILTON.

PART I.

THE character of MILTON has been scrutinized with all the minuteness of investigation, which opposite passions could suggest.. The virulent antagonist and the enraptured idolater have pursued his steps with equal pertinacity: nor have we wanted men of learning and virtue, who, devoid of prejudice and enthusiasm, both in politics and in poetry, have endeavoured to weigh his merits exactly in the balance of truth and reason.

What new light then can be thrown upon a life, whose incidents have been so eagerly collected, and so frequently retailed?　What novelty of remark can be expected in a review of poems, whose beauties and blemishes have been elaborately examined in critical dissertations, that almost

rival in excellence the poetry they difcufs? Affuredly but little; yet there remains, perhaps, one
method of giving a degree of intereft and illuftration to the life of Milton, which it has not hitherto received; a method which his accomplifhed
friend of Italy, the Marquis of Villa, in fome
meafure adopted in his interefting life of Taffo;
and which two engaging biographers of later date,
the Abbé de Sade and Mr. Mafon, have carried
to greater perfection in their refpective memoirs
of Petrarch and of Gray. By weaving into their
narrative felections of verfe and profe from the
various writings of thofe they wifhed to comme-
morate, each of thefe affectionate memorialifts
may be faid to have taught the poet he loved " to
become his own biographer;" an experiment that
may, perhaps, be tried on Milton with the hap-
pieft effect! as in his works, and particularly in
thofe that are at prefent the leaft known, he has
fpoken frequently of himfelf.— Not from vanity,
a failing too cold and low for his ardent and elevated mind; but, in advanced life, from motives
of juftice and honor, to defend himfelf againft
the poifoned arrows of flander; and, in his
younger days, from that tendernefs and fimplicity of heart, which lead a youthful poet to
make his own affections and amufements the
chief fubjects of his fong.

The great aim of the fubfequent account is to
render full and perfect juftice to the general character of Milton. His manners and caft of mind,

in various periods of life, may appear in a new and agreeable light, from the following collection and arrangement of the many little sketches, which his own hand has occasionally given us, of his passions and pursuits. Several of these, indeed, have been fondly assembled by Toland or Richardson; men, who, different as they were in their general sentiments and principles, yet sympathized completely in their zeal for the renown of Milton; delighting to dwell on his character with " that shadow of friendship, that compla-
" cency and ardor of attachment, which, as Pope
" has observed in speaking of Homer, we natu-
" rally feel for the great geniuses of former time."
— But those who have endeavoured to illustrate the personal history of the great English Author, by exhibiting passages from some of his neglected works, have almost confined themselves to selections from his prose.

There is an ampler field for the study of his early temper and turn of mind in his Latin and Italian Poetry: here the heart and spirit of Milton are displayed with all the franknefs of youth. I select what has a peculiar tendency to show, in the clearest light, his native disposition, because his character as a man appears to have been greatly mistaken. I am under no fear that the frequency or length of such citations may be exposed to censure, having the pleasure and advantage of presenting them to the English reader in the elegant and spirited version of a poet and a friend—with

pride and delight I add the name of Cowper.
This gentleman, who is prepared to oblige the
world with a complete tranflation of Milton's Latin and Italian poetry, has kindly favored me
with the liberty of tranfcribing, from his admirable work, whatever I wifh to infert in this narrative. Since I am indebted to Milton for a friendfhip,
which I regard as honorable in the higheft degree, may I be indulged in the hope of leaving a
lafting memorial of it in thefe pages.

A book, devoted to the honor of Milton, may
admit, I hope, without impropriety; the praifes
due to a living author, who is become his poetical interpreter; an office which the fpirit of the
divine bard may be gratified in his having affumed; for, affuredly, my friend bears no common
refemblance to his moft illuftrious predeceffor,
not only in the energy and hallowed ufe of poetical talents, but in that beneficent fervor and
purity of heart, which entitle the great poet to
as large a portion of affectionate efteem, as he has
long poffeffed of admiration.

JOHN MILTON was born in London, on the
9th of December, 1608, at the houfe of his father, in Bread-ftreet, and baptized on the 20th of
the fame month. His chriftian name defcended to
him from his grandfather. The family, once opu-
lent proprietors of Milton, in Oxfordfhire, loft
that eftate in the civil wars of York and Lancafter,
and was indebted, perhaps, to adverfity for much
higher diftinction than opulence can beftow. John,

the grandfather of the poet, became deputy ran-
ger in the foreft of Shotover, not far from Oxford;
and intending to educate his fon as a gentleman,
he placed him at Chrift-Church, in that univerfity; but being himfelf a rigid Papift, he difinherited
the young and devout fcholar, for an attachment
to the doctrines of the Reformation, and reduced
him to the neceffity of quitting the path of literature for a lefs honorable but more lucrative profeffion.

The difcarded ftudent applied himfelf to the
employment of a fcrivener, which has varied with
the variations, of life and manners. A fcrivener,
in remoter ages, is fuppofed to have been a mere
tranfcriber; but at the period we fpeak of, his
occupation united the two profitable branches of
drawing contracts and of lending money. The
emoluments of this profeffion enabled the father
of Milton to beftow moft abundantly on his fon
thofe advantages of education, which had been
cruelly withdrawn from himfelf. The poet was
happy in both his parents; and to the merits of
both he has borne affectionate and honorable
teftimony. The maiden name of his mother has
been difputed; but it feems reafonable to credit
the account of Philips, her grandfon, the earlieft
biographer of Milton, who had the advantage of
living with him as a relation and a difciple.

Her name, according to this author, who fpeaks
highly of her virtue, was Cafton, and her family
derived from Wales. Milton, in mentioning his

own origin, with a decent pride, in reply to one of his revilers, afferts, that his mother was a woman of exemplary character, and peculiarly diftinguifhed by her extenfive charity *. The parental kindnefs and the talents of his father he has celebrated in a Latin poem, which cannot be too warmly admired, as a monument of filial tendernefs, and poetical enthufiafm.   It is probable, that the fevere manner in which that indulgent father had been driven from the purfuits of learning induced him to exert uncommon liberality and ardor in the education of his fon.   Though immerfed himfelf in a lucrative occupation, he feems to have retained great elegance of mind, and to have amufed himfelf with literature and mufic; to the latter he applied fo fuccefsfully, that, according to Dr. Burney, the accomplifhed hiftorian of that captivating art, " 'he became a voluminous compofer, equal in fcience, if not in genius, to the beft muficians of his age." Nor did his talents pafs without celebrity or reward. Philips relates, that for one of his devotional compofitions in forty parts, he was honored with a gold chain and medal by a Polifh prince, to whom he prefented it. This mark of diftinction was frequently conferred on men, who rofe to great excellence in different arts and fciences: perhaps

* Londini fum natus, genere honefto, patre viro integerrimo, matre probatiffimâ, & eleemofynis per viciniam potiffimum nota.
Defenfio fecunda.

the ambition of young Milton was firſt awakened by theſe gifts of honor beſtowed upon his father *.

A parent, who could enliven the drudgery of a dull profeſſion by a variety of elegant purſuits, muſt have been happy to diſcern, and eager to cheriſh, the firſt dawning of genius in his child. In this point of view we may contemplate with peculiar delight the infantine portrait of Milton, by that elegant and faithful artiſt, Cornelius Janſen. Aubrey, the antiquarian, obſerving in his manuſcript memoirs of our author, that he was ten years old when this picture was drawn, affirms that " he was then a poet." This expreſſion may lead us to

---

* The father of Milton has been lately mentioned as an author. —He was thought to have publiſhed, in the year of the poet's birth, a little book, with the quaint title of " A Sixt Fold Politician."—Mr. Warton obſerved, that the curious publication aſcribed to Milton's father may be found in the Bodleian library; that " it appears to be a ſatire on characters pretending to wiſdom or policy, and is not void of learning and wit, ſuch as we often find affectedly and awkwardly blended in the eſſay-writers of that age."

By the favor of Mr. Iſaac Reed, who is moſt liberal in the communication of the literary rarities he has collected, I have peruſed this ſingular performance, and perfectly agree with its obliging poſſeſſor, and his accompliſhed friend, Dr. Farmer, that although in the records of the Stationers Company it is aſcribed to John Milton, we may rather aſſign it to John Melton, author of the Aſtrologaſter, than to the father of our poet. —The latter will loſe but little in being no longer regarded as its author, eſpecially as we have different and more honorable proofs of his attachment to literature.

imagine, that the portrait was executed to encourage the infant author; and if fo, it might operate as a powerful incentive to his future exertion. The permanent bias of an active fpirit often originates in the petty incidents of childhood; and as no human mind ever glowed with a more intenfe, or with a purer flame of literary ambition, than the mind of Milton, it may not be unpleafing to conjecture how it firft caught the fparks, that gradually mounted to a blaze of unrivalled vehemence and fplendor.

His education, as Dr. Newton has well obferved, united the oppofite advantages of private and public inftruction. Of his early paffion for letters he has left the following record, in his fecond defence *: " My father deftined me from my infancy to the ftudy of polite literature, which I embraced with fuch avidity, that from the age of twelve, I hardly ever retired from my books before midnight. This proved the firft fource of injury to my eyes, whofe natural weaknefs was attended with frequent pains of the head; but as all thefe difadvantages could not reprefs my ardor for learning, my father took care to have me inftructed by various preceptors

---

* Pater me puerulum humaniarum literarum ftudiis deftinavit; quas ita avide arripui, ut ab anno ætatis duodecimo vix unquam ante mediam noctem a lucubrationibus cubitum difcederem; quæ prima oculorum pernicies fuit, quorum ad naturalem debilitatem accefferant & crebri capitis dolores; quæ omnia cum difcendi impetum non retardarent, & in ludo literario, & fub aliis domi magiftris erudiendum quotidie curavit.

both at home and at fchool." His domeftic tutor was Thomas Young, of Effex, who, being obliged 'to quit his country on account of religious opinions, became minifter to the Englifh merchants at Hamburgh. It was probably from this learned and confcientious man, that Milton caught not only his paffion for literature, but that fteadinefs and unconquerable integrity of character, by which he was diftinguifhed through all the viciffitudes of a tempeftuous life. His reverential gratitude and affection towards this preceptor are recorded in two Latin epiftles*, and a Latin elegy

* The high opinion, which Milton entertained of his preceptor, is fo gracefully expreffed in one of thefe letters, that I felect it as a fpecimen of his epiftolary ftyle in the early period of life.

Thomæ Junio.

Infpectis literis tuis (præceptor optime) unicum hoc mihi fupervacaneum occurrebat, quod tardæ fcriptionis excufationem attuleris; tametfi enim literis tuis nihil mihi queat optabilius accedere, qui poffim tamen aut debeam fperare otii tibi tantum à rebus feriis, & fanctioribus effe, ut mihi femper refpondere vacet; præfertim cum illud humanitatis omnino fit, officii minime. Te vero oblitum effe mei ut fufpicer, tam multa tua de me recens merita nequaquam finunt. Neque enim video quorfum tantis onuftum beneficiis ad oblivionem dimitteres. Rus tuum accerfitus, fimul ac ver adoleverit, libenter adveniam, ad capeffendas anni tuique non minus colloquii delicias, & ab urbano ftrepitu fubducam me paulifper, ad ftoam tuam Icenorum, tanquam ad celeberrimam illam Zenonis porticum aut Ciceronis Tufculanum, ubi tu in re modica regio fane animo veluti Serranus aliquis aut Curius in agello tuo placide regnas, deque ipfis divitiis, ambitione, pompa, luxuria, & quicquid vulgus hominum

addreffed to him: they fuggeft a moft favorable
idea of the poet's native difpofition, and furnifh
an effectual antidote to the poifon of that moft
injurious affertion, that " he hated all whom he
was required to obey."—Could untractable pride
be the characteriftic of a mind, which has expreffed its regard for a difciplinarian fufficiently rigid,
with a tendernefs fo confpicuous in the following
verfes of the fourth Elegy?

miratur & ftupet, quafi triumphum agis fortunæ contemptor.
Cæterum qui tarditatis culpam deprecatus es, hanc mihi viciffim,
ut fpero, præcipitantiam indulgebis; cum enim epiftolam hanc
in extremum diftuliffem, malui pauca, eaque rudiufcule fcribere,
quam nihil.—Vale vir obfervande.

Cantabrigia, Julii 21, 1628.

· In perufing your letters, my excellent preceptor, this only
appeared to me fuperfluous, that you apologize for a delay in
writing; for although nothing can be more defirable to me than
your letters, yet what right have I to hope, that your ferious
and facred duties can allow you fuch leifure, that you can always find time enough to anfwer me, efpecially when your
writing is entirely an act of kindnefs, and by no means of duty.
The many and recent favors I have received from you will by
no means fuffer me to fufpect that you can forget me; nor can
I conceive it poffible that, having loaded me with fuch benefits,
you fhould now difmifs me from your remembrance. I fhall
willingly attend your fummons to your rural retirement on the
firft appearance of fpring, to enjoy with equal relish the delights
of the feafon and of your converfation. I fhall withdraw myfelf for a little time from the buftle of the city to your porch
in Suffolk, as to the famous portico of the Stoic, or the Tuf-
culum of Cicero, where ennobling a moderate eftate by an im-
perial mind, you reign contentedly in your little field, like a
Serranus or a Curius, and triumph, as it were, over opulence,

Vivit ibi antiquæ clarus pietatis honore,
  Præful, chrifticolas pafcere doctus oves;
Ille quidem eft animæ plus quam pars altera noftræ,
  Dimidio vitæ vivere cogor ego.
Hei mihi quot pelagi, quot montes interjecti,
  Me faciunt alia parte carere mei!
Charior ille mihi, quam tu, doctiffime Graium,
  Cliniadi, pronepos qui Telamonis erat;
Quamque Stagyrites generofo magnus alumno,
  Quem peperit Lybico Chaonis alma Jovi.
Qualis Amyntorides, qualis Phylirëius heros
  Myrmidonum regi, talis & ille mihi.
Primus ego Aonios illo præunte receffus
  Luftrabam, & bifidi facra vireta jugi,
Pieriofque haufi latices, Clioque favente,
  Caftalio fparfi læta ter ora mero.

There lives, deep learn'd, and primitively juft,
A faithful fteward of his Chriftian truft;
My friend, and favorite inmate of my heart,
That now is forc'd to want its better part.
What mountains now, and feas, alas! how wide!
Me from my other, dearer felf divide!
Dear as the fage, renown'd for moral truth,
To the prime fpirit of the Attic youth!

ambition, pomp, luxury (and whatever is idolized by the herd
of men) by looking down upon fortune: but as you excufe
yourfelf for delay, let me hope that you will forgive me for
hafte, fince, having deferred this letter to the laft moment, I
chofe to fend a few lines, though not very accurately written,
rather than to be filent. Farewel my revered friend.

Dear as the Stagyrite to Ammon's fon,
His pupil, who difdain'd the world he won!
Nor fo did Chiron, or fo Phœnix fhine,
In young Achilles' eyes, as he in mine:
Firft led by him, thro' fweet Aonian fhade,
Each facred haunt of Pindus I furvey'd;
Explor'd the fountain, and the Mufe my guide,
Thrice fteep'd my lips in the Caftalian tide.

And again, expreffing his regret upon the length of their feparation:

Nec dum ejus licuit mihi lumina pafcere vultu,
Aut linguæ dulces aure bibiffe fonos.

Nor yet his friendly features feaft my fight,
Nor his fweet accents my fond ear delight.

As the tendernefs of the young poet is admirably difplayed in the beginning of this Elegy, his more acknowledged characteriftic, religious fortitude, is not lefs admirable in the clofe of it.

At tu fume animos, nec fpes cadat anxia curis,
Nec tua concutiat decolor offa metus.
Sis etenim quamvis fulgentibus obfitus armis,
Intententque tibi millia tela necem,
At nullis vel inerme latus violabitur armis,
Deque tuo cufpis nulla cruore bibet;
Namque eris ipfe dei radiante fub ægide tutus,
Ille tibi cuftos, & pugil ille tibi:
Et tu (quod fupereft miferis) fperare memento,

Et tua magnanimo pectore vince mala;
Nec dubites quandoque frui melioribus annis,
Atque iterum patrios poffe videre lares.

But thou, take courage, ftrive againft defpair,
Shake not with dread, nor nourifh anxious care.
What tho' grim war on every fide appears,
And thou art menac'd by a thoufand fpears,
Not one fhall drink thy blood, not one offend
Ev'n the defencelefs bofom of my friend;
For thee the ægis of thy God fhall hide;
Jehovah's felf fhall combat on thy fide;
Thou, therefore, as the moft afflicted may,
Still hope, and triumph o'er thy evil day;
Truft thou fhalt yet behold a happier time,
And yet again enjoy thy native clime.

The reader, inclined to fymphatize in the joys of Milton, will be gratified in being informed, that his preceptor, whofe exile and poverty he pathetically lamented, and whofe profperous return he predicted, was in a few years reftored to his country, and became Mafter of Jefus College, in Cambridge.

As the year in which he quitted England (1623) correfponds with the fifteenth year of his pupil's age, it is probable that Milton was placed, at that time, under the care of Mr. Gill and his fon; the former, chief mafter of St. Paul's fchool, the latter, his affiftant, and afterwards his fucceffor. It is remarkable, that Milton, who has been fo uncandidly reprefented as an uncontrolable fpirit,

and a fpurner of all juft authority, feems to have
contracted a tender attachment to more than one
difciplinarian concerned in his education. He is
faid to have been the favorite fcholar of the
younger Gill; and he has left traces of their
friendfhip in three Latin epiftles, that exprefs
the higheft efteem for the literary character and
poetical talents of his inftructor.

On the 12th of February, 1624, he was entered,
not as a fizer, which fome of his biographers
have erroneoufly afferted, but as a penfioner of
Chrift's College, in Cambridge. "At this time,"
" fays Doctor Johnfon, "he was eminently fkil-
" led in the Latin tongue, and he himfelf, by
" annexing the dates to his firft compofitions, a
" boaft of which the learned Politian had given
" him an example, feems to commend the earli-
" nefs of his own proficiency to the notice of pof-
" terity; but the products of his vernal fertility
" have been furpaffed by many, and particularly
" by his contemporary, Cowley. Of the powers
" of the mind it is difficult to form an eftimate;
" many have excelled Milton in their firft effays,
" who never rofe to works like Paradife Loft."

This is the firft of many remarks, replete with
detraction, in which an illuftrious author has indulged his fpleen againft Milton, in a life of the
poet, where an ill-fubdued propenfity to cenfure
is ever combating with a neceffity to commend.
The partifans of the powerful critic, from a natural partiality to their departed mafter, affect to

confider his malignity as existing only in the prejudices of thofe who endeavour to counteract his
injuftice. A biographer of Milton ought therefore
to regard it as his indifpenfible duty to fhow how
far this malignity is diffufed through a long feries
of obfervations, which affect the reputation both
of the poet and the man; a duty that muft be
painful in proportion to the fincerity of our efteem
for literary genius; fince, different as they were
in their principles, their manners, and their writings, both the poet and his critical biographer
are affuredly entitled to the praife of exalted genius. Perhaps in the republic of letters there never exifted two writers more defervedly diftinguifhed, not only for the energy of their mental
faculties, but for a generous and devout defire
to benefit mankind by their exertion.

Yet it muft be lamented, and by the lovers of
Milton in particular, that a moralift, who has given us, in the Rambler, fuch fublime leffons for
the difcipline of the heart and mind, fhould be
unable to preferve his own from that acrimonious
fpirit of detraction, which led him to depreciate,
to the utmoft of his power, the rare abilities, and
perhaps the ftill rarer integrity, of Milton. It
may be faid, that the truly eloquent and fplendid encomium, which he has beftowed on the
great work of the poet, ought to exempt him
from fuch a charge. The fingular beauties and
effect of this eulogy fhall be mentioned in the proper place, and with all the applaufe they merit;

but here it is juft to recollect, that the praife of the encomiaft is nearly confined to the fentence he paffes as a critic; his more diffufive detraction may be traced in almoft every page of the biographer: not to encounter it on its firft appearance, and wherever it is vifible and important, would be to fail in that juftice and regard towards the character of Milton, which he, perhaps, of all men, has moft eminently deferved.

In the preceding citation it is evidently the purpofe of Dr. Johnfon to degrade Milton below Cowley, and many other poets, diftinguifhed by juvenile compofitions; but Mr. Warton has, with great tafte and judgment, expofed the error of Dr. Johnfon, in preferring the Latin poetry of Cowley to that of Milton. An eminent foreign critic has beftowed that high praife on the juvenile productions of our author, which his prejudiced countryman is inclined to deny. Morhoff has affirmed, with equal truth and liberality, that the verfes, which Milton produced in his childhood, difcover both the fire and judgment of maturer life: a commendation that no impartial reader will be inclined to extenuate, who perufes the fpirited epiftle to his exiled preceptor, compofed in his eighteenth year. Some of his Englifh verfes bear an earlier date. The firft of his juvenile productions, in the language which he was deftined to ennoble, is a paraphrafe of the hundred and fourteenth pfalm; it was executed at the age of fifteen, and difcovers a power that Dryden, and other

more prefumptuous critics, have unjuftly denied
to Milton, the power of moving with facility in
the fetters of rhyme: this power is ftill more confpicuous in the poem he wrote at the age of feven-
teen, on the death of his fifter's child; a compofition peculiarly entitled to the notice of thofe, who
love to contemplate the early dawn of poetical
genius. In this performance, puerile as it is in
every fenfe of the word, the intelligent reader may
yet difcern, as in the bud, all the ftriking charac-
teriftics of Milton; his affectionate fenfibility, his
fuperior imagination, and all that native tendency
to devotional enthufiafm,

> Which fets the heart on fire,
> To fpurn the fordid world, and unto Heav'n afpire.

Admirably trained as the youth of the poet was
to acquire academical honor by the union of induftry and talents, he feems to have experienced
at Cambridge a chequered fortune, very fimilar
to his deftiny in the world: It appears from fome
remarkable paffages in the Latin exercifes, which
he recited in his College, that he was at firft an
object of partial feverity, and afterwards of general admiration. He had differed in opinion concerning a plan of academical ftudies with fome
perfons of authority in his college, and thus excited their difpleafure. He fpeaks of them as highly incenfed againft him; but expreffes, with
the moft liberal fenfibility, his furprife, delight,

and gratitude, in finding that his enemies forgot
their animofity to honor him with unexpected
applaufe.

An idle ftory has been circulated concerning his
treatment in College. " I am afhamed," fays Dr.
Johnfon, " to relate what I fear is true, that Milton was the laft ftudent in either Univerfity that
fuffered the public indignity of corporal punifhment." In confirmation of this incident, which
appears improbable, though fupported by Mr.
Warton, the biographical critic alledges the following paffage from the firft Elegy:

> Jam nec arundiferum mihi cura revifere Camum,
>   Nec dudum vetiti me laris angit amor;
> Nec duri libet ufque minas perferre magiftri,
>   Cæteraque ingenio, non fubeunda meo.

> Nor zeal nor duty now my fteps impel
>   To reedy Cam and my forbidden cell;
> 'Tis time that I a pedant's threats difdain,
>   And fly from wrongs my foul will ne'er fuftain.

Dr. Johnfon confiders thefe expreffions as an
abfolute proof, that Milton was obliged to un-
dergo this indignity; but they may fuggeft a very
different idea. From all the light we can obtain
concerning this anecdote, it feems moft probable,
that Milton was threatened, indeed, with what
he confidered as a punifhment, not only difhonorable but unmerited; that his manly fpirit difdained to fubmit to it; and that he was therefore

obliged to acquiefce in a fhort exile from Cambridge.

In fpeaking of his academical life, it is neceffary to obviate another remark of a fimilar tendency.

" There is reafon," fays Johnfon, " to fufpect that he was regarded in his college with no great fondnefs." To counteract this invidious infinuation we are furnifhed with a reply, made by Milton himfelf, to this very calumny, originally fabricated by one of his contemporaries; a calumny, which he had fo fully refuted, that it ought to have revived no more! He begins with thanking his reviler for the afperfion: " It has given me,"
he fays, " an apt occafion to acknowledge public-
" ly, with all grateful mind, that more than or-
" dinary favor and refpect, which I found, above
" any of my equals, at the hand of thofe cour-
" teous and learned men, the Fellows of that
" College, wherein I fpent fome years; who, at
" my parting, after I had taken two degrees, as
" the manner is, fignified many ways how much
" better it would content them that I would ftay,
" as by many letters, full of kindnefs and loving
" refpect, both before that time and long after, I
" was affured of the fingular good affection towards
me."— Profe Works, vol. 1. p. 15.

The Latin poems of Milton are yet entitled to more of our attention; becaufe they exhibit lively proofs, that he poffeffed both tendernefs and enthufiafm, thofe primary conftituents of a poet, at an early period of life, and in the higheft degree: they have additional value, from making us acquainted with several interesting particulars of his youth, and many of his opinions, which must have had considerable influence on his moral character.

His sixth Elegy, addressed to his bosom friend, Charles Diodati, seems to be founded on the idea, which he may be said to have verified in his own conduct, that strict habits of temperance and virtue are highly conducive to the perfection of great poetical powers. To poets of a lighter class he recommends, with graceful pleasantry, much convivial enjoyment; but for those who aspire to Epic renown, he prescribes even the simple regimen of Pythagoras.

> Ille quidem parce, Samii pro more magistri,
>   Vivat, & innocuos præbeat herba cibos;
> Stet prope fagineo pellucida lympha catillo,
>   Sobriaque e puro pocula fonte bibat.
> Additur huic fcelerifque vacans & casta juventus,
>   Et rigidi mores, & sine labe manus.
> Qualis veste nitens facra, & lustralibus undis,
>   Surgis ad infensos, augur, iture Deos.

> Simply let these, like him of Samos, live;
> Let herbs to them a bloodless banquet give;
> In beechen goblets let their beverage shine;
> Cool from the crystal spring their sober wine:
> Their youth should pass in innocence, secure
> From stain licentious, and in manners pure;

Pure as Heaven's minister, arrayed in white,
Propitiating the gods with luftral rite.

In his Elegy on the Spring, our poet expreffes
the fervent emotions of his fancy in terms, that
may be almoft regarded as a prophetic defcription of his fublimeft work:

> Jam mihi mens liquidi raptatur in ardua cœli,
>   Perque vagas nubes corpore liber eo;
> Intuiturque animus toto quid agatur Olympo,
>   Nec fugiunt oculos Tartara cæca meos.
>
> I mount, and, undepreffed by cumbrous clay,
> Thro' cloudy regions win my eafy way;
> My fpirit fearches all the realms of light,
> And no Tartarean depths elude my fight.

With thefe verfes it may be pleafing to compare
a fimilar paffage in his Englifh vacation exercife,
where, addreffing his native language, as applied
to an inconfiderable purpofe, he adds,

> Yet I had rather, if I were to chufe,
> Thy fervice in fome graver fubject ufe;
> Such as may make thee fearch thy coffers round,
> Before thou clothe my fancy in fit found;
> Such, where the deep tranfported mind may foar
> Above the wheeling poles, and at Heav'n's door
> Look in, and fee each blifsful deity,
> How he before the thunderous throne doth lie.

" It is worth the curious reader's attention to obferve how much the Paradife Loft correfponds with this prophetic wifh," fays Mr. Thyer, one of the moft intelligent and liberal of Englifh commentators.

The young poet, who thus expreffed his ambition, was then in his nineteenth year. At the age of twenty-one (the period of his life when that pleafing portrait of him was executed, which the Speaker Onflow obtained from the executors of his widow) he compofed his Ode on the Nativity; a poem that furpaffes in fancy and devotional fire a compofition on the fame fubject by that celebrated and devout poet of Spain, Lopez de Vega.

The moft trifling performances of Milton are fo fingular, that we may regret even the lofs of the verfes alluded to by Aubrey, as the offspring of his childhood. Perhaps no juvenile author ever difplayed, with fuch early force,

> " The fpirit of a youth
> Who means to be of note."

His mind, even in his boyifh days, feems to have glowed, like the fancy and furnace of an alchymift, with inceffant hope and preparation for aftonifhing productions.

Such aufterity and morofenefs have been falfely attributed to Milton, that a reader, acquainted

with

with him only as he appears in the page of Johnfon, muft fuppofe him little formed for love;
but his poetry in general, and efpecially the compofitions we are now fpeaking of, may convince
us, that he felt, with the moft exquifite fenfibility, the magic of beauty, and all the force of
female attraction. His feventh Elegy exhibits a
lively picture of his firft paffion; he reprefents
himfelf as captivated by an unknown fair, who,
though he faw her but for a moment, made a
deep impreffion on his heart.

> Protinus infoliti fubierunt corda furores,
>   Uror amans intus, flammaque totus eram.
> Interea mifero quæ jam mihi fola placebat,
>   Ablata eft oculis non reditura meis.
> Aft ego progredior tacite querebundus, & excors,
>   Et dubius volui fæpe referre pedem.
> Findor & hæc remanet: fequitur pars altera votum,
>   Raptaque tam fubito gaudia flere juvat.

> A fever, new to me, of fierce defire
> Now feiz'd my foul, and I was all on fire;
> But fhe the while, whom only I adore,
> Was gone, and vanifh'd to appear no more:
> In filent forrow I purfue my way;
> I paufe, I turn, proceed, yet wifh to ftay:
> And while I follow her in thought, bemoan
> With tears my foul's delight fo quickly flown.

The juvenile poet then addreffes himfelf to love,
with a requeft that beautifully expreffes all the

inquietude, and all the irrefolution, of hopelefs attachment.

> Deme meos tandem, verum nec deme, furores;
>   Nefcio cur, mifer eft fuaviter omnis amans.

> Remove, no, grant me ftill this raging woe;
> Sweet is the wretchednefs that lovers know.

After having contemplated the youthful fancy of Milton under the influence of a fudden and vehement affection, let us furvey him in a different point of view, and admire the purity and vigor of mind, which he exerted at the age of twenty-three, in meditation on his paft and his future days.

To a friend, who had remonftrated with him on his delay to enter upon active life, he afcribes that delay to an intenfe defire of rendering himfelf more fit for it. " Yet (he fays) " that you " may fee that I am fomething fufpicious of my-" felfe, and doe take notice of a certain belated-" neffe in me, I am the bolder to fend you fome " of my night-ward thoughts, fome while fince, " becaufe they come in not altogether unfitly, " made up in a Petrarchian ftanza, which I told " you of:"

> How foon hath time, the fubtle thief of youth,
>   Stol'n on his wing my three and twentieth year!
> My hafting days fly on with full career,
> But my late fpring no bud or bloffom fhow'th.

Perhaps my femblance might deceive the truth,
That I to manhood am arriv'd fo near,
And inward ripenefs doth much lefs appear,
That fome more time'y-happy fpirits indu'th.
Yet be it lefs or more, or foon or flow,
It fhall be ftill in ftricteft meafure even
To that fame lot, however mean or high,
Towards which time leads me, and the will of
heaven ;
All is, if I have grace to ufe it fo,
As ever in my great tafk-mafter's eye.

This fonnet may be regarded, perhaps, as a refutation of that injurious criticifm, which has afferted, " the beft fonnets of Milton are entitled only to this negative commendation, that they are not bad;" but it has a fuperior value, which induced me to introduce it here, as it feems to reveal the ruling principle, which gave bias and energy to the mind and conduct of Milton; I mean the habit, which he fo early adopted, of confidering himfelf

" As ever in his great tafk-mafter's eye. "

It was, perhaps, the force and permanency with which this perfuafion was impreffed on his heart, that enabled him to afcend the fublimeft heights, both of genius and of virtue.

When Milton began his courfe of academical ftudy, he had views of foon entering the church, to " whofe fervice," he fays, " by the intentions

" of my parents and friends, I was deftined of
" a child, and in mine own refolutions. "   It
was a religious fcruple that prevented him from
taking orders; and though his mode of thinking
may be deemed erroneous, there is a refined and
hallowed probity in his conduct on this occafion,
that is entitled to the higheft efteem ; particularly
when we confider, that although he declined the
office of a minifter, he devoted himfelf, with
intenfe application, to what he confidered as the
intereft of true religion.   The fincerity and fervor with which he fpeaks on this topic muft be
applauded by every candid perfon, however differing from him on points that relate to our religious eftablifhment.

    " For me (fays this zealous and difinterefted
" advocate for fimple chriftianity) I have deter-
" mined to lay up, as the beft treafure and fo-
" lace of a good old age, if God vouchfafe it me,
" the honeft liberty of free fpeech from my youth,
" where I fhall think it available in fo dear a
" concernment as the church's good. "   In the
polemical writings of Milton there is a merit to
which few polemics can pretend ; they were the
pure dictates of confcience, and produced by
the facrifice of his favorite purfuits : this he has
ftated in the following very forcible and interefting
language :

    " Concerning therefore this wayward fubject
" againft prelaty, the touching whereof is fo dif-
" tafteful and difquietous to a number of men,

" as by what hath been faid I may deferve of
" charitable readers to be credited, that neither
" envy nor gall hath entered me upon this con-
" troverfy, but the enforcement of confcience
" only, and a preventive fear, left the omitting
" of this duty fhould be againft me, when I
" would ftore up to myfelf the good provifion
" of peaceful hours : fo left it fhould be ftill im-
" puted to be, as I have found it hath been,
" that fome felf pleafing humor of vain glory
" has incited me to conteft with men of high ef-
" timation, now while green years are upon my
" head; from this needlefs furmifal I fhall hope
" to diffuade the intelligent and equal auditor,
" if I can but fay fuccefsfully, that which in this
" exigent behoves me, although I would be
" heard, only if it might be, by the elegant
" and learned reader, to whom principally for
" a while I fhall beg leave I may addrefs myfelf:
" to him it will be no new thing, though I
" tell him, that if I hunted after praife by the
" oftentation of wit and learning, I fhould not
" write thus out of mine own feafon, when I
" have neither yet completed to my mind the
" full circle of my private ftudies (although I
" complain not of any infufficiency to the mat-
" ter in hand) or were I ready to my wifhes,
" it were a folly to commit any thing elaborate-
" ly compofed to the carelefs and interrupted
" liftening of thefe tumultuous times. Next, if
" I were wife only to my own ends, I would

" certainly take fuch a fubject, as of itfelf might
" catch applaufe; whereas this has all the difad-
" vantages on the contrary; and fuch a fubject,
" as the publifhing whereof might be delayed at
" pleafure, and time enough to pencil it over
" with all the curious touches of art, even to
" the perfection of a faultlefs picture; when ,
" as in this argument, the not deferring is of
" great moment to the good fpeeding, that if fo-
" lidity have leifure to do her office, art cannot
" have much. Laftly, I fhould not chufe this man-
" ner of writing, wherein knowing myfelf inferior
" to myfelf, led by the genial power of nature
" to another tafk, I have the ufe, as I may ac-
" count, but of my left hand." Profe Works,
" vol. I. page 62.

Such is the delineation that our author has given us of his own mind and motives in his treatife
on Church Government, which the mention of his
early defign to take orders has led me to anticipate.

Having paffed feven years in Cambridge, and
taken his two degrees, that of bachelor, in 1628,
and that of mafter, in 1632, he was admitted to
the fame degree at Oxford, in 1635. On quitting
an academical life, he was, according to his own
teftimony, regretted by the fellows of his college;
but he regarded the houfe of his father as a retreat favorable to his literary purfuits, and, at the
age of twenty-four, he gladly fhared the rural retirement, in which his parents had recently fettled,
at Horton, in Buckinghamfhire: here he devoted
himfelf, for five years, to ftudy , with that ardor

and perfeverance, to which, as he fays himfelf, in a letter to his friend, Charles Diodati, his nature forcibly inclined him. The letter I am fpeaking of was written in the laft year of his refidence under the roof of his father, and exhibits a lively picture of his progrefs in learning, his paffion for virtue, and his hope of renown.

" To give you an account of my ftudies," he fays, " I have brought down the affairs of the Greeks, in a continued courfe of reading, to the period in which they ceafed to be Greeks. I have long been engaged in the obfcurer parts of Italian hiftory, under the Lombards, the Franks, and the Germans, to the time in which liberty was granted them by the emperor Rodolphus; from this point I think it beft to purfue, in feparate hiftories, the exploits of each particular city *."

He fhows himfelf, in this letter, moft paffionately attached to the Platonic Philofophy : " As to other points, what God may have determined for me, I know not; but this I know, that if he ever inftilled an intenfe love of moral beauty into the breaft of any man, he has inftilled it into mine: Ceres, in the fable, purfued not her daughter with a greater keennefs of inquiry, than I, day and night, the idea of perfection. Hence, wherever

* De ftudiis etiam noftris fies certior, Græcorum res continuata lectione deduximus ufquequo illi Græci effe funt defiti: Italorum in obfcura re diu verfati fumus fub Longobardis & Francis & Germanis ad illud tempus quo illis ab Rodolpho Germaniæ rege conceffa libertas eft; exinde quid quæque civitas fuo marte gefferit, feparatim legere præftabit.

I find a man defpifing the falfe eftimates of the vulgar, and daring to afpire, in fentiment, language, and conduct, to what the higheft wifdom, through every age, has taught us as moft excellent, to him I unite myfelf by a fort of neceffary attachment; and if I am fo influenced by nature or deftiny, that by no exertion or labors of my own I may exalt myfelf to this fummit of worth and honor, yet no powers of heaven or earth will hinder me from looking with reverence and affection upon thofe, who have thoroughly attained this glory, or appear engaged in the fuccefsful purfuit of it.

" You inquire, with a kind of folicitude, even into my thoughts.—Hear then, Diodati, but let me whifper in your ear, that I may not blufh at my reply — I think (fo help me Heaven) of immortality. You inquire alfo, what I am about? I nurfe my wings, and meditate a flight; but my Pegafus rifes as yet on very tender pinions. Let us be humbly wife !* "

* De cætero quidem quid de me ftatuerit Deus nefcio; illud certe, δεινόν μοι ερωτα, ειπερ τω αλλω, τȣ καλȣ ενεϛαξε; nec tanto Ceres labore, ut in fabulis eft, liberam fertur quæfiviffe filiam, quanto ego hanc τȣ καλȣ ιδιαν veluti pulcherrimam quandam imaginem, per omnes rerum formas & facies; (πολλαι γαρ μορφαι των Δαιμονιων) dies noctefque indagare foleo, & quafi certis quibufdam veftigiis ducentem fector. Unde fit, ut qui, fpretis, quæ vulgus prava rerum æftimatione opinatur, id fentire, & loqui &e ffe audet, quod fumma per omne ævum fapientia optimum effe docuit, illi me protinus, ficubi reperiam, neceffitate quadam adjungam. Quod fi ego five natura, five meo fato ita

This very interesting epistle, in which Milton pours forth his heart to the favorite friend of his youth, may convince every candid reader, that he possessed, in no common degree, two qualities very rarely united, ambitious ardor of mind and unaffected modesty. The poet, who speaks with such graceful humility of his literary achievements, had at this time written Comus, a composition that abundantly displays the variety and compass of his poetical powers. After he had delineated, with equal excellence, the frolics of gaiety and the triumphs of virtue, passing with exquisite transition from the most sportive to the sublimest tones of poetry, he might have spoken more confidently of his own productions without a particle of arrogance.

We know not exactly what poems he composed during his residence at Horton. The Arcades seems to have been one of his early compositions, and it was intended as a compliment to his fair neighbour, the accomplished Countess Dowager of Derby; she was the sixth

fum comparatus, ut nulla contentione, & laboribus meis ad tale decus & faftigium laudis ipfe valeam emergere, tamen quo minus qui eam gloriam affecuti funt, aut eo feliciter afpirant, illos femper colam & fufpiciam, nec dii puto nec homines prohibuerint.—Multa folicite quæris, etiam quid cogitem. Audi, Theodate, verum in aurem ut ne rubeam, & finito paulifper apud te grandia loquar : quid cogitem quæris? Ita me bonus deus, immortalitatem quid agam vero? πlεροφυω, & volarme ditor : fed tenellis admodum adhuc pennis evehit fe nofter Pegafus : humile fapiamus.

daughter of Sir John Spencer, and allied to Spencer the poet, who, with his ufual modefty and tendernefs, has celebrated her under the title of Amarillis. At the houfe of this lady, near Uxbridge, Milton is faid to have been a frequent vifitor. The Earl of Bridgewater, before whom, and by whofe children, Comus was reprefented; had married a daughter of Ferdinando Earl of Derby, and thus, as Mr. Warton obferves, it was for the fame family that Milton wrote both the Arcades and Comus. It is probable that the pleafure, which the Arcades afforded to the young relations of the Countefs, gave rife to Comus, as Lawes, the mufical friend of Milton, in dedicating the mafk to the young Lord Brackley, her grandfon, fays, " this poem, which received its firft occafion of birth from yourfelf and others of your noble family, and much honor from your own perfon in the performance. "

Thefe expreffions of Lawes allude, perhaps, to the real incident, which is faid to have fupplied the fubject of Comus, and may feem to confirm an anecdote related by Mr. Warton, from a manufcript of Oldys; that the young and noble performers in this celebrated drama were really involved in adventures very fimilar to their theatrical fituation; that in vifiting their relations, in Herefordfhire, they were benighted in a foreft, and the Lady Alice Egerton actually loft.

Whatever might be the origin of the mafk, the modefty of the youthful poet appears very

conſpicuous in the ſollowing words of Lawes's dedication : " Although not openly acknowled-
" ged by the author, yet it is a legitimate off-
" ſpring, ſo lovely and ſo much deſired, that the
" often copying of it hath tired my pen, to give
" my ſeveral friends ſatisfaction, and brought
" me to a neceſſity of producing it to the pub-
" lic view."

Milton diſcovered a ſimilar diffidence reſpec-
ring his Lycidas, which was written while he reſided with his father, in November, 1637. This exquiſite poem, which, as Mr. Warton juſtly obſerves, " muſt have been either ſolicited as a
" favor by thoſe whom the poet had left in his
" college, or was a voluntary contribution of
" friendſhip ſent to them from the country, " appeared firſt in the academical collection of verſes on the death of Mr. Edward King, and was ſubſcribed only with the initials of its author.

An animated and benevolent veteran of criti-
ciſm, Doctor Warton, has conſidered a reliſh for the Lycidas as a teſt of true taſte in poetry; and it certainly is a teſt, which no lover of Mil-
ton will be inclined to diſpute; though it muſt exclude from the liſt of accompliſhed critics that intemperate cenſor of the great poet, who has endeavoured to deſtroy the reputation of his celebrated monody with the moſt inſulting expreſ-
ſions of ſarcaſtic contempt; expreſſions that no reader of a ſpirit truly poetical can peruſe without mingled emotions of indignation and of

pity! But the charms of Lycidas are of a texture
too firm to be annihilated by the breath of derifion; and though Doctor Johnfon has declared
the poem to be utterly deftitute both of nature
and of art, it will affuredly continue to be admired as long as tendernefs, imagination, and
harmony, are regarded as genuine fources of
poetical delight.

The effect of this favorite compofition is exactly fuch as the poet intended to produce; it firft
engages the heart with the fimplicity of juft and
natural forrow, and then proceeds to elevate the
mind with magnificent images, ennobled by affectionate and devotional enthufiafm.

The beauties of this pathetic and fublime monody are fufficiently obvious; but the reader,
who compares it with a poem on the fame fubject by Cleveland, once the popular rival of
Milton, may derive pleafure from perceiving
how infinitely our favorite poet has excelled,
on this occafion, an eminent antagonift.

Though we find no circumftances, that may
afcertain the date of the Allegro and Penforofo,
it feems probable, that thofe two enchanting
pictures of rural life, and of the diverfified delights arifing from a contemplative mind, were
compofed at Horton. It was, perhaps, in the
fame fituation, fo favorable to poetical exertions, that Milton wrote the incomparable Latin
poem addreffed to his father. There are, indeed, fome expreffions in this performance,

which may favor an opinion, that it ought to bear an earlier date; but it has such strength and manlinefs of fentiment, as incline me to fuppofe it written at this period; an idea that feems almoft confirmed by the lines, that fpeak of his application to French and Italian; after the completion of his claffical ftudies.

Whatever date may be affigned to it, the compofition deferves our particular regard, fince, of all his poems, it does the higheft honor to his heart.

With what energy and tendernefs is his filial gratitude expreffed in the following graceful exordium:

> Nunc mea Pierios cupiam per pectora fontes
> Irriguas torquere vias, totumque per ora
> Volvere laxatum gemino de vertice rivum,
> Ut tenues oblita fonos, audacibus alis
> Surgat in officium venerandi mufa parentis.
> Hoc utcunque tibi gratum, pater optime, carmen
> Exiguum meditatur opus: nec novimus ipfi
> Aptius a nobis quæ poffint munera donis
> Refpondere tuis, quamvis nec maxima poffint
> Refpondere tuis, nedum ut par gratia donis
> Effe queat, vacuis quæ redditur arida verbis.

> O that Pieria's fpring would thro' my breaft
> Pour it's infpiring influence, and rufh
> No rill, but rather an o'er-flowing flood!
> That for my venerable father's fake,
> All meaner themes renounc'd, my mufe, on wings

'Of duty borne, might reach a loftier ſtrain!
For thee, my father, howſoe'er it pleaſe,
She frames this ſlender work; nor know I aught
That may thy gifts more ſuitably requite;
Tho' to requite them ſuitably would aſk
Returns much nobler, and ſurpaſſing far
The meager gifts of verbal gratitude.

How elegant is the praiſe he beſtows on the
muſical talents of his father, and how pleaſing
the exulting and affectionate ſpirit with which he
ſpeaks of their ſocial and kindred ſtudies!

Nec tu perge, precor, ſacras contemnere Muſas,
Nec vanas inopeſque puta, quarum ipſe peritus
Munere, mille ſonos numeros componis ad aptos,
Millibus & vocem modulis variare canoram
Doctus, Arionii merito ſis nominis hæres.
Nunc tibi quid mirum, ſi me genuiſſe poetam
Contigerit, charo ſi tam prope ſanguine juncti,
Cognatas artes, ſtudiumque affine ſequamur?
Ipſe volens Phœbus ſe diſpertire duobus,
Altera dona mihi, dedit altera dona parenti;
Dividuumque deum, genitorque puerque, tenemus.
Tu tamen ut ſimules teneras odiſſe camœnas,
Non odiſſe reor; neque enim, pater, ire jubebas
Qua via lata patet, qua pronior area lucri,
Certaque condendi fulget ſpes aurea nummi:
Nec rapis ad leges, male cuſtoditaque gentis
Jura, nec inſulſis damnas clamoribus aures;
Sed magis excultam cupiens diteſcere mentem,

Me procul urbano ftrepitu, feceffibus altis
Abductum, Aoniæ jucunda per otia ripæ,
Phœbæo lateri comitem finis ire beatum.

Nor thou perfift, I pray thee, ftill to flight
The facred Nine, and to imagine vain
And ufelefs, powers, by whom infpir'd, thyfelf,
Art fkilful to affociate verfe with airs
Harmonious, and to give the human voice
A thoufand modulations! Heir by right
Indifputable of Arion's fame!
Now fay! What wonder is it if a fon
Of thine delight in verfe; if, fo conjoin'd
In clofe affinity, we fympathize
In focial arts, and kindred ftudies fweet:
Such diftribution of himfelf to us.
Was Phœbus' choice; thou haft thy gift, and I
Mine alfo, and between us we receive,
Father and fon, the whole infpiring God.
No! howfoe'er the femblance thou affume
Of hate, thou hateft not the gentle mufe,
My father! for thou never bad'ft me tread
The beaten path and broad, that leads right on
To opulence; nor didft condemn thy fon
To the infipid clamors of the bar,
To laws voluminous and ill obferv'd;
But wifhing to enrich me more, to fill
My mind with treafure, ledft me far away
From civic din to deep retreats, to banks
And ftreams Aonian, and with free confent
Didft place me happy at Apollo's fide.

The poet feems to have had a prophetic view of the fingular calumnies, that awaited his reputation, and to have anticipated his triumph, over all his adverfaries, in the following magnanimous exclamation :

Efte procul vigiles curæ ! procul efte querelæ !
Invidiæque acies tranfverfo tortilis hirquo !
Sæva nec anguiferos extende calumnia rictus:
In me trifte nihil, fœdiffima turba, poteftis,
Nec veftri fum juris ego ; fecuraque tutus
Pectora, vipereo gradiar fublimis ab ictu.

Away then, fleeplefs care ! complaint away !
And envy " with thy jealous leer malign ; "
Nor let the monfter calumny fhoot forth
Her venom'd tongue at me ! Detefted foes !
Ye all are impotent againft my peace ;
For I am privileg'd, and bear my breaft
Safe, and too high for your viperian wound.

After this high ton'd burft of confidence and indignation, how fweetly the poet finks again into the tender notes of gratitude, in the clofe of this truly filial compofition !

At tibi, chare pater, poftquam non æqua merenti
Poffe referre datur, nec dona rependere factis,
Sit memoraffe fatis, repetitaque munera grato
Percenfere animo, fidæque reponere menti.
Et vos, O noftri, juvenilia carmina, lufus,
Si modo perpetuos fperare audebitis annos,

Et

Et domini fuperefle rogo, lucemque tueri,
Nec fpiffo rapient oblivia nigra fub orco;
Forfitan has laudes, decantatumque parentis
Nomen, ad exemplum, fero fervabitis ævo.

But thou, my father, fince to render thanks
Equivalent, and to requite by deeds
Thy liberality, exceeds my power,
Suffice it that I thus record thy gifts,
And bear them treafur'd in a grateful mind.
Ye too, the favorite paftime of my youth,
My voluntary numbers, if ye dare,
To hope longevity, and to furvive
Your mafter's funeral, not foon abforb'd
In the oblivious Lethæan gulph,
Shall to futurity perhaps convey
This theme, and by thefe praifes of my fire
Improve the fathers of a diftant age.

" He began now," fays Johnfon, " to grow
" weary of the country, and had fome purpofe
" of taking chambers in the inns of court."
This wearinefs appears to have exifted only
in the fancy of his biographer. During the five
years that Milton refided with his parents, in
Buckinghamfhire, he had occafional lodgings
in London, which he vifited, as he informs us
himfelf, for the purpofe of buying books, and
improving himfelf in mathematics and in mufic,
at that time his favorite amufements. The letter, which intimates his intention of taking chambers in the inns of court, was not written from

the country, as his biographer seems to have sup-
posed; it is dated from London, and only expresses, that his quarters there appeared to him
awkward and inconvenient *.

On the death of his mother, who died in
April, 1637, and is buried in the Chancel of
Horton church, he obtained his father's permiffion to gratify his eager defire of vifiting the continent, a permiffion the more readily granted,
perhaps, as one of his motives for vifiting Italy,
was to form a collection of Italian mufic.

Having received fome directions for his travels
from the celebrated Sir Henry Wotton, he went,
with a fingle fervant, to Paris, in 1638; he was
there honored by the notice of Lord Scudamore, the Englifh ambaffador, who, at his earneft defire, gave him an introduction to Grotius, then refiding at Paris as the minifter of
Sweden.

Curiofity is naturally excited by the idea of
a conference between two perfons fo eminent
and accomplifhed. It has been conjectured,
that Milton might conceive his firft defign of
writing a tragedy on the banifhment of Adam
from this interview with Grotius; but if the
Adamus Exful of the Swedifh ambaffador were a

* Dicam jam nunc ferio quid cogitem, in hofpitium juridico-
rum aliquod immigrare, ficubi amœna & umbrofa ambulatio
eft, quod & inter aliquot fodales, commodior illic habitatio, fi
manere, & ορμητηριον ευπρεπεστερον quocunque libitum erit ex-
currere: ubi nunc fum, ut nofti, obfcure & angufte fum.

subject of their difcourfe, it is probable its author muft have fpoken of it but flightly, as a juvenile compofition, fince he does fo in a letter to his friend Voffius, in 1616, concerning a new edition of his poetry; from which he particularly excluded this facred drama, as too puerile, in his own judgment to be re-publifhed. *

The letters of Grotius, voluminous and circumftantial as they are, afford no traces of this interefting vifit; but they lead me to imagine, that the point, which the learned ambaffador moft warmly recommended to Milton, on his departure for Italy, was, to pay the kindeft attention in his power to the fufferings of Galileo, then perfecuted as a prifoner by the inquifition in Florence.

In a letter to Voffius, dated in the very month when Milton was probably introduced to Grotius, that liberal friend to fcience and humanity fpeaks thus of Galileo : " This old man, to whom the univerfe is fo deeply indebted, worn out with maladies, and ftill more with anguifh of mind, gives us little reafon to hope, that his life can be long; common prudence, therefore, fuggefts to us to make the utmoft of the time, while we can yet avail ourfelves of fuch an

---

* Chriftum patientem recudendum judico, ideoque velim aliquod ejus exemplum ad me mitti, ut errata typographica corrigam, quando ipfe nullum habeo. Adami Exulis poema juvenilius fit quam ut aufim addere. Grotii Epift. 77.

inftru&lor *. " Milton was, of all travellers, the moft likely to feize a hint of this kind with avidity, and expreffions in Paradife Loft have led an Italian biographer of the poet to fuppofe, that while he refided at Florence he caught from Galileo, or his difciples, fome ideas approaching towards the Newtonian philofophy. He has informed us himfelf, that he really faw the illuftrious fcientific prifoner of the inquifition, and it feems not unreafonable to conclude, that he was in fome degree indebted to his conference with Grotius for that mournful gratification.

From Paris our author proceeded to Italy, embarking at Nice for Genoa. After a curfory view of Leghorn and Pifa, he fettled for two months at Florence; a city, which he particularly regarded for the elegance of its language, and the men of genius it had produced; here, as he informs us, he became familiar with many perfons diftinguifhed by their rank and learning; and here, probably, he began to form thofe great, but unfettled, projects of future compofition, which were to prove the fources of his glory, and of which he thus speaks himfelf:

" In the private academies of Italy, whither I " was favoured to refort, perceiving that fome " trifles I had in memory, compofed at under

---

* Senex is, optime de univerfo meritus, morbo fra&us, infuper & animi ægritudine, haud multum nobis vitæ fuæ promittit; quare prudentiæ erit arripere tempus, dum tanto do&ore uti licet. Grotii Epift. 964.

" twenty, or thereabout (for the manner is,
" that every one muſt give ſome proof of his
" wit and reading there) met with acceptance
" above what was looked for, and other things;
" which I had-ſhifted, in ſcarcity of books and
" conveniency, to patch up amongſt them, were
" received with written encomiums, which the
" Italian is not forward to beſtow on men of
" this ſide the Alps, I began thus far to aſſent
" both to them, and divers of my friends here
" at home, and not leſs to an inward prompting,
" which now grew daily upon me, that by la-
" bour and intent ſtudy, (which I take to be
" my portion in this life) joined with the ſtrong
" propenſity of nature, I might, perhaps, leave
" ſomething ſo written to after-times as they
" ſhould not willingly let it die. Theſe thoughts
" at once poſſeſſed me, and theſe other, that if
" I were certain to write as men buy leaſes, for
" three lives and downward, there ought no re-
" gard to be ſooner had than to God's glory, by
" the honour and inſtruction of my country;
" for which cauſe, and not only for that I knew
" it would be hard to arrive at the ſecond rank
" among the Latins, I applied myſelf to that re-
" ſolution, which Arioſto followed againſt the
" perſuaſions of Bembo, to fix all the induſtry
" and art I could unite to the adorning of my
" native tongue; not to make verbal curioſities
" the end, (that were a toilſome vanity) but to
" be an interpreter and relater of the beſt and

" sageft things among mine own citizens through-
" out this ifland in the mother dialect; that
" what the greateft and choiceft wits of Athens,
" Rome, or modern Italy, and thofe Hebrews
" of old, did for their country, I in my pro-
" portion, with this over and above of being
" a Chriftian, might do for mine, not caring to
" be once named abroad, though perhaps, I
" could attain to that, but content with thefe
" Britifh iflands as my world." Profe Works,
vol. 1. p. 62.

It is delightful to contemplate fuch a character
as Milton, thus cherifhing, in his own mind,
the feeds of future greatnefs, and animating his
youthful fpirit with vifions of renown, that time
has realized and extended beyond his moft fanguine wifhes.

He appears, on every occafion, a fincere and
fervent lover of his country, and expreffes, in
one of his Latin Poems, the fame patriotic idea,
that he fhould be fatisfied with glory confined to
thefe Iflands.

> Mi fatis ampla
> Merces, & mihi grande decus (fim ignotus in ævum
> Tum licet, externo penitufque inglorius orbi)   .
> Si me flava comas legat Ufa, & potor Alauni,
> Vorticibufque frequens Abra, & nemus omne Treantæ,
> Et Thamefis meus ante omnes, & fufca metallis
> Tamara, & extremis me difcant Orcades undis.
>
> Epitaphium Damonis.

> And it shall well suffice me, and shall be
> Fame and proud recompence enough for me,
> If Ufa golden hair'd my verse may learn ;
> If Alain, bending o'er his cryftal urn ,
> Swift whirling Abra, Trent's o'erfhadow'd ftream ,
> If, lovelier far than all in my efteem ,
> Thames, and the Tamar ting'd with mineral hues,
> And northern Orcades, regard my mufe.

In tracing the literary ambition of Milton from the firft conception of his great purpofes to their accomplifhment, we feem to participate in the triumph of his genius, which, though it afpired only tô the praife of thefe British iflands, is already grown an object of univerfal admiration, and may find hereafter, in the weftern world, the ampleft theatre of his glory.

Dr. Johnfon takes occafion, from the paffage in which Milton fpeaks of the literary projects he conceived in Italy, to remark, that " he had a " lofty and fteady confidence in himfelf, perhaps not withoutfome contempt of others. " The latter part of this obfervation is evidently invidious; it is completely refuted by the various commendations, which the graceful and engaging manners of the poetical traveller received from the Italians: a contemptuous fpirit, indeed, appears utterly incompatible with the native difpofition of Milton, whofe generous enthufiafm led him to conceive the fondeft veneration for all, who were diftinguifhed by genius or virtue; a difpofition, which he has expreffed in the ftrongeft terms, as the reader may recollect, in a letter, already cited, to his friend Diodati! His prejudiced biographer endeavours to prove, that his fpirit was contemptuous, by obferving, that he was frugal of his praife. The argument is particularly defective, as applied to Milton on his travels; fince the praifes he beftowed on thofe accomplifhed foreigners, who were kind to him, are liberal in the higheft degree, and apparently dictated by the heart.

After a fhort vifit to Sienna, he refided two months in Rome, enjoying the moft refined fociety, which that city could afford. By the favor of Holftenius, the well known librarian of the Vatican (whofe kindnefs to him he has recorded in a Latin Epiftle equally grateful and elegant) he was recommended to the notice of Cardinal Barberini, who honored him with the moft flattering attention; it was at the concerts of the Cardinal that he was captivated by the charms of Leonora Baroni, whofe extraordinary mufical powers he has celebrated in Latin verfe, and whom he is fuppofed to addrefs as a lover in his Italian poetry. The moft eloquent of the paffions, which is faid to convert almoft every man who feels it into a poet, induced the imagination of Milton to try its powers in a foreign language, whofe difficulties he feems to have perfectly fubdued by the united aids of genius and of love.

His Italian fonnets have been liberally commended by natives of Italy, and one of them
contains a fketch of his own character, fo fpirited and fingular as to claim a place in this
narrative.

Giovane piano, e femplicetto amante .
  Poichè fuggir me ftcffo in dubio fono,
  Madonna a voi del mio cuor l' humil dono
  Farò divoto; io certo a prove tante
L' ebbi fedele, intrepido, coftante,
  Di Penfieri leggiadri accorto, e buono;
  Quando rugge il grand mondo, e fcocca il tuono,
  S' arma di fe, e d' intero diamante;
Tanto del forfe, e d' invidia ficuro,
  Di timori, e fperanze, al popol ufe,
  Quanto d' ingegno, e d'alto valor vago,
E di cetra fonora, e delle mufe :
  Sol troverete in tal parte men duro,
  Ove amor mife l' infanabil ago.

Enamour'd, artlefs, young, on foreign ground,
  Uncertain whether from myfelf to fly,
  To thee, dear lady, with an humble figh,
  Let me devote my heart, which I have found
By certain proofs, not few, intrepid, found,
  Good, and addicted to conceptions high :
  When tempeft fhakes the world, and fires the fky,
  It refts in adamant, felf wrapt around,
As fafe from envy and from outrage rude,
  From hopes and fears that vulgar minds abufe,

As fond of genius, and fixt folitude,
Of the refounding lyre, and every mufe:
Weak you will find it in one only part,
Now pierc'd by love's immedicable dart.

It was at Rome that Milton was compliment-
ed, in Latin verfe, by Selvaggi and Salfilli: his
reply to the latter, then fuffering from a fevere
malady, is fo remarkable for its elegance, tendernefs, and fpirit, that Mr. Warton praifes it
as one of the fineft lyrical compofitions, which
the Latin poetry of modern times can exhibit.

The circumftances that happened to our author in his travels, and, indeed, the moft ftriking particulars of his life, are related by himfelf,
in his " Second Defence." He there tells us,
that in paffing from Rome to Naples his fellow-
traveller was a hermit, who introduced him to
Baptifta Manfo, Marquis of Villa, an accomplifhed nobleman, and fingularly diftinguifhed as
the friend and the biographer of two eminent
poets, Taffo and Marini; they have both left
poetical memorials of their efteem for the Marquis, who acquired his title as a foldier in the
fervice of Spain, but retiring early, with confiderable wealth, to Naples, his native city, he
founded there a literary academy, and lived in
fplendor as its prefident.

This graceful and venerable hero, whofe politenefs and learning had been fondly celebrated
by Taffo, in a dialogue on friendfhip, that bears

the name of Manfo, was near eighty when Milton became his gueft: he feems to have been en_
deared to the imagination of our poet by the
liberal and affectionate tribute he had_ paid to
the memory of his illuftrious poetical friends; a
tribute very feelingly defcribed by Milton in the
following lines, addreffed to the noble and generous biographer—they fpeak firft of Marini:

Ille itidem moriens tibi foli debita vates
Offa, tibi foli, fupremaque vota reliquit :
Nec manes pietas tua chara fefellit amici;
Vidimus arridentem operofo ex ære poetam ;
Nec fatis hoc vifum eft in utrumque; & nec pia
    ceffant
Officia in tumulo; cupis integros rapere orco,
Qua potes, atque avidas Parcarum eludere leges;
Amborum genus, & varia fub forte peractam,
Defcribis vitam, morefque, & dona Minervæ,
Æmulus illius, Mycalen qui natus ad altam,
Retulit Æolii vitam facundus Homeri.

To thee alone the poet would intruft
His lateft vows, to thee alone his duft :
And thou with punctual piety haft paid,
In labor'ds brafs, thy tribute to his fhade ;
Nor this contented thee; thy zeal would fave
Thy bards uninjur'd from the whelming grave;
In more induring hiftory to live
An endlefs life is alfo thine to give !
And thou haft given it them; and deigned to
    teach

> The manners, fortunes, lives, and gifts of each,
> Rival to him, whofe pen, to nature true,
> The life of Homer eloquently drew!

If the two Latin verfes, in which this amiable old man expreffed his admiration of the young Englifh bard, deferve the name of a " forry diftich," which Johnfon beftows upon them, they ftill prefent Milton to our fancy in a moft favorable light. A traveller, fo little diftinguifhed by birth or opulence, would hardly have obtained fuch a compliment from a nobleman of Manfo's experience, age, and dignity, had he not been peculiarly formed to engage the good opinion and courtefy of ftrangers, by the expreffive comelinefs of his perfon, the elegance of his manners, and the charm of his converfation.

In Manfo, fays Milton, I found a moft friendly guide, who fhowed me himfelf the curiofities of Naples, and the palace of the Viceroy. He came more than once to vifit me, while I continued in that city; and when I left it, he earneftly excufed himfelf, that although he greatly wifhed to render me more good offices, he was unable to do fo in Naples, becaufe in my religion I had difdained all difguife *.

* Neapolim perrexi : illic per eremitam quendam, quicum Roma iter feceram, ad Joannem Baptiftam Manfum, Marchionem Villenfem, virum nobiliffimum atque graviffimum (ad quem Torquatus Taffus, infignis poeta Italus, de amicitia fcripfit) fum introductus; eodemque ufus, quamdiu illuc fui,

Pleafing and honorable as the civilities were
that our young countryman received from this
Neftor of Italy, he has amply repaid them in
a poem, which, to the honor of Englifh gratitude
and Englifh genius, we may juftly pronounce
fuperior to the compliments beftowed on this engaging character by the two celebrated poets, who
wrote in his own language, and were peculiarly
attached to him.

Of the five fonnets, indeed, that Taffo addreffed to his courteous and liberal friend, two
are very beautiful; but even thefe are furpaffed,
both in energy and tendernefs, by the following
conclufion of a poem, infcribed to Manfo, by
Milton.

Diis dilecte fenex, te Jupiter æquus oportet
Nafcentem, & miti luftrarit lumine Phœbus,
Atlantifque nepos; neque enim, nifi charus ab' ortu
Dii fuperis, poterit magno faviffe poetæ.
Illinc longæva tibi lento fub flore fenectus
Vernat, & Æfonios lucratur vivida fufos;
Nondum deciduos fervans tibi frontis honores,
Ingeniumque vigens, & adultum mentis acumen.
O mihi fi mea fors talem concedat amicum,
Phœbæos decoraffe viros qui tam bene norit,

fane amiciffimo; qui & ipfe me per urbis loca & proregis aulam
circumduxit, & vifendi gratia haud femel ipfe ad hofpitium ve-
nit : difcedenti ferio excufavit fe, tametfi multo plura detuliffe
mihi officia maxime cupiebat, non potuiffe illa in urbe, propterea quod nolebam in religione effe tectior. — Defenfio fecunda.

Siquando indigenas revocabo in carmina reges,
Arturumque etiam fub terris bella moventem!
Aut dicam invictæ fociali fœdere ménfæ
Magnanimos heroas; &, O modo fpiritus adfit,
Frangam Saxonicas Britonum fub marte phalanges!
Tandem ubi non tacitæ permenfus tempora vitæ,
Annorumque fatur, cineri fua jura relinquam,
Ille mihi lecto madidis aftaret ocellis,
Aftanti fat erit fi dicam, fim tibi curæ;
Ille meos artus, liventi morte folutos,
Curaret parva componi molliter urna;
Forfitan & noftros ducat de marmore vultus,
Nectens aut Paphia myrti aut Parnaffide lauri
Fronde comas; at ego fecura pace quiefcam.
Tum quoque, fi qua fides, fi præmia certa bonorum,
Ipfe ego cœlicolum femotus in æthera divum,
Quo labor & mens pura vehunt, atque ignea virtus,
Secreti hæc aliqua. Mundi de parte videbo,
Quantum fata finunt: & tota mente ferenum,
Ridens, purpureo fuffundar lumine vultus,
Et fimul æthereo plaudam mihi lætus olympo.

Well may we think, O dear to all above,
Thy birth diftinguifh'd by the fmile of Jove,
And that Apollo fhed his kindlieft power,
And Maia's fon, on that propitious hour;
Since only minds fo born can comprehend
A poet's worth, or yield that worth a friend:
Hence on thy yet unfaded cheek appears
The lingering frefhnefs of thy greener years;
Hence in thy front and features we admire

Nature unwither'd, and a mind entire.
O might fo true a friend to me belong,
So fkill'd to grace the votaries of fong,
Should I recal hereafter into rhyme
The kings and heroes of my native clime,
Arthur the chief, who even now prepares
In fubterraneous being future wars,
With all his martial knights to be reftor'd,
Each to his feat around the fed'ral board;
And O! if fpirit fail me not, difperfe
Our Saxon plunderers in triumphant verfe;
Then after all, when with the paft content,
A life I finifh, not in filence fpent,
Should he, kind mourner, o'er my death bed
    bend,
I fhall but need to fay " be ftill my friend!"
He, faithful to my duft, with kind concern,
Shall place it gently in a modeft urn;
He too, perhaps, fhall bid the marble breathe
To honor me, and with the graceful wreath,
Or of Parnaffus, or the Paphian Ifle,
Shall bind my brows—but I fhall reft the while.
Then alfo, if the fruits of faith endure,
And virtue's promis'd recompence be fure,
Borne to thofe feats, to which the bleft afpire,
By purity of foul and virtuous fire,
Thefe rites, as fate permits, I fhall furvey
With eyes illumin'd by celeftial day,
And, every cloud from my pure fpirit driven,
Joy in the bright beatitude of heaven.

The preceding verfes have various claims to attention; they exhibit a lively picture of the literary project that occupied the mind of Milton at this period; they forcibly prove with what vehemence of defire he panted for poetical immortality, and for the fuperior rewards of a laborious life, devoted to piety and virtue.

His acquaintance with Manfo may be regarded as the moft fortunate incident of his foreign excurfion. Nothing could have a greater tendency to preferve and ftrengthen the feeds of poetic enterprife in the mind of the young traveller, than his familiarity with this eminent ad engaging perfonage, the bofom friend of Taffo; the friend who had cherifhed that great and afflicted poet under his roof in a feafon of his mental calamity, had reftored his health, re-animated his fancy, and given a religious turn to the lateft efforts of his majeftic mufe. The very life of Taffo, which this noble biographer had written with the copious and minute fidelity of perfonal knowledge, and with the ardor of affectionate enthufiafm, might be fufficient to give new energy to Milton's early paffion for poetical renown: his converfation had, probably, a ftill greater tendency to produce this effect. Circumftances remote, and apparently of little moment, have often a marvellous influence on the works of imagination; nor is it too wild a conjecture to fuppofe, that the zeal of Manfo, in fpeaking to Milton of his departed friend, might give force and permanence

to

to that literary ambition, which ultimately rendered his afpiring gueft the great rival of Taffo, and ,
in the eftimation of Englifhmen , his fuperior.

From Naples it was the defign of Milton to
pafs into Sicily and Greece; but receiving intelligence of the civil war in England, he felt it inconfiftent with his principles to wander abroad,
even for the improvement of his mind, while his
countrymen were contending for liberty at home.

In preparing for his return to Rome , he was
cautioned againft it by fome mercantile friends,
whofe letters intimated , that he had much to
apprehend from the machinations of Englifh je-
fuits , if he appeared again in that city ; they
were incenfed againft him by the freedom of his
difcourfe on topics of religion : " I had made it
a rule (fays Milton) never to ftart a religious
fubject in this country; but if I were queftioned
on my faith , never to diffemble , whatever I
might fuffer. I returned , neverthelefs, to Rome,"
continues the undaunted traveller , " and , whenever I was interrogated , I attempted no difguife;
if any one attacked my principles, I defended
the true religion in the very city of the pope,
and, during almoft two months , with as much
freedom as I had ufed before. By the protection
of God I returned fafe again to Florence, re-vifit-
ing friends , who received me as gladly as if I
had been reftored to my native home *. "

* In Siciliam quoque & Græciam trajicere volentem me, triftis
ex Anglia belli civilis nuntius revocavit; turpe enim exiftimabam

After a second refidence of almoft two months in Florence, whence he made an excurfion to Lucca, a place endeared to him by having produced the anceftors of his favorite friend Diodati, he extended his travels through Bologna and Ferrara to Venice. Here, he remained a month, and having fent hence a collection of books, and particularly of Mufic, by fea, he proceeded himfelf through Verona and Milan to Geneva. In this city he was particularly gratified by the fociety and kindnefs of John Diodati, uncle of his young friend, whofe untimely death he lamented in a Latin poem, of which we fhall foon have occafion to fpeak. Returning by his former road through France, he reached England at a period that feems to have made a ftrong impreffion on his mind, when the king was waging, in favor of epifcopacy, his unprofperous war with the Scots. The time of Milton's

dum mei cives domi de libertate dimicarent, ne animi caufa etiofe peregrinari. Romam autem reverfurum, monebant mercatores fe didiciffe per literas parari mihi ab jefuitis Anglis infidias, fi Romam reverterem, eo quod de religione nimis libere loquutus effem. Sic enim mecum ftatueram, de religione quidem iis in locis fermones ultro non inferre; interrogatus de fide, quicquid effem paffurus, nihil diffimulare. Romam itaque nihilominus redii : quid effem, fi quis interrogabat, nemine celavi; fi quis adoriebatur, in ipfa urbe pontificis, alteros prope duos menfes, orthodoxam religionem, ut antea, liberrime tuebar : deoque fic volente, incolumis Florentiam rurfus perveni; haud minus mei cupientes revifens, ac fi in patriam revertiffem. — Defenfio fecunda.

abfence from his native country exceeded not, by his own account, a year and three months.

In the relation that he gives himfelf of his return, the name of Geneva recalling to his mind one of the moft flanderous of his political adverfaries, he animates his narrative by a folemn appeal to heaven·on his unfpotted integrity; he protefts that, during his refidence in foreign fcenes, where licentioufnefs was univerfal, his own conduct was perfectly irreproachable ⁎. I dwell the more zealoufly on whatever may elucidate the moral character of Milton, becaufe, even among thofe who love and revere him, the fplendor of the poet has.in fome meafure eclipfed the merit of the man; but in proportion as the particulars of his life are ftudied with intelligence and candor, his virtue will become, as it ought to be, the friendly rival of his genius, and receive its due fhare of admiration and efteem. Men, indeed of narrow minds, and of fervile principles, will for ever attempt to depreciate a character fo abfolutely the reverfe of their own; but liberal fpirits, who allow to others that freedom of fentiment, which they vindicate for themfelves, however they difapprove or oppofe the opinions of the fectary and the republican,

---

⁎ Quæ urbs, cum in mentem mihi hinc veniat Mori calumniatoris, facit ut deum hic rurfus teftem invocem, me his omnibus in locis, ubi tam multa licent, ab omni flagitio ac probro integrum atque intactum vixiffe, illud perpetuo cogitantem, fi hominum latere oculos poffem, dei certe non poffe.

will render honorable and affectionate juftice to the patriotic benevolence, the induftry,
and the courage, with which Milton endeavoured
to promote what he fincerely and fervently regarded as the true intereft of his country.

We have now attended him to the middle
ftage of his life, at which it may not be improper
to paufe, and make a few remarks on the years
that are paffed; and thofe that are yet in profpect. We behold him, at the age of thirty-two,
recalled to England, from a foreign excurfion of
improvement and delight, by a manly fenfe of
what he owed to his country in a feafon of difficulty and, danger. His thoughts and conduct on
this occafion are the more noble and becoming,
as all his preceding years had been employed in
forming, for the moft important purpofes, a
firm and lofty mind, and in furnifhing it abundantly with whatever might be ufeful and honorable to himfelf and others, in the various exigencies and viciffitudes both of private and public
life. We have traced him through a long courfe
of infantine, academical, domeftic, and foreign
ftudy; we have feen him diftinguifhed by application, docility, and genius; uncommonly
attached to his inftructors, and moft amiably grateful to his parents; in friendfhip, ardent and
fteady; in love, though tender not intemperate;
as a poet, fenfible of his rare mental endowments, yet peculiarly modeft in regard to his

own productions; enamoured of glory, yet as ready to beftow as anxious to merit praife; in his perfon and manners fo fafhioned to prepoffefs all men in his favor, that even foreigners gave him credit for thofe high literary atchievements, which were to fhed peculiar luftre on his latter days, and confidered him already as a man, of whom his country might be proud.

With fuch accomplifhments, and fuch expectations in his behalf, Milton returned to England. the fubfequent portion of his life, however gloomy and tempeftuous, will be found to correfpond, at leaft in the clofe of it, with the radiant promife of his youth. We fhall fee him deferting his favorite haunts of Parnaffus to enter the thorny paths of ecclefiaftical and political diffenfion : his principles as a difputant will be condemned and approved, according to the prevalence of oppofite and irreconcileable opinions, that fluctuate in the world; but his upright confiftency of conduct deferves applaufe from all honeft and candid men of every perfuafion. The Mufe, indeed, who had bleft him with fingular endowments, and given him fo lively a fenfe of his being conftituted a poet by nature, that when he wrote not verfe, he had the ufe, (to borrow his own forcible expreffion) " but of his left hand;" the Mufe alone might have a right to reproach him with having acted againft inward conviction; but could his mufe have vifibly appeared to reprove his defertion of her fervice in a parental remonſtrance, he might have anſwered her, as the young Harry of Shakeſpeare anſwers the tender and keen reproof of his royal father,

" I will redeem all this,
" And in the cloſing of ſome glorious day
" Be bold to tell you that I am your ſon. "

END OF THE FIRST PART.

PART II.

———

INCONCUSSA TENENS DUBIO VESTIGIA MUNDO.

LUCAN.

THE narrative may proceed from the information of Milton himfelf. On his return he procured a refidence in London, ample enough for himfelf and his books, and felt happy in renewing his interrupted ftudies *. This firft eftablifhment (as we learn from his nephew) was a lodging in St. Bride's Church-yard, where he received, as his difciples, the two fons of his fifter, John and Edward Philips; the latter is his biographer; but although he has written the life of his illuftrious relation with a degree of laudable

---

* Ipfe, ficubi poffem, tam rebus turbatis & fluctuantibus, locum confiftendi circumfpiciens mihi librifque meis, fat amplam in urbe domum conduxi; ibi ad intermiffa ftudia beatulus me recepi; rerum exitu deo, imprimis & quibus id muneris populus dabat, facile permiffo.

pride and affectionate spirit, he does not communicate that abundance of information, which might have been expected from the advantage he possessed. In one article his pride has a ludicrous effect, as it leads him into an awkward attempt to vindicate his uncle from the fancied opprobrium of having engaged professionally in the education of youth; a profession which, from its utility and importance, from the talents and virtues it requires, is unquestionably entitled to respect. Philips, will not allow that his uncle actually kept a school, as he taught only the sons of his particular friends. Johnson ridicules this distinction, and seems determined to treat Milton as a profest schoolmaster, for the sake of attempting to prove, that he did not sustain the character with advantage, but adopted a vain and preposterous plan of education.

" Let me not be censured," says the Doctor, " as pedantic or paradoxical; for if I have Mil- " ton against me, I have Socrates on my side : " it was his labor to turn philosophy from the " study of nature to speculations upon life; but " the innovators, whom I oppose, are turning " off attention from life to nature; they seem to " think that we are placed here to watch the " growth of plants, or the motions of the stars; " Socrates was rather of opinion, that what we " had to learn was, how to do good and avoid " evil."

Ὅττι τοι ἐν μεγάροισι κακόν τ' ἀγαθόν τε τέτυκται.

This infidious artifice of reprefenting Milton and Socrates as antagonifts is peculiarly unfortunate, fince no man appears to have imbibed the principles of Socratic wifdom more deeply than our poet; his regard and attachment to them is fervently expreffed, even in his juvenile letters; the very maxims of moral truth, he is accufed of counteracting, never fhone with more luftre than in the following paffage of the Paradife Loft:

> But apt the mind or fancy is to rove
> Uncheck'd, and of her roving is no end,
> Till warn'd; or by experience taught, fhe learn,
> That not to know at large of things remote
> From ufe, obfcure and fubtle, but to know
> That, which before us lies in daily life,
> Is the prime wifdom; what is more is fume,
> Or emptinefs, or fond impertinence,
> And renders us in things that moft concern,
> Unpractis'd, unprepar'd, and ftill to feek.

. Thefe beautiful lines are built in fome meafure, as Bentley has remarked, upon a verfe of Homer, the very verfe admired by Socrates, which Dr. Johnfon has not fcrupled to quote, as a part of his fingular ill-grounded attempt to prove that Milton's ideas of education were in direct oppofition to thofe of the great moralift of Greece; an attempt that arofe from a very inoffenfive boaft of Milton's nephew, who gives a long lift of books perufed by the fcholars of his uncle, which merely proves, that they read more books than are ufually read in our common fchools; and that their diligent inftructor thought it advifable for boys, as they approach towards fixteen, to blend a little knowledge of the fciences with their Greek and Latin.

That he taught the familiar and ufeful doctrine of the Attic philofopher, even in his lighter poetry, we have a pleafing inftance in the following lines of his fonnet to Syriac Skinner, who was one of his fcholars :

    " To meafure life learn thou betimes and know
    " Toward folid good what leads the neareft way."

But his brief treatife, addreffed to Hartlib, affords, perhaps, the beft proof that his ideas of moral difcipline were perfectly in unifon with thofe of Socrates; he fays, in that treatife, " I " call a complete and generous education that, " which fits a man to perform juftly, fkilfully, " and magnanimoufly, all the offices, both pri-" vate and public, of peace and war. " Who can define a good education in terms more truly Socratic ?

Milton, however in his attachment to morality, forgot not the claims of religion; his Sundays were devoted to theology, and Johnfon duly praifes the care, with which he inftructed his fcholars in the primary duties of men.

With a critic fo fincerely devout as Johnfon unqueftionably was, we might have hoped that

the sublime piety of our author would have secured him from sarcastic attacks; but we have yet
to notice two insults of this kind, which the
acrimony of uncorrected spleen has lavished upon
Milton as a preceptor.

" From this wonder-working academy," says
the biographer, " I do not know that there ever
" proceeded any man very eminent for knowledge;
" its only genuine product, I believe, is a small
" history of poetry, written in Latin by his
" nephew, of which, perhaps, none of my read-
" ers ever heard. " The contemptuous spirit
and the inaccuracy of this sarcasm are equally
remarkable. The scholars of Milton were far from
being numerous. Can it be just to speak with
derision of a small academy, merely because it
raises no celebrated author, when we consider
how few of that description every nation produces? We know little of those, who were under
the tuition of our poet, except his two nephews;
these were both writers; and a biographer of
Milton should not have utterly forgotten his obli-
tion to Edward Philips, if he allowed no credit
to his brother, for the spirited Latin treatise in
which that young man appeared as the defender
of his uncle. But the striking inaccuracy of the
critic consists in not giving a just account of a
book that particularly claimed his attention,
Philips's Theatrum Poetarum, a book that, under a Latin title, contains in English a very com-
prehensive list of poets, ancient and modern,

with reflections upon many of them, particularly thofe of our own nation. It is remarkable that this book was licenfed Sep. 14, 1674, juft two months before the death of Milton, and printed the following year. The author affigns an article both to his uncle and his brother. After enumerating the chief works of the former, he modeftly fays, " how far he hath revived the majefty and " true decorum of heroic poefy and tragedy, it " will better become a perfon lefs related than " myfelf to deliver his judgment. "

Though he here fupprefles a defire to praife his moft eminent relation, it burfts forth in an amiable manner, when he comes to fpeak of his brother; for he calls him, " the maternal nephew " and difciple of an author of moft deferved " fame, late deceafed, being the exacteft of heroic " poets (if the truth were well examined , and " it is the opinion of many, both learned and " judicious perfons) either of the ancients or mo- " derns, either of our own or whatever nation elfe."

I tranfcribe with pleafure this honeft and fimple eulogy; it does credit to the intelligence and affection of the poet's difciple, and it in fome meafure vindicates the good fenfe of our country, by fhowing that in the very year of Milton's deceafe, when fome writers have fuppofed that his poetical merit was almoft utterly unknown, there were perfons in the nation, who underftood his full value.

Let us return to the author in his little academy, and the fecond farcaftic infult, which his biographer has beftowed upon him as the mafter of a fchool. The lodging in which he fettled, on his arrival from the continent, was foon exchanged for a more fpacious houfe and garden, in Alderfgate-ftreet, that fupplied him with conveniencies for the reception of fcholars : on this occafion Johnfon exclaims, " let not our venera- " tion for Milton forbid us to look with fome " degree of merriment on great promifes and " fmall performance; on the man who haftens " home, becaufe his countrymen are contending " for their liberty, and, when he reaches the " fcene of action, vapors away his patriotifm " in a private boarding-fchool. "

To excite merriment by rendering Milton ridiculous for having preferred the pen to the fword was an enterprife that furpaffed the powers of Johnfon ; the attempt affords a melancholy proof how far prejudice may miflead a very vigorous underftanding. What but the blind hatred of bigotry could have tempted one great author to deride another, merely for having thought that he might ferve his country more effentially by the rare and highly cultivated faculties of his mind, than by the ordinary fervice of a foldier. But let us hear Milton on this fubject. We have this obligation to the malice of his contemporaries, that it led him to fpeak publicly of himfelf, and to relate, in the moft manly and explicit manner, the real motives of his conduct.

Speaking of the Englifh people, in the commencement of his Second Defence, he

fays * " it was the juft vindication of their laws
" and their religion , that neceffarily led them
" into civil war; they have driven fervitude from
" them by the moft honorable arms; in which
" praife, though I can claim no perfonal fhare,
" yet I can eafily defend myfelf from a charge
" of timidity or indolence, fhould any fuch be
" alledged againft me; for I have avoided the
" toil and danger of military life only to render
" my country affiftance more ufeful, and not
" lefs to my own peril, exerting a mind never
" dejected in adverfity , never influenced by
" unworthy terrors of detraction or of death;

* Quos non legum contemptus aut violatio in effrænatam li-
centiam effudit; non virtutis & gloriæ falfa fpecies, aut ftulta
veterum æmulatio inani nomine libertatis incendit, fed innocentia
vitæ morumque fanctitas rectum atque folum iter ad libertatem
veram docuit, legum & religionis juftiffima defenfio neceffario
armavit. Atque illi quidem Deo perinde confifi, fervitutem ho-
neftiffimis armis pepulere : cujus laudis etfi nullam partem mihi
vindico, a reprehenfione tamen vel timiditatis vel ignaviæ, fi
qua infertur, facile me tueor. Neque enim militiæ labores &
pericula fic defugi, ut non alia ratione, & operam, multo utilio-
rem, nec minore cum periculo meis civibus navarim, & animum
dubiis in rebus neque demiffum unquam, neque ullius invidiæ,
vel etiam mortis plus æquo metuentem præftiterim. Nam cum ab
adolefcentulo humanioribus effem ftudiis, ut qui maxime dedi-
tus, & ingenio femper quam corpore validior, pofthabita caftrenfi
opera, qua me gregarius quilibet robuftior facile fuperaffet,
ad ea me contuli, quibus plus potui; ut parte mei meliore ac
potiore, fi faperem, non deteriore, ad rationes patriæ, caufamque
hanc præftantiffimam, quantum maxime poffem momentum ac-
cederem.

" fince from my infancy I had been addicted to
" literary purfuits, and was ftronger in mind than
" in body, declining the duties of a camp, in
" which every mufcular common man muft have
" furpaffed me, I devoted myfelf to that kind
" of fervice for which I had the greateft ability,
" that, with the better portion of myfelf, I
" might add all the weight I could to the pleas
" of my country and to this moft excellent
" caufe. "

He thus juftifies, on the nobleft ground, the
line of life he purfued. In the fame compofition
he frankly ftates the motives which prompted
him to execute each particular work that raifed
him to notice in his new field of controverfy;
but before we attend to the order in which he
treated various public queftions that he confidered of high moment to his country, it is juft
to obferve his fidelity and tendernefs in firft
difcharging, as a poet, the duties of private
friendfhip.

Before he quitted Florence, Milton received
intelligence of the lofs he had to fuftain, by the
untimely death of Charles Diodati, the favorite
affociate of his early ftudies. On his arrival in
England, the bitternefs of fuch a lofs was felt
with redoubled fenfibility by his affectionate
heart, which relieved and gratified itfelf by com-
memorating the engaging character of the deceafed, in a poem of confiderable length, entitled, Epitaphium Damonis, a poem mentioned

by Johnson with supercilious contempt, yet possessing such beauties as render it pre-eminent in that species of composition.

Many poets have lamented a friend of their youth, and a companion of their studies, but no one has surpassed the affecting tenderness with which Milton speaks of his lost Diodati.'

>   ——Quis mihi fidus
> Hærebit lateri comes, ut tu sæpe solebas,
> Frigoribus duris, & per loca fœta pruinis,
> Aut rapido sub sole, siti morientibus herbis ?
>
> Pectora cui credam ? Quis me lenire docebit
> Mordaces curas, quis longam fallere noctem
> Dulcibus alloquiis, grato cum sibilat igni
> Molle pyrum, & nucibus strepitat focus, & malus
>   Auster
> Miscet cuncta foris, & desuper intonat ulmo ?
>
> Aut æstate, dies medio dum vertitur axe,
> Cum Pan æsculea somnum capit abditus umbra,
> Quis mihi blanditiasque tuas, quis tum mihi risus,
> Cecropiosque sales referet, cultosque lepores ?

Who now my pains and perils shall divide
As thou wast won't, for ever at my side,
Both when the rugged frost annoy'd our feet,
And when the herbage all was parch'd with heat ?

In whom shall I confide, whose counsel find
A balmy medicine to my troubled mind?

Or

Or whofe difcourfe with innocent delight
Shall fill me now, and cheat the wintry night?
While hiffes on my hearth the pulpy pear,
And black'ning chefnuts ftart and crackle there;
While ftorms abroad, the dreary fcene o'erwhelm,
And the wind thunders thro' the riven elm?

Or who, when fummer funs their fummit reach,
and Pan fleeps hidden by the fhelt'ring beech,
Who then fhall render me thy Attic vein
Of wit, too polifh'd to inflict a pain?

With the fpirit of a man moft able to feel, and
moft worthy to enjoy, the delights of true friendfhip, he defcribes the rarity of that ineftimable
bleffing, and the anguifh we fuffer from the untimely lofs of it.

Vix fibi quifque parem de millibus invenit unum;
Aut fi fors dederit tandem non afpera votis,
Illum inopina dies, qua non fperaveris hora,
Surripit, æternum linquens in fæcula damnum.

Scarce one in thoufands meets a kindred mind.
And if the long-fought good at laft he find,
When leaft he fears it, death his treafure fteals,
And gives his heart a wound that nothing heals.

There is, indeed, but one effectual lenitive
for wounds of this nature, which Milton happily
poffeffed in the fincerity and fervor of his religion. He clofes his lamentation for his favorite

friend, as he had clofed his Lycidas, with juft and foothing reflections on the purity of life, by which the object of his regret was diftinguifhed, and with a fublime conception of that celeftial beatitude, which he confidently regarded as the infallible and immediate recompence of departed virtue.

Having paid what was due to friendfhip in his poetical capacity, he devoted his pen to public affairs, and entered on that career of controverfy, which eftranged him fo long, and carried him fo far from thofe milder and more engaging ftudies, that nature and education had made the *darlings of his mind*. If to facrifice favorite purfuits that promifed great glory, purfuits in which acknowledged genius had qualified an ambitious fpirit to excel; if to facrifice thefe to irkfome difputes, from a fenfe of what he owed to the exigencies of his country; if fuch conduct deferve, as it affuredly does, the name of public virtue, it may be as difficult, perhaps, to find an equal to Milton in genuine patriotifm as in poetical power.: for who can be faid to have facrificed fo much, or to have fhown a firmer affection to the public good? If he miftook the mode of promoting it; if his fentiments, both on ecclefiaftical and civil policy, are fuch as the majority of our countrymen think it juft and wife to reject, let us give him the credit he deferves for the merit of his intention; let us refpect, as we ought to do, the probity of an exalted underftanding , animated by a fervent, fteady, and laudable defire to enlighten mankind , and to render them more virtuous and happy.

In the year 1640 , when Milton returned to England , the current of popular opinion ran with great vehemence againft epifcopacy. He was prepared to catch the fpirit of the time, and to become an advocate for ecclefiaftical re-formation , by having peculiar and domeftic grounds of complaint againft religious oppreffion. His favorite preceptor had been reduced to exile, and his father difinherited, by intolerance and fuperftition. He wrote, therefore, with the indig-nant enthufiafm of a man refenting the injuries of thofe, who are moft entitled to his love and veneration. The ardor of his affections confpi-red with the warmth of his fancy to enflame him with that puritanical zeal, which blazes fo in-tenfely in his controverfial productions : no lefs than four of thefe were publifhed within two years after his return; and he thus fpeaks of the motives, that led him to this fpecies of compofi-tion, in his Second Defence.

" Being * animated by this univerfal outcry againft the bifhops , as I perceived that men

* Ut primum loquendi faltem cæpta eft libertas concedi, omnia in epifcopos aperiri ora; alii de ipforum vitiis, alii de ipfius ordinis vitio conqueri — — — Ad hæc fane experrectus, cum veram affectari viam ad libertatem cernerem , ab his initiis , his paffibus , ad liberandam fervitute vitam omnem mortalium rectiffime procedi, fi ab religione difciplina orta, ad

were taking the true road to liberty, and might proceed with the utmoſt rectitude from theſe beginnings to deliver human life from all baſe ſubjection, if their diſcipline, drawing its ſource from religion, proceeded {to morals and political inſtitutions ; as I had been trained from my youth to the particular knowledge of what belonged to divine, and what to human juriſdiction; and as I thought I ſhould deſerve to forfeit the power of being uſeful to mankind, if I now failed to aſſiſt my country and the church, and ſo many brethren, who for the ſake of the goſpel were expoſing themſelves to peril, I reſolved, though my thoughts had been pre-engaged by

mores & inſtituta reipublicæ emanaret, cum etiam me ita ab adolcſcentia paraſſem, ut quid divini, quid humani eſſet juris, ante omnia poſſem non ignorare, meque conſuluiſſem ecquando ullius uſus eſſem futurus, ſi nunc patriæ, immo vero eccleſiæ totque fatribus evangelii cauſa periculo ſeſe objicientibus deeſſem, ſtatui, etſi tunc alia quædam meditabar, huc omne ingenium, omnes induſtriæ vires transferre. Primum itaque de reformanda eccleſia Anglicana, dnos ad amicum quendam libros conſcripſi ; deinde, cum duo præ cæteris magni nominis epiſcopi ſuum jus contra miniſtros quoſdam primarios aſſererent, ratus de iis rebus, quas amore ſolo veritatis, & ex officii chriſtiani ratione didiceram, haud pejus me dicturum quam qui de ſuo quæſtu & injuſtiſſimo dominatu contendcbant, ad hunc libris duobus, quorum unus De Epiſcopatu Prælatico, alter De Ratione Diſciplinæ Eccleſiaſticæ, inſcribitur, ad illum ſcriptis quibuſdam animadverſionibus, & mox Apologia reſpondi, & miniſtris facundiam hominis, ut ferebatur ægrc ſuſtinentibus, ſuppetias tuli, & ab eo tempore, ſi quid poſtea reſponderent, interfui.

other defigns, to transfer to this object all my talents and all my application : firft, therefore, I wrote of reformation in England two books addreffed to a friend; afterwards when two bifhops of eminence had afferted their caufe againft the leading minifters of the oppofite party, as I conceived that I could argue, from a love of truth and a fenfe of chriftian duty, not lefs forcibly than my antagonift (who contended for lucre and their own unjuft dominion) I anfwered one of them in two books with the following titles, Of Prelatical Epifcopacy, Of Church Government ; and the other, firft in Animadverfions upon the Remonftrants Defence againft Smectymnuus, and fecondly, in my Apology. As the minifters were thought hardly equal to their opponent in eloquence, I lent them my aid, and from that time, if they made any farther reply, I was a party concerned. "

I have inferted this paffage at full length, becaufe it gives us a clear infight into the motives of Milton on his firft engaging in controverfy, and difcovers the high opinion which he entertained, both of the chriftian purity and the argumentative powers of his own cultivated mind: the two bifhops to whom he alludes were, Hall bifhop of Norwich, famous as our firft fatirift, and the learned Ufher, primate of Ireland. Hall publifhed, in 1640, " An humble Remonftrance to the High Court of Parliament in Behalf of Epifcopacy " — an anfwer to this appeared written by fix minifters, under the title of Smectymnuus, a word cafually formed from the initial letters of their refpective names. This little band of religious writers included Thomas Young, the beloved preceptor of Milton; fo that perfonal attachment confpired with public enthufiafm to make our author vehement in his reply to the two bifhops, who failed not to encounter the confederate antagonifts of their order. He probably recollected the fufferings of his favorite inftructor, when he exclaimed in his treatife of reformation, " What numbers of faithful and free born Englifhmen and good chriftians have been conftrained to forfake their deareft home, their friends and kindred, whom nothing but the wide ocean, or the favage deferts of America, could hide and fhelter from the fury of the bifhops. "

However furious the perfecution might be, which excited antipathy and abhorrence in Milton againft the order of bifhops, it muft be confeffed that he frequently fpeaks with that intemperance of zeal, which defeats its own purpofe. There are fome paffages in his controverfial writings, that muft be read with concern by his moft paffionate admirers; yet even the gloom and feverity of thefe are compenfated by fuch occafional flafhes of ardent fancy, of found argument, and of fublime devotion, as may extort commendation even from readers who love not the author.

In his firſt Ecclefiaſtical Treatife of Reformation, he makes the following very folemn appeal to heaven on his integrity as a writer:
" And here withal I invoke the immortal deity,
" revealer and judge of fecrets, that wherever I
" have in this book plainly and roundly, though
" worthily and truly, laid open the faults and
" blemifhes of fathers, martyrs, or chriſtian
" emperors, or have otherways inveighed againſt
" error and fuperſtition with vehement expref-
" fions, I have done it neither out of malice,
" nor lift to fpeak evil, nor any vain glory, but
" of mere neceffity, to vindicate the fpotlefs
" truth from an ignominious bondage. "
Towards the clofe of this performance he gives
a diſtant myſterious hint of his great and unfettled poetical defigns, with a very ſtriking mixture of moral, political, and religious enthufiafm.

" Then, amidſt the hymns and hallelujahs
" of faints, fome one may, perhaps, be heard
" offering at high ſtrains, *in new and lofty*
" *meafures*, to fing and celebrate thy divine
" mercies and marvellous judgments in this land
" throughout all ages. "
In his fubfequent work, on the Reafon of
Church Government, he gratifies us with a
more enlarged view of his literary projects, not
yet moulded into form, but, like the unarran-
ged elements of creation, now floating at large
in his capacious mind.

I tranfcribe the long paffage alluded to, becaufe it illuftrates the mental character of Milton, with a mild energy, a folemn fplendor of fentiment and expreffion peculiar to himfelf.

" Time ferves not now, and, perhaps, I
" might feem too profufe to give any certain
" account of what the mind at home, in the
" fpacious circuits of her mufing, hath liberty
" to propofe to herfelf, though of higheft hope
" and hardeft attempting; whether that epic
" form, whereof the two poems of Homer,
" and thofe other two of Virgil and Taffo,
" are a diffufe, and the book of Job a brief,
" model; or whether the rules of Ariftotle here-
" in are ftrictly to be kept, or nature to be
" followed; which in them that know art, and
" ufe judgment, is no tranfgreffion, but an en-
" riching of art: and laftly, what king or knight,
" before the Conqueft, might be chofen, in
" whom to lay the pattern of a chriftian hero.
" And as Taffo gave to a prince of Italy his
" choice, whether he would command him to
" write of Godfrey's expedition againft the infi-
" dels, Belifarius againft the Goths, or Charle-
" main againft the Lombards; if to the inftinct
" of nature, and the emboldning of art aught
" may be trufted, and that there be nothing
" adverfe in our climate, or the fate of this age,
" it haply would be no rafhnefs, from an equal
" diligence and inclination, to prefent the like
" offer in our antient ftories. Or whether thofe

" dramatic conftitutions, wherein Sophocles and
" Euripides reign, fhall be found more doctrinal
" and exemplary to a nation — Or, if occafion
" fhall lead, to imitate thofe magnific odes and
" hymns, wherein Pindarus and Callimachus are
" in moft things worthy. But thofe frequent
" fongs throughout the law and prophets, beyond
" all thefe, not in their divine argument alone,
" but in the very critical art of compofition,
" may be eafily made appear over all the kinds
" of lyric poefy to be incomparable. Thefe abi-
" lities, wherefoever they be found, are the in-
" fpired gift of God, rarely beftowed, but yet
" to fome (though moft abufe) in every nation;
" and are of power, befides the office of a
" pulpit, to inbreed and cherifh in a great
" people the feeds of virtue and public civility,
" to allay the perturbations of the mind, and
" fet the affections in right tune; to celebrate
" in glorious and lofty hymns the throne and
" equipage of God's almightinefs, and what he
" works, and what he fuffers to be wrought
" with high providence in his church; to fing
" victorious agonies of martyrs and faints, the
" deeds and triumphs of juft and pious nations
" doing valiantly through faith againft the ene-
" mies of Chrift; to deplore the general relapfes
" of kingdoms and ftates from juftice and God's
" true worfhip. Laftly, whatfoever in religion is
" holy and fublime, in virtue amiable or grave,
" whatfoever hath paffion or admiration in all

" the changes of that, which is called fortune
" from without , or the wily fubtleties and re-
" fluxes of man's thoughts from within ; all
" thefe things, with a folid and treatable fmooth-
" nefs to paint out and defcribe , teaching
" over the whole book of fanctity and virtue ,
" through all the inftances of example , with
" fuch delight, to thofe efpecially of foft and
" delicious temper, who will not fo much as
" look upon truth herfelf, unlefs they fee her
" elegantly dreft ; that whereas the paths of
" honefty and good life appear now rugged
" and difficult , though they be indeed eafy
" and pleafant , they will then appear to all
" men both eafy and pleafant , though they
" were rugged and difficult indeed. "

" The thing which I had to fay, and thofe
" intentions, which have lived within me ever
" fince I could conceive myfelf any thing worth
" to my country, I return to crave excufe that
" urgent reafon hath pluckt from me by an
" abortive and fore-dated difcovery; and the
" accomplifhment of them lies not but in a
" power above man's to promife; but that none
" hath by more ftudious ways endeavoured, and
" with more unwearied fpirit that none fhall ,
" that I dare almoft aver of myfelf, as far as
" life and free leifure will extend. Neither do
" I think it fhame to covenant with any knowing
" reader that for fome few years yet I may go
" on truft with him toward the payment of what

" I am now indebted, as being a work not to
" be raifed from the heat of youth, or the va-
" pours of wine, like that which flows at wafte
" from the pen of fome vulgar amourift, or the
" trencher fury of a rhyming parafite; nor to be
" obtained by the invocation of dame Memory
" and her firen daughters; but by devout prayer
" to that eternal fpirit, who can enrich with all
" utterance and knowledge , and fends out his
" Seraphim with the hallowed fire of his altar to
" touch and purify the lips of whom he pleafes;
" to this muft be added induftrious and felect
" reading, fteady obfervation, infight into all
" feemly and generous arts and affairs; till which
" in fome meafure be compaffed at mine own
" peril and coft I refufe not to fuftain this ex-
" pectation from as many as are not loth to
" hazard fo much credulity upon the beft pledges
" that I can give them. Although it nothing
" content me to have difclofed thus much before
" hand; but that I truft hereby to make it ma-
" nifeft with what fmall willingnefs I endure to
" interrupt the purfuit of no lefs hopes than thefe,
" and leave a calm and pleafing folitarinefs, fed
" with chearful and confident thoughts, to em-
" bark in a troubled fea of noife and hoarfe dif-
" putes, put from beholding the bright coun-
" tenance of truth, in the quiet and ftill air of
" delightful ftudies."

Mr. Warton, who has cited the laft fentence
of this very interefting paffage, as a proof that

Milton, then engaged in controversy, sighed for his more congenial pursuits, laments, " that the " vigorous portion of his life, that those years " in which imagination is on the wing, were " unworthily and unprofitably wasted on tem- " porary topics. " Many lovers of poetry will sympathize with this amiable writer in his regret; but others may still entertain very different sensations on the subject. Allowing for a moment that the controversial writings of Milton deserve to be neglected and forgotten, reasons may yet be found to rejoice, rather than lament, that he exerted his faculties in composing them. The occupation, however it might suspend his poetical enterprises, cherished the ardor and energy of his mind, and above all, confirmed in him that well founded and upright self-esteem, to which we are principally indebted for his sublimest production. The works I allude to were, in his own estimation, indispensible and meritorious; had he not written them, as he frankly informs us, " he would have heard within him- " self, all his life after, of discourage and re- " proach. " Nothing, perhaps, but this retrospect on a life passed, as his own conscience assured him, in the faithful discharge of arduous and irksome duties, could have afforded to the declining days of Milton that confident vigor of mind, that intense and inextinguishable fire of imagination, which gave existence and perfection to his Paradise Lost.

He appears to have thought with a celebrated ancient, that perfect morality is neceſſary to the perfection of genius; and that ſublimity in com_ poſition may be expected only from the man, who has attained the ſublime in the ſteady prac- tice of virtue.

Theſe noble and animating ideas ſeem to have had great influence on his conduct very early in life; for in ſpeaking of the ſtudies and ſentiments of his youth, he ſays,

" I was confirmed in this opinion, that he who
" would not be fruſtrate of his hope to write
" well hereafter in laudable things, ought himſelf
" to be a true poem; that is, a compoſition
" and pattern of the honourableſt things; not pre-
" ſuming to ſing high praiſes of heroic men, or
" famous cities, unleſs he have in himſelf the ex-
" perience and the practice of all that which is
" praiſe worthy."

In reply to the abſurd charge of his leading a diſſolute life, he gives an engaging and ſpirited account of his domeſtic conduct. " Thoſe morn-
" ing haunts are where they ſhould be, at home;
" not ſleeping or concocting the ſurfeits of an ir-
" regular feaſt, but up and ſtirring; in winter
" often ere the ſound of any bell awake men to
" labor or to devotion; in ſummer, as oft with
" the bird that firſt rouſes, or not much tar-
" dier, to read good authors, or cauſe them to
" be read, till the attention be weary; or me-
" mory have its full fraught; then with uſeful

" and generous labours, preferving the body's
" health and hardinefs, to render lightfome,
" clear, and not lumpifh obedience to the mind."

Had the profe works of Milton no merit but
that of occafionally affording us little fketches
of his fentiments, his manners, and occupations,
they would on this account be highly valuable
to every reader, whom a paffionate admiration
of the poet has induced to wifh for all poffible
acquaintance with the man. To gratify fuch
readers, I felect very copioufly from his various
works thofe paffages that difplay, in the ftrongeft
point of view, his moral and domeftic character.
It is my firm belief, that as this is more known,
it will become more and more an object of affection and applaufe; yet I am far from furveying it with that blind idolatry, which fees
no defect, or with that indifcreet partiality, which
labors to hide the failing it difcovers; a biographer muft have ill underftood the nature of
Milton, who could fuppofe it poffible to gratify
his fpirit by homage fo unworthy; for my own
part, I am perfuaded his attachment to truth
was as fincere and fervent as that of the honeft
Montaigne, who fays, " I would come again
" with all my heart from the other world to give
" any one the lie, who fhould report me other
" than I was, though he did it to honor me."

I fhall not therefore attempt to deny or to
excufe the fatiguing heavinefs or the coarfe afperity of his ecclefiaftical difputes. The fincereft

friends of Milton may here agree with Johnfon, who fpeaks of his controverfial merriment as difgufting; but when the critic adds, fuch is his malignity, that "Hell grows darker at his frown," they muft abhor this bafe mifapplication, I had almoft faid, this profanation, of Miltonic verfe.

In a controverfial treatife that gave rife to fuch an imputation, we fhould expect to find the polemic favagely thirfting for the blood of his adverfaries : it is juft the reverfe. Milton's antagonift had, indeed, fuggefted to the public, with *infernal malignity*, that he was a mifcreant, " who ought, in the name of Chrift, to be " ftoned to death. " This antagonift, as Milton fuppofed, was a fon of bifhop Hall," and fcrupled not to write thus outrageoufly againft one, who (to ufe the milder words of our author) " in all his writing fpake not that any man's " fkin fhould be rafed. "

" The ftyle of his piece, " fays Johnfon, in " fpeaking of this apology," is rough, and fuch, " perhaps, is that of his antagonift. " The different degrees of roughnefs that the two writers difplayed give a fingular effect to this obfervation of the critic, who confounds the coarfe and intemperate vehemence of the one with the outrageous barbarity of the other. Milton fometimes wrote with the unguarded and ungraceful afperity of a man in wrath, but let equity add, that when he did fo, he was exafperated by

foes, who exerted againſt him all the perſecu-
ting ferocity of a fiend.

The incidents of his life were calculated to
put his temper and his fortitude to the moſt
arduous trials, and in the ſevereſt of theſe he
will be found conſtant and exemplary in the
exerciſe of gentle and beneficent virtue. From
the thorns of controverſy he was plunged into
the ſtill ſharper thorns of connubial diſſenſion.
During the Whitſuntide of the year 1643, at
the age of thirty - five, he married Mary, the
daughter of Richard Powell, a gentleman who
reſided at Foreſt Hill, near Shotover, in Ox-
fordſhire. This ill-ſtarr'd union might ariſe from
an infantine acquaintance, as the grandfather of
Milton had probably lived very near the ſeat
of the Powells. What led to the connexion
we can only conjecture, but we know it was
unhappy, as the lady, after living only a few
weeks with her huſband in London, deſerted
him, under the decent pretence of paſſing the
ſummer months on a viſit to her father, with
whom the indulgent poet gave her permiſſion
to remain till Michaelmas : during the interval
he was engaged in kind attention to his father,
whom he now eſtabliſhed under his own roof.
The old man had been ſettled at Reading, with
his younger ſon Chriſtopher, a lawyer and a
royaliſt, but thought it expedient to quit that
place on its being taken by Eſſex, the parliamentary general, and found a comfortable
aſylum

afylum for the refidue of his long life in the filial piety and tender protection of the poet. .

. At the time appointed, Milton folicited the return of his wife; fhe did not condefcend even to anfwer his letter : he repeated his requeft by a meffenger, who, to the beft of my remembrance (fays Philips) reported; that he was difmiffed with fome fort of contempt. This proceeding, in all probability (continues the biographer, whofe fituation made him the beft judge of occurrences fo extraordinary) was grounded " upon no other caufe but this ; " namely, that the family, being generally ad- " dicted to the cavalier party, as they called it, " and fome of them poffibly engaged in the " king's fervice, who by this time had his head- " quarters at Oxford, was in fome profpect of " fuccefs, they began to repent them of having " matched the eldeft daughter of the family to " a perfon fo contrary to them in opinion, and " thought it would be a blot in their efcutcheon " whenever that Court came to flourifh again; " however, it fo incenfed our author, that he " thought it would be difhonorable ever to re- " ceive her again after fuch a repulfe. "

Milton had too tender and too elevated a fpirit not to feel this affront with double poignancy, as it affected both his happinefs and his dignity; but it was one of his noble characterif- tics to find his mental powers rather invigorated than enfeebled by injury and affliction : he

thought it the prerogative of wifdom to find
remedies againft every evil, however unexpected,
by which vice or infirmity can embitter life.
In reflecting on his immediate domeftic trouble,
he conceived the generous defign of making it
fubfervient to the public good. He found that
in difcordant marriage there is mifery, for which
he thought there exifted a very eafy remedy,
and perfectly confiftent both with reafon and
religion : with thefe ideas he publifhed, in 1644,
the Doctrine and Difcipline of Divorce. He addreffes the work to the Parliament, with great
fpirit and eloquence, and after afferting the purity of his precepts, and the beneficence of his
defign, he fays, with patriotic exultation, " let
" not England forget her precedence of teaching
" nations how to live. "

Sanguine as Milton was in the hope of promoting the virtue and happinefs of private life
by this publication, the Prefbyterian clergy,
notwithftanding their paft obligations to the author, endeavoured to perfecute him 'for the novelty and freedom of his fentiments." The affembly of divines fitting at Weftminfter, impa-
" tient," fays Antony Wood, " of having the
" clergy's jurifdiction, as they reckoned it, in-
" vaded, did, inftead of anfwering or difproving
" what thofe books had afferted, caufe him to
" be fummoned before the Houfe of Lords; but
" that houfe, whether approving the doctrine,
" or not favouring his accufers, did foon difmifs
" him. "

Milton, whom no oppofition could intimidate when he believed himfelf engaged in the caufe, of truth and juftice, endeavoured to fupport his doctrine by fubfequent publications; firft, " The " Judgment of Martin Bucer concerning Di- " vorce;" this alfo he addreffes to the Parlia- ment, and fays, with his ufual fpirit, " God, it " feems, intended to prove me, whether I durft " alone take up a rightful caufe againft a world " of difefteem, and found I durft. My name I " did not publifh, as not willing it fhould fway " the reader either for me or againft me; but " when I was told that the ftile (which what " it ails to be fo foon diftinguifhable I cannot " tell) was known by moft men, and that " fome of the clergy began to inveigh and ex- " claim on what I was credibly informed they " had not read, I took it then for my proper " feafon, both to fhow them a name that could " eafily contemn fuch an indifcreet kind of cen- " fure, and to reinforce the queftion with a " more accurate diligence; that if any of them " would be fo good as to leave railing, and to " let us hear fo much of his learning and chrif- " tian wifdom, as will be ftrictly demanded of " him in his anfwering to this problem, care " was had he fhould not fpend his preparations " againft a namelefs pamphlet. "

Thefe expreffions difplay the franknefs and fortitude of a noble mind, perfectly confcious of its own integrity, in difcuffing a very delicate point, that materially affects the comfort of human life. This integrity he had indeed pro-tested very solemnly in his former Addrefs to the Parliament, where, after afferting that the fub-ject concerned them chiefly as redreffers of griev-ances, he proceeds thus, " Me it concerns next, " having, with much labour and faithful dili- " gence, firft found out, or at leaft with a " fearlefs communicative candour firft publifhed, " to the manifeft good of chriftendom, that " which, calling to witnefs every thing mortal " and immortal, I believe unfeignedly to be " true. " The folemnity of this proteftation, confirmed as it was by the fingular regularity of his morals, and the fincerity of his zeal as a chriftian, could not fecure him from cenfures of every kind, which, vehement as they were, he feems to have defpifed. His ideas were de-rided by libertines, and calumniated by hypo-crites and bigots; but, fuperior to ridicule and to flander, he proceeded refolutely in what he thought his duty, by fhowing how completely his doctrine was confonant, in his own opinion, to that gofpel, which he had feduloufly made not only the favorite ftudy, but the conftant guide of his life. With this view he publifhed in 1645, his Tetrachordon, expofitions upon the four chief places of fcripture, which fpeak of marriage. He introduces this work by a third Addrefs to the Parliament, and, fpeaking of their juftice and candor in difdaining to think of perfecuting him for his doctrine, according to the inftigation of his enemies, he expreffes his gratitude in the following animated terms : " For which uprightnefs and incorrupt refufal " of what ye were incenfed to, lords and com- " mons (though it were done to juftice, not " to me, and was a peculiar demonftration how " far your ways are different from the rafh " vulgar) befides thofe allegiances of oath and " duty, which are my public debt to your " public labours, I have yet a ftore of gratitude " laid up, which cannot be exhaufted, and " fuch thanks, perhaps, they may live to be, as " fhall more than whifper to the next ages. " This fentence is remarkable in various points of view, but chiefly as it fhows us that the peculiar eagernefs and energy with which Milton, at a future period, defended the parliament, origin- ated not only in his paffionate attachment to freedom, but in his ardent fenfe of perfonal gratitude to the legiflature of his country. He was however; too magnanimous to wifh for fhel- ter under any authority, without vindicating his innocence and the merit of his caufe; he there- fore fays to the parliament, in fpeaking of an antagonift who, in their prefence, had traduced him from the pulpit, " I fhall take licence by " the right of nature, and that liberty wherein " I was born, to defend myfelf publicly againft " a printed calumny, and do willingly appeal " to thofe judges to whom I am accufed. "

The preacher had reprefented the doctrine of divorce as a wicked book, for allowing other caufes of divorce than Chrift and his Apoftles mentioned, and the parliament as finners for not punifhing its authors.

This induces Milton to exclaim with devotion-al fpirit, which feems predominant in his mind upon every occafion, " Firft, lords and com-
" mons, I pray to that God, before whom ye
" then were proftrate, fo to forgive ye thofe
" omiffions and trefpaffes, which ye defire moft
" fhould find forgivenefs, as I fhall foon fhow
" to the world how eafily ye abfolve yourfelves
" of that, which this man calls your fin, and
" is indeed your wifdom and noblenefs, where-
" of to this day ye have done well not to
" repent. "

The fcope of Milton, in his doctrine of divorce, is thus explained by himfelf : " This fhall be
" the tafk and period of this difcourfe to prove,
" firft, that other reafons of divorce befides
" adultery were by the law of Mofes, and are
" yet to be allowed by the Chriftian magiftrate,
" as a piece of juftice, and that the words of
" Chrift are not hereby contraried ; next that,
" to prohibit abfolutely any divorce whatfoe-
" ver, except thofe which Mofes excepted, is
" againft the reafon of law. "

This doctrine he firft delivered as the refult of his own diligent ftudy of the fcripture. He afterwards found and declared it confonant to

what many eminent divines of the reformed church, particularly Martin Bucer and Erafmus, had maintained; laftly, to grace his opinions with the higheft human fupport, he afferts;
" they were fanctioned by the whole affembled
" authority of England, both church and ftate,
" and in thofe times which are on record for
" the pureft and fincereft that ever fhone yet
" on the Reformation of his land, the time of
" Edward the Sixth. That worthy prince,
" having utterly abolifhed the canon law out of
" his dominions, as his father did before him,
" appointed by full vote of parliament a com-
" mittee of two-and-thirty chofen men, divines
" and lawyers, of whom Cranmer the arch-
" bifhop, Peter Martyr, and Walter Haddon,
" not without the affiftance of Sir John Cheek,
" the king's tutor, a man at that time accounted
" the learnedeft of Englifhmen, and for piety
" not inferior, were the chief to frame anew
" fome ecclefiaftical laws, that might be inftead
" of what was abrogated. The work with great
" diligence was finifhed, and with as great ap-
" probation of that reforming age was received,
" and had been doubtlefs, as the learned preface
" thereof teftifies, eftablifhed by act of parlia-
" ment, had not the good king's death fo foon
" enfuing arrefted the farther growth of religion
" alfo from that feafon to this. Thofe laws,
" thus founded on the memorable wifdom and
" piety of that religious parliament and fynod,

" allow divorce and fecond marriage not only
" for adultery and defertion, but for any capital
" enmity or plot laid againft the other's life,
" and likewife for evil and fierce ufage. Nay,
" the twelfth chapter of that title, by plain
" confequence declares, that leffer contentions,
" if they be perpetual, may obtain divorce,
" which is all one really with the pofition by
" me held in the former treatife publifhed on
" this argument, herein only differing, that
" there the caufe of perpetual ftrife was put,
" for example, in the unchangeable difcord of
" fome natures; but in thefe laws, intended us
" by the beft of our anceftors, the effect of
" continual ftrife is determined no unjuft plea
" of divorce, whether the caufe be natural or
" wilful. "

The author exults fo much in this authority,
that he concludes with the following expreffions
of confidence and triumph:

" Henceforth let them, who condemn the
" affertion of this book for new and licentious,
" be forry, left, while they think to be of the
" graver fort, and take on them to be teachers,
" they expofe themfelves rather to be pledged
" up and down by men who intimately know
" them, to the difcovery and contempt of their
" ignorance and prefumption. "

I have dwelt the longer on this fubject, becaufe it occupied fo deeply the mind and heart
of Milton. In thefe treatifes the energy of his

language is very ſtriking; it forcibly proves how keenly he felt the anguiſh of connubial infelicity, and how ardently he labored to remove from himſelf and others that " ſecret afflinion " (to uſe one of his own expreſſive phraſes). " of an " unconſcionable ſize to human ſtrength. "

He argues, indeed, for what the majority of modern legiſlators and divines have thought inconſiſtent with ſound' morality and true religion; but they who deem his arguments inconcluſive, may yet admire the powers and the probity of the advocate. His view of the queſtion is as extenſive and liberal as his intention was pure and benevolent: if a few words of our Saviour, in their literal ſenſe, are againſt him, the ſpirit of the goſpel may be thought, by ſincere Chriſtians, to allow him all the latitude for which he contends; the moſt rigid opponent of his doſrine may be frequently charmed with his rich vein of fervid eloquence and chriſtian philanthropy.

His three publications on divorce were followed by Colaſterion, a reply to a nameleſs anſwer againſt his doſrine. This work is an angry inveſtive, in which he endeavours, but not happily, to overwhelm his antagoniſt with ridicule.

In the account which he gives of his own compoſitions, in his Second Defence, he ſpeaks of this treatiſe on divorce, as forming a part of his progreſſive labor to vindicate liberty in various points of view; he confidered it in three different fhapes, ecclefiaftical, domeftic, and civil; he thought it of high moment to eftablifh a more enlarged fyftem of domeftic liberty, at a time when connubial difcord was fo common, in confequence of civil diffenfion; when, to ufe his own forcible expreffion, alluding probably to his particular fituation, " the wife might be " found in the camp of the enemy, threatening " ruin and flaughter to her hufband." He feems to exult in faying, that his doctrine of divorce was more abundantly demonftrated, about two years after his publication, by the illuftrious Selden, in his Uxor Hebræa *.

* Cum itaque tres omnino animadverterem libertatis effe fpecies, quæ nifi adfint, vita ulla tranfigi commode vix poffit, ecclefiafticam, domefticam, feu privatam, atque civilem, deque prima jam fcripfiffem, deque tertia magiftratum fedulo agere viderem, quæ reliqua fecunda erat, domefticam mihi defumpfi; ea quoque tripartita, cum videretur effe, fi res conjugalis, fi liberorum inftitutio recte fe haberet, fi denique libere philofophandi poteftas effet, de conjugio non folum rite contrahendo, verum etiam, fi neceffe effet, diffolvendo, quid fentirem explicui; idque ex divina lege, quam Chriftus non fuftulit, nedum aliam, tota lege Mofaica graviorem civiliter fauxit; quid item de excepta folum fornicatione fentiendum fit, & meam aliorumque fententiam exprompfi, & clariffimus vir Seldenus nofter, in Uxore Hebræa plus minus biennio poft edita, uberius demonftravit. Fruftra enim libertatem in comitiis & foro crepat, qui domi fervitutem viro indigniffimam, inferiori etiam fervit; ea igitur de re aliquot libros edidi; eo præfertim tempore cum vir fæpe & conjux hoftes inter fe acerrimi, hic domi

Those who love not Milton affect to speak scornfully of his writings on this subject, and intimate, that they were received at first with universal contempt; but this was far from being the case; they were applauded by many, on whose judgment the author set the highest value, though they were made a source of indecent mirth by the vulgar; and we may reasonably conclude, it was this circumstance that induced him to wish he had written them in Latin. To the low ribaldry, with which they were attacked, he alludes in the sonnet, celebrated for the following admirable lines on the hypocritical or intemperate assertors of liberty,

> That bawl for freedom in their senseless mood,
> And still revolt when truth would set them free;
> Licence they mean, when they cry liberty,
> For who loves that, must first be wise and good.

This noble sentiment he has inculcated more than once in prose; and as his life was in harmony with his precept, it might have taught his enemies to avoid the gross absurdity of representing him as the lover of anarchy and confusion. Never was a mind better constituted, than Milton's, to set a just value on the prime blessings of peace and order; if he ran into political

cum liberis, illa in castris hostium materfamilias versaretur, viro cædem atque perniciem minitans. — Prose Works, vol. 2. p. 385. folio Edit. London, 1738. vol. 2. p. 333.

errors, they arofe not from any fondnefs for fcenes of turbulence, but rather from his generous
credulity refpecting the virtue of mankind; from
believing that many hypocrites, who affected a
wifh to eftablifh peace and order in his country,
on what he efteemed the fureft foundation, were
as fincere and difinterefted as himfelf.

"From this time (fays Johnfon) it is obfer-
" ved, that he became an enemy to the Prefby-
" terians, whom he had favored before. He
" that changes his party by his humor is not
" much more virtuous than he that changes it
" by his intereft; he loves himfelf rather than
" truth." Notwithftanding the air of morality
in this remark, it may be queftioned, if ever an
obfervation was made on any great character
more invidios or more unjuft. When the
Prefbyterians were favored by Milton, they
fpake the language of the oppreffed; on their
being invefted with power, they forgot their own
pleas for liberty of confcience, and became, in
their turn, perfecutors; it was the confiftency of
virtue, therefore, in Milton, that made him at
one time their advocate, and at another their
opponent: fo far from loving himfelf better than
truth, he was perhaps of all mortals the leaft
felfifh. — He contended for religion without
feeking emoluments from the church; he contended for the ftate without aiming at any civil
or military employment: truth and juftice were
the idols of his heart and the ftudy of his life;

if he fometimes failed of attaining them, it was not becaufe he loved any thing better; it was becaufe he overfhot the object of fincere affection from the fondnefs and ardor of his purfuit.

His wife ftill perfifted in her defertion, but he amufed his mind under the mortification her conduct had occafioned by frequent vifits to the Lady Margaret Ley, whofe manners and converfation were peculiarly engaging. Her father, the Earl of Marlborough, had held the higheft offices in a former reign, and of his virtues fhe ufed to fpeak with fuch filial eloquence as infpired Milton with a fonnet in her praife.

He continued alfo to manifeft his firm affection to the public good, by two compofitions intended to promote it; the little tractate on education, addreffed to Mr. Hartlib, who had requefted his thoughts upon that interefting fubject, and his Areopagitica, a fpeech for the liberty of unlicenfed printing. The latter has been re-printed, with a fpirited preface by Thomfon, a poet whom a paffion for freedom, united to genius, had highly qualified as an editor and eulogift of Milton.

Had the author of the Paradife Loft left us no compofition but his Areopagitica, he would be ftill entitled to the affectionate veneration of every Englifhman, who exults in that intellectual light, which is the nobleft characteriftic of his country, and for which England is chiefly indebted to the liberty of the prefs. Our conftant advocate for freedom , in every department of 'life, vindicated this moſt important privilege with a mind fully fenſible of its value; he poured all his heart into this vindication, and, to ſpeak of his work in his own energetic language, we may juſtly call it, what he has defined a good book to be, " the precious life-blood of a maſter " ſpirit, embalmed and treaſured up on purpoſe " to a life beyond life."

His late biographer, inſtead of praiſing Milton for a ſervice ſo honorably rendered to literature, ſeems rather deſirous of annihilating its merit, by directing his ſarcaſtic animoſity againſt the liberty of the preſs. " It ſeems not more " reaſonable, ſays Johnſon, " to leave the right " of printing unreſtrained, becauſe writers may " be afterwards cenſured, than it would be to " ſleep with doors unbolted, becauſe by our " laws we can hang a thief."

This is ſervile ſophiſtry; the author's illuſtration of a thief may be turned againſt himſelf. To ſuffer no book to be publiſhed without a licence, is tyranny as abſurd as it would be to ſuffer no traveller to paſs along the highway without producing a certificate that he is not a robber.

Even bad books may have their uſe, as Milton obſerves; and I mention this obſervation, chiefly to ſhow how liberally he introduces a juſt compliment to a great author of his own time in ſupport of this idea. " What better witneſs," ſays the advocate for unlicenſed printing, " can

" ye expect I fhould produce, than one of your
" own, now fitting in parliament, the chief of
" learned men reputed in this land, Mr. Selden,
" whofe volume of natural and national laws
" proves, not only by great authorities brought
" together, but by exquifite reafons and theorems
" almoft mathematically demonftrative, that all
" opinions, yea errors, known, read, and col-
" lated, are of main fervice and affiftance to-
" wards the fpeedy attainment of what is trueft."
This eulogy alone appears fufficient to refute a
remark unfriendly to Milton, that he was frugal
of his praife; fuch frugality will hardly be found
united to a benevolent heart and a glowing
imagination.

In 1645, his early poems, both Englifh and
Latin, were firft publifhed in a little volume by
Humphry Mofely, who informs the reader in
his advertifement, that he had obtained them by
folicitation from the author, regarding him as a
fuccefsful rival of Spencer.

Milton had now paffed more than three years
in that fingular ftate of mortification, which the
difobedience of his wife occafioned. His time
had been occupied by the inceffant exercife of his
mental powers; but he probably felt with peculiar poignancy

" A craving void left aching in the breaft."

As he entertained ferious thoughts of enforcing,
by his own example, his doctrine of divorce,

and of marrying another wife who might be
worthy of the title, he paid his addreſſes to the
daughter of Doctor Davies : the father ſeems to
have been a convert to Milton's arguments; but
the lady had ſcruples. She poſſeſſed, according
to Philips, both wit and beauty. A noveliſt could
hardly imagine circumſtances more ſingularly
diſtreſſing to ſenſibility, than the ſituation of the
poet, if, as we may reaſonably conjecture, he
was deeply enamoured of this lady; if her father,
was inclined to accept him as a ſon-in-law; and
if the object of his love had no inclinatioh to
reject his ſuit, but what aroſe from a dread of
his being indiſſolubly united to another.

Perhaps Milton alludes to what he felt on this
occaſion in thoſe affecting lines of Paradiſe Loſt,
where Adam, prophetically enumerating the
miſeries to ariſe from woman, ſays, in cloſing
the melancholy liſt, that man ſometimes

> " His happieſt choice too late
> " Shall meet, already link'd and wedlock-bound
> " To a fell adverſary, his hate or ſhame !
> " Which infinite calamity ſhall cauſe
> " To human life, and houſehold peace confound."

However ſtrong the ſcruples of his new favorite
might have been, it ſeems not improbable that
he would have triumphed over them, had not
an occurrence, which has the air of an incident
in romance, given another turn to the emotions
of

of his heart. While he was converfing with a relation, whom he frequently vifited in St. Martin's-lane, the door of an adjoining apartment
was fuddenly opened : he beheld his repentant
wife kneeling at his feet, and imploring his forgivenefs. After the natural ftruggles of honeft
pride and juft refentment, he forgave and received her, " partly from the interceffion of
" their common friends, and partly, " fays his
nephew, " from his own generous nature, more
" inclinable to reconciliation, than to perfeve-
" rance in anger and revenge. "

Fenton juftly remarks, that the ftrong impreffion which this interview muft have made
on Milton, " contributed much to the painting
" of that pathetic fcene in Paradife Loft, in
" which Eve addreffes herfelf to Adam for pardon
" and peace; " the verfes, charming as they are,
acquire new charms, when we confider them
as defcriptive of the poet himfelf and the penitent deftroyer of his domeftic comfort.

> " Her lowly plight
> " Immoveable, till peace obtain'd from fault
> " Acknowledg'd and deplor'd, in Adam wrought
> " Commiferation ; foon his heart relented
> " Towards her, his life fo late and fole delight,
> " Now at his feet fubmiffive in diftrefs !
> " Creature fo fair his reconcilement feeking,
> " His counfel whom fhe had difpleas'd, his aid
> " As one difarm'd, his anger all he loft. "

It has been said, that Milton resembled his own Adam in the comeliness of his person; but he seems to have resembled him still more in much nobler endowments, and particularly in uniting great tenderness of heart to equal dignity of mind. Soon after he had pardoned, and lived again with his wife, he afforded an asylum, in his own house, to both her parents, and to their numerous family. They were active royalists, and fell into great distress by the ruin of their party: these were the persons who had not only treated Milton with contemptuous pride, but had imbittered his existence for four years, by instigating his wife to persist in deserting him. The mother, as Wood intimates, was his greatest enemy, and occasioned the perverse conduct of her daughter. The father, though sumptuous in his mode of life when he first received Milton as his son-in-law, had never paid the marriage portion of a thousand pounds, according to his agreement, and was now stript of his property by the prevalence of the party he had opposed. On persons thus contumelious and culpable towards him, Milton bestowed his favor and protection. Can the records of private life exhibit a more magnanimous example of forvigeness and beneficence?

At the time of his wife's unexpected return, he was preparing to remove from Aldersgate to a larger house in Barbican, with a view of

increafing the number of his fcholars. It was in this new manfion that he received the forgiven penitent, and provided a refuge for her relations, whom he retained under his roof, according to Fenton, " till their affairs were ac-
" commodated by his intereft with the victo-
" rious party. "

They left him foon after the death of his father, who ended a very long life, in the year 1647, and not without the gratification, peculiarly foothing to an affectionate old man, of beftowing his benediction on a grand-child; for, within the year of Milton's re-union with his wife, his family was increafed by a daughter, Anne, the eldeft of his children, born July 29th, 1646.

When his apartments were no longer occupied by the guefts, whom he had fo generoufly received, he admitted more fcholars; but their number was fmall, and Philips imagines, that he was induced to withdraw himfelf from the bufinefs of education by a profpect of being appointed adjutant general in Sir William Waller's army : whatever might have been the motive for his change of life, he quitted his large houfe in Barbican for a fmaller in Holborn, " among thofe (fays his nephew) that
" open bakwards into Lincoln's Inn Fields, " where he lived, according to the fame author, in great privacy, and perpetually engaged in a variety of ftudies.

Three years elapfed without any new publication from his pen; a filence which the various affecting occurrences in his family would naturally produce. In 1649 he publifhed The Tenure of Kings and Magiftrates; and in his fummary account of his own writings, he relates the time and occafion of this performance. He declares, that without any perfonal malevolence againft the deceafed monarch, who had been tried and executed before this publication appeared, it was written to compofe the minds of the people, difturbed by the duplicity and turbulence of certain prefbyterian minifters, who affected to confider the fentence againft the king as contrary to the principles of every proteftant church, " a falfhood (fays Milton) which, without " inveighing againft Charles, I refuted by the " teftimony of their moft eminent theologians*."

* Tum vero tandem, cum prefbyteriani quidam miniftri, Carolo prius infeftiffimi, nunc independentium partes fuis an-teferri, & in fenatu plus poffe indignantes, parliamenti fententiæ de rege latæ (non facto irati, fed quod ipforum factio non feciffet) reclamitarent, & quantum in ipfis erat tumultuarentur, aufi affirmare proteftantium doctrinam, omnefque ecclefias reformatas ab ejufmodi in reges atroci fententia abhorrere, ratus falfitati tam apertæ palam eundem obviam effe, ne tum quidem de Carolo quicquam fcripfi aut fuafi, fed quid in genere contra tyrannos liceret, adductis haud paucis fummorum theologorum teftimoniis, oftendi; & infignem hominum meliora profitentium, five ignorantiam five impudentiam prope concionabundus inceffi. Liber ifte non nifi poft mortem regis prodiit, ad componendos potius hominum animos

His obfervations on the articles of peace between the Earl of Ormond and the Irifh papifts
appeared in the fame year; a performance that
he probably thought too inconfiderable to enumerate in his own account of what he had pub-
liflied; it includes, however, fome remarkably
keen ftriftures on a letter written by Ormond,
to tempt Colonel Jones, the governor of Dub-
lin, to defert the Parliament, who had intrufted
him with his command. Ormond, having imputed to the prevailing party in England a defign to eftablifh a perfeft Turkifh tyranny, Milton, with great dexterity, turns the expreffion
againft Ormond, obferving, that the defign of
bringing in that tyranny is a monarchical defign, and not of thofe who have diffolved monarchy. " Witnefs (fays he) that confultation
" had in the court of France, under Charles
" the IXth, at Blois, wherein Poncet, a certain
" court projeftor, brought in fecretly by the
" chancellor Biragha, after many praifes of the
" Ottoman government, propofes ways and
" means at large, in the prefence of the king,
" the queen regent, and Anjou the king's bro-
" ther; how, with beft expedition and leaft noife,
" the Turkifh tyranny might be fet up in France."
I tranfcribe the paffage as an example of Milton's
applying hiftorical anecdotes with peculiar felicity.

factus, quam ad ftatuendum de Carolo quicquam, quod non
mea, fed magiftratuum intererat, & peractum jam tum erat
—Profe Works, vol. ii. p. 385.

He now began to employ himſelf in one of the great works, with which he hoped to enrich his native language. The ſketch that he has drawn of himſelf and his ſtudies, at this period, is ſo intereſting and honorable, that it would be injurious not to tranſlate the Latin expreſſions to which I allude.

" * Thus (ſays Milton) as a private citizen,
" I gratuitouſly gave my aſſiſtance to the church
" and ſtate; on me, in return, they beſtowed
" only the common benefit of protection; but
" my conduct aſſuredly gave me a good con-
" ſcience, a good reputation among good men,
" and this honorable freedom of diſcourſe: others

* Hanc intra privatos parietes meam operam nunc eccleſiæ, nunc reipublicæ, gratis dedi; mihi viciſſim vel hæc vel illa præter incolumitatem nihil; bonam certe conſcientiam, bonam apud bonos exiſtimationem, & honeſtam hanc dicendi libertatem facta ipſa reddidere : commoda alii, alii honores gratis ad ſe trahebant; me nemo ambientem, nemo per amicos quicquam petentem, curiæ foribus affixum petitoris vultu aut minorum conventuum veſtibulis hærentem nemo me unquam vidit. Domi fere me continebam; meis ipſe facultat bus, tametſi hoc civili tumultu magna ex parte ſæpe detentis, & cenſum fere iniquius mihi impoſitum & vitam utcunque frugi tolerabam. His rebus confectis, cum jam abunde otii exiſtimarem mihi futurum, ad hiſtoriam gentis ab ultima origine repetitam ad hæc uſque tempora, ſi poſſem, perpetuo filo deducendam me converti : Quatuor jam libros abſolveram, cum ecce nihil tale cogitantem me Caroli regno in rempublicam redacto, concilium ſtatus quo dicitur cum primum authoritate parliamenti conſtitutum ad ſe vocat, meaque opera ad res præſertim externas uti voluit. — Proſe Works, vol. ii. p. 386.

" have been bufy in drawing to themfelves un-
" merited emoluments and honor; no one has
" ever beheld me foliciting any thing, either in
" perfon or by my friends; I have confined my-
" felf much at home; and by my own property,
" though much of it has been withheld from
" me in this civil tumult, I have fupported life,
" however fparingly, and paid a tax impofed
" upon me, not in the moft equitable pro-
" portion.

" Having now a profpect of abundant lei-
" fure, I directed my ftudies to the hiftory of my
" country, which I began from its remoteft
" fource, and intended to bring down, if pof-
" fible, in a regular procefs, to the prefent times.
" I had executed four books, when, on the
" fettlement of the republic, the council of ftate,
" then firft eftablifhed by the authority of par-
" liament, called me moft unexpectedly to its
" fervice, and wifhed to employ me chiefly in
" its foreign concerns.". It has not yet, I believe, been afcertained to whom Milton was particularly indebted for a public appointment. " He
" was (fays Wood) without any feeking of his,
" by the endeavours of a private acquaintance,
" who was a member of the new council of ftate,
" chofen Latin fecretary." The new council confifted of thirty-nine members, including two perfons, whom we may fuppofe equally inclined to
promote the intereft of Milton; thefe were Ser-
jeant Bradfhaw and Sir Harry Vane the younger:

it feems probable that he owed his ftation of fecretary to the former, fince, in his Second Defence, he mentions him as a friend entitled to his particular regard, and draws his character in colors fo vivid, that the portrait may be thought worthy of prefervation, even by thofe who have no efteem for the original.

The character of a man fo extraordinary, derived from perfonal intimacy, and delineated by a hand fo powerful, can hardly fail to be interefting; yet it becomes ftill more fo, if we confider it as a monument of Milton's gratitude to the friend who fixed him in that public ftation, which gave fignal exercife to the energy of his mind, and firft made him, as a Latin writer, the admiration of Europe.

Whatever influence gratitude might have on the defcription, and however different the ideas may be, that are commonly entertained of Bradfhaw, the eulogy beftowed on him by Milton was certainly fincere; for though not frugal of his praife, yet fuch was his probity, that it may, I think, be fairly proved, he never beftowed a particle of applaufe where he did not think it deferved; a point that I hope to eftablifh, by refuting, in the courfe of this narrative, the charge of fervile flattery, which he is falfely accufed of having lavifhed upon Cromwell.

To praife, indeed, appears to have been an occupation peculiarly fuited to his fpirit, which was naturally fanguine, free from the gloom of farcaftic melancholy, and ever ready to glow with affectionate enthufiafm. His character of Bradfhaw may illuftrate this remark; it is written with peculiar elegance and affection; the following portion of it will be fufficient to fhow, not only the fervency of his friendfhip, but his facility and force of pencil in the delineation of character *.

" He had, united to the knowledge of law,
" a liberal difpofition, an elevated mind, and
" irreproachable integrity of morals, neither
" gloomy nor fevere, but courteous and mild.

* " Attulerat ad legum fcientiam ingenium liberale, animum
" excelfum, mores integros ac nemini obnoxios; ———— nec
" triftis, nec feverus, fed comis ac placidus. In confiliis ac
" laboribus publicis maxime omnium indefeffus, multifque
" par unus; domi, fi quis alius, pro fuis facultatibus hof-
" pitalis ac fplendidus; amicus longe fideliffimus, atque in
" omni fortuna certiffimus; bene merentes quofcunque nemo
" citius aut libentius agnofcit, neque majore benevolentia
" profequitur; nunc pios, nunc doctos, aut quamvis ingenii
" laude cognitos, nunc militares etiam & fortes viros ad ino-
" piam redactos fuis opibus fublevat; iis, fi non indigent,
" colit tamen libens atque amplectitur; alienas laudes perpetuo
" prædicare, fuas tacere folitus. Quod fi caufa oppreffi
" cujufpiam defendenda palam, fi gratia aut vis potentiorum
" oppugnanda, fi in quemquam benemeritum ingratitudo pu-
" blica objurganda fit, tum quidem in illo viro, vel facun-
" diam vel conftantiam nemo defideret, non patronum, non
" amicum, vel idoneum magis & intrepidum, vel difertiorem
" alium quifquam fibi optet, habet, quem non minæ dimovere
" recto, non metus aut munera propofito bono atque officio,
" vultufque ac mentis firmiffimo ftatu dejicere valeant. "—
Profe Works. vol. ii. p. 389.

" In public councils and labors he is the moſt
" indefatigable of men, and alone equal to many;
" in his houſe he, if any man, may be eſteemed
" hoſpitable and ſplendid, in proportion to his
" fortune ; as a friend faithful in the higheſt
" degree, and moſt ſurely to be depended upon
" in every emergency ; no man ſooner or more
" freely acknowledges merit, wherever it may
" be found ; no man rewards it with greater
" benevolence ; he raiſes from indigence at his
" own coſt, ſometimes men of piety, learning,
" and talents, ſometimes thoſe brave military
" men, whoſe proſperity has not been equal
" to their valor : ſuch perſons, if they are not
" indigent, he ſtill honors with his regard; it is
" his nature to proclaim the deſert of others,
" and to be ſilent on his own.

" If the cauſe of any one under oppreſſion
" is to be openly defended, if the influence or
" authority of men in power is to be oppoſed,
" if the ingratitude of the public towards any
" individual of merit is to be reproved, no want
" will be found in this man, either of eloquence
" or courage; nor can any ſufferer wiſh to find,
" on ſuch occaſions, a patron and a friend
" more ſuited to his neceſſities, more reſoᵗte,
" or more accompliſhed; he already poſſeſſes ſuch
" a friend, and ſuch a patron as no menaces can
" drive from the line of rectitude, whom neither
" terrors nor bribes can divert from the duty he is

" purfuing, or fhake from his fettled firmnefs
" of mind and countenance. "

A writer of a fanguine imagination, who
delineates a public character he admires in the
glowing colors of affection, has rarely the good
fortune to find the perfonage whom he has
praifed acting in perfect conformity to his
panegyric; but Milton, in one particular circumftance, had this rare felicity, in regard to
the friend whom he fo fervently commended;
for Bradfhaw refifted the tyrannical orders o
Cromwell, in the plenitude of his power, with
fuch firmnefs, that we might almoft fuppofe him
animated by a defire to act up to the letter of
the eulogy, with which he had been honored
by the eloquence and the efteem of Milton.
This will fufficiently appear by the following
anecdote in Ludlow's Memoirs, who after fpeaking of Oliver's ufurpation, and the univerfal
terror he infpired, relates how he himfelf was
fummoned, with Bradfhaw, Sir Henry Vane,
and colonel Rich, to appear before the ufurper
in council. " Cromwell (fays Ludlow) as foon as
" he faw the lord prefident, required him to
" take out a new commiffion for his office of
" chief juftice of Chefter, which he refufed, al-
" ledging that he held that place by a grant
" from the parliament of England, to continue,
" 'quamdiu fe bene gefferit;' and whether he
" had carried himfelf with that integrity, which
" his commiffion exacted, he was ready to fubmit

" to a trial by twelve Englishmen, to be chosen
" even by Cromwell himself."

This opposition to the usurper was assuredly
magnanimous, and the more so as Bradshaw per-
sisted in it, and actually went his circuit as chief
justice without paying any regard to what Cromwell had required. The odium which the pre-
sident justly incurred in the trial of Charles seems
to have prevented even our liberal historians from
recording with candor the great qualities he possessed : he was undoubtedly not only an intrepid
but a sincere enthusiast in the cause of the commonwealth. His discourse on his death-bed is a
sanction to his sincerity; he regarded it as meritorious to have pronounced sentence on his king,
in those awful moments when he was passing
himself to the tribunal of his God. Whatever
we may think of his political tenets, let us render
justice to the courage and the consistency with
which he supported them. — The mind of Milton was in unison with the high-toned spirit of
this resolute friend, and we shall soon see how
little ground there is to accuse the poet of ser-
vility to Cromwell; but we have first to notice
the regular series of his political compositions.

Soon after his public appointment, he was requested by the council to counteract the effect
of the celebrated book, entitled, Icon Basilike,
the Royal Image, and in 1649 he published his
Iconoclastes, the Image Breaker. The sagacity of
Milton enabled him to discover, that the pious

work imputed to the deceafed king was a political artifice to ferve the caufe of the royalifts; but as it was impoffible for him to obtain fuch evidence to detect the impofition as time has fince produced, he executed a regular reply to the book, as a real production of the king, intimating at the fame time his fufpicion of the fraud.

This reply has recently drawn on the name of Milton much liberal praife, and much injurious obloquy. A Scottifh critic of great eminence, Lord Monboddo, has celebrated the opening of the Iconoclaftes as a model of Englifh profe, or, to ufe his own juft expreffions, " a fpecimen of " noble and manly eloquence." Johnfon, from the fame work, takes occafion to infinuate, that Milton was a difhoneft man. A charge fo ferious, and from a moralift who profeffed fuch an attachment to truth, deferves fome difcuffion. " As " faction (fays the unfriendly biographer) feldom " leaves a man honeft, however it might find " him, Milton is fufpected of having interpolat- " ed the book called Icon Bafilike, by inferting " a prayer taken from Sidney's Arcadia, and im- " puting it to the king, whom he charges, in " his Iconoclaftes, with the ufe of this prayer as " with a heavy crime, in the indecent language " with which profperity had emboldened the " advocates for rebellion to infult all that is ve- " nerable and great."

A fimple queftion will fhow the want of candor in this attempt to impeach the moral credit

of Milton. By whom is he fufpected of this dif-
honefty? His fevere biographer finks the name
of his own old and difhonorable affociate in depreciating Milton, and does not inform us that it
was the infamous Lauder, who, having failed to
blaft the reputation of the poet, with equal im-
potence and fury purfued his attack againft the
probity of the man in an execrable pamphlet entitled " King Charles the Firft vindicated from the
" Charge of Plagiarifm brought againft him by
" Milton, and Milton himfelf convicted of For-
" gery." Inftead of naming Lauder, who perfifted in trying to fubftantiate this moft improbable charge, Johnfon would infidioufly lead us
to believe, that the refpectable Dr. Birch fupported it, though Birch, who had indeed printed in the appendix to his Life of Milton, the
idle ftory which Lauder urges as a proof of Milton's impofture, had properly rejected that ftory
from the improved edition of his work, and
honorably united with another candid biographer of the poet, the learned bifhop of Briftol,
in declaring that " fuch contemptible evidence
" is not to be admitted againft a man, who had
" a foul above being guilty of fo mean an
" action."

There are fome calumnies fo utterly defpicable
and abfurd, that to refute them elaborately is
almoft a difgrace : did not the calumny I am
now fpeaking of belong to this defcription, it
might be here obferved, that a writer who

publiſhed remarks on Johnſon's Life of Milton , in which the aſperity of that biographer is op⸱poſed with ſuperior aſperity, has proved , with new arguments , the futility of the charge in queſtion. Inſtead of repeating theſe ; let me obſerve , that the attempt of Johnſon to revive a baſe and ſufficiently refuted imputation againſt the great author whoſe life he was writing , is one of the moſt extraordinary proofs that lite⸱rature can exhibit how far the virulence of po⸱litical hatred may pervert a very powerful mind , even a mind which makes moral truth its principal purſuit , and aſſiduouſly labors to be juſt. This remark is not made in enmity to Johnſon , but to ſhow how cautious the moſt cultivated underſtanding ſhould be in watching the influence of any hoſtile prejudice. Milton himſelf may be alſo urged as an example to enforce the ſame caution ; for though he was certainly no impoſtor in imputing the prayer in queſtion to the king , yet his conſidering the king's uſe of it as an offence againſt heaven , is a pitiable abſurdity ; an abſurdity as glaring as it would be to affirm , that the divine poet is himſelf profane in alſigning to a ſpeech of the Almighty , in his poem , the two following verſes :

Son of my boſom , ſon who art alone
My word, my wiſdom , and effectual might—

Becaufe they are partly borrowed from a line in Virgil, addreffed by a heathen goddefs to her child:

" Nate, meæ vires, mea magna potentia folus. "

The heat of political animofity could thus throw a mift over the bright intellects of Milton; yet his Iconoclaftes, taken all together, is a noble effort of manly reafon, it uncanonized a fictitious faint, who affuredly had no pretenfion to the title.

Having thus fignalized himfelf as the literary antagonift of Charles, when the celebrated Salmafius was hired to arraign the proceedings of England againft him, every member of the Englifh council turned his eyes upon Milton, as the man from whofe fpirit and eloquence his country might expect the moft able vindication. In 1651, he publifhed his defence of the people, the moft elaborate of all his Latin compofitions; the merits and defects of this fignal performance might be moft properly difcuffed in a preliminary difcourfe to the profe works of Milton; here I fhall only remark, that in the compofition of it he gave the moft fingular proof of genuine public fpirit that ever patriot had occafion to difplay; fince, at the time of his engaging in this work, the infirmity in his eyes was fo alarming, that his phyficians affured him he muft inevitably lofe them if he perfifted in

his

his labor. " On this occafion, " (fays Milton
to a favage antagonift, who had reproached
him with blindnefs) " * I reflected that many
" had purchafed with a fuperior evil a lighter
" good, glory with death; to me, on the con-
" trary, greater good was propofed with an
" inferior evil; fo that, by incurring blindnefs
" alone, I might fulfil the moft honorable of
" all duties, which, as it is a more folid ad-
" vantage than glory itfelf, ought to be more
" eligible in the eftimation of every man; I
" refolved therefore to make what fhort ufe I
" might yet have of my eyes as conducive as

* Unde fic mecum reputabam, multos graviore malo minus
bonum, morte gloriam, redemiffe ; mihi contra majus bonum
minore cum malo proponi; ut poffem cum cæcitate fola vel
honeftiffimum officii munus implere quod ut ipfa gloria per
fe eft folidius, ita cuique optatius atque antiquius debet eff.
Hac igitur tam brevi luminum ufura quanta maxima quivi
cum utilitate publica, quoad liceret, fruendum effe ftatui.
Videtis quid prætulerim, quid amiferim, qua inductus ratione,
defignant ergo judiciorum Dei calumniatores maledicere, deque
me fomnia fibi fingere : fic denique habendo me fortis meæ
neque pigere neque pænitere; immotum atque fixum in fententia perftare ; Deum iratum neque fentire, neque habere,
immo maximis in rebus clementiam ejus & benignitatem
erga me paternam experiri atque agnofcere; in hoc præfertim
quod folante ipfo atque animum confirmante in ejus divina
voluntate acquiefcam ; quid is largitus mihi fit quam quid
negaverit fæpius cogitans; poftremo nolle me cum fuo quovis
rectiffime facto, facti mei confcientiam permutare, aut recor-
dationem ejus gratam mihi femper atque tranquillam depo-
nere. — Profe Works, vol. 2. p. 376.

" poffible to public utility : you fee what I
" preferred, and what I loft, with the principle
" on which I acted ; let flanderers therefore
" ceafe to talk irreverently on the judgment of
" God, and to make me the fubject of their
" fictions; let them know that I am far from
" confidering my lot with forrow or repentance;
" that I perfift immoveable in my fentiment; that
" I neither fancy nor feel the anger of God,
" but, on the contrary, experience and ac-
" knowledge his paternal clemency and kindnefs
" in my moft important concerns, in this efpe-
" cially, that, by the comfort and confirmation
" which he himfelf infufes into my fpirit, I ac-
" quiefce in his divine pleafure, continually
" confidering rather what he has beftowed upon
" me, than what he has denied. Finally, that
" I would not exchange the confcioufnefs of my
" own conduct for their merit, whatever it may
" be, or part with a remembrance, which is to
" my own mind a perpetual fource of tran-
" quillity and fatisfaction. "
Whenever he is induced to mention himfelf,
the purity and vigor of Milton's mind appear
in full luftre, whether he fpeaks in verfe or in
profe : the preceding paffage from his Second
Defence is confonant to the fonnet on his blindnefs, addreffed to Syriac Skinner, which, though
different critics have denied the author to excel
in this minute fpecies of compofition, has hardly

been furpaffed ; it deferves double praife or
energy of expreffion and heroifm of fentiment.

> Cyriac, this three-years day thefe eyes, tho' clear
>   To outward view of blemifh or of fpot,
>   Bereft of fight their feeing have forgot,
>   Nor to their idle orbs does day appear ,
> Or fun , or moon, or ftar, throughout the year ,
>   Or man or woman ; yet I argue not
>   Againft Heav'n's hand or will, nor bate one jot,
>   Of heart or hope, but ftill bear up and fteer
>   Right onward. What fupports me doft thou afk?
>   The confcience, friend , to have loft them over-ply'd
>   In liberty's defence , my noble tafk.
> Of which all Europe talks from fide to fide:
> This thought might lead me thro' theworld's vain
>   mafk
>   Content, tho' blind, had I no better guide."

The ambition of Milton was as pure as his
genius was fublime ; his firft object on every occafion was to merit the approbation of his confcience and his God ; when this moft important
point was fecured, he feems to have indulged
the predominant paffion of great minds, and to
have exulted, with a triumph proportioned to
his toil, in the celebrity he acquired : he muft
have been infenfible indeed to public applaufe,
had he not felt elated by the fignal honors which
were paid to his name in various countries, as

the eloquent defender of the Englifh nation. " * This I can truly affirm, " (fays Milton, in mentioning the reception of his great political performance) " that as foon as my defence of " the people was publifhed , and read with " avidity, there was not, in our metropolis , " any ambaffador from any ftate or fovereign , " who did not either congratulate me if we met " by chance , or exprefs a defire to receive me " at his houfe, or vifit me at mine."

Toland relates, that he received from the parliament a prefent of a thoufand pounds for the defence. The author does not include this circumftance among the many particulars he mentions of himfelf; and if fuch a reward was ever beftowed upon him, it muft have been after the publication of his Second Defence, in which he affirms, that he was content with having difcharged what he confidered as an honorable public duty, without aiming at a pecuniary recompence ; and that inftead of having acquired the opulence with which his adverfary reproached him, he received not the flighteft gratuity for that production †. Yet he appears to have been

---

* Hoc etiam vere poffum dicere, quo primum tempore noftra defenfio eft edita, & legentium ftudia incaluere, nullum vel principis vel civitàtis legatum in urbe tum fuiffe, qui non vel forte obvio mihi gratularetur, vel conventum apud fe cuperet vel domi inviferet.—Profe Works, vol. 2. p. 394.

† Contentus quæ honefta factu funt, ea propter fe folum appetiffe, & gratis perfequi : id alii viderent tuque fcito me

perfectly satisfied with the kindnefs of his affociates; for, in fpeaking of his blindnefs, he fays, that " far from being neglected on this account by " the highest characters in the republic, they " conftantly regarded him with indulgence and " favor, not feeking to deprive him either of " diftinction or emolument, though his powers " of being ufeful were diminifhed; " hence he compares himfelf to an ancient Athenian, fup- ported by a decree of honor at the expenfe of the public *. Among the foreign compliments he received, the applaufe of Chriftina afforded him the higheft gratification; for he regarded it as an honorable proof of what he had ever af- firmed, that he was a friend to good fovereigns, though an enemy to tyrants : he underftood that the queen of Sweden had made this diftinction in commending his book, and in the warmth

illas " opimitates, " atque " opes, " quas mihi exprobas, non attigiffe neque eo nomine quo maxime accufas obole factum ditiorem. — Profe Works, vol. ii. p. 378.

* Quin & fummi quoque in republica viri quandoquidem non otio torpentem me, fed impigrum & fumma difcrimina pro li- bertate inter primos adeuntem oculi deferuerunt, ipfi non de- ferunt; verum humana qualia! fint! fecum reputantes, tanquam emerito favent, indulgent vacationem atque otium faciles con- cedunt; fi quid publici muneris, non adimunt; fi quid ex ea re commodi, non minuunt; & quamvis non aeque nunc utili praebendum nihilo minus benigne cenfent; eodem plane honore, ac fi, ut olim Athenienfibus mos erat, in Prytaneo alendum decreviffent. — Profe Works, vol. ii. pag. 376.

of his gratitude he beftowed on the northern
princefs a very fplendid panegyric, of which the
fubfequent conduct of that fingular and fantaftic
perfonage too clearly proved her unworthy; yet
Milton cannot fairly be charged with fervile
adulation. Chriftina, when he appeared as her
eulogift, was the idol of the literary world. The
candor with which fhe fpake as a queen on his
defence of the people would naturally ftrike the
author as an engaging proof of her difcernment
and magnanimity; he was alfo gratified in no common degree by the coolnefs with which fhe treated his adverfary; for Salmafius, whom fhe had
invited to her court for his erudition, was known
to have loft her favor, when his literary arrogance and imbecility were expofed and chaftifed
by the indignant fpirit of Milton. The wretched
Salmafius, indeed, was utterly overwhelmed in
the encounter : he had quitted France, his native
country, where he honorably difdained to pur-
chafe a penfion by flattering the tyranny of Rich-
lieu, and had fettled in Leyden as an afylum
of liberty; he feemed, therefore, as one of his
Parifian correfpondents obferved to him, " to
" cancel the merit of his former conduct by
" writing againft England. " Salmafius was extravagantly vain, and trufted too much to his
great reputation as a fcholar; his antagonift,
on the contrary, was fo little known as a Latin
writer before the defence appeared, that feveral
friends advifed Milton not to hazard his credit

againſt a name ſo eminent as that of Salmaſius.
Never did a literary conflict engage the attention
of a wider circle; and never did victory declare
more decidedly in favor of the party from whom
the public had leaſt expectation. Perhaps no
author ever acquired a more rapid and extenſive
celebrity than Milton gained by this conteſt. Let
us however remark, for the intereſt of literature,
that the two combatants were both to blame in
their reciprocal uſe of weapons utterly unworthy
of the great cauſe that each had to ſuſtain; not
content to wield the broad and bright ſword of
national argument, they both deſcended to uſe
the mean and envenomed dagger of perſonal malevolence. They have indeed great authorities of
modern time to plead in their excuſe, not to
mention the bitter diſputants of antiquity. It was
the opinion of Johnſon, and Milton himſelf
ſeems to have entertained the ſame idea, that it
is allowable in literary contention to ridicule,
vilify, and depreciate as much as poſſible the
character of an opponent. Surely this doctrine
is unworthy of the great names who have endeavoured to ſupport it, both in theory and practice; a doctrine not only morally wrong, but
prudentially defective; for a malevolent ſpirit in
eloquence is like a dangerous varniſh in painting,
which may produce, indeed a brilliant and forcible effect for a time, but ultimately injures
the ſucceſs of the production; a remark that may
be verified in peruſing the Latin proſe of Milton,

where elegance of language and energy of
fentiment fuffer not a little from being blended
with the tirefome afperity of perfonal invective.

It is a pleafing tranfition to return from his
enemies to his friends.   He had a mind and
heart peculiarly alive to the duties and delights
of friendfhip, and feems to have been peculiarly
happy in this important article of human life. In
fpeaking of his blindnefs, he mentions, in the
moft interefting manner, the affiduous and tender
attention, which he received on that occafion
from his friends in general; fome of them he regarded as not inferior in kindnefs to Thefeus and
Pylades, the ancient demigods of amity.   We
have loft, perhaps, fome little poems that flowed
from the heart of Milton, by their being addreffed to perfons who, in the viciffitudes of public fortune, were fuddenly plunged into obfcuri-
ty with the honors they had received. Some of his
fonnets that we poffefs did not venture into public till many years after the death of their author
for political reafons; others might be concealed
from the fame motive, and in fuch concealment
they might eafily perifh. I can hardly believe that
he never addreffed a verfe to Bradfhaw, whom
we have feen him praifing fo eloquently in profe;
and among thofe whom he mentions with efteem
in his Latin works, there is a lefs known military
friend, who feems ftill more likely to have been
honored with fome tribute of the poet's affection, that time and chance may have deftroyed;

I mean his friend Overton, a foldier of eminence in the fervice of the parliament, whom Milton defcribes " as endeared to him through many " years by the fimilitude of their purfuits, by " the fweetnefs of his manners, and by an inti- " macy furpaffing even the union of brothers. *" A character fo highly and tenderly efteemed by the poet has a claim to the attention of his biographer. Overton is commended by the frank ingenuous Ludlow as a brave and faithful officer; he is alfo ridiculed in a ballad of the royalifts as a religious enthufiaft. He had a gratuity of 300 l. a year conferred on him for his bravery by the parliament, and had rifen to the rank of a major general. Cromwell, apprehenfive that Overton was confpiring againft his ufurpation, firft imprifoned him in the tower, and afterwards confined him in the ifland of Jerfey. A letter, in which Marvel relates to Milton his having prefented to the Protector at Windfor a recent copy of the Second Defence, expreffes at the fame time an affectionate curiofity concerning the bufinefs of Overton, who was at that time juft brought to London by a myfterious order of Cromwell. He did not efcape from confinement till after the death of Oliver, when, in confequence of a petition from his fifter to the

* Te, Overtone, mihi multis ab hinc annis & ftudiorum fimilitudine, & morum fuavitate, concordia plufquam fraterna conjunctiffime. ——Profe Works, Vol. II. p. 400.

parliament, he obtained his releafe. Soon after
the reftoration , he was again imprifoned in the
Tower with Colonel Defborow, on a rumor
of their being concerned in a treafonable com-
motion; but as that rumor feems to have been
a political device of the royalifts, contrived to
ftrengthen the new government, he probably
regained his freedom , though we know not how
his active days were concluded. The anxiety
and anguifh that Milton muft have indured in
the various calamities to which his friends were
expofed on the viciffitude of public affairs, formed, I apprehend, the fevereft fufferings of his
extraordinary life, in which genius and affliction
feem to have contended for pre-eminence.

Some traces of the fufferings I allude to, though
myfterioufly veiled, are yet vifible in his poetry,
and will be noticed hereafter. Not to anticipate
the fevereft evil of his deftiny, let me now fpeak
of a foreign friend, in whofe lively regard he
found only honor and delight. On the publication of his defence, Leonard Philaras, a native
of Athens, who had diftinguifhed himfelf in Italy,
and rifen to the rank of envoy from the duke
of Parma to the court of France, conceived a
flattering defire to cultivate the friendfhip of Milton. With this view he fent him his portrait,
with very engaging letters, and the higheft commendation of the recent defence. The reply of
Milton is remarkable for its elegance and fpirit;
after thanking his correfpondent for prefents fo

agreeable, he fays, " * If Alexander in the midſt
" of his martial toil confeſſed, that he labored
" but to gain an eulogy from Athens, I may
" think myſelf fortunate indeed, and eſteem it
" as the higheſt honor, to be thus commended
" by the man in whom alone the genius and
" virtue of the ancient Athenians feem, after fo

* Cum enim Alexander ille magnus in terris ultimis bellum
gerens, tantos fe militiæ labores pertuliſſe teſtatus fit, της παρ'
Αθηναίων ευ δοξίας ἕνεκα ; quidni ergo mihi gratuler, meque
ornari quam maxime putem, ejus viri laudibus, in quo jam
uno priſcorum Athenienſium artes, atque virtutes illæ celebra-
tiſſimæ, renaſci tam longo intervallo, & reflorefcere videntur.
Qua ex urbe cum tot viri difertiſſimi prodierint, eorum potiſ-
fimum fcriptis ab adolefcentia pervolvendis, didiciſſe me libens
fateor quicquid ego literis profeci. Quod fi mihi tanta vis dicendi
accepta ab illis & quaſi transfuſa ineſſet, ut exercitos noſtros
& claſſes ad liberandam ab Ottomanico tyranno Græciam, elo-
quentiæ patriam, excitare poſſem; ad quod facinus egregium
noſtras opes pene implorare videris, facerem profecto id quo
nihil mihi antiquius aut in votis prius eſſet. Quid enim vel
fortiſſimi olim viri, vel eloquentiſſimi glorioſius aut fe dignius
eſſe duxerunt, quam vel fuadendo vel fortiter faciendo
ἐλευθερȣς καὶ αὐτονόμȣς ποιεῖσθαι τȣς Ἕλληνας? Verum & aliud
quiddam præterea tentandum eſt, mea quidem fententia longe
maximum, ut quis antiquam in animis Græcorum virtutem,
induſtriam, laborum tolerantiam, antiqua illa ſtudia dicendo,
fufcitare atque accendere poſſit. Hoc fi quis effecerit, quod a
nemine potius quam abs te, pro tua illa inſigni erga patriam
pietate, cum fumma prudentia reique militaris peritia, fummo
denique recuperandæ libertatis priſtinæ ſtudio conjuncta, ex-
pectare debemus; neque ipfos fibi Græcos neque ullam gentem
Græcis defuturam eſſe confido. Vale.—Profe Works, vol. 2. p. 575.

" long an interval, to revive and flourish. As
" your city has produced many moſt eloquent
" men, I am perfectly willing to confeſs, that
" whatever proficiency I have made in literature
" is chiefly owing to my long and inceſſant
" ſtudy of their works. Had I acquired from
" them ſuch powers of language as might enable
" me to ſtimulate our fleets and armies to deliver
" Greece, the native ſeat of eloquence, from the
" tyranny of the Turks (a ſplendid enterpriſe,
" for which you almoſt ſeem to implore our
" aſſiſtance) I would aſſuredly do what would
" then be among the firſt objects of my deſire;
" for what did the braveſt or moſt eloquent men
" of antiquity conſider as more glorious or more
" worthy of themſelves, than by perſuaſive lan-
" guage or bold exploits to render the Greeks
" free, and their own legiſlators. " He cloſes
his letter by obſerving very juſtly, that " it is
" firſt neceſſary to kindle in the minds of the
" modern Greeks the ſpirit and virtue of their
" anceſtors, " (politely adding) that " if this
" could be accompliſhed by any man, it might
" be moſt reaſonably expected from the patriotic
" enthuſiaſm, and the experience, civil and mi-
" litary, of his accompliſhed correſpondent. "
This letter is dated June, 1652. Milton had ſoon
afterwards the gratification of a viſit from this
liberal Athenian, who took ſo tender an intereſt in the blindneſs of his friend, that, on his
return to Paris, he wrote to him on the ſubject.

The following anſwer of Milton relates the particulars of his diſorder, and ſhows at the ſame time with what cheerful magnanimity he ſupported it.

" * To Leonard Philaras.

" As I have chériſhed from childhood (if ever mortal did) a reverential fondneſs for the Greciau

---

* Leonardo Philaræ Athenienſi.

Cum ſim a pueritia totius Græci nominis, tuarumque in primis Athenarum cultor, ſi quis alius, tum una hoc ſemper mihi perſuaſiſſimum habebam, fore ut illa urbs præclaram aliquando redditura vicem eſſet benevolentiæ erga ſe meæ. Neque defuit ſanc tuæ patriæ nobiliſſimæ antiquus ille genius augurio meo; deditque te nobis & germanum Atticum & noſtri amantiſſimum; qui me, ſcriptis duntaxat notum, & locis ipſe disjunctus, humaniſſime per literas compellens & Londinum poſtea inopinatus adveniens; viſenſque non videntem, etiam in ea calamitate, propter quam conſpectior nemini, deſpectior multis fortaſſis ſim, eadem benevolentia proſequaris. Cum itaque author mihi ſis, ut viſus recuperandi ſpem omnem ne abjiciam, habere te amicum ac neceſſarium tuum Pariſiis Tevenotum medicum, in curandis præſertim oculis præſtantiſſimum, quem ſis de meis luminibus conſulturus, ſi modo acceperis a me unde, is cauſas morbi & ſymptomata poſſit intelligere, faciam equidem quod hortaris, ne oblatam undecunque divinitus fortaſſis opem repudiare videar. Decennium, opinor, plus minus eſt, ex quo debilitari atque hebeſcere viſum ſenſi, eodemque tempore lumen, viſceraque omnia gravari, flatibuſque vexari; & mane quidem, ſi quid pro more legere cœpiſſem, oculi ſtatim penitus dolere; lectionemque refugere, poſt mediocrem deinde corporis exercitationem recreari; quam aſpexiſſem lucernam, iris quædam viſa

name, and for your native Athens in particular, so have I continually perſuaded myſelf, that at ſome period I ſhould receive from that city a very ſignal return for my benevolent regard : nor has the ancient genius of your moſt noble

eſt redimere : haud ita multo poſt ſiniſtra in parte oculi ſiniſtri (is enim oculus aliquot annis prius altera nubilavit) caligo oborta, quæ ad latus illud ſita erant, omnia eripiebat. Anteriora quoque, ſi dexterum forte oculum clauſiſſem, minora viſa ſunt. Deficiente per hoc fere triennium ſenſim atque paulatim altero quoque lumine, aliquot ante menſibus quam viſus omnis aboleretur, quæ immotus ipſe cernerem, viſa ſunt omnia nunc dextrorſum, nunc ſiniſtrorſum natare; frontem totam atque tempora inveterati quidem vapores videntur inſediſſe; qui ſomnolenta quadam gravitate oculos, a cibo præſertim uſque ad veſperam, plerumque urgent atque deprimunt; ut mihi haud raro veniat in mentem Salmydeſſii vatis Phinei in Argonauticis:

$$
\begin{aligned}
&\text{— κάρος δέ μιν ἀμφεκάλυψεν} \\
&\text{Πορφύρεος. γαίην δὲ πέριξ ἐδόκησε φέρεσθαι} \\
&\text{Νειόθεν, ἀβληχρῷ δ'ἐπι κώματι κέκλιτ' ἄναυδος.}
\end{aligned}
$$

Sed neque illud omiſerim, dum adhuc viſus aliquantulum ſupererat, ut primum in lecto decubuiſſem meque in alterutrum latus reclinaſſem, conſueviſſe copioſum lumen clauſis oculis emicare; deinde, imminuto indies viſu, colores perinde obſcuriores cum impetu & fragore quodam intimo exilire; nunc autem, quaſi extincto lucido, merus nigror, aut cineraceo diſtinctus, & quaſi intectus ſolet ſe affundere : caligo tamen quæ perpetuo obſervatur, tam noctu, quam interdiu albenti ſemper quam nigricanti proprior videtur; & volvente ſe oculo aliquantulum lucis quaſi per rimulam admittit. Ex quo tametſi medico tantundem quoque ſpei poſſit elucere, tamen ut in ire

country failed to realize my prefage; he has given me in you an Attic brother, and one moft tenderly attached to me. Though I was known to you only by my writings; and though your refidence was far diftant from mine, you firft addreffed me in the moft engaging terms by letter; and afterwards coming unexpectedly to London, and vifiting the ftranger, who had no eyes to fee you, continued your kindnefs to me under that calamity, which can render me a more eligible friend to no one, and to many, perhaps, may make me an object of difregard.

" Since, therefore, you requeft me not to reject all hope of recovering my fight, as you have an intimate friend at Paris, in Thevenot the phyfician, who excels particularly in relieving ocular complaints, and whom you wifh to confult

plane infanabili ita me paro atque compono; illudque fæpe cogito, cum deftinati cuique dies tenebrarum, quod monet fapiens multi fint, meas adhuc tenebras, fingulari numinis benignitate, inter otium & ftudia, vocefque amicorum & falutatione, illis lethalibus multo effe mitiores. Quod fi, ut fcriptum eft, non folo pane vivit homo, fed omni verbo prodeunte per os Dei, quid eft, cur quis in hoc itidem non acquiefcat, non folis fe oculis, fed Dei ductu an providentiæ fatis oculatum effe. Sane dummodo ipfe mihi profpicit, ipfe mihi providet, quod facit, meque per omnem vitam quafi manu ducit atque deducit, ne ego meos oculos, quandoquidem ipfi fic vifum eft, libens feriari juffero. Teque, mi Philara, quocunque res cecidit, non minus forti & confirmato animo, quam fi Lynceus effem, valere jubeo.

Weftmonafterio, Septemb. 28, 1654.

Profe Works, Vol. II. p. 577.

concerning my eyes, after receiving from me such an account as may enable him to underſtand the ſource and ſymptoms of my diſorder, I will certainly follow your kind ſuggeſtion, that I may not appear to rejeȼt aſſiſtance thus offered me, perhaps providentially.

" It is about ten years, I think, ſince I perceived my ſight to grow weak and dim, finding at the ſame time my inteſtines afflicȻed with flatulence and oppreſſion.

" Even in the morning, if I began as uſual to read, my eyes immediately ſuffered pain, and ſeemed to ſhrink from reading; but, after ſome moderate bodily exerciſe, were refreſhed; whenever I looked at a candle I ſaw a ſort of iris around it. Not long afterwards, on the left ſide of my left eye (which began to fail ſome years before the other) a darkneſs aroſe, that hid from me all things on that ſide; — if I chanced to cloſe my right eye, whatever was before me ſeemed diminiſhed.— In the laſt three years, as my remaining eye failed by degrees ſome months before my ſight was utterly gone, all things that I could diſcern, though I moved not myſelf, appeared to fluȼtuate, now to the right, now to the left. Obſtinate vapors ſeem to have ſettled all over my forehead and my temples, overwhelming my eyes with a ſort of ſleepy heavineſs, eſpecially after food, till the evening; ſo that I frequently recolleȼt the condition of the prophet Phineus in the Argonautics:

Him

Him vapors dark
Envelop'd, and the earth appeared to roll
Beneath him, finking in a lifelefs trance.

But I fhould not omit to fay, that while I had fome little fight remaining, as foon as I went to bed, and reclined on either fide, a copious light ufed to dart from my clofed eyes; then, as my fight grew daily lefs, darker colors feemed to burft forth with vehemence, and a kind of internal noife; but now, as if every thing lucid were extinguifhed, blacknefs either abfolute or chequered, and interwoven, as it were with afh-color, is accuftomed to pour itfelf on my eyes; yet the darknefs perpetually before them, as well during the night as in the day, feems always approaching rather to white than to black, admitting, as the eye rolls, a minute portion of light as through a crevice.

"Though from your phyfician fuch a portion of hope alfo may arife, yet, as under an evil that admits no cure, I regulate and tranquillize my mind, often reflecting, that fince the days of darknefs allotted to each, as the wife man reminds us, are many, hitherto my darknefs, by the fingular mercy of God, with the aid of ftudy, leifure, and the kind converfation of my friends, is much lefs oppreffive than the deadly darknefs to which he alludes. For if, as it is written, man lives not by bread alone, but by every word that proceeds from the mouth of

11

God, why should not a man acquiesce even in this? not thinking that he can derive light from his eyes alone, but esteeming himself sufficiently enlightened by the conduct or providence of God.

" As long, therefore, as he looks forward, and provides for me as he does, and leads me backward and forward by the hand, as it were through my whole life, shall I not cheerfully bid my eyes keep holiday, since such appears to be his pleasure? But whatever may be the event of your kindness, my dear Philaras, with a mind not 'less resolute and firm than if I were Lynceus himself, I bid you farewel.

" Westminster, Sept. 28, 1654."

We have no reason to imagine that Milton received any kind of medical benefit from the friendly intention of this amiable foreigner. Strange as the idea may at first appear, perhaps it was better for him, as a man and as a poet, to remain without a cure; for his devout tenderness and energy of mind had so far converted his calamity into a blessing, that it seems rather to have promoted than obstructed both the happiness of his life and the perfection of his genius. We have seen, in the admirable sonnet on his blindness, how his reflections on the conscientious labor by which he lost his eyes gave a dignified satisfaction to his spirit. In one of his prose works he expresses a sentiment on the same subject, that shows, in the most striking point of view, the meeknefs and fublimity of his devotion. He exults in his misfortune, and feels it endeared to him by the perfuafion, that to be blind is to be placed more immediately under the conduct and providence of God * : when regarded in this manner, it could not fail to quicken and invigorate his mental powers. Blindnefs, indeed, without the aid of religious enthufiafm, has a natural tendency to favor that undifturbed, intenfe, and continual meditation, which works of magnitude require. Perhaps we fometimes include in the catalogue of difadvantages the very circumftances that have been partly inftrumental in leading extraordinary men to diftinction. In examining the lives of illuftrious fcholars we may difcover, that many of them arofe to glory by the impulfe of perfonal misfortune; Bacon and Pope were deformed ; Homer and Milton were blind.

* Sed neque ego cæcis afflictis mœrentibus imbecillis tametfi vos id miferum ducitis aggregari me difcrucior ; quando quidem fpes eft, eo me proprius ad mifericordiam fummi patris atque tutelam pertinere. Eft quoddam per imbecillitatem præeunte apoftolo ad maximas vires iter : fim ego debiliffimus; dummodo in mea debilitate immortalis ille & melior vigor eo fe efficacius exerat; dummodo in meis tenebris divini vultus lumen eo clarius eluceat, tum etim infirmiffimus ero fimul & validiffimus cæcus eodem tempore & perfpicaciffimus; hac poffim ego infirmitate confummari, hac perfici poffim in hac obfcuritate fic ego irradiari. Et fane haud ultima Dei cura cæci fumus ; qui nos quo minus quicquam aliud præter ipfum cernere valemus, eo clementius atque benignius refpicere dignatur. — Profe Works, vol. 2. p. 376.

It has been frequently remarked, that the blind are generally cheerful; it is not therefore marvellous that Milton was very far from being dispirited by the utter extinction of his sight; but his unconquerable vigor of mind was signally displayed in continuing to labor under all the pains and inconveniencies of approaching blindnefs, a ftate peculiarly unfavorable to mental exertion.

From the very eloquent preface to his Defence we learn, that while he was engaged on that compofition, and eager to throw into it all the force of his exalted mind, " his infirmity obli-
" ged him to work only by ftarts, and scarce
" to touch, in fhort periods of ftudy broken by
" hourly interruptions, what he wifhed to purfue
" with continued application *. " In this moft uneafy and perilous labor he exerted his failing eyes to the utmoft, and, to repeat his own triumphant expreffion,

> Loft them overply'd
> In liberty's defence.

His left eye became utterly blind in 1651, the year in which the book that he alludes to was

---

* Quod fi quis miretur forte cur ergo tam diu intactum & ovantem, noftroque omnium filentio inflatum volitare paffi fumus de aliis fane nefcio, de me audacter poffum dicere, non mihi verba aut argumenta quibus caufam tuerer tam bonam diu quærenda aut inveftiganda fuiffe fi otium & valetudinem (quæ

published, and he loft the ufe of the other in
1654, the year in which he wrote concerning
his blindnefs to his Athenian friend. In this interval he repeatedly changed his abode. As
every fpot inhabited by fuch a man acquires a
fort of confecration in the fancy of his admirers,
I fhall here tranfcribe from his nephew the particulars of his refidence.

" Firft he lodged at one Thomfon's, next
" door to the Bull Head tavern at Charing
" Crofs, opening into the Spring Garden, which
" feems to have been only a lodging taken till
" his defigned apartment in Scotland Yard was
" prepared for him; for hither he foon removed
" from the aforefaid place, and here his third
" child, a fon, was born, which, through the
" ill-ufage or bad conftitution of an ill-chofen
" nurfe, died an infant. From this apartment,
" whether he thought it not healthy or other-
" wife convenient for his ufe, or whatever elfe
" was the reafon, he foon after took a pretty
" garden-houfe in Petty France; in Weftminfter,
" next door to the Lord Scudamore's, and
" opening into St. James's Park, where he re-
" mained no lefs than eight years, namely, from
" the year 1652 till within a few weeks of King
" Charles the Second's reftoration. "

quidem fcribendi laborem ferre poffit) naftus effem. Qua cum
adhuc etiam tenui admodum utar carptim hæc cogor & intercifis
pene fingulis horis vix attingere, quæ continenti ftylo atque
ftudio perfequi debuiffem.— Profe Works, vol. 2. p. 278.

Philips alfo informs us, that while his uncle lodged at Thomfon's he was employed in revifing and polifhing the Latin work of his youngeft nephew John, who, on the publication of a fevere attack upon Milton, afcribed to Bramhall, Bifhop of Derry, vindicated his illuftrious relation, and fatirized his fuppofed adverfary with a keennefs and vehemence of invective, which induced, perhaps, fome readers to fufpect that the performance was written entirely by Milton. The traces, however, of a young hand are evident in the work; and John Philips, at the time it appeared, 1652, was a youth of nineteen or twenty, eager (as he declares) to engage unfolicited in a compofition, which, however abounding in juvenile defects, proves him attached to his country, and grateful to his friends.

In 1654, Milton, now utterly blind, appeared again in the field of controverfy, firft, in his Second Defence of the Englifh People, and the following year in a defence of himfelf, " Autoris " pro fe defenfio." The firft of thefe productions is in truth his own vindication; it is the work in which he fpeaks moft abundantly of his own character and conduct; it difplays that true eloquence of the heart, by which probity and talents are enabled to defeat the malevolence of an infolent accufer; it proves that the mind of this wonderful man united to the poetic imagination of Homer the argumentative energy of Demofthenes.

It muft however be allowed, that while Milton defended himfelf with the fpirit of the Grecian orator, in imitating the eloquent Athenian he promifcuoufly caught both his merits and defeels. It is to be regretted, that thefe mighty mafters of rhetoric permitted fo large an alloy of perfonal virulence to debafe the dignity of national argument; yet as the great orators of an age more humanized are apt, we fee, to be hurried into the fame failing, we may conclude that it is almoft infeparable from the weaknefs of nature, and we muft not expeel to find, though we certainly fhould endeavour to introduce, the charity of the Gofpel in political contention.

If the utmoft acrimony of inveelive could in any cafe be juftified, it might affuredly be fo by the calumnies which hurried both Demofthenes and Milton into thofe intemperate expreffions, which appear in their refpeelive vindications like fpecks of a meaner mineral in a mafs of the richeft ore. The outrages that called forth the vindielive thunders of the eloquent Athenian are fufficiently known. The indignation of Milton was awakened by a Latin work, publifhed at the Hague in 1652, entitled, " Regii Sanguinis " Clamor ad Coelum;" The Cry of Royal Blood to Heaven. In this book all the bitter terms of abhorrence and reproach, with which the malignity of paffion can difhonor learning, were lavifhed on the eloquent defender of the Englifh commonwealth. The fecret author of this scurrility was Peter du Moulin, a proteftant divine, and fon of a French author, whom the biographers of his own country defcribe as a fatirift without tafte and a theologian without temper. Though du Moulin feems to have inherited the acrimonious fpirit of his father, he had not the courage to publifh himfelf what he had written as the antagonift of Milton, but fent his papers to Salmafius, who intrufted them to Alexander More, a French proteftant of Scotch extraction, and a divine, who agreed in his principles with the author of the manufcript.

Moft unfortunately for his own future comfort, More publifhed, without a name, the work of Du Moulin, with a dedication to Charles 'the Second, under the Signature of Ulac, the Dutch printer.. He decorated the book with a portrait of Charles, and applied at the fame time to Milton the Virgilian delineation of Polypheme :

> Monftrum horrendum informe ingens, 'cui lumen
> ademptum.

> A monftrous bulk deform'd, depriv'd of fight.
>
> DRYDEN.

Never was a favage infult more completely avenged; for Milton, having difcovered that More was unqueftionably the publifher of the work, confidered him as its author, which, according to legal maxims he had a right to do, and in return expofed, with fuch feverity of reproof, the irregular and licentious life of his adverfary, that, lofing, his popularity as a preacher, he feems to have been overwhelmed with public contempt.

There is a circumftance hitherto unnoticed in this controverfy, that may be confidered as a proof of Milton's independent and inflexible fpirit. More having heard accidentally, from an acquaintance of the Englifh author, that he was preparing to expofe him as the editor of the fcurrilous work he had publifhed, contrived to make great intereft in England, firft, to prevent the appearance, and again, to foften the perfonal feverity of Milton's Second Defence. The Dutch ambaffador endeavoured to prevail on Cromwell to fupprefs the work. When he found that this was impoffible, he conveyed to Milton the letters of More, containing a proteftation that he was not the author of the invective, which had given fo much offence, the ambaffador at the fame time made it is particular requeft to Milton, that, in anfwering the book, as far as it related to the Englifh government, he would abftain from all hoftility againft More. — Milton replied, " that no unbecoming words fhould " proceed from his pen ; " but his principles would not allow him to fpare, at any private interceffion, a public enemy of his country. Thefe particulars are collected from the laft of our author's political treatifes in Latin, the defence of himfelf, and they form, I truft, a favorable introduction to a refutation, which it is time to begin, of the fevereft and moft plaufible charge, that the recent enemies of Milton have urged againft him; I mean the charge of fervility and adulation, as the fycophant of an ufurper.

I will ftate the charge in the words of his moft bitter accufer, and without abridgment, that it may appear in its full force.

" Cromwell (fays Johnfon) had now difmiffed
" the parliament, by the authority of which he
" had deftroyed monarchy, and commenced mo-
" narch himfelf under the title of protector,
" but with kingly, and more than kingly,
" power.—That his authority was lawful never
" was pretended; he himfelf founded his right
" only in neceffity : but Milton, having now
" tafted the honey of public employment, would
" not return to hunger and philofophy, but,
" continuing to exercife his office under a mani-
" feft ufurpation, betrayed to his power that li-
" berty which he had defended. Nothing can
" be more juft than that rebellion fhould end
" in flavery; that he who had juftified the mur-
" der of the king for fome acts, which to him
" feemed unlawful, fhould now fell his fervices
" and his flatteries to a tyrant, of whom it was
" evident that he could do nothing lawful. "

Let us obferve, for the honor of Milton, that the paragraph, in which he is arraigned with fo

much rancor, contains a political dogma, that, if it were really true, might blaft the glory of all the illuftrious characters who are particularly endeared to every Englifh heart. If nothing can be more juft than that rebellion fhould end in flavery, why do we revere thofe anceftors, who contended againft kings? why do we not refign the privileges that we owe to their repeated rebellion? but the dogma is utterly unworthy of an Englifh moralift; for affuredly we have the fanction of truth, reafon, and experience, in faying, that rebellion is morally criminal or meritorious, according to the provocation by which it is excited, and the end it purfues. This doctrine was fupported even by a fervant of the imperious Elizabeth. " Sir Thomas Smith" (fays Milton in his tenure of Kings and Magiftrates) " a pro-
" teftant and a ftatefman, in his Commonwealth
" of England, putting the queftion, whether
" it be lawful to rife againft a tyrant, anfwers,
" that the vulgar judge of it according to the
" event, and the learned. according to the pur-
" pofe of them that do it." Dr. Johnfon, though one of *the learned*, here fhows not that candor which the liberal ftatefman had defcribed as the characteriftic of *their* judgment. The biographer, uttering himfelf political tenets of the moft fervile complexion, accufes Milton of fervility; and, in his mode of ufing the words honey and hunger, falls into a petulant meannefs of expreffion, that too clearly difcovers how cordially he detefted

him. But perhaps, this deteſtation was the mere effeɕt of political prejudice, the common but unchriſtian abhorrence that a vehement royaliſt thinks it virtue to harbour and to manifeſt againſt a republican. We might indeed eaſily believe that Johnſon's rancor againſt Milton was merely political, had he not appeared as the biographer of another illuſtrious republican; but when we find him repreſenting as honorable in Blake the very principles and conduɕt which he endeavours to make infamous and contemptible in Milton, can we fail to obſerve, that he renders not the ſame juſtice to the heart of the great republican author which he had nobly rendered to the gallant admiral of the republic. To Blake he generouſly aſſigns the praiſe of intrepidity, honeſty, contempt of wealth, and love of his country. Aſſuredly theſe virtues were as eminent in Milton — and however different their lines in life may appear, the celebrated ſpeech of Blake to his ſeamen, " It is our buſineſs to hinder foreigners from fooling us," by which he juſtified his continuance in his poſt under Cromwell, is ſingularly applicable to Milton, who, as a ſervant engaged by the ſtate to conduɕt in Latin its foreign correſpondence, might think himſelf as ſtrongly bound in duty and honor as the juſtly applauded admiral, " to hinder his country " from being fooled by foreigners." " But Milton," ſays his uncandid biographer, " conti-" nuing to exerciſe his office under a manifeſt

" ufurpation, betrayed to his power that liberty
" which he had defended." Was the ufurpation
more manifeft to Milton than to Blake? Or is
it a deeper crime againft liberty to write the
Latin defpatches, than to fight the naval battles
of a nation under the control of an ufurper?
Affuredly not: nor had either Blake or Milton
the leaft intention of betraying that liberty,
which was equally the darling idol of their elevated and congenial fpirits; but in finding the
learned and eloquent biographer of thefe two immortal worthies fo friendly to the admiral, and
fo inimical to the author, have we not reafon to
lament and reprove fuch inconfiftent hoftility.

That the Latin fecretary of the nation deferved
not this bitternefs of cenfure for remaining in
his office may be thought fufficiently proved by
the example of Blake.—If his conduct in this
article required farther juftification, we might
recollect with the candid bifhop Newton, that
the blamelefs Sir Matthew Hale, the favorite
model of integrity, exercifed under Cromwell
the higher office of a judge; but the heavieft
charge againft Milton is yet unanfwered, the
charge of lavifhing the moft fervile adulation on
the ufurper.

In replying to this moft plaufible accufation,
let me be indulged in a few remarks, that may
vindicate the credit not only of a fingle poet
but of all Parnaffus. The poetical fraternity
have been often accufed of being ever ready to

flatter ; but the general charge is in fome meafure inconfiftent with a knowledge of human nature. As poets, generally fpeaking, have more fenfibility and lefs prudence than other men, we fhould naturally expect to find them rather diftinguifhed by abundance than by a want of fincerity ; when they are candidly judged, they will generally be found fo ; a poet indeed is as apt to applaud a hero as a lover is to praife his miftrefs, and both, according to the forcible and true expreffion of Shakfpeare,

" Are of imagination all compact. "

Their defcriptions are more faithful to the acutenefs of their own feelings than to the real qualities of the objects defcribed. Paradoxical as it may found, they are often deficient in truth, in proportion to the excefs of their fincerity ; the charm or the merit they celebrate is partly the phantom of their own fancy ; but they believe it real, while they praife it as a reality ; and as long as their belief is fincere, it is unjuft to accufe them of adulation. Milton himfelf gives us an excellent touchftone for the trial of praife in the following paffage of his Areopagitica ; " there " are three principal things, without which all " praifing is but courtfhip and flattery : firft, " when that only is praifed, which is folidly " worth praife ; next, when greateft likelihoods " are brought that fuch things are truly and

" really in thofe perfons to whom they are af-
" cribed; the other, when he who praifes, by
" fhewing that fuch his actual perfuafion is of
" whom he writes, can demonftrate that he
" flatters not. " If we try Milton by this his
own equitable law; we muft honorably acquit
him of the illiberal charge that might almoft be
thought fufficiently refuted by its apparent inconfiftency with his elevated fpirit.

Though in the temperate judgment of pofterity, Cromwell appears only a bold bad man,
yet he dazzled and deceived his contemporaries
with fuch a ftrong and continued blaze of real
and vifionary fplendor, that almoft all the power and all the talents on earth feemed eager
to pay him unfolicited homage : but I mean not
to reft the vindication of Milton on the prevalence of example, which, however high and
dignified it might be, could never ferve as a
fanction for the man, to whom the rare union
of fpotlefs integrity with confummate genius had
given an elevation of character that no rank and
no powers unfupported by probity could poffibly
beftow; though all the potentates and all the
literati of the world confpired to flatter the ufurper, we might expect Milton to remain, like
his own faithful Abdiel,

Unfhaken, unfeduc'd, unterrified.

Affuredly he was fo; and in praifing Cromwell he praifed a perfonage, whofe matchlefs hypo-crify affumed before him a mafk that the arch apoftate of the poet could not wear in the pre-fence of Abdiel, the mafk of affectionate zeal to-wards man, and of devout attachment to God; a mafk that Davenant has defcribed with poeti-cal felicity in the following couplet:

> Diffembled zeal, ambition's old difguife,
> The vizard in which fools outface the wife.

It was more as a faint than as an hero that Cromwell deluded the generous credulity of Milton; and, perhaps, the recollection of his having been thus deluded infpired the poet with his admirable apology for Uriel deceived by Satan.

> For neither man nor angel can difcern
> Hypocrify, the only evil that walks
> Invifible, except to God alone,
> By his permiffive will, thro' heav'n and earth:
> And oft, tho' wifdom wake, fufpicion fleeps
> At wifdom's gate, and to fimplicity
> Refigns her charge, while goodnefs thinks no ill
> Where no ill feems.

That fublime religious enthufiafm, which was the predominant characteriftic of the poet,
expofed

expofed him particularly to be duped by the prime artifice of the political impoftor, who was indeed fo confummate in the art of deception, that he occafionally deceived the prudent unheated Ludlow and the penetrating inflexible Bradfhaw; nay, who carried his habitual deception to fuch a length, that he is fuppofed, by fome acute judges of human nature, to have been ultimately the dupe of his own hypocritical fervor, and to have thought himfelf, what he induced many to think 'him, the felected fervant of God, exprefsly chofen to accomplifh wonders, not only for the good of his nation, but for the true intereft of Chriftendom.

Though Cromwell had affumed the title of Protector, when Milton in his fecond defence fketched a mafterly portrait of him (as we have feen he did of Bradfhaw in the fame production) yet the new potentate had not, at this period, completely unveiled his domineering and oppreffive character; on the contrary, he affected, with the greateft art, fuch a tender concern for the people; he reprefented himfelf, both in his public and private proteflations, fo perfectly free from all ambitious defires, that many perfons, who poffeffed not the noble unfufpecting fimplicity of Milton, believed the Protector fincere in declaring, that he reluctantly fubmitted to the cares of government, merely for the fettlemeut and fecurity of the nation. With a mind full of fervid admiration for his marvellous achievements, and generally difpofed to give him credit for every upright intention, Milton hailed him as the father of his country, and delineated his character: if there were fome particles of flattery in this panegyric, which, if we adhere to our author's juft definition of flattery we cannot allow, it was completely purified from every cloud or fpeck of fervility by the moft fplendid and fublime admonition that was ever given to a man poffeffed of great talents and great power by a genuine and dauntlefs friend, to whom talents and power were only objects of reverence, when under the real or fancied direction of piety and virtue.

" * Revere (fays Milton to the Protector) the great expectation, the only hope, which our

* Reverere tantam de te expectationem, fpem patriæ de te unicam; reverere vultus & vulnera tot fortium virorum, quotquot, te duce, pro libertate tam ftrenue decertarunt; manes etiam eorum qui in ipfo certamine occubuerunt; reverere exterarum quoque civitatum exiftimationem. de nobis atque fermones, quantas res de libertate noftra tam fortiter parta, de noftra republica tam gloriofe exorta fibi polliceantur; quæ fi tam cito quafi aborta evanuerit, profecto nihil æque dedecorofum huic genti, atque pudendum fuerit; teipfum denique reverere, ut pro qua adipifcenda libertate tot ærumnas pertulifti, tot pericula adiifti, eam adeptus violatam per te. ✦ ut ulla in parte imminutam aliis ne finas effe. Profecto tu ipfe liber fine nobis effe non potes, fic enim. natura comparatum eft, ut qui aliorum libertatem occupat; fuam ipfe primum omnium amittat; feque primum omnium intelligat ferviri; atque id quidem non injurja. At vero, fi patronus ipfe libertatis, & quafi tutelaris deus, fi

country now refts upon you — revere the fight
and the fufferings of fo many brave men, who,
under your guidance, have fought fo ftrenuoufly
for freedom — revere the credit we have gained
in foreign nations — reflect on the great things
they promife themfelves from our liberty, fo
bravely acquired; from our republic, fo glorioufly
founded, which, fhould it perifh like an abor-
tion, muft expofe our country to the utmoft
contempt and difhonor.

is, quo nemo juftior, nemo fanctior eft habitus; nemo vir melior,
quam vindicavit ipfe, eam poftmodum invaferit, id non ipfi
tantum fed univerfæ virtutis ac pietatis rationi perniciofum ac
lethale prope modum fit neceffe eft : ipfa honeftas ipfa virtus
decoxiffe videbitur religionis augufta fides, exiftimatio perexigua
in pofterum erit, quo gravius generi humano vulnus, poft illud
primum, infligi nullum poterit. Onus longe graviffimum fuf-
cepifti, quod te penitus explorabit totum te atque intimum per-
fcrutabitur atque oftendet, quid tibi animi, quid virium infit,
quid ponderis; vivatne in te vere illa pietas, fides, juftitia,
animique moderatio, ob quas evectum te præ cæteris Dei nu-
mine ad hanc fummam dignitatem credimus. Tres nationes
validiffimas confilio regere, populos ab inftitutis pravis ad me-
liorem, quam antehac, frugem ac difciplinam velle perducere,
remotiffimas in partes, follicitam mentem, cogitationes immit-
tere, vigilare, prævidere, nullum laborem recufare, nulla vo-
luptatum blandimenta non fpernere, divitiarum atque potentiæ
oftentationem fugere, hæc funt illa ardua, præ quibus bellum
ludus eft; hæc te ventilabunt atque excutient, hæc virum pof-
cunt divino fultum auxilio, divino pene colloquio monitum atque edoctum. Quæ tu, & plura, fæpenumero quin tecum re-
putes atque animo revolvas, non dubito; uti & illud, quibus
potiffimum queas modis & illa maxima perficere & libertatem
falvam nobis reddere & auctiorem. — Profe Works, vol. 2.
pag. 399.

" Finally, revere yourfelf; and having fought
and fuftained every hardfhip and danger for the
acquifition of this liberty, let it not be violated
by yourfelf, or impaired by others, in the fmal-
left degree. In truth, it is impoffible for you
to be free yourfelf unlefs we are fo; for it is the
ordinance of nature, that the man who firft in-
vades the liberty of others muft firft lofe his
own, and firft feel himfelf a flave. This indeed
is juft. But if the very patron and tutelary angel of liberty, if he who is generally regarded
as pre-eminent in juftice, in fanctity, and virtue; if he fhould ultimately invade that liberty
which he afferted himfelf, fuch invafion muft indeed be pernicious and fatal, not only to himfelf, but to the general intereft of piety and
virtue. Truth, probity, and religion would
then lofe the eftimation and confidence of mankind, the worft of wounds, fince the fall of our
firft parents, that could be inflicted on the human race. You have taken upon you a burden
of weight inexpreffible; it will put to the fevereft
perpetual teft the inmoft qualities, virtues, and
powers of your heart and foul; it will determine
whether there really exifts in your character that
piety, faith, juftice, and moderation, for the
fake of which we believe you raifed above others,
by the influence of God, to this fupreme charge.

" To direct three moft powerful nations by
your counfel, to endeavour to reclaim the people
from their depraved inftitutions to better conduct

and difcipline, to fend forth into remoteft regions your anxious fpirit and inceffant thoughts, to watch, to forefee, to fhrink from no labor, to fpurn every allurement of pleafure, to avoid the oftentation of opulence and power, thefe are the arduous duties, in comparifon of which war itfelf is mere fport, thefe will fearch and prove you; they require, indeed, a man fupported by the affiftance of heaven, and almoft admonifhed and inftructed by immediate intercourfe with God. Thefe and more I doubt not but you diligently revolve in your mind, and this in particular, by what methods you may be moft able to accomplifh things of higheft moment, and fecure to us our liberty not only fafe but enlarged."

If a private individual thus fpeaking to a man of unbounded influence, whom a powerful nation had idolized and courted to affume the reins of government, can be called a flatterer, we have only to wifh that all the flatterers of earthly power may be of the fame complexion. The admonition to the people, with which Milton concludes his fecond defence, is by no means inferior in dignity and fpirit to the advice he beftowed on the protector. The great misfortune of the monitor was, that the two parties, to whom he addreffed his eloquent and patriotic exhortation, were neither of them fo worthy of his counfel as he wifhed them to be, and endeavoured to make them. For Cromwell, as his fubfequent conduct fufficiently proved, was a

political impoftor with an arbitrary foul; and as to
the people, they were alternately the difhonored
inftruments and victims of licentioufnefs and fa-
naticifm. The protector, his adherents, and his
enemies, to fpeak of them in general, were as
little able to reach the difinterefted purity of
Milton's principles, as they were to attain, and
even to eftimate, the fublimity of his poetical
genius. But Milton, who paffionately loved his
country, though he faw and lamented the various corruptions of his contemporaries, ftill continued to hope; with the native ardor of a fanguine fpirit, that the mafs of the Englifh people
would be enlightened and improved. His real
fentiments of Cromwell, I am perfuaded, were
thefe : he long regarded him as a perfon not
only poffeffed of wonderful influence and ability,
but difpofed to attempt, and likely to accomplifh, the pureft and nobleft purpofes of policy
and religion; yet often thwarted and embarraf-
fed in his beft defigns, not only by the power
and machinations of the enemies with whom he
had to contend, but by the want of faith, morality, and fenfe in the motley multitude, whom
he endeavoured to guide and govern. As religious enthufiafm was the predominant characteriftic of Milton, it is moft probable that his
fervid imagination beheld in Cromwell a perfon
deftined by heaven to reduce, if not to annihilate, what he confidered as the moft enormous
grievance of earth, the prevalence of popery and

superftition. The feveral humane and fpirited letters which he wrote, in the name of Cromwell, to redrefs the injuries of the perfecuted proteftants, who fuffered in Piedmont, were highly calculated to promote, in equal degrees, his zeal for the purity of religion, and his attachment to the protector.

Yet great as the powers of Cromwell were to dazzle and delude, and willing as the liberal mind of Milton was to give credit to others for that pure public fpirit, which he poffeffed himfelf, there is great reafon to apprehend, that his veneration and efteem for the protector were entirely deftroyed by the treacherous defpotifm of his latter days. But however his opinion of Olver might change, he was far from betraying liberty, according to Johnfon's ungenerous accufation, by continuing to exercife his office; on the contrary, it ought to be efteemed a proof of his fidelity to freedom, that he condefcended to remain in an office, which he had received from no individual, and in which he juftly confidered himfelf as a fervant of the ftate. From one of his familiar letters, written in the year preceding the death of Cromwell, it is evident that he had no fecret intimacy or influence with the protector; and that, inftead of engaging in ambitious machinations, he confined himfelf as much as poffible to the privacy of domeftic life. Finally, on a full and fair review of all the intercourfe between Milton and Cromwell, there is not the smallest ground to suspect, that Milton ever spoke or acted as a sycophant or a slave; he bestowed, indeed, the most liberal eulogy, both in prose and rhyme, upon the protector; but at a period when it was the general opinion, that the utmost efforts of panegyric could hardly equal the magnitude and the variety of the services rendered to his country by the acknowledged hero and the fancied patriot; at a period when the eulogist, who understood the frailty of human nature, and foresaw the temptations of recent power, might hope that praise so magnificent, united to the noblest advice, would prove to the ardent spirit of the protector the best preservative against the delirium of tyranny. These generous hopes were disappointed; the despotic proceedings of Cromwell convinced his independent monitor, that he deserved not the continued applause of a free spirit; and though the achievements of the protector were so fascinating, that poetical panegyrics encircled even his grave, yet Milton praised him no more, but after his decease fondly hailed the revival of parliamentary independence, as a new dawning of God's providence on the nation. In contemplating these two extraordinary men together, the real lover of truth and freedom can hardly fail to observe the striking contrast of their characters; one was an absolute model of false, and the other of true, grandeur. Mental dignity and public virtue were in Cromwell fictitious and delusive; in Milton they were genuine and unchangeable; Cromwell fhows the formidable wonders that courage and cunning can perform, with the affiftance of fortune; Milton, the wonders, of a fuperior kind, that integrity and genius can accomplifh, in defpite of adverfity and affliction.

An eager folicitude to vindicate a moft noble mind from a very bafe and injurious imputation has led me to anticipate fome public events. From thefe obfervations on the native and incorruptible independence of Milton's mind, let us return to the incidents of his domeftic life.

Soon after his removal to his houfe in Weftminfter, his fourth child, Deborah, was born, on the 2d of May, 1652. The mother, according to Philips, died in child-bed. The fituation of Milton at this period was fuch as might have depreffed the mind of any ordinary man : at the age of forty-four he was left a widower, with three female orphans, the eldeft about fix years old, deformed in her perfon, and with an impediment in her fpeech ; his own health was very delicate ; and with eyes that were rapidly finking into incurable blindnefs, he was deeply engaged in a literary conteft of the higheft importance. With what fpirit and fuccefs he triumphed over his political and perfonal enemies the reader is already informed. When thefe, in 1654, were all filenced and fubdued by the irrefiftible power of his fuperior talents and probity, " he had

" leifure again (fays his nephew) for his own
" ftudies and private defigns. "

It feems to have been the habit of Milton to devote as many hours in every day to intenfe ftudy as the mental faculties could bear, and to render fuch conftant exertion lefs oppreffive to the mind, by giving variety to the objects of its application, engaging in different works of magnitude at the fame time, that he might occafionally relieve and infpirit his thoughts by a tranfition from one fpecies of compofition to another. If we may rely on the information of Philips, he now began to employ himfelf in this manner on three great works; a voluminous Latin Dictionary, a hiftory of England, and an Epic poem ; of the two laft I fhall fpeak again, according to the order of their publication. The firft and leaft important, a work to which blindnefs was peculiarly unfavorable, was never brought to maturity, yet ferved to amufe this moft diligent of authors, by a change of literary occupation, almoft to the clofe of his life. His collection of words amounted to three folios; but the papers, after his deceafe, were fo difcompofed and deficient (to ufe the expreffion of his nephew) that the work could not be made fit for the prefs. They proved ferviceable, however, to future compilers, and were ufed by thofe who publifhed the Latin Dictionary at Cambridge, in 1693.

Though he had no eyes to chufe a fecond wife, Milton did not long continue a widower. He married Catherine, the daughter of Captain Woodcock, a rigid fectarift, fays Mr. Warton, of Hackney. This lady appears to have been the moft tender and amiable of the poet's three wives, and fhe is the only one of the three whom the mufe of Milton has immortalized with an affectionate 'memorial. Within the year of their marriage fhe gave birth to a daughter, and very foon followed her infant to the grave. " Her hufband" (fays Johnfon) " has honored her me- " mory with a poor fonnet;" an expreffion of contempt, which only proves that the rough critic was unable to fympathize with the tendernefs that reigns in the pathetic poetry of Milton: in the opening of this fonnet;

Methought I faw my late efpoufed faint
  Brought to me, like Alceftis, from the grave,
  Whom Jove's great fon to her glad hufband gave,
Refcued from death by force, tho' pale and faint:

and in the latter part of it,

Her face was veil'd, yet to my fancied fight
  Love, fweetnefs, goodnefs, in her perfon fhin'd
So clear, as in no face with more delight,
  But O, as to embrace me fhe inclin'd
I wak'd, fhe fled, and day brought back my night.

Milton has equalled the mournful graces of Petrarch and of Camoens, who have each of them left a plaintive compofition on a fimilar idea. The curious reader, who may wifh to compare the three poets on this occafion, will find the fimilarity I fpeak of in the 79th fonnet of Petrarch, and the 72d of Camoens.

The lofs of a wife fo beloved, and the fevere inthralment of his country under the increafing defpotifm of Cromwell, muft have wounded very deeply the tender and patriotic feelings of Milton. His variety of affliction from thefe fources might probably occafion his being filent, as an author, for fome years. In 1655 he is fuppofed to have written a national manifefto in Latin, to juftify the war againft Spain. From that time, when his defence of himfelf alfo appeared, we know not of his having been engaged in any publication till the year 1659, excepting a political manufcript of Sir Walter Raleigh, called the Cabinet Council, which he printed in 1658, with a brief advertifement. What his fentiments were concerning the laft years of Cromwell, and the following diftracted period, we have a ftriking proof in one of his private letters, written not long after the death of the protector. In reply to his foreign friend Oldenburg (he fays) *

* Ab hiftoria noftrorum motuum concinnanda, quod hortari videris, longe abfum; funt enim filentio digniores quam præconio: nec nobis qui motuum hiftoriam concinnare, fed qui motus ipfos componere feliciter poffit eft opus; tecum enim vereor ne libertatis ac religionis hoftibus nunc nuper focietatis, nimis opportuni inter has noftras civiles difcordias vel potius infanias,

" I am very far from preparing a hiflory of our
commotions, as you feem to advife, for they
are more worthy of filence than of panegyric;
nor do we want a perfon with ability to frame
a hiflory of our troubles, but to give thofe
troubles a happy termination; for I fympathize
with you in the fear, that the enemies of our
liberty and our religion; who are recently combined, may find us too much expofed to their
attack in thefe our civil diffenfions, or rather our
fits of frenzy; they cannot, however, wound our
religion more than we have done ourfelves by
our own enormities. " The intereft of religion appears on every occafion to have maintained its
due afcendency in the mind of Milton, and to
have formed, through the whole courfe of his
life, the primary objedt of his purfuit; it led
him to publifh, in 1659, two diftindt treatifes, the
firft on civil power in ecclefiaftical caufes; the fecond, on the likelieft means to remove hirelings
out of the church; performances which Johnfon
prefumes to charadterize by an expreffion not very
confonant to the fpirit of Chriftianity, reprefenting
them as written merely to gratify the author's
malevolence to the clergy; a coarfe reproach,
which every bigot beftows upon enlightened folicitude for the purity of religion, and particularly

videamur; verum non illi gravius quam nofmetipfi jamdiu fla-
gitiis noftris religioni vultus intulerint — Profe Works,
vol. 2. p. 585.

uncandid in the prefent cafe, becaufe the devout author has confcientioufly explained his own motives in the following expreffions, addreffed to the long parliament reftored after the deceafe of Cromwell.

" Of civil liberty I have written heretofore by the appointment, and not without the approbation, of civil power; of Chriftian liberty I write now, which others long fince having done with all freedom under heathen emperors, I fhould do wrong to fufpect that I now fhall with lefs under Chriftian governors, and fuch epecially as profefs openly their defence of Chriftian liberty; although I write this not otherways appointed or induced than by an inward perfuafion of the Chriftian duty, which I may ufefully difcharge herein to the common Lord and Mafter of us all, and the certain hope of his approbation, firft and chiefeft to be fought." Milton was not a being of that common and reptile clafs, who affume an affected devotion as the mafk of malignity. In addreffing his fecond treatife alfo to the Parliament, he defcribes himfelf as a man under the protection of the legiflative affembly, who had ufed, during eighteen years, on all occafions to affert the juft rights and freedom both of church and ftate.

Had be been confcious of any bafe fervility to Cromwell, he would certainly have abftained from this manly affertion of his own patriotic integrity, which, in that cafe, would have been only ridiculous and contemptible. His opinions might be erroneous, and his ardent mind over heated; but no man ever maintained, with more fteadinefs and refolution, the native dignity of an elevated fpirit, no man more feduloufly endeavoured to difcharge his duty both to earth and heaven.

In February 1659, he publifhed The ready and eafy Way to eftablifh a Free Commonwealth, a work not approved even by republican writers: I will only make one obfervation upon it : the motto to this performance feems to difplay the juft opinion that Milton entertained concerning the tyranny of Cromwell :

> ———& nos,
> Confilium Syllæ dedimus, demus populo nunc.

> —g'en we have given
> Counfel to Sylla—to the people now;

a very happy allufion to the noble but neglected advice which he beftowed on the Protector.

Amidft the various political diftractions towards the end of the year 1659, he addreffed a letter to a namelefs friend, who had converfed with him the preceding evening on the dangerous ruptures of the commonwealth: This letter and a brief paper, containing a fketch of a commonwealth, addreffed to general Monk, were, foon after the author's death communicated by his nephew to Toland, who imparted them to the public.

Milton gave yet another proof of his unwearied attention to public affairs, by publishing brief notes on a sermon preached by Dr. Griffith, at Mercer's Chapel, March 25th, 1660, " wherein (says the annotator) " many notorious wreslings " of scripture, and other falsities, are observed."

When the repeated proteslations of Monk to support the republic had ended in his introduction of the king, the anxious friends of Milton, who thought the literary champion of the parliament might be exposed to revenge from the triumphant royalists, hurried him into concealment. The solicitude of those who watched over his safety was so great, that, it is said, they deceived his enemies by a report of his death, and effectually prevented a search for his person (during the first tumultuary and vindictive rage of the royalists) by a pretended funeral. A few weeks before the restoration (probably in April) he quitted his house in Weftminster, and did not appear in public again till after the act of oblivion, which passed on the 29th of August. In this important interval some events occurred, which greatly affected both his security and reputation. The House of Commons, on the 16th of June, manifested their resentment against his person as well as his writings, by ordering the attorney general to commence a prosecution against him, and petitioning the king, that his two

books,

books, the Defence of the People, and his Anfwer to Eikon Bafilike, might be publicly burnt.

Happily for the honor of England, the perfon of the great author was more fortunate than
his writings in efcaping from the fury of perfecution. Within three days after the burning of his
books, he found himfelf relieved from the neceffity of concealment, and fheltered under the
common protection of the law by the general
act of indemnity, which had not included his
name in the lift of exceptions. It has been
thought wonderful by many, that a writer, whofe
celebrated compofitions had rendered him an object of abhorrence to the royal party, could elude
the activity of their triumphant revenge, and various conjectures have been ftarted to account
for the fafety of Milton, after his enemies had
too plainly difcovered an inclination to crufh him.
One of thefe conjectural caufes of his efcape reprefents two contemporary poets in fo amiable a
light, that though I am unable to confirm the
anecdote entirely by any new evidence, I fhall
yet dwell upon it with pleafure. Richardfon,
whofe affectionate veneration for the genius and
virtue he celebrates makes ample amends for all
the quaintnefs of his ftyle, has the following paffage on the fubject in queftion:

" Perplexed and inquifitive as I was, I at
" length found the fecret, which he from whom
" I had it thought he had communicated to me
" long ago, and wondered he had not. I will no

" longer keep you in expectation :—'twas Sir
" William Davenant obtained his remiffion, in
" return for his own life procured by Milton's
" intereft, when himfelf was under condemna-
" tion, anno 1650—a life was owing to Milton
" (Davenant's) and 'twas paid nobly; Milton's for
" Davenant's , at Davenant's interceffion. — It
" will now be expected I fhould declare what
" authority I have for this ftory;—my firft anfwer
" is, Mr. Pope told it me. Whence had he it?
" From Mr. Betterton — Sir William faw his
" patron — Betterton was prentice to a book-
" feller, John Holden, the fame who printed
" Davenant's Gondibert. There Sir William faw
" him, and, perfuading his mafter to part with
" him, brought him firft on the ftage. Betterton
" then may be well allowed to know this tranf-
" action from the fountain head."

On this interefting anecdote Johnfon makes
the following remark : " Here is a reciprocation
" of generofity and gratitude fo pleafing, that the
" tale makes its own way to credit, but if help
" were wanted I know not where to find it ;
" the danger of Davenant is certain from his own
" relation, but of his efcape there is no account."

This paffage of the critical biographer affords
a fingular proof, that he is fometimes as inac-
curate in narration as he is defective in fentiment.
Impreffed as I am with the cleareft conviction of
his repeated endeavours to depreciate the character
of Milton, I will not fuppofe that Johnfon could
defignedly fupprefs an evidence of the poet's

generofity, which, while he is fpeaking of it in terms of admiration, he ftill endeavours to render problematical ; yet certain it is, that of Milton's protection of Davenant a very obvious evidence exifts in Antony Wood, who fays, under the article Davenant, " he was carried prifoner to " the Ifle of Wight, anno 1650, and afterwards " to the Tower of London, in order to be tried " for his life in the High Court of Juftice, anno " 1651; but upon the mediation of John Mil- " ton, and others, efpecially two godly alder- " men of York (to whom he had fhown great " civility when they had been taken prifoners in " the north by fome of the forces under Wil- " liam Marquis of Newcaftle) he was faved, and " had liberty allowed him as a prifoner at large."

Thus far the pleafing ftory is fufficiently proved to the honor of Milton. That Davenant endeavoured to return the favor is highly probable, from the amiable tendernefs and benevolent acti-vity of his character. Perhaps this probability may feem a little ftrengthened by the follow-ing verfes of Davenant, in a poem addreffed to the king on his happy return:

> Your clemency has taught us to believe
> It wife as well as virtuous to forgive ;
> And now the moft offended fhall proceed
> In great forgiving, till no laws we need ;
> For laws flow progreffes would quickly end
> Could we forgive as faft as men offend.

If Davenant was in any degree inftrumental to the fecurity of Milton, it is probable that he ferved him rather from gratitude than affection, as no two writers of the time were more different from each other in their religious and political opinions. That the poet-laureat of Charles was utterly unconfcious of thofe ineftimable poetic powers, which the blind fecretary of the republic was providentially referved to difplay, we may infer from a very remarkable couplet, towards the clofe of a fecond poem, addreffed by Davenant to the King, where, fpeaking of Homer, he ventures to affert that

> Heav'n ne'er made but one, who, being blind
> Was fit to be a painter of the mind.

It is however very poffible that Davenant might doubly conduce to the production' of Paradife Loft; firft, as one of thofe who exerted their influence to fecure the author from moleftation; and fecondly, as affording by his Gondibert an incentive to the genius of Milton to fhow how infinitely he could furpafs a poem which Hobbs (whofe opinions he defpifed) had extravagantly extolled as the moft exquifite production of the epic mufe. In Aubrey's manufcript anecdotes of Milton it is faid, that he began his Paradife Loft about two years before the return of the king, and finifhed it about three years after that event; the account appears the more probable, as the following lines in the commencement of the seventh book pathetically allude to his present situation:

More safe I sing with mortal voice unchang'd
To hoarse or mute, though fall'n on evil days,
On evil days though fall'n, and evil tongues,
In darkness and with dangers compass'd round,
And solitude; yet not alone, while thou
Visit'st my slumbers nightly, or when morn
Purples the east: still govern thou my song,
Urania, and fit audience find, though few.
But drive far off the barbarous diffonance
Of Bacchus and his revellers, the race
Of that wild rout that tore the Thracian bard
In Rhodope, where rocks and woods had ears
To rapture, till the savage clamor drown'd
Both harp and voice; nor could the Mufe defend
Her son. So fail not thou, who thee implores:
For thou art heav'nly, she an empty dream.

How peculiarly affecting are these beautiful verses, when the history of the poet suggests that he probably wrote them while he was concealed in an obscure corner of the city, that refounded with the triumphant roar of his intoxicated enemies, among whom drunkenness arose to such extravagance, that even the festive royalists found it necessary to issue a proclamation, which forbade the drinking of healths. How poignant at this time must have been the personal and

patriotic feelings of Milton, who had paſſed his
life in animating himſelf and his country to habits
of temperance, truth, and public virtue, yet had
the mortification of finding that country, ſo dear
to him, now doubly diſgraced; firſt, by the hy-
pocriſy and treacherous ambition of republicans,
to whoſe pretended virtues he had given too eaſy
credit; and now, by the mean licentious ſervility
of royaliſts, whoſe more open though not more
dangerous vices his upright and high-toned ſpirit
had ever held in abhorrence. For his country
he had every thing to apprehend from the blind
infatuation with which the parliament had rejected the patriotic ſuggeſtion of Hale (afterwards
the illuſtrious chief juſtice) to eſtabliſh conſtitu-
tional limitations to the power of the king·at the
critical period of his reception. The neglect of
this meaſure contributed not a little to ſubſequent
evils, and the reign of Charles the Second was
in truth deformed with all the public miſery and
diſgrace which Milton had predicted, when he
argued on the idea of his re-admiſſion. For his
own perſon, the literary champion of the people
had no leſs to dread from the barbarity of public
vengeance, or from the private dagger· of ſome
overheated royaliſt, who, like the aſſaſſins of
Doriſlaus in Holland, and of Aſcham in Spain,.
might think it meritorious to ſeize any opportunity
of deſtroying a ſervant of the Engliſh republic.
When royal government, reſtored to itſelf, could
yet deſcend to authorize a mean and execrable

indignity againſt the dead body of a man ſo magnanimous and ſo innocent as Blake, it was ſurely
·natural, and by no means unbecoming the ſpirit
of Milton, to ſpeak as he does, in the preceding
verſes, of evil days and evil tongues, of darkneſs·
and of danger.

   " This darkneſs (ſays Johnſon) had his eyes
" been better employed, had undoubtedly· deſer-
" ved compaſſion." What! had Milton, no title
to compaſſion for his perſonal calamity, becauſe
he. had ·nobly ſacrificed his ſight to what he eſteemed an important diſcharge of his public duty?
—Oh egregious morality! to which no feeling,
heart can ſubſcribe. No, ſay his implacable enemies, he loſt his eyes in the vindication of wic-·
kedneſs : but admitting their aſſertion in its full
force, juſtice and humanity ſtill contend, that,
inſtead of diminiſhing, it rather doubles his claim
to compaſſion; to ſuffer in a ſpirited defence of
guilt, that we miſtake and eſteem as virtue, is
perhaps, of all pitiable misfortunes, what a candid
and conſiderate mind ſhould be moſt willing to
pity.

   But Johnſon proceeds to ſay, " of evil tongues
" for Milton to complain required ·impudence.
" at leaſt equal to his other powers; Milton
" whoſe warmeſt advocates muſt allow, that he
" never ſpared any aſperity of reproach or bru-
" tality of inſolence."

   Theſe are, perhaps, the moſt bitter words
that were ever applied by an author, illuſtrious

himself for great talents, and still more for christian virtue, to a character pre-eminent in genius and in piety. By showing to what a marvellous degree a very cultivated and devout mind may be exasperated by party rage; may they serve to caution every fervid spirit against that outrageous animosity, which a difference of sentiment in politics and religion is so apt to produce. It would seem almost an affront to the memory of Milton to vindicate him elaborately from a charge, whose very words exhibit so palpable a violation of decency and truth.

His coldest advocates, instead of allowing that he never spared any brutality of insolence, may rather contend, that his native tenderness of heart, and very graceful education, rendered it hardly possible for him at any time to be insolent and brutal. It would have been wonderful indeed, had he not written with some degree of asperity, when his antagonist Salmasius asserted, that he ought to suffer an ignominious and excruciating death. Against the unfortunate (but not innocent) Charles the first, he expressly declares that he published nothing till after his decease; and that he meant not, as he says in one of his Latin works, to insult the Manes of the king, is indeed evident to an unprejudiced reader, from the following very beautiful and pathetic sentence, with which he begins his answer to the Eikon Basilike:

" To defcant on the misfortunes of a perfon fallen from fo high a dignity, who hath alfo paid his final debt, both to nature and his faults, is neither of itfelf a thing commendable, nor the intention of this difcourfe. " Thofe who fairly confider the exafperated ftate of the contending parties, when Milton wrote, and compare his political compofitions with the favage ribaldry of his opponents, however miftaken they may think him in his ideas of government, will yet find more reafon to admire his temper than to condemn his afperity.

If in a quiet ftudy, at a very advanced period of life, and at the diftance of more than a century from the days of the republic; if a philofopher fo fituated could be hurried by political heat to fpeak of Milton with fuch harfh intemperance of language, though writing under the friendly title of his biographer, with what indulgence ought we to view that afperity in Milton himfelf, which arofe from the immediate preffure of public oppreffion and of private outrage; for his fpirit had been enflamed, not only by the fight of many national vexations, but by feeing his own moral character attacked with the moft indecent and execrable calumny that can incite the indignation of infulted virtue. If the fafcinating powers of his facred poem, and the luftre of his integrity, have failed to foften the virulence of an aged moralift againft him in our days, what muft he not have had to apprehend from the raging paffions of his own time, when his poetical genius had not appeared in its meridian fplendor, and when moft of his writings were confidered as recent crimes againft thofe, who were entering on their career of triumph and revenge? Johnfon, indeed, afferts in his barbarous cenfure of Milton's exquifite picture of his own fituation, that the poet, in fpeaking of his danger, was ungrateful and unjuft; that the charge. itfelf feems to be falfe, for it would be hard to recollect any reproach caft upon him, either ferious or ludicrous, through the whole remaining part of his life; yet Lauder, once the affociate of Johnfon in writing againft Milton, exprefsly affirms, that it was warmly debated for three days, whether he fhould fuffer death with the regidices, or not, as many contended that his guilt was fuperior to theirs. Lauder, indeed, mentions no authority for his affertion; and the word of a man fo fupremely infamous would deferve no notice, were not the circumftance rendered probable by the rancor and atrocity of party fpirit. To what deteftable exceffes this fpirit could proceed we have not only an example in Lauder himfelf (of whofe malignity to the poet I fhall have fubfequent occafion to fpeak) but in that collection of virulent invectives againft Milton, compofed chiefly by his contemporaries, which Lauder added as an appendix to his own moft malignant pamphlet. The moft fingular and indecent of thefe invectives, whofe fcurrility is too

grofs to be tranfcribed, has been imputed to that
very copious writer, Sir Roger L'Eftrange; and
if a pen employed fo favagely againft Milton
could obtain public encouragement and applaufe,
he might furely, without affectation or timidity,
think himfelf expofed to the dagger of. fome
equally hoftile and more fanguinary royalift.
L'Eftrange, for fuch fufferings in the caufe of
royalty as really entitled him to reward, obtained, not long after the reftoration, the revived
but unconftitutional office of licenfer to the prefs.
It was happy for literature that he poffeffed
not that oppreffive jurifdiction when the author
of the Paradife Loft was obliged to folicit an
imprimatur, fince the excefs of his malevolence
to Milton might have then exerted itfelf in fuch
a manner as to entitle both the office and its pof-
feffor to the execration of the world. The licenfer
of that period, Thomas Tomkyns, chaplain to
archbifhop Sheldon, though hardly fo full of rancor as L'Eftrange (if L'Eftrange was the real author of the ribaldry afcribed to him) was abfurd
or malignant enough to obftruct, in fome meafure, the publication of Paradife Loft. " He,
among other frivolous exceptions (fays Toland)
would needs fupprefs the whole poem, for ima-
ginary treafon in the following lines:

———as when the fun new rifen
  Looks thro' the horizontal mifty air
  Shorn of his beams, or from behind the moon
  In dim eclipfe difaftrous twilight fheds

> On half the nations, and with fear of change
> Perplexes monarchs——"

By what means the poet was happily enabled to triumph over the malevolence of an enemy in office we are not informed by the author, who has recorded this very interefting anecdote; but from the peril to which his immortal work was expofed, and which the mention of a licen-fer to the prefs has led me to anticipate, let us return to his perfonal danger: the extent of this danger, and the particulars of his efcape, have never been completely difcovered. The account that his nephew gives of him at this momentous pe-riod is chiefly contained in the following fentence:

" It was a friend's houfe in Bartholomew Clofe where he lived till the act of oblivion came forth, which, it pleafed God, proved as favor-able to him as could be hoped or expected, through the interceffion of fome that ftood his friends both in council and parliament; particu-larly in the Houfe of Commons, Mr. Andrew Marvel, a member for Hull, acted vigoroufly in his behalf, and made a confiderable party for him."

Marvel, like the fuperior author whom he fo nobly protected, was himfelf a poet and a patriot. He had been affociated with Milton in the office of Latin fecretary in 1657, and cultivated his friendfhip by a tender and refpectful attachment. As he probably owed to that friendfhip the improvement of his own talents and virtues, it is highly pleafing to find, that he exerted them on different occafions in eftablifhing the fecurity, and in celebrating the genius of his incomparable friend. His efforts of regard on the prefent emergency are liberally defcribed in the preceding expreflion of Philips; and his friendly verfes on the publication of the Paradife Loft deferve no common applaufe; for the records of literature hardly exhibit a more juft, a more fpirited, or a more generous compliment paid by one poet to another.

But the friendfhip of Marvel, vigilant, active, and beneficial as it was, could not fecure Milton from being feized and hurried into confinement. It appears from the minutes of the Houfe of Commons, that he was prifoner to their ferjeant on the 15th of December. The particulars of his imprifonment are involved in darknefs; but Dr. Birch (whofe copious life of Milton is equally full of intelligence and candor) conjectures, with great probability, that on his appearing in public after the act of indemnity, and adjournment of Parliament, on the 13th of September, he was feized in confequence of the order formerly given by the Commons for his profecution.

The exact time of his continuing in cuftody no refearches have afcertained. The records of Parliament only prove, that on the 15th of December the Houfe ordered his releafe; but the fame upright and undaunted fpirit, which had made Milton in his younger days a refolute

oppofer of injuftice and oppreffion, ftill continued
a characteriftic of his declining life, and now induced him, difadvantageoufly fituated as he was
for fuch a conteft, to refift the rapacity of the
parliamentary officer, who endeavoured to extort from him an exorbitant fee on his difcharge.
He remonftrated to the houfe on the iniquity of
their fervant; and as the affair was referred to
the committee of privileges, he probably obtained the redrefs that he had the courage to
demand.

In this fortunate efcape from the grafp of
triumphant and vindictive power, Milton may
be confidered as terminating his political life:
commencing from his return to the continent, it
had extended to a period of twenty years; in
three of thefe he had been afflicted with partial
but increafing blindnefs, and in fix he had been
utterly blind. His exertions in this period of his
life had expofed him to infinite obloquy, but
his generous and enlightened country, whatever
may be the ftate of her political opinions, will
remember with becoming equity and pride, that
the fublimeft of her poets, though deceived as he
certainly was by extraordinary pretenders to public virtue, and fubject to great illufion in his
ideas of government, is entitled to the firft of
encomiums, the praife of being truly an honeft
man : fince it was affuredly his conftant aim to
be the fteady difinterefted adherent and encomiaft
of truth and juftice; hence we find him continually

difplaying thofe internal bleffings, which have been happily called, " the clear witneffes of a benign nature," an innocent confcience, and a fatisfied underftanding.

Such is the imperfection of human exiftence, that miftaken notions and principles are perfectly compatible with elevation, integrity, and fatisfaction of mind. The writer muft be a flave of prejudice, or a fycophant to power, who would reprefent Milton as deficient in any of thefe noble endowments. Even Addifon feems to lofe his rare Chriftian candor, and Hume his philofophical precifion, when thefe two celebrated though very different authors fpeak harfhly of Milton's political character, without paying due acknowledgment to the rectitude of his heart. I truft, the probity of a very ardent but uncorrupted enthufiaft is in fome meafure vindicated in the courfe of thefe pages, happy if they promote the completion of his own manly wifh to be perfectly known, if they imprefs a juft and candid eftimate of his merits and miftakes on the temperate mind of his country.

END OF THE SECOND PART.

PART III.

TASSO.

In beginning to contemplate the latter years of Milton, it may be useful to remark, that they afford, perhaps, the moſt animating leſſon, which biography, inſtructive as it is, can ſupply; they ſhow to what noble uſe a cultivated und religious mind may convert even declining life, though embittered by a variety of afflictions, and darkened by perſonal calamity.

On regaining his liberty, he took a houſe in Holborn, near Red Lion Fields, but ſoon removed to Jewin-ſtreet, and there married, in his 54th year, his third wife, Elizabeth Minſhall, the daughter of a gentleman in Cheſhire. As the miſfortune of blindneſs ſeems particularly to require a female companion, and yet almoſt precludes the unhappy ſufferer from ſelecting ſuch as might ſuit him, Milton is ſaid to have formed this attachment on the recommendation of

his

his friend Dr. Paget, an eminent phyfician of the city, to whom the lady was related. Some biographers have fpoken harfhly of her temper and conduct; but let me obferve, in juftice to her memory, that the manufcript of Aubrey, to whom fhe was probably known, mentions her as a gentle perfon, of a peaceful and agreeable humor. That fhe was particularly attentive to her hufband, and treated his infirmities with tendernefs, is candidly remarked by Mr. Warton, in a pofthumous note to the teftamentary papers relating to Milton, which his indefatigable refearches at length difcovered, and committed to the prefs, a few months before his own various and valuable labors were terminated by death. Thefe very curious and interefting papers afford information refpecting the latter days of the poet, which his late biographers were fo far from poffeffing, that they could not believe it exifted. Indeed, Mr. Warton himfelf had concluded, that all farther inquiries for the will muft be fruitlefs, as he had failed in a tedious and intricate fearch. At laft, however; he was enabled, by the friendfhip of Sir William Scott, to refcue from oblivion a curiofity fo precious to poetical antiquarians. He found in the prerogative regifter the will of Milton, which, though made by his brother Chriftopher, a lawyer by profeffion, was fet afide from a deficiency in point of form — the litigation of this will produced a collection of evidence relating to the

14

teftator, which renders the difcovery of thofe long forgotten papers peculiarly interefting; they fhow very forcibly, and in new points of view, his domeftic infelicity, and his amiable difpofition. The tender and fublime poet, whofe fenfibility and fufferings were fo great, appears to have been almoft as unfortunate in his daughters as the Lear of Shakefpeare. A fervant declares in evidence, that her deceafed mafter, a little before his laft marriage, had lamented to her the ingratitude and cruelty of his children. He complained, that they combined to defraud him in the œconomy of his houfe, and fold feveral of his books in the bafeft manner. His feelings on fuch an outrage, both as a parent and as a fcholar, muft have been fingularly painful; perhaps they fuggefted to him thofe very pathetic lines, where he feems to paint himfelf, in Samfon Agoniftes:

> I dark in light, expos'd
> To daily fraud, contempt, abufe, and wrong,
> Within doors or without; ftill as a fool,
> In power of others, never in my own,
> Scarce half I feem to live, dead more than half.

Unfortunate as he had proved in matrimony, he was probably induced to venture once more into that ftate by the bitter want of a domeftic protector againft his inhuman daughters, under which defcription I include only the two eldeft;

and in palliation even of their conduct, deteſtable as it appears, we may obſerve, that they are entitled to pity, as having been educated without the ineſtimable guidance of maternal tenderneſs, under a father afflicted with loſs of ſight; they were alſo young : at the time of Milton's laſt marriage his eldeſt daughter had only reached the age of fifteen, and Deborah, his favorite, was ſtill a child of nine years.

His new connexion ſeems to have afforded him what he particularly ſought; that degree of domeſtic tranquillity and comfort eſſential to his perſeverance in ſtudy, which appears to have been, through all the viciſſitudes of fortune, the prime object of his life; and while all his labors were under the direction of religion or of philanthropy, there was nothing too arduous or too humble for his mind. In 1661 he publiſhed a little work, entitled, " Accidence commenced Grammar," benevolently calculated for the relief of children, by ſhortening their very tedious and irkſome progreſs in learning the elements of Latin. He publiſhed alſo, in the ſame year, another brief compoſition of Sir Walter Raleigh's, containing (like the former work of that celebrated man, which the ſame editor had given to the public) a ſeries of political maxims; one of theſe I am tempted to tranſcribe, by a perſuaſion that Milton regarded it with peculiar pleaſure, from its tendency to juſtify the parliamentary contention with Charles the Firſt. Had the mifguided monarch obferved the maxim of Raleigh, he would not, like that illuftrious victim to the vices of his royal father, have perifhed on the fcaffold. — The maxim is the feventeenth of the collection, and gives the following inftruction to a prince for preferving an hereditary kingdom.

" To be moderate in his taxes and impofitions, and, when need doth require to ufe the fubjects purfe, to do it by parliament, and with their confent, making the caufe apparent to them, and fhowing his unwillingnefs in charging them. Finally, fo to ufe it, that it may feem rather an offer from his fubjects, than an exaction by him."

However vehement the enmity of various perfons againft Milton might have been, during the tumult of paffions on the recent reftoration, there is great reafon to believe, that his extraordinary abilities and probity fo far triumphed over the prejudices againft him, that, with all his republican offences upon his head, he might have been admitted to royal favor had he been willing to accept it. Richardfon relates, on very good authority, that the poft of Latin fecretary, in which he had obtained fo much credit as a fcholar, was again offered to him after the Reftoration; that he rejected it, and replied to his wife, who advifed his acceptance of the appointment, " You, as other women, would ride in your coach; for me, my aim is to live and die

an honeft man." Johnfon difcovers an inclination to difcredit this ftory, becaufe it does honor
to Milton, and feemed inconfiftent with his own
ideas of probability. " He that had fhared authority, either with the Parliament or Cromwell,"
fays Johnfon, " might have forborne to talk very
loudly of his honefty." How miferably narrow
is, the prejudice, that cannot allow perfect honefty
to many individuals on both fides in a conteft
like that, which divided the nation in the civil
wars. Undoubtedly there were men in each party,
and men of great mental endowments, who acted,
during that calamitous contention, according to
the genuine dictates of confcience. Thofe who
examine the conduct of Milton with impartiality
will be ready to allow, that he poffeffed not
only one of the moft cultivated,. but one of the
moft upright minds, which the records of human
nature have taught us to revere. His retaining
his employment under Cromwell has, I truft,
been fo far juftified, that it can no more be reprefented as a blemifh on his integrity. His office, indeed, was of fuch a nature, that he might,
without a breach of honefty, have refumed it
under the king; but his return to it, though not
abfolutely difhonorable, would have ill accorded
with that refined purity and elevation of character, which, from his earlieft youth, it was
the nobleft ambition of Milton to acquire and
fupport. He would have loft much of his title
to the reverence of mankind for his magnanimity,

had he accepted his former office under Charles the Second, whom he muſt have particularly deſpiſed as a profligate and ſervile tyrant, as ready to betray the honor of the nation as he was careleſs of his own; a perſonage whom Milton could never have beheld without horror, on re-flecting on his ſingular barbarity to his celebrated friend, that eccentric but intereſting character, Sir Henry Vane. The king, ſo extolled for his mercy, had granted the life of Sir Henry to the joint petition of the Lords and Commons; but, after promiſing to preſerve him, ſigned a warrant for his execution — one of the moſt inhuman and deteſtable acts of duplicity that was ever practiſed againſt a ſubject by his ſovereign. It is to the fate of Vane, with others of that party, and to his own perſonal ſufferings, that the great poet alludes in the following admirable reflections, aſſigned to the chorus in his Samſon Agoniſtes:

> Many are the ſayings of the wife
> In ancient and in modern books enroll'd,
> Extolling patience as the trueſt fortitude:
> And to the beai ing well of all calamities,
> All chances incident to man's frail life,
> Conſolatories writ
> With ſtudied argument, and much perſuaſion ſought
> Lenient of grief, and anxious thought:
> But with th' afflicted in his pangs their ſound
> Little prevails, or rather ſeems a tune
> Harſh, and of diſſonant mood from his complaint;

Unlefs he feel within
Some fource of confolation from above,
Secret refrefhings that repair his ftrength,
And fainting fpirits uphold.
God of our fathers, what is man!
That thou towards him with hand fo various,
Or might I fay contrarious,
Temper'ft thy Providence through his fhort courfe,
Not evenly, as thou rul'ft
The angelic orders and inferior creatures mute,
Irrational and brute.
Nor do I name of men the common rout,
That wandering loofe about,
Grow up and perifh, as the fummer fly,
Heads without name, no more remember'd;
But fuch as thou haft folemnly elected,
With gifts and graces eminently adorn'd
To fome great work, thy glory,
And people's fafety, which in part they effect:
Yet toward thefe, thus dignified, thou oft
Amidft their height of noon
Changeft thy countenance, and thy hand, with no
  regard
Of higheft favors paft
From thee on them, or them to thee of fervice.
  Nor only doft degrade them, or remit
To life obfcur'd, which were a fair difmiffion,
But throw'ft them lower than thou didft exalt them
  high,
Unfeemly falls in human eye,
Too grievous for the trefpafs or omiffion;

Oft leav'ft them to the hoftile fword
Of heathen and profane, their carcafes
To dogs and fowls a prey, or elfe captiv'd;
Or to th' unjuft tribunals under change of times,
And condemnation of th' ungrateful multitude.
If thefe they fcape, perhaps in poverty,
With ficknefs and difeafe thou bow'ft them down,
Painful difeafes and deform'd,
In crude old age;
Though not difordinate, yet caufelefs fuff'ring
The punifhment of diffolute days.

Warburton was the firft, I believe, to remark how exactly thefe concluding lines defcribe
the fituation of the poet himfelf, afflicted by his
lofs of property, and " his gout, not caufed by
intemperance." The fame acute but very unequal critic is by no means fo happy in his obfervation, that Milton feems to have chofen the
fubject of this fublime drama for the fake of the
fatire on bad wives; it would be hardly lefs abfurd to fay, that he chofe the fubject of Paradife
Loft for the fake of defcribing a connubial altercation. The nephew of Milton has told us, that
he could not afcertain the time when this drama
was written; but it probably flowed from the
heart of the indignant poet foon after his fpirit
had been wounded by the calamitous deftiny of
his friends, to which he alludes with fo much
energy and pathos. He did not defign the drama
for a theatre, nor has it the kind of action

requisite for theatrical interest; but in one point of view the Samson Agonistes is the most singularly affecting composition, that was ever produced by sensibility of heart and vigor of imagination. To give it this peculiar effect, we must remember, that the lot of Milton had a marvellous coincidence with that of his hero; in three remarkable points; first (but we should regard this as the most inconsiderable article of resemblance) he had been tormented by a beautiful but disaffectionate and disobedient wife; secondly, he had been the great champion of his country, and as such the idol of public admiration; lastly, he had fallen from that height of unrivalled glory, and had experienced the most humiliating reverse of fortune:

His foes' derision, captive, poor, and blind.

In delineating the greater part of Samson's sensations under calamity, he had only to describe his own. No dramatist can have ever conformed so literally as Milton to the Horatian precept.

Si vis me flere, dolendum est
Primum ipsi tibi.

And if, in reading the Samson Agonistes, we observe how many passages, expressed with the most energetic sensibility, exhibit to our fancy the fufferings and real fentiments of the poet, as well as thofe of his hero, we may derive from this extraordinary compofition a kind of pathetic delight, that no other drama can afford; we may applaud the felicity of genius, that contrived, in this manner, to relieve a heart overburdened with anguifh and indignation, and to pay a half concealed yet hallowed tribute to the memories of dear though difhonored friends, whom the ftate of the times allowed not the afflicted poet more openly to deplore.

The concluding verfes of the beautiful chorus (which I have already cited in part) appear to me particularly affecting, from the perfuafion that Milton, in compofing them, addreffed the two laft immediately to Heaven, as a prayer for himfelf :

In fine,

Juft or unjuft alike feem miferable,
For oft alike both come to evil end.
So deal not with this once thy glorious champion,
The image of thy ftrength, and mighty minifter.
What do I beg? how haft thou dealt already?
Behold him in this ftate calamitous, and turn
His labors, for thou can'ft, to peaceful end.

If the conjecture of this application be juft, we may add, that never was the prevalence of a righteous prayer more happily confpicuous; and let me here remark, that however various the

opinions of men may be concerning the merits
or demerits of Milton's political character, the
integrity of his heart appears to have secured to
him the favor of Providence, since it pleased the
Giver of all good not only to turn his labors to
a peaceful end, but to irradiate his declining
life with the most abundant portion of those pure
and sublime mental powers, for which he had
constantly and fervently prayed, as the choicest
bounty of Heaven.

At this period, his kind friend and physician,
who had proved so serviceable to him in the recommendation of an attentive and affectionate wife,
introduced to his notice a young reader of
Latin, in that singular character, Thomas Ellwood, the quaker, who has written a minute
history of his own life : a book, which suggests
the reflection, how strangely a writer may sometimes mistake his way in his endeavours to engage
the attention of posterity. Had the honest quaker
bequeathed to the world as circumstantial an account of his great literary friend, as he has done
of himself, his book would certainly have engros-
sed no common share of public regard : we are
indebted to him, however, for his incidental
mention of the great poet; and as there is a pleasing air of simplicity and truth in his narrative,
I shall gratify the reader by inserting it with very
little abridgment :

" JOHN MILTON, a gentleman of great note
for learning throughout the learned world, having

filled a public station in former times, lived now a private and retired life in London; and having wholly lost his sight, kept always a man to read to him, which usually was the son of some gentleman of his acquaintance, whom in kindness he took to improve in his learning.

" By the mediation of my friend, Isaac Penington, with Dr. Paget, and of Dr. Paget with John Milton, was I admitted to come to him, not as a servant to him, which at that time he needed not, nor to be in the house with him, but only to have the liberty of coming to his house at certain hours, when I would, and to read to him what books he should appoint me, which was all the favor I desired."

Ellwood was at this time an ingenuous but undisciplined young man, about three-and-twenty; —his father, a justice of Oxfordshire, had taken him, very unseasonably, from school, with a view to lessen his own expenses, and this his younger son, after wasting some years at home, attached himself, with great fervency, to the sect of quakers. His religious ardor involved him in a long and painful quarrel with his father, and in many singular adventures — he united with his pious zeal a lively regard for literature; and being grieved to find that his interrupted education had permitted him to acquire but a slender portion of classical learning, he anxiously sought the acquaintance of Milton, in the hope of improving it.

" I went, therefore (fays the candid quaker)
and took myfelf a lodging near to his houfe,
which was then in Jewin-ftreet as conveniently as I
could, and from thence forward went every day
if the afternoon, except on the firft days of the
week, and fitting by him in his dining-room,
read to him fuch books in the Latin tongue as
he pleafed to hear me read.

" At my firft fitting to read to him, obferving
that I ufed the Englifh pronunciation, he told
me, if I would have the benefit of the Latin
tongue, not only to read and underftand Latin
authors, but to converfe with foreigners, either
abroad or at home, I muft learn the foreign pronunciation; to this I confenting, he inftructed
me how to found the vowels: this change of pronunciation proved a new difficulty to me; but,

Labor omnia vincit
Improbus;

And fo did I; which made my reading the more
acceptable to my mafter. He, on the other hand,
perceiving with what earneft defire I purfued
learning, gave me not only all the encouragement, but all the help he could; for having a
curious ear, he underftood by my tone when I
underftood what I read, and when I did not,
and accordingly would ftop me, examine me,
and open the moft difficult paffages to me."

Tle clearnefs and fimplicity of Ellwood's narrative brings us, as it were, into the company of Milton, and fhows, in a very agreeable point of view, the native courtefy and fweetnefs of a temper, that has been ftrangely·mifreprefented as morofe and auftere.

Johnfon, with his accuftomed afperity to Milton, difcovers an inclination to cenfure him for his mode of teaching Latin to Ellwood; but Milton, who was inftructing an indigent young man, had probably very friendly reafons for wifhing him to acquire immediately the foreign pronunciation; and affuredly the patience, good nature, and fuccefs, with which he condefcended to teach this fingular attendant, do credit both to the difciple and the preceptor.

Declining health foon interrupted the ftudies of Ellwood, and obliged him to retire to the houfe of a friend and phyfician in the country. Here, after great fuffering from ficknefs, he revived, and returned again to London.

" I was very kindly received by my Mafter (continues the interefting quaker) who had conceived fo good an opinion of me, that my converfation, I found, was acceptable, and he feemed heartily glad of my recovery and return, and into our old method of ftudy we fell again, I reading to him, and he explaining to me, as occafion required. "

But learning (as poor Ellwood obferves) was almoft a forbidden fruit to him.   His intercourfe

with Milton was again interrupted by a second
calamity; a party of soldiers rushed into a meet-
ing of quakers, that included this unfortunate
scholar, and he was hurried, with his friends,
from prison to prison. Though ten-pence was all
the money he possessed, his honest pride prevented his applying to Milton for relief in this
exigence, and he contrived to support himself by
his industry, in confinement, with admirable
fortitude.

Moderate prosperity, however, visited at last
this honest and devout man, affording him an
agreeable opportunity of being useful to the great
poet, who had deigned to be his preceptor.

An affluent quaker, who resided at Chalfont,
in Buckinghamshire, settled Ellwood in his family, to instruct his children, and in 1665, when
the pestilence raged in London, Milton requested
his friendly disciple to find a refuge for him in
his neighbourhood.

" I took a pretty box for him," says this affectionate friend, " in Giles Chalfont, a mile
from me, of which I gave him notice, and intended to have waited on him, and seen him
well settled in it, but was prevented by impri-
sonment."

This was a second captivity that the unfortunate young man had to sustain; for in conse-
quence of a recent and most iniquitous persecu-
tion of the quakers, he was apprehended at the
funeral of a friend, and confined in the gaol of
Aylesbury.

" But being now releafed," continues Ellwood, " I foon made a vifit to him, to welcome him into the country.

" After fome common difcourfes had paffed between us, he called for a manufcript of his, which, being brought, he delivered to me, bidding me take it home with me, and read it at my leifure, and when I had fo done, return it to him, with my judgment thereupon.

" When I came home, and fet myfelf to read it, I found it was that excellent poem, which he entitled Paradife Loft.

" After I had, with the beft attention, read it through, I made him another vifit, and returned him his book, with due acknowledgment of the favor he had done me in communicating it to me. He afked me how I liked it, and what I thought of it? which I modeftly and freely told him; and after fome farther difcourfe about it, I pleafantly faid to him, ' Thou haft faid much here of Paradife Loft, but what haft thou to fay of Paradife found.' He made me no anfwer, but fat fome time in a mufe, then brake off that difcourfe, and fell upon another fubjeĉt.

" After the ficknefs was over, and the city well cleanfed, and become fafely habitable again, he returned thither; and when afterwards I went to wait on him there (which I feldom failed of doing, whenever my occafions led me to London) he fhowed me his fecond poem, called Paradife Regain'd, and in a pleafant tone faid to me,

me,

me, ' This is owing to you, for you put it into my head by the queftion you put to me at Chalfont, which before I had not thought of'."

The perfonal regard of this ingenuous quaker for Milton, and his giving birth to a compofition of fuch magnitude and merit as Paradife Regain'd, entitle him to diftinction in a life of his great poetical friend, and I have therefore rather tranf-cribed than abridged his relation. My reader, I doubt not, will join with me in wifhing that we had more fketches of the venerable bard, thus minutely delineated from the life, in the colors of fidelity and affection.

The laft of Milton's familiar letters in Latin relates to this period; it fpeaks with devotional gratitude of the fafe afylum from the plague, which he had found in the country; it fpeaks alfo with fo much feeling of his paft political adventures, and of the prefent inconvenience which he fuffered from the lofs of fight, that I apprehend an entire tranflation of it can hardly fail of being acceptable to the Englifh reader. It is dated from London, Auguft 15, 1666, and addreffed to Heimbach, an accomplifhed German, who is ftyled counfellor to the elector of Brandenburgh. An expreffion in a former letter to the fame correfpondent feems to intimate, that this learned foreigner, who vifited England in his youth had refided with Milton, perhaps in the character of a difciple—But here is the interefting letter:

* " If, among so many funerals of my countrymen, in a year so full of pestilence and sor-
row, you were induced, as you say, by rumor
to believe that I also was snatched away, it is

* Ornatissimo Viro Petro Heimbachio, Electoris Brandenbur-
gici Consiliario.

Si inter tot funera popularium meorum, anno tam gravi ac
pestilenti, abreptum me quoque, ut scribis, ex rumore præser-
tim aliquo credidisti, mirum non est, atque ille rumor apud
vestros, ut videtur, homines, si ex eo quod de salute mea soli-
citi essent, increbuit, non displicet; indicium enim suæ erga me
benevolentiæ fuisse existimo. Sed Dei benignitate, qui tutum
mihi receptum in agris paraverat, & vivo adhuc & valeo; uti-
nam ne inutilis, quicquid muneris in hac vita restat mihi pera-
gendum. Tibi vero tam longo intervallo venisse in mentem
mei, pergratum est; quamquam prout rem verbis exornas, præ-
bere aliquem suspicionem videris, oblitum mei te potius esse,
qui tot virtutum diversarum conjugium in me, ut scribis, ad-
mirere. Ego certe ex tot conjugiis numerosam nimis prolem
expavescerem, nisi constaret in re arcta, rebusque duris, virtutes ali maxime & vigere : tametsi earum una non ita belle
charitatem hospitii mihi reddidit : quam enim politicam tu vo-
cas, ego pietatem in patriam dictam abs te mallem, ea me pul-
chro nomine delinitum prope, ut ita dicam, expatriavit. Reli-
quarum tamen chorus clare concinit. Patria est, ubicunque est
bene. Finem faciam, si hoc prius abs te impetravero, ut, si
quid mendose descriptum aut non interpunctum repereris, id
puero, qui hæc excepit, Latine prorsus nescienti velis impu-
tare; cui singulas plane literulas annumerare non sine miseria
dictans cogebar. Tua interim viri merita, quem ego adolescen-
tem spei eximiæ cognovi, ad tam honestum in principis gratia
provexisse te locum, gaudeo, cæteraque fausta omnia & cupio
tibi, & spero vale.

Londini, Aug. 15, 1666.

not furprifing; and if fuch a rumor prevailed among thofe of your nation, as it feems to have done, becaufe they were folicitous for my health, it is not unpleafing, for I muft efteem it as a proof of their benevolence towards me. But by the gracioufnefs of God, who had prepared for me a fafe retreat in the country, I am ftill alive and well; and I truft not utterly an unprofitable fervant, whatever duty in life there yet remains for me to fulfil. That you remember me, after fo long an interval in our correfpondence, gratifies me exceedingly, though, by the politenefs of your expreflion, you feem to afford me room to fufpect, that you have rather forgotten me, fince, as you fay, you admire in me fo many different virtues wedded together. From fo many weddings I fhould affuredly dread a family too numerous, were it not certain that, in narrow circumftances and under feverity of fortune, virtues are moft excellently reared, and are moft flourifhing. Yet one of thefe faid virtues has not very handfomely rewarded me for entertaining her; for that which you call my political virtue, and which I fhould rather wifh you to call my devotion to my country (enchanting me with her captivating name) almoft, if I may fay fo, expatriated me. Other virtues, however, join their voices to affure me, that wherever we profper, in rectitude there is our country. In ending my letter, let me obtain from you this favor, that if you find any parts of it incorrectly written, and without ʃtops, you will impute it to the boy who writes for me, who is utterly ignorant of Latin, and to whom I am forced (wretchedly enough) to repeat every ʃingle ʃyllable that I dictate. I ʃtill rejoice that your merit as an accompliʃhed man, whom I knew as a youth of the higheʃt expectation, has advanced you ʃo far in the honorable favor of your prince. For your proʃperity in every other point you have both my wiʃhes and my hopes. Farewel.

" London, Auguʃt 15, 1666."

How intereʃting is this complaint, when we recollect that the great writer, reduced to ʃuch irkʃome difficulties in regard to his ʃecretary, was probably engaged at this period in poliʃhing the ʃublimeʃt of poems.

From Ellwood's account it appears, that Paradiʃe Loʃt was complete in 1665. Philips and Toland aʃʃert, that it was actually publiʃhed the following year; but I believe no copy has been found of a date ʃo early. The firʃt edition on the liʃt of the very accurate Mr. Loʃt was printed by Peter Parker in 1667, and, probably, at the expenʃe of the author, who ʃold the work to Samuel Simmons, by a contract dated the 27th of April, in the ʃame year.

The terms of this contract are ʃuch as a lover of genius can hardly hear without a ʃigh of pity and indignation. The author of the Paradiʃe Loʃt received only an immediate payment of five pounds for a work, which is the very maʃter - piece

of fublime and refined imagination ; a faculty not only naturally rare, but requiring an
extraordinary coincidence of circuftances to cherifh
and ftrengthen it for the long and regular exercife effential to the production of fuch a poem.
The bookfeller's agreement, however, entitled
the author to a conditional payment of fifteen
pounds more; five to be paid after the fale of
thirteen hundred copies of the firft edition, and
five, in the fame manner', both on a fecond and
a third. The number of each edition was li-
mited to fifteen hundred copies.

The original fize of the publication was a
fmall quarto, and the poem was at firft divided
into ten books; but in the fecond edition the
author very judicioufly increafed the number to
twelve, by introducing a paufe in the long nar-
nation of the feventh and of the tenth, fo that
each of thefe books became two.

Simmons was a printer, and his brief advertifement to the work he had purchafed is curious
enough to merit infertion :

" Courteous Reader, there was no argument
at firft intended to the book; but for the fatisfaction of many that have defired it, I have procured it, and withal a reafon of that, which
ftumbled many others, why the poem rhymes
not. " Here we may plainly fee that the novelty of blank verfe was confidered as an un-
palatable innovation. The book, however, advanced fo far in its fale, that thirteen hundred

were difperfed in two years. In April, 1669, the author received his fecond payment of five pounds. The fecond edition came forth in the year of his death, and the third in four years after that event : his widow, who inherited a right to the copy, fold all her claims to Simmons for eight pounds, in December, 1680; fo that twenty-eight pounds, paid at different times in the courfe of thirteen years, is the whole pecuniary reward which this great performance produced to the poet and his widow.

But although the emolument, which the author derived from his nobleft produ&ion, was moft deplorably inadequate to its merit, he was abundantly gratified with immediate and fervent applaufe from the feveral accomplifhed judges of poetical genius. It has been generally fuppofed, that Paradife Loft was negle&ed to a mortifying degree on its firft appearance ; and that the exalted poet confoled his fpirit under fuch mortification by a magnanimous confidence in the juftice of future ages, and a fanguine anticipation of his poetical immortality. The ftrength and dignity of his mind would indeed have armed him againft any poffible difappointment of his literary ambition ; but fuch was the reception of his work, that he could not be difappointed. Johnfon has vindicated the public on this point with judgement and fuccefs : " The fale of books (he ob- " ferves) was not in Milton's age what it is in " the prefent ; the nation had been fatisfied,

" from 1623 to 1664, that is forty-one years,
" with only two editions of the works of Shak-
" fpeare, which probably did not together make
" one thoufand copies. The fale of thirteen
" hundred copies in two years, in oppofition to
" fo much recent enmity, and to a ftyle of ver-
" fification new to all, and difgufting to many,
" was an uncommon example of the prevalence
" of genius." Thefe remarks are perfectly juft;
but when their author proceeds to fay; " the
" admirers of Paradife Loft did not dare to pub-
" lifh their opinion," he feems to forget the very
fpirited eulogies that were, during the life of the
poet, beftowed on that performance. Panegyric
can hardly affume a bolder tone than in the
Englifh and Latin verfes addreffed to Milton by
Marvel and Barrow. He received other compliments not inferior to thefe. The mufe of
Dryden affured him, that he poffeffed the united
excellencies of Homer and of Virgil; and, if we
may rely on an anecdote related by Richardfon,
the Paradife Loft was announced to the world
in a very fingular manner, that may be thought
not ill-fuited to the pre-eminence of the work.
Sir John Denham, a man diftinguifhed as a foldier, a fenator, and a poet, came into the
Houfe of Commons with a proof-fheet of Milton's new compofition wet from the prefs, and
being queftioned concerning the paper in his
hand, he faid, it was " part of the nobleft poem
" that ever was written in any language or in

any age." ¬ Richardson, whofe active and liberal
affection for the poet led him to fearch with intelligent alacrity and fuccefs for every occurrence that could redound to his honor, has recorded another incident, which muft be particularly interefting to every lover of literary anecdote, as it difcovers how the Paradife Loft was
firft introduced to Dryden, and with what fervency of admiration he immediately fpoke of it.
The Earl of Dorfet and Fleetwood Shepard, the
friend of Prior, found the poem, according to
this ftory, at a bookfeller's in Little Britain, who,
lamenting its want of circulation, entreated the
Earl to recommend it ; Dorfet, after reading
it himfelf, fent it to Dryden, who faid, in returning the book, " This man cuts us all out,
and the ancients too." Thefe were probably the
real fentiments of Dryden on his firft perufal of
the poem; but as that unhappy genius was not
bleft with the independent magnanimity of Milton, his opinions were apt to fluctuate according to his intereft, and we find him occafionally
difpofed to exalt or degrade the tranfcendent performance, which he could not but admire. As
the fix celebrated verfes, in which he has com-
plimented the Englifh Homer, fo much refemble
what he faid of him to Lord Dorfet, it is probable that thofe verfes were written while his
mind was glowing with admiration from his firft
furvey of the Paradife Loft; and as long as Milton lived, Dryden feems to have paid him the

deference fo juftly due to his age, his genius, and his virtue. Aubrey relates, in the manufcript which I have repeatedly cited, that the poet laureat waited on Milton for the purpofe of foliciting his permiffion to put his Paradife Loft into a drama. " Mr. Milton (fays Aubrey) received him civilly, and told him, he would give him leave to tag his verfes," an expreffion that probably alluded to a couplet of Marvel's, in his poetical eulogy on his friend. The opera which Dryden wrote, in confequence of this permiffion, entitled the ftate of Innocence, was not exhibited in the theatre, and did not appear in print till two years after the death of Milton, who is mentioned in becoming terms of veneration and gratitude in the preface. The drama itfelf is a very fingular and ftriking performance; with all the beauties and all the defects of Dryden's animated unequal verfification, it has peculiar claims to the attention of thofe, who may wifh to inveftigate the refpective powers of Englifh rhyme and blank verfe, and it may furnifh arguments to the partifans of each; for, if in many paffages the images and harmony of Milton are deplorably injured by the neceffity of rhyming, in a few inftances, perhaps, rhyme has imparted even to the ideas of Milton new energy and grace. There are prefixt to this opera fome very animated but injudicious verfes by poor Nat. Lee, who has lavifhed the moft exaggerated praife on his friend Dryden, at the expenfe of the fuperior poet.

It is highly pleaſing to reflect, that Milton, who had ſo many evils to ſuſtain in the courſe of his chequered life, had yet the high gratification of being aſſured, by very competent judges, that he had glorioufly ſucceeded in the prime object of his literary ambition, the great poetical achievement, which he projected in youth, and accompliſhed in old age. He probably received ſuch animating aſſurances from many of his friends, whoſe applauſe, being intended for his private ſatisfaction, has not deſcended to our time; but when we recollect the honors already mentioned, that were paid to the living poet by Denham, Dryden, and Marvel, we may reſt ſatisfied in the perſuaſion, that he enjoyed a grateful earneſt of his future renown, and according to the petition he addreſſed to Urania,

" Fit audience found tho' few."

If the ſpirit of a departed bard can be gratified by any circumſtances of poſthumous renown, it might gratify Milton to perceive, that his divine poem was firſt indebted for general celebrity to the admiration of Sommers and of Addiſon, two of the moſt accompliſhed and moſt amiable of Engliſh names. Sommers promoted the firſt ornamented edition of Paradiſe Loſt in 1688; and Addiſon wrote his celebrated papers on Milton in 1712.

But to return to the living author; in the year 1670, the great poet aspired to new distinction, by appearing in the character of an historian.—He had long meditated a work, which, in his time, was particularly wanted in our language, and which the greater cultivation bestowed by the present age on this branch of literature has not yet produced in perfection—an eloquent and impartial history of England. Milton executed only six books, beginning with the most early fabulous period, and closing with the Norman conquest. " Why he should have given the first part (says Johnson) which he seems not to believe, and which is universally rejected; it is difficult to conjecture." Had the critic taken the trouble to peruse a few pages of the work in question his difficulty would have vanished; he would at least have found the motive of the author, if he had not esteemed it satisfactory :

" I have determined (says Milton) in speaking of the ancient and rejected British fables, to bestow the telling over even of these reputed tales, be it for nothing else but in favor of our English poets and rhetoricians, who by their art will know how to use them judiciously." This sentiment implies a striking fondness for works of imagination, and a good natured disposition to promote them.

The historian discovers higher aims as he advances in his work, and expresses a moral and patriotic desire to make the lessons suggested by the early calamities of this nation a fource of wifdom and virtue to his improving countrymen. The very paffage, which was moft likely to produce fuch an effect, was ftruck out of the publication by the Gothic hand of the licenfer, an incident that feems to give new energy to all the noble arguments, which the injured author had formerly adduced in vindicating the liberty of the prefs.

The paffage in queftion contained a very mafterly fketch of the long parliament and affembly of divines, contrafting their fituation and their mifconduct, after the death of Charles the Firft, with thofe of the ancient Britons, when, by the departure of the Roman power, " they were left (according to the expreffion of the hiftorian) to the fway of their own councils." The author gave a copy of this unlicenfed parallel to the celebrated Earl of Anglefey, a man diftinguifhed by erudition, with a liberal refpect for genius, and though a minifter of Charles the Second, a frequent vifiter of Milton. This curious fragment was publifhed in 1681, with a fhort preface, declaring, that it originally belonged to the third book of Milton's Hiftory; and in the edition of his profe works, in 1738, it was properly replaced. The poet would have fucceeded more eminently as an hiftorian, had his talents been exercifed on a period more favorable to their exertion. We have reafon to regret his not having executed the latter part of his original intention, inſtead of dwelling on the meager and dark annals of Saxon barbarity. In his early hiſtory, however, there are paſſages of great force and beauty; his character of Alfred in particular is worthy that engaging model of an accompliſhed monarch, and verifies a ſentiment, which Milton profeſſed, even while he was defending the commonwealth, that although a reſolute enemy to tyrants, he was a ſincere friend to ſuch kings as merited the benediction of their people *.

* The attractive merit of Alfred, and the affectionate zeal, with which Milton appears to have delineated his character, form a double motive for inſerting it in a note, as a ſpecimen of the great author's ſtyle in hiſtorical compoſition.

" After which troubleſome time Alfred enjoying three years of peace, by him ſpent, as his manner was, not idly or voluptuously, but in all virtuous employments both of mind and body, becoming a prince of his renown, ended his days in the year nine hundred, the fifty-firſt of his age, the thirtieth of his reign, and was buried regally at Wincheſter : he was born at a place called Wanading, in Berkshire, his mother Osburga, the daughter of Oslac the king's cup-bearer, a Goth by nation, and of noble deſcent. He was of perſon comelier than all his brethren, of pleaſing tongue, and graceful behaviour, ready wit and memory; yet, through the fondneſs of his parents towards him, had not been taught to read till the twelfth year of his age ; but the great deſire of learning which was in him ſoon appeared, by his conning of Saxon poems day and night, which, with great attention, he heard by others repeated. He was beſides excellent at hunting, and the new art then of hawking, but more exemplary in devotion, having collected into a book certain prayers and pſalms, which he carried ever with him in his boſom to uſe on all occaſions. He thirſted after all

In 1671, the year after the firſt appearence of his hiſtory, he publiſhed the Paradiſe Regained, and Samſon Agoniſtes.

liberal knowledge, and oft complained, that in his youth he had no teachers, in his middle age ſo little vacancy from wars and the cares of his kingdom; yet leiſure he found ſometimes, not only to learn much himſelf, but to communicate thereof what he could to his people, by translating books out of Latin into English, Oroſius, Boethius, Beda's hiſtory, and others; permitted none unlearned to bear office, either in court or commonwealth. At twenty years of age, not yet reigning, he took to wife Egelſwitha, the daughter of Ethelred, a Mercian earl. The extremities which befel him in the ſixth of his reign, Neothan Abbot told him were juſtly come upon him for neglecting, in his younger days, the complaint of ſuch as, injured and oppreſſed, repaired to him, as then ſecond perſon in the kingdom, for redreſs; which neglect, were it ſuch indeed, were yet excuſable in a youth, through jollity of mind, unwilling perhaps to be detained long with ſad and ſorrowful narrations; but from the time of his undertaking regal charge no man more patient in hearing cauſes, more inquiſitive in examining, more exact in doing juſtice, and providing good laws, which are yet extant; more ſevere in puniſhing unjuſt judges or obſtinate offenders, thieves eſpecially and robbers, to the terror of whom in croſs ways were hung upon a high poſt certain chains of gold, as it were daring any one to take them thence; ſo that juſtice ſeemed in his days not to flouriſh only, but to triumph: no man can be more frugal of two precious things in man's life, his time and his revenue; no man wiſer in the diſpoſal of both. His time, the day and night, he diſtributed by the burning of certain tapers into three equal portions; the one was for devotion, the other for public or private affairs, the third for bodily refreſhment; how each hour paſt he was put in mind by one who had that office. His whole annual

Many groundlefs remarks have been made on the fuppofed want of judgment in Milton to form a proper eftimate of his own compofitions. " His laft poetical offspring (fays Johnfon) was his favorite; he could not, as Ellwood relates, endure to have Paradife Loft preferred to Paradife

revenue, which his firft care was should be juftly his own, he divided into two equal parts; the firft he employed to fecular ufes, and fubdivided thofe into three; the firft to pay his foldiers, houfehold fervants, and guards, of which, divided into three bands, one attended monthly by turn; the fecond was to pay his architects and workmen, whom he had got together of feveral nations, for he was alfo an elegant builder, above the cuftom and conceit of Englishmen in thofe days; the third he had in readinefs to relieve or honor ftrangers, according to their worth, who came from all parts to fee him, and to live under him. The other equal part of his yearly wealth he dedicated to religious ufes; thofe of four forts; the firft to relieve the poor, the fecond to the building and maintenance of two monafteries, the third of a fchool, where he had perfuaded many noblemen to ftudy facred knowledge and liberal arts, fome fay at Oxford; the fourth was for the relief of foreign churches, as far as India to the shrine of St. Thomas, fending thither Sigelm bishop of Sherburn, who both returned fafe and brought with him many rich gems and fpices; gifts alfo, and a letter, he received from the patriarch at Jerufalem; fent many to Rome, and from them received relics. Thus far, and much more, might be faid of his noble mind, which rendered him the mirror of princes. His body was difeafed in his youth with a great forenefs in the feige, and that ceafing of itfelf, with another inward pain of unknown caufe, which held him by frequent fits to his dying day; yet not difenabled to fuftain thofe many glorious labors of his life both in peace and war.—Profe Works, Vol. II. p. 97.

Regained." In this brief paſſage, there is more than one miſrepreſentation. It is not Ellwood, but Philips, who ſpeaks of Milton's eſteem for his latter poem; and inſtead of ſaying that the author preferred it to his greater work, he merely intimates, that Milton was offended with the general cenſure, which condemned the Paradiſe Regained as infinitely inferior to the other. Inſtead of ſuppoſing, therefore, that the great poet was under the influence of an abſurd predilection, we have only reaſon to conclude, that he heard with lively ſcorn ſuch idle witticiſm as we find recorded by Toland, " That Milton might be ſeen in Paradiſe Loſt, but not in Paradiſe Regained." His own accompliſhed mind, in which ſenſibility and judgment were proportioned to extraordinary imagination, moſt probably aſſured him what is indiſputably true, that uncommon energy of thought and felicity of compoſition are apparent in both performances, however different in deſign, dimenſion, and effect. To cenſure the Paradiſe Regained, becauſe it does not more reſemble the preceding poem, is hardly leſs abſurd than it would be to condemn the moon for not being a ſun, inſtead of admiring the two different luminaries, and feeling that both the greater and the leſs are viſibly the work of the ſame divine and inimitable power.

Johnſon has very liberally noticed one peculiarity in Milton, and calls it, with a benevolent happineſs of expreſſion, " a kind of humble
dignity,

" dignity, which did not difdain the meaneft
" fervices to literature. The epic poet, the con-
" trovertift, the politician, having already def-
" cended to accommodate children with a book
" of rudiments, now, in the laft years of his
" life, compofed a book of Logic, for the initia-
" tion of ftudents in philofophy, and publifhed,
" 1672, Artis logicæ plenior Inftitutio ad Petri
" Rami Methodum concinnata, that is, a new
" fcheme of Logic, according to the method of
" Ramus."

It is fo pleafing to find one great author fpeaking of another in terms, which do honor to both,
that I tranfcribe, with fingular fatisfaction, the
preceding paffage of the eminent biographer,
whofe frequent and injurious afperity to Milton I
have fo repeatedly noticed, and muft continue
to notice, with reprehenfion and regret.

In the very moment of delivering the juft
encomium I have commended, the critic difcovers an intemperate eagernefs to revile the object
of his praife; for he proceeds to fay of Milton,
" I know not whether, even in this book, he
" did not intend an act of hoftility againft the
" univerfities, for Ramus was one of the firft
" oppugners of the old philofophy, who difturbed
" with innovations the quiet of the fchools." Is
there not a vifible want of candor in fhowing fo
wildly a wifh to impute a very inoffenfive and
meritorious work of fcience to a malevolent
motive?

16

Ramus was a man, whofe writings and memory were juftly regarded by Milton, for he refembled our great countryman in temperance,
in fortitude, in paffion for ftudy, and, above
all, in a brave and inflexible oppofition to ignorance, tyranny, and fuperftition; his life was
a continued ftuggle with thefe mercilefs enemies,
and he perifhed at laft with circumftances of peculiar barbarity, in the atrocious maffare of St.
Bartholomew.

A defire of rendering juftice to the talents and
virtues of fuch a fufferer in the caufe of learning
might furely be afcribed to Milton, as a more
probable and becoming motive on this occafion,
than dark intentions of hoftility againft the univerfities. It is but a forry compliment to thofe
univerfities to infinuate, that he engaged in war-
fare againft them, who republifhed a fimple and
feafonable treatife on the management of human
reafon. Milton with great judgment augmented
the logic of Ramus, and added to his fyftem an
abridgment of the Latin life, which Fregius had
written, of its unfortunate author.

The long literary career of Milton was now
drawing towards its termination, and it clofed as
it began, with a fervent regard to the intereft of
religion.—Alarmed by that encroachment, which
the Romifh fuperftition was making under the
connivance of Charles the Second, and with the
aid of his apoftate brother, Milton publifhed
" A treatife of true Religion, Herefy, Schifm,

" Toleration, and the beft means to prevent the
" Growth of Popery." The patriotic fcope of
this work was to unite and confolidate the jar-
rings fects of the proteftants, by perfuading them
to reciprocal indulgence, and to guard them
againft thofe impending dangers from Rome,
which, in a fhort period, burft upon this ifland,
and very happily terminated. in our fignal deli-
verance from many of thofe religious and political
evils, which the fpirit of Milton had, through
a long life, moft refolutely and confcientioufly
oppofed.

His treatife againft the growth of popery,
which was publifhed in 1673, was the laft confiderable performance that he gave to the world;
but publication in fome fhape feems to have contributed to his amufement as long as he exifted.
In the fame year he reprinted his fmaller poems
with the Tractate on Education ; and in the year
following, the laft of his laborious life, he publifhed his Familiar Letters, and a Declaration of
the Poles in praife of their heroic fovereign, John
Sobiefki, tranflated from the Latin original. A
brief hiftory of Mofcovia, which he appears to
have compiled, in the early parts of his life,
from various travellers who had vifited that country, was publifhed a few years after his death,
and two of his compofitions (both perhaps intended for the prefs) have probably perifhed; the
firft, a Syftem of Theology in Latin, that feems
to have been intrufted to his friend Cyriac

Skinner; the fecond, an Anfwer to a fcurrilous libel upon himfelf, which his nephew fuppofes him to have fuppreffed from a juft contempt of his reviler.

Soon after his marriage in 1661, he had removed from Jewin-ftreet to a houfe in the Artillery-walk, leading to Bunhill-fields, a fpot that to his enthufiaftic admirers may appear confecrated by his genius : here he refided in that period of his days, when he was peculiarly entitled to veneration; here he probably finifhed no lefs than three of his admirable works; and here, with a diffolution fo eafy that it was unperceived by the perfons in his chamber, he clofed a life, clouded indeed by uncommon and various calamities, yet ennobled by the conftant exercife of fuch rare endowments as render his name, perhaps, the very firft in that radiant and comprehenfive lift, of which England, the moft fertile of countries in the produce of mental power, has reafon to be proud.

For fome years he had fuffered much from the gout, and in July, 1674, he found his conftitution fo broken by that diftemper, that he was willing to prepare for his departure from the world. With this view he informed his brother Chriftopher, who was then a bencher in the Inner Temple, of the difpofition he wifhed to make of his property. " Brother (faid the invalid) the portion due to me from Mr. Powell, my firft wife's father, I leave to the unkind children I had by her; but I have received no part of it; and my will and meaning is, they shall have no other benefit of my eftate than the faid portion, and what I have befides done for them, they having been very undutiful to me; and all the refidue of my eftate I leave to the difpofal of Elizabeth, my loving wife." Such is the brief teftament, which Milton dictated to his brother, about the 20th of July, but which Chriftopher does not appear to have committed to paper till a few days after the deceafe of the teftator, who expired on Sunday night, the 15th of November, 1674. " All his learned and great friends in London, (fays Toland) not without a friendly concourfe of the vulgar, accompanied his body to the church of St. Giles, near Cripplegate, where he lies buried in the chancel." This bio-grapher, who, though he had the misfortune to think very differently from Milton on the great article of religion, yet never fails to fpeak of him with affectionate refpect, indulged a pleafing ex-pectation, when he wrote his life in the clofe of. the laft century, that national munificence would fpeedily raife a monument worthy of the poet, to protect and to honor his remains. To the difcredit of our country fhe has failed to pay this decent tribute to the memory of a man, from whofe genius fhe has derived fo much glory; but an individual, Mr. Benfon, in the year 1737, placed a buft of the great author in Weftminfter Abbey; an act of liberality that does him credit, though Johnfon and Pope have both fatirized

the monumental infcription with a degree of cy-
nical afperity : fuch afperity appears unfeafonable,
becaufe all the oftentation, fo feverily cenfured
in Mr. Benfon, amounts merely to his having
faid, in the plaineft manner, that he raifed the
monument; and to his having added to his own
name a common enumeration of the offices he poffeffed ; a circumftance in which candor might have
difcovered rather more modefty than pride. —
Affluence appears particularly amiable when
paying a voluntary tribute to neglected genius,
even in the grave; nor is Benfon the only individual of ample fortune, who has endeared
himfelf to the lovers of literature by generous
endeavours to promote the celebrity of Milton.
Affectionate admirers of the poet will honor the
memory of the late Mr. Hollis, in recollecting
that he devoted much time and money to a fimilar purfuit; and they will regret that he was
unable to difcover the Italian verfes, and the
marble buft, which he diligently fought for in
Italy, on a fuggeftion that fuch memorials of
our poetic traveller had been carefully preferved
in that country. But from this brief digreffion
on the recent admirers of Milton, let us return
to his family at the time of his deceafe.

His will was contefted by the daughters,
whofe undutiful conduct it condemned : being
deficient in form, it was fet afide, and letters
of adminiftration were granted to the widow,
who is faid to have allotted a hundred pounds

to each daughter, a fum which, being probably too little in their opinion, and too much in her's, would naturally produce reciprocal animofity and cenfure between the contending parties.

It has been already obferved, that the recent difcovery of this forgotten will, and the allegations annexed to it, throw confiderable light on the domeftic life of Milton; and the more infight we can gain into his focial and fequeftered hours, the more we fhall difcover, that he was not lefs entitled to private affection, than to public efteem; but let us contemplate his perfon, before we proceed to a minuter examination of his mind. and manners.

So infatuated with rancor were the enemies of this illuftrious man, that they delineated his form, as. they reprefented his character, with the utmoft extravagance of malevolent falfhood: he was not only compared to that monfter of deformity, the eyelefs Polypheme, but defcribed as a diminutive, bloodlefs, and fhrivelled creature. Expreffions of this kind, in which abfurdity and malice are equally apparent, induced him to expofe the contemptible virulence of his revilers by a brief defcription of his own figure [*].

---

[*] Veniamus nunc ad mea crimina; eftne quod in vita aut moribus reprehendat? Certe nihil. Quid ergo? Quod nemo nifi immanis ac barbarus feciffet, formam mihi ac cæcitatem obje&at.

Monftrum horrendum, informe, ingens, cui lumen ademptum. Nunquam exiftimabam quidem fore, ut de forma, cum Cyclope certamen mihi effet; verum ftatim fe revocat. " Quanquam

He reprefents himfelf as a man of moderate ftature, not particularly flender, and fo far endued
with ftrength and fpirit, that as he always wore
a fword, he wanted not, in his healthy feafon
of life, either fkill or courage to ufe it; having
practifed fencing with great affiduity, he confidered

nec ingens, quo nihil eft exilius exfanguius contractius." Tametfi virum nihil attinet de forma dicere, tandem quando hic
quoque eft unde gratias deo agam & mendaces redarguam ne
quis (quod Hifpanorum vulgus de hereticis, quos vocant, plus
nimio facerdotibus fuis credulum opinatur) me forte cynocepha-
lum quempiam aut rhinocerota effe putet, dicam. Deformis quidem a nemine quod fciam, qui modo me vidit fum unquam habitus; formofus necne minus laboro; ftatura fateor non fum
procera; fed quæ mediocri tamen quam parvæ propior fit; fed
quid fi parva, qua & fummi fæpe tum pace tum bello viri
fuere, quanquam parva cur dicitur, quæ ad virtutem fatis magna eft? Sed neque exilis admodum eo fane animo iifque viribus ut cum ætas vitæque ratio fic ferebat, nec ferrum tractare,
nec ftringere quotidiano ufu exercitatus nefcirem; eo accinctus ut
plerumque eram cuivis vel multo robuftiori exæquatum me pu-
tabam, fecurus quid mihi quis injuriæ vir viro inferre poffet.
Idem hodie animus, cædem vires; oculi non iidem; ita tamen
extrinfecus illæfi, ita fine nube clari ac lucidi, ut eorum qui
acutiffimum cernunt; in hac folum parte, memet invito, fimu-
lator fum. In vultu quo " nihil exfanguius" effe dixit, is
manet etiamnum color exfangui & palenti plane contrarius, ut
quadragenario major vix fit cui non denis prope annis videar
natu minor; neque corpore contracto neque cute. In his ego
fi ulla ex parte mentior multis millibus popularium meorum
qui de facie me norunt, exteris etiam non paucis, ridiculus merito fim : fin ifte in re minime neceffaria tam impudenter gra-
tuito mendax comperietur poteritis de reliquo eandem conjectu-
ram facere. Atque hæc de forma mea vel coactus.

himfelf as a match for any antagonift, however fuperior to him in mufcular force; his countenance (he fays) was fo far from being bloodlefs, that when turned of forty he was generally allowed to have the appearance of being ten years younger; even his eyes (he adds) though utterly deprived of fight, did not betray their imperfection, but on the contrary appeared as fpecklefs and as lucid as if his powers of vifion had been peculiarly acute — " In this article alone" (fays Milton) " and much againft my will, I am an " hypocrite."

Such is the interefting portrait, which this great writer has left us of himfelf. Thofe who had the happinefs of knowing him perfonally, fpeak in the higheft terms even of his perfonal endowments, and feem to have regarded him as a model of manly grace and dignity in his figure and deportment.

" His harmonical and ingenuous foul" (fays Aubrey) " dwelt in a beautiful and well pro-" portioned body."

" In toto nufquam corpore menda fuit. "

His hair was a light brown, his eyes dark grey, and his complexion fo fair, that at college, according to his own expreffion, he was flyled " The Lady," an appellation which he could not relifh; but he confoled himfelf under abfurd raillery on the delicacy of his perfon, by recollecting that fimilar raillery had been lavifhed on thofe manly and eminent characters of the ancient world, Demofthenes and Hortenfius. His general appearance approached not in any degree to effeminacy. " His deportment " (fays Anthony Wood) " was affable, and his gait erect and " manly , befpeaking courage and undaunt- " ednefs. " Richardfon, who labored with affectionate enthufiafm to acquire and communicate all poffible information concerning the perfon and manners of Milton , has left the two following fketches of his figure at an advanced period of life.

" An ancient clergyman of Dorfetfhire (Dr. Wright) found John Milton in a fmall chamber hung with rufty green, fitting in an elbow chair, and dreffed neatly in black, pale but not cadaverous, his hands and fingers gouty and with chalk ftones. ".

" He ufed alfo to fit, in a grey coarfe cloth coat, at the door of his houfe near Bunhill fields, in warm funny weather, to enjoy the frefh air , and fo, as well as in his room, received the vifits of people of diftinguifhed parts as well as quality. " It is probable, that Milton , in his youth, was, in fome meafure, indebted to the engaging graces of his perfon for that early introduction into the politeft fociety, both in England and abroad, which improved the natural fweetnefs of his character (fo vifible in all his genuine portraits) and led him to unite with profound erudition, and with the fublimeft talents, an endearing and cheerful delicacy of manners, very rarely attained by men, whofe application to ftudy is continual and intenfe.

The enemies of Milton indeed (and his late biographer I muft reluctantly include under that defcription) have labored to fix upon him a fictitious and moft unamiable character of aufterity and harfhnefs. " What we know (fays John-" fon) of Milton's character in domeftic relations " is, that he was fevere and arbitrary. His fa-" mily confifted of women, and there appears " in his books fomething like a Turkifh contempt " of females, as fubordinate and inferior beings; " that his own daughters might not break the " ranks, he fuffered them to be depreffed by a " mean and penurious education. He thought " woman made only for obedience, and man " for rebellion." This is affuredly the intemperate language of hatred, and very far from being confonant to truth.

As it was thought a fufficient defence of Sophocles, when he was barbaroufly accufed of mental imbecility by his unnatural children, to read a portion of his recent dramatic works, fo, I am confident, the citation of a few verfes from our Englifh bard may be enough to clear him from a charge equally groundlefs, and almoft as ungenerous.

No impartial reader of genuine fenfibility will deem it poffible, that the poet could have

entertained a Turkiſh contempt of females, who
has thus delineated woman :

> All higher knowledge in her preſence falls
> Degraded; wiſdom, in diſcourſe with her,
> Loſes diſcountenanc'd, and like folly ſhows;
> Authority and reaſon on her wait,
> As one intended firſt, not after made
> Occaſionally; and to conſummate all,
> Greatneſs of mind and nobleneſs their ſeat
> Build in her lovelieſt, and create an awe
> About her, as a guard angelic plac'd.

A description ſo complete could ariſe only
from ſuch exquiſite feelings in the poet, as inſured
to every deſerving female his tendereſt regard.
This argument might be ſtill more enforced by
a paſſage in the ſpeech of Raphael; but the preceding verſes are, I truſt, ſufficient to counteract the uncandid attempt of the acrimonious
biographer to prejudice the faireſt part of the
creation againſt a poet, who has ſurpaſſed his
peers in delineating their charms, whoſe poetry,
a more enchanting mirror than the lake that he
deſcribes in Paradiſe, repreſents their mental
united to their perſonal graces, and exhibits in
perfection all the lovelineſs of woman.

As to Milton's depreſſing his daughters by a
mean and penurious education, it is a calumny
reſting only on a report, that he would not allow
them the advantage of learning to write. This is

evidently falfe, fince Aubrey, who was perfon-
nally acquainted with the poet, and who had
probably confulted his widow in regard to many
particulars of his life, exprefsly affirms, that his
youngeft daughter was his amanuenfis; a circumftance of which my friend Romney has happily availed himfelf to decorate the folio edition
of this life with a production of his pencil. The
youngeft daughter of Milton had the moft frequent opportunities of knowing his temper, and
fhe happens to be the only one of his children
who has delivered a deliberate account of it; but
her account, inftead of confirming Johnfon's idea
of her father's domeftic feverity, will appear to
the candid reader to refute it completely. " She
fpoke of him (fays Richardfon) with great tendernefs; fhe faid he was delightful company;
the life of the converfation, and that on account
of a flow of fubject, and an unaffected cheerful-
nefs and civility." It was this daughter who related the extraordinary circumftance, that fhe
and one of her fifters read to their father feveral languages, which they did not underftand:
it is remarkable, that fhe did not fpeak of it as
a hardfhip; nor could it be thought an intolerable
grievance by an affectionate child, who thus affifted a blind parent in laboring for the maintenance of his family. Such an employment, however, muft have been irkfome; and the confide-
rate father, in finding that it was fo, " fent
out his children (according to the expreffion of

his nephew) to learn some curious and ingenious sorts of manufacture, particularly embroideries in gold or silver." That he was no penurious parent is strongly proved by an expression that he made use of in speaking of his will, when he declared, that " he had made provision for his children in his life-time, and had spent the greatest part of his estate in providing for them." It is the more barbarous to arraign the poet for domestic cruelty, because he appears to have suffered from the singular tenderness and generosity of his nature... He had reason to lament that excess of indulgence, with which he forgave and received again his disobedient and long-alienated wife, since their re-union not only disquieted his days, but gave birth to daughters, who seem to have inherited the perversity of their mother:

> The wisest and best men full oft beguil'd
> With goodness principled, not to reject
> The penitent, but ever to forgive,
> Are drawn to wear out miserable days,
> Intangled with a pois'nous bosom-snake.

These pathetic lines, in a speech of his Samson Agonistes, strike me as a forcible allusion to his own connubial infelicity. If in his first marriage he was eminently unhappy, his success in the two last turned the balance of fortune in his favor. That his second wife deserved, possessed, and retained his affection, is evident from his

fonnet occafioned by her death; of the care and
kindnefs which he had long experienced from
the partner of his declining life, he fpoke with
tender gratitude to his brother, in explaining
his teftamentary intention; and we are probably
indebted to the care and kindnefs, which the
aged poet experienced from this affectionate guardian, for the happy accomplifhment of his ineftimable works.   A blind and defolate father
muft be utterly unequal to the management of
difobedient daughters confpiring againft him; the
anguifh he endured from their filial ingratitude,
and the bafe deceptions, with which they continually tormented him, muft have rendered even
the ftrongeft mind very unfit for poetical application.   The marriage, which he concluded by
the advice and the aid of his friend Dr. Paget,
feems to have been his only refource againft a
moft exafperating and calamitous fpecies of domeftic difquietude; it appears, therefore, not
unreafonable to regard thofe immortal poems,
which recovered tranquillity enabled him to produce, as the fruits of that marriage.   As matrimony has, perhaps, annihilated many a literary
defign, let it be remembered to its honor, that
it probably gave birth to the brighteft offspring
of literature.

The two eldeft daughters of Milton appear to
me utterly unworthy of their father; but thofe
who adopt the dark prejudices of Johnfon, and
believe with him, that the great poet was an

auftere domeftic tyrant, will find, in their idea of the father, an apology for his children, whofe deftiny in the world I fhall immediately mention, that I may have occafion to fpeak of them no more. Anne, the eldeft, who with a deformed perfon had a pleafing face, married an architect, and died, with her firft infant, in child-bed. Mary, the fecond, and apparently the moft deficient in affection to her father, died unmarried. Deborah, who was the favorite of Milton, and who, long after his deceafe, difcovered, on a cafual fight of his genuine portrait, very affecting emotions of filial tendernefs and enthufiafm, even Deborah deferted him without his knowledge, not in confequence of his paternal feverity, of which fhe was very far from complaining, but, as Richardfon intimates, from a difguft fhe had conceived againft her mother-in-law. On quitting the houfe of her father, fhe went to Ireland with a lady, and afterwards became the wife of Mr. Clarke, a weaver, in Spital-fields. As her family was numerous, and her circumftances not affluent, the liberal Addifon made her a prefent, from his regard to the memory of her father, and intended to procure her fome decent eftablifhment, but died before he could accomplifh his generous defign. From Queen Caroline, fhe received fifty guineas, a donation as ill proportioned to the rank of the donor as to the mental dignity of the great genius, whofe indigent daughter was the object of this unprincely munificence. —

Mrs.

Mrs Clarke had ten children, but none of them appear} to have attracted public regard, till Dr. Birch and Dr. Newton, two benevolent and refpectable biographers of the poet, difcovered his grand-daughter, Mrs. Elizabeth Fofter, keeping a little chandler's-fhop in the city, poor, aged, and infirm; they publicly fpoke of her condition; Johnfon was then writing as the coadjutor of Lauder in his attempt to fink the glory of Milton; but as the critic's charity was ftill greater than his fpleen, he feized the occafion of recommending, under Lauder's name, this neceffitous defcendant of the great poet to the beneficence of his country; Comus was reprefented for her benefit, in the year 1750, and Johnfon, to his honor, contributed a prologue on the occafion, in which noble fentiments are nobly expreffed.

The poor grand-daughter of Milton gained but one hundred and thirty pounds by this public benefaction; this fum, however, fmall as it was, afforded peculiar comfort to her declining age, by enabling her to retire to Iflington with her hufband: fhe had feven children, who died before her, and by her own death it is probable that the line of the poet became extinct. Let us haften from this painful furvey of his progeny to the more enlivening contemplation of his rare mental endowments. The moft diligent refearches into all that can elucidate the real temper of Milton only confirm the opinion, that his

17

native characteristics were mildness and magnanimity, In controversy his mind was undoubtedly overheated, and passages may be quoted from his prose works, that are certainly neither mild nor magnanimous; but if his controversial asperity is compared with the outrageous insolence of his opponents, even that asperity will appear moderation; in social intercourse he is represented as peculiarly courteous and engaging. When the celebrity of his Latin work made him esteemed abroad, many inquiries were made concerning his private character among his familiar acquaintance, and the result of such inquiry was, that mildness and affability were his distinguishing qualities. " Virum esse miti comique ingenio aiunt," says the celebrate Heinsius, in a letter that he wrote concerning Milton, in the year 1651, to Gronovius. Another eminent foreigner represents him in the same pleasing light, and from the best information. Vossius, who was at that time in Sweden, and who mentions the praise, which his royal patroness Christina bestowed on Milton's recent defence of the English people, informs his friend Heinsius, that he had obtained a very particular account of the author from a relation of his own, the learned Junius, who wrote the elaborate and interesting history of ancient painting, resided in England, and particularly cultivated the intimacy of Milton.

Indeed, when we reflect on the poet's uncommon tenderness towards his parents, and all

the advantages of his early life, both at home
and abroad, we have every reafon to believe,
that his manners were fingularly pleafing.   He
was fond of refined female fociety, and appears
to have been very fortunate in two female friends
of diftinction; the Lady Margaret Ley, whofe
fociety confoled him when he was mortified by
the defertion of his firft wife, and the no lefs accomplifhed Lady Ranelagh, who had placed her
fon under his care, and who probably affifted
him, when he was a widower and blind, with
friendly directions for the management of his female infants.   A paffage in one of his letters to
her fon fuggefts this idea; for he condoles with
his young correfpondent, then at the Univerfity,
on the lofs they would both fuftain by the long
abfence of his moft excellent mother, paffing at
that time into Ireland; " her departure muft
grieve us both," fays Milton, " for to me alfo
fhe fupplied the place of every friend*; " an expreffion full of tendernefs and regret, highly honorable to the lady, and a pleafing memorial of
that fenfibility and gratitude, which I am perfuaded we fhould have feen moft eminent in the
character of Milton, if his Englifh letters had
been fortunately preferved, particularly his letters to this interefting lady, whofe merits are com-
memorated in an eloquent fermon, preached by
bifhop Burnet, on the death of her brother, that
mild and accofnplifhed model of virtue and learning,

* Nam & mihi omnium neceffitudinum loco fuit.

Robert Boyle. Lady Ranelagh muſt have been one of the moſt exemplary and engaging characters that ever exiſted, ſince we find ſhe was the darling ſiſter of this illuſtrious philoſopher, and the favorite friend of a poet ſtill more illuſtrious. Four of Milton's Latin letters are addreſſed to her ſon, and they blend with moral precepts to the young ſtudent reſpectful and affectionate praiſe of his mother *.

In the Latin correſpondence of Milton we have ſome veſtiges of his ſentiments concerning the authors of antiquity; and it is remarkable, that in a deliberate opinion on the merits of Salluſt †, he prefers him to all the Roman hiſtorians. Milton, however, did not form himſelf

---

* In the quarto edition of Boyle there are a few letters from his favorite ſiſter, Lady Ranelagh; one very intereſting, in which ſhe ſpeaks of the poet Waller; but ſhe does not mention the name of Milton in the whole collection. Her ſon (the firſt and laſt Earl of Ranelagh) who was in his childhood a diſciple of the great poet, proved a man of talents, buſineſs, and pleaſure.

† De Salluſtio quod ſcribis, dicam libere; quoniam ita vis plane ut dicam quod ſentio, Salluſtium cuivis Latino hiſtorico me quidem anteferre; quæ etiam conſtans fere antiquorum ſententia fuit. Habet ſuas laudes tuus Tacitus, ſed eas meo quidem judicio maximas, quod Salluſtium nervis omnibus ſit imitatus. Cum hæc tecum coram diſſererem perfeciſſe videor quantum ex eo quod ſcribis conjicio, ut de illo cordatiſſimo ſcriptore ipſe jam idem prope ſentias : adeoque ex me quæris, cum is in exordio belli Catilinarii perdifficile eſſe dixerit hiſtoriam ſcribere, propterea quod facta dictis exæquanda ſunt qua potiſſimum ratione id aſſequi hiſtoriarum ſcriptorem poſſe exiſtimem.

as a writer on any Roman model : being very
early moſt anxious to excel in literature, he wiſe-
ly attached himſelf to thoſe prime examples of.
literary perfeſtion, the Greeks; among the poets
he particularly delighted in Euripides and Homer;
his favorites in proſe ſeem to have been Plato
and Demoſthenes; the firſt peculiarly fit to give
richneſs, purity, and luſtre to the fancy; the ſecond, to invigorate the underſtanding, and in-
ſpire the fervid energy of public virtue.   It is a
very juſt remark of Lord Monboddo, that even
the poetical ſpeeches in Paradiſe Loſt derive their
conſummate propriety and· eloquence from the
fond and enlightened attention with which the

Ego vero ſic exiſtimo; qui geſtas res dignas digne ſcripſerit,
cum animo non minus magno rerumque uſu præditum ſcribere
oportere quam is qui eas geſſerit : ut vel maximas pari animo
comprehendere atque metiri poſſit, & comprehenſas ſermone
puro atque caſto diſtinſte graviterque narrare : nam ut ornate
non admodum laboro; hiſtoricum enim, non oratorem requiro.
Crebras etiam ſententias, & judicia de rebus geſtis interjeſta
prolixe nollem, ne, interrupta rerum ſerie, quod politici ſcri;-
toris munus eſt hiſtoricus invadat; qui ſi ,in conſiliis explicen-
dis, faſtiſque ennarrandis, non ſuum ingenium aut conjeſturam,
ſed veritatem potiſſimum ſequitur, ſuarum profeſto partium ſa-
·tagit.   Addiderim & illud Salluſtianum, qua in re ipſe Cato-
tonem maxime laudavit, poſſe multa paucis abſolvere; id quod
ſine acerrimo judicio, atque etiam temperantia quadam neminem
poſſe arbitror.   Sunt multi in quibus vel· ſermonis elegantiam
vel congeſtarum rerum copiam non deſideres, qui brevitatem cum
copia conjunxerit, id eſt qui, multa paucis abſolverit, princeps
meo judicio eſt Salluſtius.—Proſe Works, vol. 2. p. 582.

poet had ftudied the moft perfect orator of Athens: the ftudies of Milton, however, were very extenfive; he appears to have been familiar not only with all the beft authors of antiquity, but with thofe of every refined language in Europe; Italian, French, Spanifh, and Portugueze. Great erudition has been often fuppofed to operate as an incumbrance on the finer faculties of the mind; but let us obferve to its credit, the fublimeft of poets was alfo the moft learned: of Italian literature he was particularly fond, as we may collect from one of his letters to a profeffor of that language, and from the eafe and fpirit of his Italian verfes. To the honor of modern Italy it may he faid, that fhe had a confiderable fhare in forming the genius of Milton. In Taffo, her brighteft ornament, he found a character highly worthy of his affectionate emulation, both as a poet and as a man; this accomplifhed perfonage had, indeed, ended his illuftrious and troubled life feveral years before Milton vifited his country; but he was yet living in the memory of his ardent friend Manfo, and through the medium of Manfo's converfation his various excellencies made, I am perfuafed, a forcible and permanent impreffion on the heart and fancy of our youthful countryman. It was hardly the example of Triffino, as Johnfon fuppofes, that tempted Milton to his bold experiment of blank verfe; for Triffino's epic poem is a very heavy performance, and had funk into fuch oblivion in Italy, that the literary friend and biographer of Taſſo conſiders that greater poet as the firſt perſon who enriched the Italian language with valuable blank verſe: " our early works of, that kind ," ſays Manſo, " are tranſlations from the Latin , and thoſe not ſucceſsful. ". The poem in blank verſe, for which this amiable biographer applauds his friend, is an extenſive work, in ſeven books, on the Seven Days of the Creation, a ſubject. that has engaged the poets of many countries. The performance of Taſſo was begun at the houſe of his friend Manſo, and at the ſuggeſtion of a lady, the accompliſhed mother of the Marquis. As this poem is formed from the Bible, and full of religious enthuſiaſm, it probably influenced the Engliſh viſiter of Manſo in his choice of blank verſe. Taſſo was a voluminous author, and we have reaſon to believe that Milton was familiar with all his compoſitions, as the exquiſite eulogy on connubial affection, in the Paradiſe Loſt, is founded on a proſe compoſition in favor of marriage, addreſſed by the Italian poet to one of his relations*; but Milton, who was perhaps of all authors the leaſt

---

* Taſſo begins this intereſting diſcourſe, by informing his kinſman Ercole, that he firſt heard the news of his having taken a wife, and then was ſurpriſed by reading a compoſition of his, in which he inveighs not only againſt the ladies, but againſt matrimony. The poet, with great politeneſs and ſpirit, aſſumes the defence of both, and in the cloſe of a learned and eloquent panegyric, indulges his heart and fancy in a very

addicted to imitation, rarely imitates even Taſſo in compoſition : in life, indeed, he copied him more cloſely, and to his great poetical compeer of Italy he diſcovers a very ſtriking reſemblance in application to ſtudy, in temperance of diet, in purity of Morals, and in fervency of devotion. The Marquis of Villa, in cloſing his life of Taſſo, has enumerated all the particular virtues by which he was diſtinguiſhed; theſe were all equally conſpicuous in Milton; and we may truly ſay of him, what Manſo ſays of the great Italian poet, that the preference of virtue to every other conſideration was the predominant paſſion of his life.

Enthuſiaſm was the characteriſtic of his mind; in politics, it made him ſometimes too generouſly credulous, and ſometimes too rigorouſly deciſive; but in poetry it exalted him to ſuch a degree of excellence as no man has hitherto ſurpaſſed; nor is it probable that in this province he will ever be excelled; for although in all the arts there are undoubtedly points of perfection much higher than any mortal has yet attained, ſtill it requires ſuch a coincidence of ſo many advantages depending on the influence both of nature and of deſtiny to raiſe a great artiſt of any kind, that the world has but little reaſon to expect productions of poetical genius ſuperior to the Paradiſe Loſt. There was a bold yet refined originality of conception, which characterized the

animated and beautiful addreſs to wedded love, which Milton has copied with his uſual dignity and ſweetneſs of expreſſion.

mental powers of Milton, and gives him the highest claim to distinction : we are not only indebted to him for having extended and ennobled the province of epic poetry, but he has another title to our regard, as the founder of that recent and enchanting English art, which has embellished our country, and, to speak the glowing language of a living bard very eloquent in its praise,

———— Made Albion smile,
One ample theatre of sylvan grace.

The elegant historian of modern gardening, Lord Orford, and the two accomplished poets, who have celebrated its charms both in France and England, de Lille and Mason, have, with great justice and felicity of expression, paid their homage to Milton, as the beneficent genius, who bestowed upon the world this youngest and most lovely of the arts. As a contrast to the Miltonic garden, I may point out to the notice of the reader, what has escaped, I think, all the learned writers on this engaging subject, the garden of the imperious Duke of Alva, described in a poem of the celebrated Lope de Vega. The sublime vision of Even, as Lord Orford truly calls it, proves indeed, as the same writer observes, how little the poet suffered from the loss of light. The native disposition of Milton, and

his perfonal infirmity, confpired to make contemplation his chief bufinefs and chief enjoyment: few poets have devoted fo large a portion
of their time to intenfe and regular ftudy; yet
he often made a paufe of fome months in the
progrefs of his great work, if we may confide
in the circumftantial narrative of his nephew. " I
had the perufal of it from the very beginning,"
fays Philips, " for fome years, as I went from
time to time to vifit him, in parcels of ten,
twenty, or thirty verfes at a time (which, being
written by whatever hand came next, might
poffibly want correction as to the orthography
and pointing). Having, as the fummer came
on, not been fhowed any for a confiderable
while, and defiring the reafon thereof, was anfwered that his vein never happily flowed but
from the autumnal equinox to the vernal."

Johnfon takes occafion, from this anecdote,
to treat the fenfations of Milton with farcaftic
feverity, and to deride him for fubmitting to the
influence of the feafons; he lavifhes ridicule, not
lefs acrimonious, on the great poet, for having
yielded to a fafhionable dread of evils ftill more
fantaftic. " There prevailed in his time (fays
the critic) an opinion that the world was in its
decay, and that we have had the misfortune to be
born in the decrepitude of nature." Johnfon ex-
pofes, with great felicity of expreffion, this abfurd idea, of which his own frame of body and
mind was a complete refutation; but inftead of

deriding the great poet for harbouring fo weak
a conceit, he might have recollected that Milton
himfelf has fpurned this chimera of timid imagination in very fpirited Latin verfe, written in
his twentieth year, and exprefsly againft the folly
of fuppofing nature impaired.

> Ergone marcefcet, fulcantibus obfita rugis,
> Naturæ facies & rerum publica mater,
> Omniparum contracta uterum, fterilefcet ab ævo
> Et fe fafſa fenem male certis paffibus ibit,
> Sidereum tremebunda caput!

> How! fhall the face of nature then be plough'd
> Into deep wrinkles, and fhall years at laft
> On the great parent fix a fteril curfe;
> Shall even fhe confefs old age, and halt
> And palfy-fmitten fhake her ftarry brows!

COWPER.

The fpirit of the poet was, in truth, little
formed for yielding to any weakneffes of fancy
that could impede mental exertion; and we may
confider it as one of the ftriking peculiarities of
his character, that with an imagination fo excur-
five he poffeffed a mind fo induftrious.

His ftudious habits are thus defcribed by his
acquaintance Aubrey and others, who collected
their account from his widow : — He rofe at
four in the fummer, at five in the winter, and
regularly began the day by hearing a chapter

in the Hebrew Bible; it was read to him by a man, who, after this duty, left him to meditation of some hours, and, returning at seven, either read or wrote for him till twelve; he then allowed himself an hour for exercise, which was usually walking, and when he grew blind, the occasional resource of a swing: after an early and temperate dinner he commonly allotted some time to music, his favorite amusement; and his own musical talents happily furnished him with a pleasing relaxation from his severer pursuits; he was able to vary his instrument, as he played both on the bass viol and the organ, with the advantage of an agreeable voice, which his father had probably taught him to cultivate in his youth. This regular custom of the great poet, to indulge himself in musical relaxation after food, has been recently praised as favorable to mental exertion, in producing all the good effects of sleep, with none of its disadvantages, by an illustrious scholar, who, like Milton, unites the passion and the talent of poetry to habits of intense and diversified application. Sir William Jones, in the third volume of Asiatic Researches, has recommended, from his own experience, this practice of Milton, who from music returned to study; at eight he took a light supper, and at nine retired to bed.

If such extreme regularity could be preserved at any period, it must have been in the closing years of his life. While he was in office his time was undoubtedly much engaged, not only by official attendance, but by his intercourse with learned foreigners, as the parliament allowed him a weekly table for their reception. The Latin compofitions of Milton had rendered him, on the continent, an object of idolatry; " and ftrangers (fays Wood, who was far from being partial to his illuftrious contemporary) vifited the houfe where he was born." Even in his latter days, when he is fuppofed to have been neglected by his countrymen, intelligent foreigners were folicitous to converfe with him as an object of their curiofity and veneration; they regarded him, and very juftly, as the prime wonder of England; for he was, in truth, a perfon fo extraordinary, that it may be queftioned if any age or nation has produced his parallel. Is there, in the records of literature, an author to be found, who, after gaining such extenfive celebrity as a political difputant, caft off the mortal vefture of a polemic, and arofe in the pureft fplendor of poetical immortality?

Biographers are frequently accufed of being influenced by affection for their fubject; to a certain degree it is right that they fhould be fo; for what is biography in its faireft point of view? a tribute paid by juftice and efteem to genius and to virtue; and never is this tribute more pleafing or more profitable to mankind, than when it is liberally paid, with all the fervor and all the fidelity of friendfhip: the chief delight

and the chief utility that arifes from this attractive branch of literature confifts in the affectionate
intereft, which it difplays and communicates in
favor of the talents and probity that it afpires to
celebrate; hence the moft engaging pieces of biography are thofe that have been written by relations of the deceafed. This remark is exem-
plified in the life of Agricola by Tacitus, and
in that of Racine, the dramatic poet, written
by his fon, who, was alfo a poet, and addreffed
to his grandfon.

It has been the lot of Milton to have his life
frequently defcribed, and recently, by a very
powerful author, who, had he loved the character he engaged to delineate, might, perhaps,
have fatisfied the admirers of the poet, and clofed
the lift of his numerous biographers. But the
very wonderful mind of Johnfon was fo embittered by prejudice, that in delineating a character confeffedly pre-eminent in eminent accomplifhments, in genius, and in piety, he perpetually endeavours to reprefent him as unamiable,
and inftead of attributing any miftaken opinions
that he might entertain to fuch fources as charity
and reafon confpire to fuggeft, imputes them to fuppofed vices in his mind, moft foreign to his nature,
and the very worft that an enemy could imagine.

In the courfe of this narrative I have confidered it as a duty incumbent upon me to notice and counteract, as they occurred, many important ftrokes of the hoftility which I am now

lamenting, thefe become ftill more remarkable in that portion of the biographer's labor to which I am at length arrived ; it is in diffecting the mind of Milton, if I may ufe fuch an expreffion, that Johnfon indulges the injurious intemperance of his hatred. " It is to be fufpected (he fays) that " his predominant defire was to deftroy rather " than eftablifh; and that he felt not fo much " the love of liberty as repugnance to authority." Such a fufpicion may indeed be harboured by political rancor, but it muft be in direct oppofition to juftice and truth; for of all men who have written or acted in the fervice of liberty, there is no individual, who has proved more completely, both by his language and his life, that he made a perfect diftinction between liberty and licentioufnefs. No human fpirit could be more fincerely a lover of juft and beneficent authority; for no man delighted more in peace and order; no man has written more eloquently in their praife, or given fublimer proofs of his own perfonal attachment to them by the regulation of his own orderly and peaceful ftudies. If he hated power (as Johnfon afferts in every eftablifhed form, he hated not its falutary influence, but its pernicious exertions. Vehement as he occafionally was againft kings and prelates, he fpoke of the fectaries with equal indignation and abhorrence when they alfo became the agents of perfecution; and as he had fully feen, and has forcibly expofed, the grofs failings of republican reformers,

had his life been extended long enough to witnefs the revolution, which he might have beheld
without fuffering the decrepitude or imbecility
of extreme old age, he would probably have
exulted as warmly as the ftauncheft friend of
our prefent conftitution can exult, in that temperate and happy reformation of monarchical
enormities.

Johnfon alfo intimates, that he was a fhallow
politician, who fuppofed money to be the chief
good, though with fingular inconfiftency he at
the fame time confeffes, " that fortune feems not
to have had much of his care."

Money, in fact, had fo little influence over
the elevated mind of Milton, that from his want
of attention to it he fuftained fuch loffes as, according to his nephew's expreffion, " might
have ruined a man lefs temperate than he was."
Two thoufand pounds he is faid to have loft by
intrufting it to government, and as much in a
private loan, without fufficient fecurity.

" Towards the latter part of his time," fays
one of his early biographers, " he contracted
his library, both becaufe the heirs he left could
not make a right ufe of it, and that he thought
he might fell it more to their advantage than
they could be able to do themfelves. His enemies reported, that poverty conftrained him thus
to part with his books; and were this true it
would be a great difgrace, not to him (for perfons
of the higheft merits have been often reduced to
that

that condition) but to any country that should
have no more regard to probity or learning. This
story, however, is so false, that he died worth
fifteen hundred pounds, besides all his goods."

Such are the remarks of Toland on the pecuniary circumstances of the poet; they show with
becoming spirit, that he was not reduced by absolute indigence to the sale of his library; yet
every reader, whose literary feelings are acute,
must regret, that the old age of Milton was not
guarded and enlivened by such affluence as might
have saved him from a measure, in which those
who have a passion for books must suppose him
to have suffered some degree of mortification.

The necessities into which many deserving men
of letters have fallen towards the close of life,
and in various countries, may be regarded as an
universal disgrace to civilized society, which the
improving refinement and liberality of mankind
ought effectually to remove. Literature, which
is so eminently beneficial to a nation, is frequently
ruinous to worthy individuals most fervently attached to it; and it should be regarded as a duty,
therefore, by every polished people, to provide
a public fund, which might afford a becoming
competence to the advanced life of every illustrious scholar, whose public labors entitle him to
that honorable distinction. Such meritorious ve-
terans in literature as Milton and his late aged
biographer should have been preserved, in their
declining days, from every shadow of indigence,

by the public gratitude of the nation to whom they had devoted their intellectual fervice. What friend to letters and to genius could fail to wifh affluent comfort to the clofing life of fuch au thors, however he might condemn the excelfes of republican feverity in the one, or thofe of fervile and cenforial bigotry in the other?

There can hardly be any contemplation more painful, than to dwell on the virulent excelfes of eminent and good men; yet the utility of fuch contemplation may be equal to its pain. What mildnefs and candor fhould it not inftil into ordinary mortals to obferve, that even genius and virtue weaken their title to refpect, in proportion as they recede from that evangelical charity, which, fhould influence every man in his judgement of another.

The ftrength and the acutenefs of fenfation, which partly conftitute genius, have a great tendency to produce virulence; if the mind is not perpetually on its guard againft that fubtle, infinuating, and corrofive paffion, hatred againft all whofe opinions are oppofite to our own. Johnfon profeffed, in one of his letters, to love a good hater; and in the Latin correfpondence of Milton, there are words that imply a fimilarity of fentiment; they both thought there might be a fanctified bitternefs, to ufe an expreffion of Milton, towards political and religious opponents; yet furely thefe two devout men were both wrong, and both in fome degree unchriftian in this principle. To what singular iniquities of judgment such a principle may lead, we might, perhaps, have had a most striking, and a double proof, had it been possible for these two energetic writers to exhibit alternately a portrait of each other. Milton, adorned with every graceful endowment, highly and holily accomplished. as he was, appears, in the dark coloring of Johnson, a most unamiable being; but could he revisit earth in his mortal character, with a wish to retaliate, what a picture might be drawn, by that sublime and offended genius, of the great moralist, who has treated him with such excess of asperity. The passions are powerful colorists, and marvellous adepts in the art of exaggeration; but the portraits executed by love (famous as he is for overcharging them) are infinitely more faithful to nature, than gloomy sketches from the heavy hand of hatred; a passion not to be trusted or indulged even in minds of the highest purity or power; since hatred, though it may enter the field of contest under the banner of justice, yet generally becomes so blind and outrageous, from the heat of contention, as to execute, in the name of virtue, the worst purposes of vice : Hence arises that species of calumny the most to be regretted, the calumny lavished by men of talents and worth on their equals or superiors, whom they have rashly and blindly hated for a difference of opinion. To such hatred the fervid and opposite characters, who gave rife to this obfervation, were both more inclined, perhaps, by nature and by habit, than chriftianity can allow. The freedom of thefe remarks on two very great, and equally devout, though different writers, may poffibly offend the partifans of both : in that cafe my confolation will be, that I have endeavoured to fpeak of them with that temperate, though undaunted fincerity, which may fatisfy the fpirit of each in a purer ftate of exiftence. There is one characteriftic of Milton, which ought to be confidered as the chief fource of his happinefs and his fame; I mean his early and perpetual attachment to religion. It muft gratify every Chriftian to reflect, that the man of our country moft eminent for energy of mind, for intenfenefs of application, and for franknefs and intrepidity in afferting whatever he believed to be the caufe of truth, was fo confirmedly devoted to chriftianity, that he feems to have made the Bible, not only the rule of his conduct, but the prime director of his genius. His poetry flowed from the fcripture, as if his unparalleled poetical powers had been exprefsly given him by Heaven for the purpofe of imparting to religion fuch luftre as the moft fplendid of human faculties could beftow. As in the Paradife Loft he feems to emulate the fublimity of Mofes and the prophets, it appears to have been his wifh, in the Paradife Regained, to copy the fweetnefs and fimplicity of the milder evangelifts. If the futile remarks that were made upon the latter work, on its firſt appearance, excitd the ſpleen of the great author, he would probably have felt ſtill more indignant, could he have ſeen the comment of Warburton. That diſguſting writer, whoſe critical dictates form a fantaſtic medley of arrogance, acuteneſs, and abſurdity, has aſſerted, that the plan of Paradiſe Regained is very unhappy, and that nothing was eaſier than to have invented a good one.

Much idle cenſure ſeems to have been thrown on more than one of Milton's poetical works, from want of due attention to the chief aim of the poet : — if we fairly conſider it in regard to Paradiſe Regained, the aim I allude to, as it probably occaſioned, will completely juſtify, the plan which the preſumptuous critic has ſo ſuperciliouſly condemned. Milton had already executed one extenſive divine poem, peculiarly diſtinguiſhed by richneſs and ſublimity of deſcription; in framing a ſecond, he would naturally wiſh to vary its effect; to make it rich in moral ſentiment, and ſublime in its mode of unfolding the higheſt wiſdom that man can learn; for this purpoſe it was neceſſary to keep all the ornamental parts of the poem in due ſubordination to the preceptive. This delicate and difficult point is accompliſhed with ſuch felicity, they are blended together with ſuch exquiſite harmony and mutual aid, that inſtead of arraigning the plan, we might rather doubt if any poſſible change could improve it; aſſuredly, there is no poem of epic form, where the fublimeft moral inftruction is fo forcibly and abundantly united to poetical delight : the fplendor of the poet does not blaze, indeed, fo intenfely as in his larger production; here he refembles the Apollo of Ovid, foftening his glory in fpeaking to his fon, and avoiding to dazzle the fancy, that he may defcend into the heart. His dignity is not impaired by his tendernefs. The Paradife Regained is a poem, that deferves to be peculiarly recommended to ardent and ingenuous youth, as it is admirably calculated to infpire that fpirit of felf-command, which is, as Milton efteemed it, the trueft heroifm, and the triumph of chriftianity.

It is not my intention to enter into a critical analyfis of the beauties and the blemifhes that are vifible in the poetry of Milton, not only becaufe Addifon and Johnfon have both written admirably on his greateft work, but becaufe my moft excellent friend, the poet (whofe fpirit I efteem moft congenial to that of Milton) is engaged in fuch illuftration of his honored predeceffor; I fhall therefore confine myfelf to a fingle effay, detached from this narrative, under the title of " Conjectures on the Origin of the Paradife Loft."

I muft not, however, omit to fpeak here, as I have engaged to do, of the character beftowed by Johnfon on the principal performance of the poet; the greateft part of that character is, perhaps, the moft fplendid tribute that was ever paid by one powerful mind to another. Ariftotle, Longinus, and Quintilian, have not fpoken of their favorite Homer with more magnificence of praife; yet the character, taken altogether, is a golden image, that has lower parts of iron and of clay. The critic feems to prepare a diadem of the richeft jewels; he places them, moft liberally, on the head of the poet; but in the moment of adjufting his radiant gift, he breathes upon it fuch a vapor of fpleen, as almoft annihilates its luftre.

After difplaying, in the nobleft manner, many of the peculiar excellencies in the poem, he fays, " its perufal is a duty rather than a pleafure; we read Milton for inftruction, retire haraffed and overburdened, and look elfewhere for recreation; we defert our mafter, and feek for companions."

Injurious as thefe remarks are to the poet, let us afcribe them, not to the virulence of intended detraction, but to the want of poetical fenfibility in the critic; a want that may be fufficiently proved, by comparing this account of the effect produced by Paradife Loft on his own feelings with its effect on a fpirit truly poetical. That enchanting poem, The Tafk, very happily furnifhes fuch an illuftration; it is thus that a mind attuned by nature to poetry defcribes the effect in queftion, as produced even in childhood.

Then Milton had indeed a poet's charms
New to my tafte; his Paradife furpaffed

> The ftruggling efforts of my boyifh tongue
> To fpeak its excellence : I danc'd for joy."

But the little delight that Johnfon confeffes himfelf to have taken in the poetry of Milton was rather his misfortune than his fault; it merits pity more than reproach, as it partly arofe from conftitutional infelicity, and the very wide difference between the native turn of his mind and that of the poet : never were two fpirits lefs congenial, or two chriftian fcholars, who differed more completely in their fentiments of poetry, politics, and religion. In temperament, as well as in opinions, they were the reverfe of each other; the one was fanguine to excefs, the other melancholy in the extreme. Milton

> " Might fit in the centre and enjoy bright day;"

but Johnfon,

> " Benighted walk'd under the mid-day fun;
> " Himfelf was his own dungeon."

Such was the great contraft between thefe two extraordinary men, that although they were both equally fincere in their attachment to chriftianity, and both diftinguifhed by noble intellectual exertions in the fervice of mankind, the critic was naturally difqualified from being a fair and a perfect judge of the poet. My regard for a departed and meritorious writer (of great powers, but conſtitutionally unhappy) is ſuch, that I would rather aſcribe to any cauſe, than to mere envious malignity, his outrages againſt the poetical glory of Milton, which from the force and celebrity of the very admirable but too auſtere work that contains them, it becomes the duty of a more recent biographer to expoſe.

For example, when Johnſon ſays that Milton "wrote no language, but formed a Babyloniſh dialefl, harſh and barbarous," though it would be difficult to pronounce a critical cenſure more bitter or more injurious, we may impute it, not to a malevolent deſire of depreciating the poet, but to a natural want of ear for that harmony, which the critic condemns as diſcord. On this article, the moſt harmonious of our bards has been very happily vindicated by men of ſcience and taſte. Dr. Foſter and Lord Monboddo have ſhown Milton to be one of the moſt conſummate artificers of language, that ever gave either energy or grace to words; and Mr. Loft, in the preface to his recent edition of Paradiſe Loſt, deſcribes the majeſtic flow of his numbers with ſuch truth and eloquence, as render ample juſtice to the inſulted dignity of the poet.

The inſult, groſs as it may be thought, loſes much of its force when we recollefl the inconſiſtency of the critic, who, though in his latter work he condemns the language of Milton as harſh and barbarous, had before obſerved, with more truth, in the Rambler, that the poet " excelled as much in the lower as in the higher parts of his art, and that his ſkill in harmony was not leſs than his invention or his learning;" but the praiſe as well as the cenſure of Johnſon, on this article, could not be the reſult of perfect perception, for the monotony of his own blank verſe, and ſome of his remarks in the Rambler on particular lines of Milton, are ſtriking proofs, that although he was a melodious writer himſelf in the common meaſures of rhyme, and in dignified proſe, yet he never entered with perfect intelligence and feeling into the muſical graces of Miltonic compoſition; he was, indeed, as far from enjoying the poet's ear for the varied modulation and extenſive compaſs of metrical harmony, as he was from poſſeſſing the mild elegance of his manners, or the cheerful elevation of his mind.

There is a ſtriking reſemblance between the poetical and the moral character of Milton; they were both the reſult of the fineſt diſpoſitions for the attainment of excellence that nature could beſtow, and of all the advantages that ardor and perſeverance in ſtudy and diſcipline could add, in a long courſe of years, to the beneficent prodigality of nature : even in infancy he diſcovered a paſſion for glory; in youth he was attached to temperance; and, arriving at manhood, he formed the magnanimous deſign of building a lofty name upon the moſt ſolid and ſecure foundation.

> —— " He all his ſtudy bent
> To worſhip God aright, and know his works
> Not hid; nor thoſe things laſt that might preſerve
> Freedom and peace to men.

In a noble conſciouſneſs of his powers and intentions, he was not afraid to give, in his early life, a moſt ſingular promiſe to his country of producing ſuch future works as might redound to her glory; and though ſuch perſonal calamities fell upon him, as might fairly have abſolved him from that engagement, yet never was any promiſe more magnificently fulfilled. Seneca has conſidered a man of reſolution ſtruggling with adverſity as a ſpectacle worthy of God; our reſolute countryman not only ſtruggled with adverſity, but, under a peculiar load of complicated calamities, he accompliſhed thoſe works, that are juſtly reckoned among the nobleſt offſpring of human genius. In this point of view, with what pathetic grandeur is the poet inveſted. In contemplating the variety of his ſufferings, and his various mental achievements, we may declare, without any extravagance of praiſe, that although ſublimity is the predominant characteriſtic of Milton's poem, his own perſonal character is ſtill more ſublime.

His majeſtic pre eminence is nobly deſcribed in the following verſes of Akenſide, a poet who bore ſome affinity to Milton in the ardor of his mind, whoſe ſentiments are always noble, though not always accompanied by a graceful felicity of .expreffion.

> Mark hòw the dread Pantheon ftands
> Amid the domes of modern han's,
> Amid the toys of idle ftate.
> How fimply, how feverely great!
> Then turn, and while each weftern clime
> Prefents her tuneful fons to time,
> So mark thou MILTON'S name,
> And add, thus differs from the thiong
> The fpirit which inform'd thy awful fong,
> Which bade thy potent voice piotect thy country's
> fame.

The powers of Milton, indeed, are fo irrefiftible, that even thofe, whom the blindnefs of prejudice has rendered his enemies, are conftrained to regard him as an object of admiration. In this article pofterity, to whom he made a very interefting appeal, has done him ample juftice; ftill he is more admired than beloved; yet in granting him only admiration, we ungeneroufly withhold the richeft half of that pofthumous reward for which he labored fo fervently: we may be confident that he rather wifhed to excite the affection than the applaufe of mankind; and affuredly he has the nobleft title to both, the title of having exerted fuperlative genius and literary ambition, under the conftant influence of religious philantropy. In proportion as our country has advanced in purity of tafte, fhe has applauded the poet; and in proportion as fhe advances in liberality of fentiment, fhe will love the man; but love in this afpect is more volatile than admiration, and a beneficent genius may be eafily deprived of it by the detraction of an enemy, or the miftake of a friend: Milton has fuffered not a little from both; and indeed, if one fingular miftake of his friends fhould prevail, he could hardly become an object of general affection. What votary of the Mufes could love a poet, however excellent in that capacity, who reprefented it as a crime in a captive monarch to have made the poetry of Shakefpeare the companion of his folitude? Credulity has imagined that Milton was fuch a barbarous Goth. Nor is this the fuggeftion of his enemies; even Warton, the liberal defender of his poetical reputation, and feveral living writers of eminence, have lavifhed their cenfures on Milton, from a too hafty belief, that puritanical prejudices had hurried him into this rancorous abfurdity.

Their cenfures are all founded on a miftake; but the merit of correcting it belongs not to me; Mr. Waldron, the fenfible and modeft editor of a mifcellany, entitled, The Literary Mufeum, in a note to Rofcius Anglicanus, has, in a very liberal manner, collected and refuted the charges againft Milton on this point, and abundantly proved, that inftead of cenfuring the unfortunate Charles for amufing himfelf with Shakefpeare, he only cenfured him for imitating the religious hypocrify of Richard the Third fo clofely as to utter the very fentiments that are affigned to Richard in the page of the dramatic poet.

Milton, undoubtedly thought, what an ardent political writer of the prefent age has not fcrupled to affert, that " Charles the Firft lived and died an hypocrite." Thefe two acute judges of mankind were, I believe, miftaken in this idea : it feems more probable, that this unfortunate prince was flattered into a perfuafion, that he was really the meritorious martyr his adherents endeavoured to reprefent him. But whatfoever his genuine character might be, the fevere fentiments which Milton entertained of the king, and the delufive hopes that he cherifhed of the protector, had equally their fource in the virtuous ardor of his own fpirit. The confcioufnefs of his integrity, when time had fully unveiled to him fome illufions, gave that tranquillity and vigor to his declining days, which enabled him to produce his aftonifhing poems, not more aftonifhing for their intrinfic merit, than for the period of their production ; fo that his poetry, in this point of view, may be regarded both as the offspring and the witnefs of his virtue. The world had never been enriched with his two poems on Paradife, if their great author, when he was, according to his own true and pathetic defcription,

" In darknefs and with dangers compafs'd round. "

had not, in fome little degree, refembled the hero
of his latter poem, and like that hallowed perfonage, whom he delineates fo divinely, amid
the darknefs and the fiends of the defert,

" Sat unappall'd in calm and finlefs peace. "

Yet to fuch mifreprefentations has the life and
the poetry of Milton been expofed, that both
have been confidered as too auftere to be amiable,
though. affuredly, both in the one, and the other,
the moft engaging qualities are admirably united
to the moft aweful—the graceful and the tender:
to the grand and the fublime.

The attractions of his mufe have triumphed:
over obloquy, and in the eftimation of the,
world fhe is juftly thought to refemble. the enchanting Eve of the poet,

——— Adorn'd
With what all earth or heav'n could beftow
To make her amiable.

But equal juftice has not hitherto been rendered to the perfonal virtues of the author; it
has, therefore, been my chief aim, in a delineation of his life, to make Milton rather more
beloved than more admired; and I may the more
reafonably hope to fucceed in that idea, becaufe,
though I have never been attached to his political opinions, yet, in proportion to my refearches into his character as a man, he has advanced
in my efteem and my affection.

I lament that the neceffity of inveftigating many mifreprefentations, and of correcting much afperity againft him, has frequently obliged me to fpeak rather in the tone of an advocate, than of a common biographer; but I may fay, in the words of the great Roman author, pleading the caufe of a poet infinitely lefs entitled to love and admiration; *Hunc ego non diligam, non admirer, non omni ratione defendendum putem? Atque fic a fummis hominibus eruditiffimifque accepimus, cæterarum rerum ftudia & doctrina, & præceptis, & arte conftare; poetam naturâ ipfa valere, & mentis viribus excitari, & quafi divino quodam fpiritu afflari*—if poetical powers may ever deferve to be regarded as heavenly infpiration, fuch undoubtedly were thofe of Milton, and the ufe to which he applied them was worthy of the fountain whence they flowed. He is pre-eminent in that clafs of poets, very happily defcribed in the two following verfes by the amiable lord Falkland;

> Who, while of heav'n the glories they recite,
> Find it within, and feel the joys they write.

It is by the epic compofitions of Milton alone that England may efteem herfelf as a rival to antiquity in the higheft province of literature; and it appears therefore juft, that the memory of the man, to whom fhe is indebted for the pureft, the moft extenfive, and permanent glory, fhould for ever excite her affectionate veneration.

CONJECTURES

CONJECTURES

ON THE

ORIGIN

OF THE

PARADISE LOST.

CONJECTURES, &c.

⸺

To write an Epic Poem was the prime object of MILTON's ambition at an early period of life; a paffionate attachment to his country made him firft think of celebrating its ancient heroes; but in the long interval between the dawn of fuch a project in his thoughts, and the commencement of his work, a new train of images got poffeffion of his fancy; Arthur yielded to Adam, and England to Paradife.

To confider what various caufes might confpire to produce this revolution in the ideas of the great poet may be a pleafing fpeculation, if it is purfued with due refpect to the noble mind that it afpires to examine.

An inveftigation of a fimilar nature was undertaken fome years ago, upon very different principles, when a fingular attempt was made to annihilate the poetical glory of Milton, by proving him a plagiary. This attempt was fo extraordinary in its nature, and in its end fo honorable to the poet and his country, that a brief account of it fhould, I think, be annexed to the Life of Milton; whofe admirers may fay, on that occafion, to the flanderers of genius,

"Difcite juftitiam moniti, & non temnere divos."

I fhall give, therefore, a fketch of the literary tranfactions to which I allude, as an introduction to thofe conjectures, that a long and affectionate attachment to Milton has led me to form, concerning the origin of his greateft work.

In 1746, William Lauder, an unfortunate adventurer, whom a furious temper, confiderable learning, and greater indigence, converted into an audacious impoftor, attacked the originality of the chief Englifh poet. Having afferted, in a periodical mifcellany, that Milton had borrowed all his ideas from the juvenile work of Grotius, or from other lefs known writers of Latin verfe, and finding the novelty of his charge attract the attention of the public, he endeavoured to enforce it in a pamphlet, entitled, " An Effay on Milton's Ufe and Imitation of the Moderns," printed in 1750, and addreffed to the two univerfities of Oxford and Cambridge. In the clofe of this effay he fcrupled not to fay of Milton :

" His induftrious concealment of his helps,
" his peremptory difclaiming all manner of af-
" fiftance, is highly ungenerous, nay criminal
" to the laft degree, and abfolutely unworthy of

" any man of common probity and honor. By
" this mean practice, indeed, he has acquired
" the title of the Britiſh Homer, nay, has been.
" preferred to Homer and Virgil both, and con-
" ſequently to every other poet of every age and
" nation. Cowley, Waller, Denham, Dryden,
" Prior, Pope, in compariſon with Milton,
" have borne no greater proportion, than that
" of dwarfs to a giant, who, now he is reduced
" to his true ſtandard, appears mortal and
" uninſpired, and in ability little ſuperior to the
" poets above-mentioned, but in honeſty and
" open dealing, the beſt quality of the human
" mind, not inferior, perhaps, to the moſt un-
" licenſed plagiary that ever wrote."

In a publication, containing *ſuch language*,
Lauder was able to engage the great critic and
moraliſt, Samuel Johnſon, as his confederate;
for the preface and poſtſcript to the Eſſay, from
which the preceding paragraph is cited, are con-
feſſedly the compoſition of that elaborate and
nervous writer.

This confederacy, unbecoming as it may at
firſt appear, will, on candid reflection, ſeem
rather a credit than a diſgrace to Johnſon; for
we certainly ought to believe that the primary
motive, which prompted him to the aſſiſtance
of Lauder, was that true and noble compaſſion
for indigence, which made him through life ſo
generouſly willing to afford all the aid in his
power to literary mendicants; but in rendering

juftice to that laudable charity, which he conftantly exercifed to the neceffitous , we cannot
fail to obferve, that his malevolent prejudices
againft Milton were equally vifible on this fignal
occafion. Had he not been under the influence
of fuch prejudice, could his ftrong underftanding
have failed to point out to his affociate, what
a liberal monitor very juftly obferved to Lauder,
in convicting him of fraud and falfhood, that,
allowing his facts to have been true, his inference from them was unfair. Lauder, with an
unexampled audacity of impofture, had corrupt-
ed the text of the poets, whom he produced
as evidence againft Milton, by interpolating feveral verfes, which he had taken from a neglected
Latin tranflation of the Paradife Loft. Expecting
probably to efcape both difcovery and fufpicion by
the daring novelty of his deception, and the mental
dignity of his patron and coadjutor, he exulted in
the idea of blafting the laurels of Milton; but thofe
laurels were proof, indeed, againft the furious and
repeated flafhes of malevolence and hoftility. More
than one defence of the injured poet appeared; the
firft, I believe, was a pamphlet by Mr. Richardfon, of Clare Hall, printed in 1747, and entitled Zoilomaftix, or, a Vindication of Milton,
confifting of letters inferted in the mifcellany,
where the charge of Lauder had made its firft
appearance; but the complete overthrow of that
impoftor was accomplifhed by Dr. Douglas, the
prefent bifhop of Salifbury, who publifhed, in

1750, a letter addreſſed to Lord Bath, with the title of "Milton vindicated from the Charge of Plagiariſm;" a performance that, in many points of view, may be regarded as a real honor to literature—it unites what we find very rarely united in literary contention, great modeſty with great fervor; and magnanimous moderation with the ſeverity of vindictive juſtice. The author ſpeaks with amiable liberality of Mr. Bowle, in ſaying, " that gentleman had firſt collected " materials for an anſwer to Lauder, " and " has the juſteſt claim to the honor of being " the original detector of this ungenerous critic." The writer of this valuable pamphlet gave alſo an admonition to Johnſon, which breathes the manly ſpirit of intelligence, of juſtice, and of candor. " It is to be hoped (he ſaid) nay it is " to be expected, that the elegant and nervous· " writer, whoſe judicious ſentiments and inimi- " table ſtyle point out the author of Lauder's " preface and poſtſcript, will no longer allow " one to plume himſelf with his feathers, who " appeareth ſo little to have deſerved his aſſiſt- " ance; an aſſiſtance which, I am perſuaded, " would never have been communicated had " there been the leaſt ſuſpicion of thoſe facts, " which I have been the inſtrument of con- " veying to the world in theſe ſheets, a peruſal " of which will ſatisfy our critic, who was plea- " ſed to ſubmit his book to the judgment of the " two univerſities, that it has been examined

" and carefully read at leaft by fome members
" of the univerfity of. Oxford." The defence of
Milton, which I have mentioned, by Mr. Richardfon, proves alfo, for the honor of Cambridge,
that *her men of letters* were by no means deficient in fuch regard, as they peculiarly owe to
the reputation of the poet, who " flames in the
van" of the poetical hoft, which has contributed
to her renown.

When the pamphlet of Dr. Douglas had completely unveiled the moft impudent of literary
frauds, Johnfon, whom his prejudice againft
Milton could no longer render blind to the un-
worthinefs of Lauder, recoiled from the wretch
whom he had too creduloufly befriended, and
finding him as deficient in the truth of facts as
he was in propriety of fentiment, and decency
of language, made him addrefs to his antagonift,
who had convicted him of fome forgeries, an
ample avowal of more extenfive fraud, and a
moft humble fupplication for pardon. This ex-
piatory addrefs was dictated by Johnfon, whofe
conduct on the occafion was manly and moral—
but it failed to correct his affociate, for prejudice againft Milton in Lauder arofe almoft to
madnefs; in Johnfon it amounted only to a degree of malevolence, too commonly produced
by political difagreement; it had induced him to
cherifh too eagerly a detractive deception, fabricated to fink an illuftrious character, without
allowing himfelf the due exercife of his keen

underſtanding to inveſtigate its falſhood, or to perceive its abſurdity.   Lauder ſeems to have hoped, for ſome time, that a full confeſſion of his offences would reſtore him to the favor of the public; for in the year 1751 he ventured to publiſh an apology, addreſſed to the Archbiſhop of Canterbury, ſoliciting patronage for his projected edition of the ſcarce Latin authors, from whom he had accuſed Milton of borrowing.   The chief purpoſe of ſo extraordinary an attack on the re-nown of the poet, appears to have been a deſire, prompted by indigence, to intereſt the public in the re-appearance of theſe neglected writers, whom he meant to republiſh.   In cloſing his apology to the Archbiſhop, he ſays, with ſingular confidence:

" As for the interpolations (for which I am ſo
" highly blamed) when paſſion is ſubſided, and
" the minds of men can patiently attend to truth,
" I promiſe amply to replace them, with paſ-
" ſages equivalent in value that are genuine, that
" the public may be convinced that it was ra-
" ther paſſion and reſentment, than a penury of
" evidence, the twentieth part of which has not
" as yet been produced, that obliged me to
" make uſe of them."

He printed the collection of Latin poets as he propoſed, one volume in 1752, and a ſecond in 1753. The book may be regarded as a literary curioſity, but it ſeems to have contributed little to the emolument of its miſerable editor, who had thoroughly awakened univerfal indignation; and as Dr. Douglas obferved, in a poftfcript to his pamphlet, reprinted in 1756, " The curiofity " of the public to fee any of thefe poems was " at an end; the only thing which had ftamped " a value upon them, was a fuppofition that Mil- " ton had thought them worthy of his imitation. " As therefore it now appeared, by the detection " of Lauder's fyftem of forgery, that Milton had " not imitated them, it is no wonder that the " defign of reprinting them fhould meet with " little or no fuccefs."

The affertion of this learned and amiable writer, that Milton had not imitated thefe poets, is not to be underftood in a ftrict and liberal fenfe; for affuredly there are paffages in fome of them that Milton may be fairly fuppofed to have copied, though his obligations to thefe Latin poets are very far from being confiderable; and had they been infinitely greater, the inference drawn by the malevolent reviler of Milton would ftill have been prepofteroufly fevere.

The detected flanderer was foon overwhelmed with the utter contempt he deferved; but, contemptible as he was, the memory of his offences and of his punifhment ought to be preferved, not fo much for the honor of Milton, as for the general intereft of literature, that if the world can produce a fecond Lauder, he may not hope for impunity,

Part of his fubfequent hiftory is related in the following words by Dr. Douglas:

"Grown defperate by his difappointment, this "very man, whom but a little before we have feen "as abject in the confeflion of his forgeries, as he "had been bold in the contrivance of them, with "an inconfiftence, equalled only by his impu- "dence, renewed his attack upon the author "of the Paradife Loft, and in a pamphlet, pub- "lifhed for that purpofe, acquainted the world, "that the true reafon which had excited him "to contrive his forgery was, becaufe Milton "had attacked the character of Charles the Firft, "by interpolating Pamela's prayer from the Ar- "cadia, in an Edition of the Eicon Bafilike; "hoping, no doubt, by this curious key to his "conduct, to be received into favor, if not by "the friends of truth, at leaft by the idolaters "of the royal martyr—the zeal of this wild party- "man againft Milton having at the fame time "extended itfelf againft his biographer, the very "learned Dr. Birch, for no other reafon but "becaufe he was fo candid as to exprefs his "difbelief of a tradition unfupported by evi- "dence."

Were it requifite to give new force to the many proofs of that malignant prejudice againft Milton in a late writer, which I have had too frequent occafion to examine and regret, fuch force might be drawn from the words juft cited from Dr. Douglas. That gentleman here informs us, that Lauder directed his intemperate zeal againſt Dr. Birch, for rejecting the ill-ſupported ſtory that repreſented Milton as an impoſtor, concerned in forging the remarkable prayer of the king. Yet Johnſon ungenerouſly labored to fix this ſuſpicion of diſhoneſty on the great cha-racter whoſe life he delineated, by inſinuating that Dr. Birch believed the very ſtory, which Lauder reviled him for having candidly rejected. Is it not too evident from this circumſtance, that Lauder's intemperate hatred of Milton had in ſome degree infected his noble coadjutor? though he very juſtly diſcarded that impoſtor, when con-victed of forgery, after writing for him a ſuppli-catory confeſſion of his fraud, for which he was afterwards cenſured by the half-frantic offender, who, finding that it procured him no favor from the public, declared it infinitely too general and too abject for the occaſion.

The malevolence of Johnſon towards the great poet has been repreſented as a mere fiction of party rage, acrimoniouſly reviling an illuſtrious biographer: but inſtead of being an injurious fiction of that evil ſpirit, it is a reality univerſally felt, and ſincerily lamented by thoſe lovers of literature, who, being exempt from all party rage themſelves, would willingly annihilate the influence of that inſidious foe to truth and juſtice in the republic of letters. It ſhould afford us an antidote againſt the poiſon of party rage in all literary diſcuſſions, to obſerve, that by indulging it, a very ftrong and a very devout mind was hurried into the want of clear moral perception, and of true Chriftian charity, in defcribing the conduct, and in fcrutinizing the motives, of Milton. It feems as if the good angel of this extraordinary poet had determined that his poetical renown fhould pafs (like his virtue and his genius) through trials moft wonderfully adapted to give it luftre; and hence (as imagination at leaft may pleafe itfelf in fuppofing) hence might fuch enemies be combined againft him, as the world, perhaps, never faw before in a fimilar confederacy. A bafe artificer of falfhood, and a magnanimous teacher of moral philofophy, united in a wild endeavour to diminifh his reputation; but, like the rafh affailants of Jupiter, in the fables of paganifm, they only confirmed the pre-eminence they attacked with prepofterous temerity. The philofopher, indeed, made an honorable retreat; and no candid mind will feverely cenfure him for an ill-ftarred alliance, which however clouded by prejudice, he might originally form in compaffion to indigence, and which he certainly ended by rejection of impofture.

The miferable Lauder was punifhed by events fo calamitous, that even thofe admirers of Milton, who are moft offended by the enormity of the fraud, muft wifh that penitence and amendment had fecured to this unhappy being, who feems to have poffeffed confiderable fcholarfhip, a milder deftiny. Finding himfelf unable to ftruggle with public odium in this country, he fought an afylum in the Weft Indies, and there died, an indigent outcaft, and a memorable example, how dangerous it is to incur the indignation of mankind, by bafe devices to blaft the reputation of departed genius. — May his wretched cataftrophe preferve the literary world from being difhonored again by artifice fo deteftable!

I have faid, that the collection he publifhed of Latin poets is entitled to fome regard as a literary curiofity: and it may here be proper to enumerate the authors comprifed in that collection. The firft volume contains the Poemata Sacra of Andrew Ramfay, from a copy printed at Edinburgh, 1633; and the Adamus Exul of Grotius, from the edition of the Hague, 1601. In the fecond volume we have the Sarcotis of Mafenius, from the edition of Cologne, 1644, omitting the 4th and 5th books, which may be found in a copy of the Sarcotis printed at Paris, by Barbou, 1771: the firft book of Dæmonomachia, a poem by Odoricus Valmarana, printed at Vienna, in 25 books, 1627 : Paradifus Jacobi Catfii, a celebrated Dutch poet—the Paradife of Catfius is a fpirited and graceful epithalamium on the nuptials of Adam and Eve, originally written in the native language of the author; this Latin verfion of it was executed by the learned Barlæus, and firft printed in 1643 : Bellum Angelicum, Auctore Frederico Taubmanno; a poem, confifting of two books, and a fragment of a third, originally printed in 1604.

Lauder, in publishing this collection of curious Latin verse, has occasionally seasoned it with remarks of his own, both in Latin and English —the tenor of them has a great tendency to confirm the apology, with which Johnson excused the implicit and hasty credit that he gave to the gross forgeries of the impostor : " He " thought the man too frantic to be fraudulent." The language used by Lauder, in the publication I am speaking of, shows indeed that the contemptuous abhorrence, which this unhappy scholar had conceived of Milton, really bordered upon insanity. Without pointing to any particular instances of plagiarism, he bestows on the poet the extraordinary title of the arch felon; and inserts a singular epigram, written by a servile foreigner, to prove Milton an atheist. Not contented with reviling the great author himself, he extends the virulent attack to his nephew Philips, whom he accuses of having favored, by a suspicious silence, the secret practice of his uncle, in rifling the treasures of others, " Phi-" lips (says Lauder) every where in his 'Thea-" trum Poetarum,' either wholly passes over in " silence such authors as Milton was most obliged " to, or, if he chances to mention them, does it " in the most slight and superficial manner ima-" ginable."

There is fome acutenefs, and more truth, in this obfervation concerning Philips, than Lauder was himfelf aware of. Though Milton was indeed no plagiary, and his nephew of courfe had no thefts to conceal, it is very remarkable that Philips, giving an account of poets in all languages, omits fuch of their works as were built on fubjects refembling thofe of his uncle. This omiffion is not only ftriking in the brief account he gives of the Latin poets collected by Lauder; it extends to fome Italian writers, of whom I fhall prefently have occafion to fpeak more at large. Let me firft obferve, in apology for the omiffions of Philips, which are too frequent to be confidered as accidental, that he probably chofe not to enumerate various poems relating to angels, to Adam, and to Paradife, left ignorance and malice fhould abfurdly confider the mere exiftence of fuch poetry as a derogation from the glory of Milton. That Philips had himfelf no inconfiderable fhare of poetical tafte, and that he was laudably zealous for the honor of his uncle, appears, I think, from the following remarks, which I tranfcribe with pleafure, from his preface to the little book I am fpeaking of, as they feem to contain an oblique and graceful compliment to his renowned relation:—" A poetical " fancy is much feen in a choice of verfe proper " to a chofen fubject.

" Wit, ingenuity, and learning in verfe, even " elegance itfelf, though that comes neareft, are " one

" one thing, true native poetry is another, in
" which there is a certain air and fpirit, which,
" perhaps, the moft learned and judicious in
" other arts do not perfectly apprehend, much
" lefs is it attainable by any ftudy or induftry."

This certain air and fpirit are affuredly moft
confpicuous in Milton : he was a poet of nature's
creation, but one who added to all her endowments every advantage that ftudy could acquire.

By the force and opulence of his own fancy
he was exempted from the inclination and the
neceffity of borrowing and retailing the ideas of
other poets ; but, rich as he was in his own
proper fund, he chofe to be perfectly acquainted,
not only with the wealth, but even with the
poverty of others. He feems to have read, in
different languages, authors of every clafs; and I
doubt not but he had perufed every poem collected by Lauder, though fome of them hardly
afford ground enough for a conjecture, that he
remembered any paffage they contain, in the
courfe of his nobler compofition. Johnfon, in
his preface to Lauder's pamphlet, reprefents the
Adamus Exul of Grotius as " the firft draught,
" the *prima ftamina* of the Paradife Loft." The
fame critic obferves, in touching on this fubject,
in his life of Milton— " Whence he drew the
" original defign has been varioufly conjectured
" by men, who cannot bear to think themfelves
" ignorant of that, which, at laft, neither dili-
" gence nor fagacity can difcover. Some find

" the hint in an Italian tragedy. Voltaire tells
" a wild, unauthorized ftory of a farce feen by
" Milton in Italy, which opened thus: ' Let
" the rainbow be the fiddle-ftick of the fiddle
" of heaven'."

The critic was perfectly right in relinquifhing
his former idea concerning the Adamus Exul of
Grotius; but, in his remark on Voltaire, he
fhows how dangerous it is to cenfure any writer
for what he fays concerning books, which the
cenfurer has no opportunity of examining. Voltaire, indeed, from his predominant paffion for
ridicule, and from the rafh vivacity, that often
led him to fpeak too confidently of various works
from a very flight infpection of their contents,
is no more to be followed implicitly in points
of criticifm, than he is on the more important
article of religion : but his opinions in literature
are generally worth examination, as he poffeffed
no common degree of tafte, a perpetual thirft
for univerfal knowledge, and though not the
moft intimate, yet, perhaps, the moft extenfive
acquaintance with literary works and literary men
that was ever acquired by any individual.

When Voltaire vifited England in the early
part of his life, and was engaged in foliciting a
fubfcription for his Henriade, which firft appeared
under the title of " The League," he publifhed,
in our language, an Effay on Epic Poetry, a
work which, though written under fuch difad-
vantage, poffeffes the peculiar vivacity of this

extraordinary writer, and is indeed fo curious a
fpecimen of his verfatile talents, that although
it has been fuperfeded by a French compofition
of greater extent, under the fame title, it ought,
I think, to have found a place in that fignal monument to the name of Voltaire, the edition of
his works in ninety-two volumes.

As my reader may be gratified in feeing the
Englifh ftyle of this celebrated foreigner, I will
tranfcribe, without abridgment, what he fays of
Andreini :

" Milton, as he was travelling through Italy
" in his youth, faw at Florence a comedy called
" Adamo, writ by one Andreini, a player, and
" dedicated to Mary de Medicis, Queen of France.
" The fubject of the play was the Fall of Man;
" the actors, God, the devils, the angels, Adam,
" Eve, the Serpent, Death, and the feven mor-
" tal fins : that topic, fo improper for a drama,
" but fo fuitable to the abfurd genius of the Ita-
" lian ftage (as it was at that time) was handled
" in a manner entirely conformable to the ex-
" travagance of the defign.   The fcene opens
" with a chorus of angels, and a cherubim thus
" fpeaks for the reft :—' Let the rainbow be the
" fiddle-ftick of the fiddle of the heavens ! let
" the planets be the notes of our mufic ! let time
" beat carefully the meafure, and the winds
" make the fharps, &c. Thus the play begins,

and every scene rifes above the laft in profufion of impertinence.

" Milton pierced through the abfurdity of that
" performance to the hidden majefty of the
" fubject, which, being altogether unfit for the
" ftage, yet might be (for the genius of Milton,
" and for his only) the foundation of an epic
" poem.

" He took from that ridiculous trifle the firft
" hint of the nobleft work, which human ima-
" gination has ever attempted, and which he
" executed more than twenty years after.

" In the like manner, Pythagoras owed the
" invention of mufic to the noife of the ham-
" mer of a Blackfmith; and thus, in our days,
" Sir Ifaac Newton, walking in his garden, had
" the firft thought of his fyftem of gravitation
" upon feeing an apple falling from a tree. "

It was thus that, in the year 1727, Voltaire, then ftudying in England, and collecting all poffible information concerning our great epic poet, accounted for the origin of Paradife Loft. Rolli, another foreign ftudent in epic poetry, who refided at that time in London, and was engaged in tranflating Milton into Italian verfe, publifhed fome fevere cenfures, in Englifh, on the Englifh effay of Voltaire, to vindicate both Taffo and Milton from certain ftrictures of farcaftic raillery, which the volatile Frenchman had lavifhed upon both. Voltaire, indeed, has fallen himfelf into the very inconfiftency, which he

mentions as unaccountable in Dryden; I mean
the inconfiftency of fometimes praifing Milton
with fuch admiration as approaches to idolatry,
and fometimes reproving him with fuch keennefs
of ridicule as borders on contempt. In the
courfe of this difcuffion we may find, perhaps,
a mode of accounting for the inconfiftency both
of Dryden and Voltaire; let us attend at prefent
to what the latter has faid of Andreini!—If the
Adamo of this author really gave birth to the
divine poem of Milton, the Italian dramatift,
whatever rank he might hold in his own country, has a fingular claim to our attention and
regard. Johnfon indeed calls the report of Voltaire a wild and unauthorized ftory; and Rolli
afferts, in reply to it, that if Milton faw the
Italian Drama, it muft have been at Milan, as
the Adamo, in his opinion, was a performance
too contemptible to be endured at Florence.
" Adreini (fays the critic of Italy) was a ftroller
(un iftrione) of the worft age of the Italian letters." Notwithftanding thefe terms of contempt,
which one of his countrymen has beftowed upon
Andreini, he appears to me highly worthy of
our notice; (for although in uniting, like Shakfpeare and Moliere, the two different arts of
writing and of acting plays, he difcovered not
fuch extraordinary powers as have juftly immortalized thofe idols of the theatre) he was yet en-
dowed with one quality, not only uncommon,
but fuch as might render him, if I may hazard

the expreſſion, the poetical parent of Milton. The quality I mean is, enthuſiaſm in the higheſt degree, not only poetical but religious. Even the preface that Andreini prefixed to his Adamo may be thought ſufficient to have acted like lightning on the inflammable ideas of the Engliſh poet, and to have kindled in his mind the blaze of celeſtial imagination.

I am aware, that in reſearches like the preſent, every conjecture may abound in illuſion; the petty circumſtances, by which great minds are led to the firſt conception of great deſigns, are ſo various and volatile, that nothing can be more difficult to diſcover : fancy in particular is of a nature ſo airy, that the traces of her ſtep are hardly to be diſcerned; ideas are ſo fugitive, that if poets, in their life-time, were queſtioned concerning the manner in which the ſeeds of conſiderable productions firſt aroſe in their mind, they might not always be able to anſwer the inquiry; can it then be poſſible to ſucceed in ſuch an inquiry concerning a mighty genius, who has beeu conſigned more than a century to the tomb, eſpecially when, in the records of his life, we can find no poſitive evidence on the point in queſtion? However trifling the chances it may afford of ſuccefs, the inveſtigation is aſſuredly worthy our purſuit; for, as an accompliſhed critic has ſaid, in ſpeaking of another poet, with his uſual felicity of diſcernment and expreſſion, " the inquiry cannot be void of entertainment

" whilft Milton is our conftant theme : what-
" ever may be the fortune of the chafe, we are
" fure it will lead us through pleafant profpects
" and a fine country."

It has been frequently remarked, that accident
and genius generally confpire in the origin of great
performances; and the accidents that give an impulfe to fancy are often fuch as are hardly within
the reach of conjecture. Had Ellwood himfelf
not recorded the occurrence, who would have
fuppofed that a few words, which fell from a
fimple youth in converfation, were the real fource
of Paradife Regained? Yet the offsprings of imagination, in this point of view, have a ftriking
analogy to the productions of nature. The noble
poem juft mentioned refembles a rare and valua-
ble-tree, not planted with care and forecaft, but
arifing vigoroufly from a kernel dropt by a ram-
bling bird on a fpot of peculiar fertility. We
are perfectly affured that Milton owed one of his
great poems to the ingenuous queftion of a young
quaker; and Voltaire, as we have feen, has afferted, that he was indebted for the other to
the fantaftic drama of an Italian ftroller. It does
not appear that Voltaire had any higher authority for his affertion than his own conjecture from
a flight infpection of the drama, which he haftily
defcribes; yet, it is mere juftice to this rapid
entertaining writer to declare, that in his conjecture there is great probability, which the Englifh reader, I believe, will be inclined to admit,

in proportion as he becomes acquainted with Andreini and his Adamo; but before we examine
their merit, and the degree of influence that we
may fuppofe them to have had on the fancy of
Milton, let us contemplate, in one view, all the
fcattered hints which the great poet has given us
concerning the grand project of his life, his defign
of writing an epic poem.

His firft mention of this defign occurs in the
following verfes of his poetical compliment to
Manfo:

> O mihi fi mea fors talem concedat amicum,
> Phœbæos decoraffe viros qui tam bene norit,
> Si quando indigenas revocabo in carmina reges,
> Arturumque etiam fub terris bella moventem,
> Aut dicam invictæ fociali fœdere menfæ
> Magnanimos heroas; & O modo fpiritus adfit,
> Frangam Saxonicas Britonum fub marte phalanges!

> O might fo true a friend to me belong,
> So fkill'd to grace the votaries of fong,
> Should I recal hereafter into rhyme
> The kings and heroes of my native clime,
> Arthur the chief, who even now prepares
> In fubterraneous being future wars,
> With all his martial knights to be reftor'd,
> Each to his feat around the fed'ral board;
> And, O! if fpirit fail me not, difperfe
> Our Saxon plund'rers in triumphant verfe.

COWPER

Mr. Warton fays, in his comment on this paffage, " it is poffible that the advice of Manfo,
" the friend of Taffo, might determine our poet
" to a defign of this kind." The conjecture of
this refpectable critic may appear confirmed
by the following circumftance : — In the difcourfes on Epic Poetry, which are included in
the profe works of Taffo, Arthur is repeatedly
recommended as a proper hero for a poem. Thus
we find that Italy moft probably fuggefted to Milton his firft epic idea, which he relinquifhed; nor
is it lefs probable that his fecond and more arduous enterprife, which he accomplifhed, was
fuggefted to him by his perufal of Italian authors.
If he faw the Adamo of Andreini reprefented at
Milan, we have reafon to believe that performance did not immediately infpire him with the
project of writing an epic poem on our Firft Parents; becaufe we find that Arthur kept poffeffion
of his fancy after his return to England.

In the following verfes of his Epitaphium Damonis, compofed at that period, he ftill fhows
himfelf attached to romantic heroes, and to
Britifh ftory :

Dicam, & Pandrafidos regnum vetus Inogeniæ,
Brennumque Arviragumque duces, prifcumque Belinum
Et tandem Armoricos Britonum fub lege colonos,
Tum gravidam Arturo, fatali fraude, Iögernen,
Mendaces vultus, affumptaque Gorlöis arma
Merlini dolus.

Of Brutus, Dardan chief, my fong fhall be,
How with his barks he plough'd the Britifh fea;
Firft from Rutupia's tow'ring headland feen,
And of his confort's reign, fair Inogen;
Of Brennus and Belinus, brothers bold,
And of Arviragus; and how of old
Our hardy fires th'Armorican controll'd;
And of the wife of Gorlois who, furpris'd
By Uther in her hufband's form difguis'd,
(Such was the force of Merlin's art) became
Pregnant with Arthur of heroic fame:
Thefe themes I now revolve.

COWPER.

In one of his controverfial works, publifhed in 1641, Milton informs us what poetical ideas were then fluctuating in his mind; particularly " what king or knight before the Conqueft might " be chofen, in whom to lay the pattern of a " chriftian hero." This project of delineating in a hero a model of chriftian perfection, was fuggefted to the Englifh poet, not only by the example, but by the precepts, of Taffo, as they are delivered in his critical difcourfes. The epic defigns of Milton were fufpended, we know, for many years, by very different purfuits; and when he efcaped from " the troubled fea of noife " and hoarfe difpute to the quiet and ftill air of " delighful ftudies," Arthur had fo far ceafed to be his favorite, that he probably exclaimed, in the words of Taffo:

Taccia Artù quei fuoi
Erranti, che di fogni empion le carte.

Arthur no more thy errant knights rehearfe,
Who fill, with idle dreams, delufive verfe.

For Adam now reigned in his fancy, not immediately as the fubject of an epic poem, but as a
capital perfonage in the plan of a dramatic compofition, that inftead of being formed on the
narrow ground of Grotius, in his Adamus Exul,
allowed a wider range to the fancy, and included allegorical characters, like the Adamo of
Andreini.

This compofition, firft printed at Milan, in
1613, and again in 1617, refembles the myfteries
of our early ftage; and is denominated in Italian, *Rapprefentazione*, a name which the writers
of Italy apply to dramas founded on the fcripture. — Dr. Pearce has faid, in the preface to his
review of Milton's text, that he was informed
an Italian tragedy exifted, entitled *Il Paradifo
Perfo*, Paradife Loft; but, in a very extenfive
refearch, I can difcover no fuch performance.
There is indeed another Italian drama on the
fubject, which I have not feen, entitled *Adamo
Caduto*, tragedia facra; but this was not printed
until 1647, fome years after the return of our
poet from the continent *. It feems very probable

* For the benefit of commentators on our divine bard, let
me here infert a brief lift of fuch Italian compofitions, as may
poffibly have afforded him fome ufeful hints:

that Milton, in his collection of Italian books, had brought the Adamo of Andreini to England; and that the perufal of an author, wild indeed, and abounding in grotefque extravagance, yet now and then fhining with pure and united rays of fancy and devotion, firft gave a new bias to the imagination of the Englifh poet, or, to ufe the expreffive phrafe of Voltaire, firft revealed to him the *hidden majefty of the fubject*. The apoftate angels of Andreini, though fometimes hideoufly and abfurdly difgufting, yet occafionally fparkle

1. Adamo Caduto, tragedia facra, di Serafino della Salandra. Cozenza, 1647. Octavo.

2. La Battaglia Celefte tra Michele e Lucifero, di Antonio Alfani, Palermitano. Palermo, 1568. Quarto.

3. Dell' Adamo di Giovanni Soranzo, i due primi libri. Genova 1604. Duodecimo.

Thefe little known productions on the fubject of Milton are not to be found in the royal library, nor in the princely collection of Lord Spencer, who poffeffes that remarkable rarity of Italian literature, the *Tefeide* of Boccaccio; and whofe liberal paffion for books is ennobled by his politenefs and beneficence to men of letters.

The poets of Italy were certainly favorites with Milton; and perhaps his Samfon Agoniftes was founded on a facred drama of that country, La Rapprefentazione di Sanfone, per Aleffandro Rofelli. Siena, 1616. Quarto.— There is probably confiderable poetical merit in this piece, as I find two confequent editions of it recorded in the hiftorians of Italian literature; yet I am unable to fay whether Milton is indebted to it or not, as I have never been fo fortunate as to find a copy of Rofelli's compofition. Yet the mention of it here may be ufeful to future editors of the English poet.

with fuch fire as might awaken the emulation of Milton.

I fhall not attempt to produce parallel paffages from the two poets, becaufe the chief idea that I mean to inculcate is, not that Milton tamely copied the Adamo of Andreini, but that his fancy caught fire from that fpirited, though irregular and fantaftic, compofition—that it proved in his ardent and fertile mind the feed of Paradife Loft;—this is matter of mere conjecture, whofe probability can only be felt in examining the Adamo—to the lovers of Milton it may prove a fource of amufing fpeculation.

And as the original work of Andreini is feldom to be found, it may be pleafing to the reader, both of Englifh and Italian, to fee in thefe pages a brief analyfis of his drama; with a fhort felection from a few of the moft remarkable fcenes.

The CHARACTERS.

God the Father.
Chorus of Seraphim, Cherubim, and Angels.
The archangel Michael.
Adam.
Eve.
A Cherub, the guardian of Adam.
Lucifer.
Satan.
Beelzebub.

The SEVEN mortal SINS.
The WORLD.
The FLESH.
FAMINE.
LABOR.
DESPAIR.
DEATH.
VAIN GLORY.
SERPENT.
VOLANO, an infernal meſſenger.
CHORUS of PHANTOMS.
CHORUS of fiery, airy, aquatic, and infernal
SPIRITS.

ACT I. SCENE 1. Chorus of Angels, ſinging the glory of God. — After their hymn, which ſerves as a prologue, God the Father, Angels, Adam and Eve.—God calls to Lucifer, and bids him ſurvey with confuſion the wonders of his power.—He creates Adam and Eve—their delight and gratitude.

SCENE 2. Lucifer, ariſing from hell—he expreſſes his enmity againſt God, the Good Angels, and Man.

SCENE 3. Lucifer, Satan, and Beelzebub. — Lucifer excites his aſſociates to the deſtruction of Man, and calls other Demons from the abyſs to conſpire for that purpoſe.

SCENE 4, 5, and 6. Lucifer, ſummoning ſeven diſtinct Spirits, commiſſions them to act under the character of the ſeven mortal Sins, with the following names :

MELECANO	-	PRIDE.
LURCONE	-	ENVY.
RUSPICANO	-	ANGER.
ARFARAT	-	AVARICE.
MALTEA	-	SLOTH.
DULCIATO	-	LUXURY.
GULIAR	-	GLUTTONY.

ACT II. SCENE 1. The Angels, to the number of fifteen, separately sing the grandeur of God, and his munificence to Man.

SCENE 2. Adam and Eve, with Lurcone and Guliar watching unseen.—Adam and Eve expreſs their devotion to God so fervently, that the evil Spirits, though inviſible; are put to flight by their prayer.

SCENE 3. The Serpent, Satan, Spirits.—The Serpent, or Lucifer, announces his deſign of circumventing Woman.

SCENE 4. The Serpent, Spirits, and Volano. —Volano arrives from hell, and declares that the confederate powers of the abyſs deſigned to ſend a goddeſs from the deep, entitled Vain Glory, to vanquiſh Man.

SCENE 5. Vain Glory, drawn by a giant, Volano, the Serpent, Satan, and Spirits.—The Serpent welcomes Vain Glory as his confederate, then hides himſelf in the tree to watch and tempt Eve.

SCENE 6. The Serpent and Vain Glory at firſt concealed, the Serpent diſcovers himſelf to

Eve, tempts and feduces her.—Vain Glory clofes the act with expreffions of triumph.

ACT III. SCENE 1. Adam and Eve.—After a dialogue of tendernefs fhe produces the fruit.—Adam expreffes horror, but at laft yields to her temptation.—When both have tafted the fruit, they are overwhelmed with remorfe and terror: they fly to conceal themfelves.

SCENE 2. Volano proclaims the Fall of Man, and invites the powers of darknefs to rejoice, and pay their homage to the prince of hell.

SCENE 3. Volano, Satan, chorus of Spirits, with enfigns of victory.—Expreffion of their joy.

SCENE 4. Serpent, Vain Glory, Satan, and Spirits.—The Serpent commands Canoro, a mufical fpirit, to fing his triumph, which is celebrated with fongs and dances in the 4th and 5th fcenes; the latter clofes with expreffions of horror from the triumphant demons, on the approach of God.

SCENE 6. God the Father, Angels, Adam and Eve.—God fummons and rebukes the finners, then leaves them, after pronouncing his malediction.

SCENE 7. An Angel, Adam and Eve.—The Angel gives them rough fkins for clothing, and exhorts them to penitence.

SCENE 8. The archangel Michael, Adam and Eve.—Michael drives them from Paradife with a fcourge of fire. Angels clofe the act with a chorus, exciting the offenders to hope in repentance.

ACT

ACT IV. Scene 1. Volano, chorus of fiery, airy, earthly, and aquatic Spirits.—They exprefs their obedience to Lucifer.

Scene 2. Lucifer rifes, and utters his abhorrence of the light; the demons confole him—he, queftions them on the meaning of God's words and conduct towards Man—He fpurns their conjectures, and announces the incarnation, then proceeds to new machinations againft Man.

Scene 3. Infernal Cyclops, fummoned by Lucifer, make a new world at his command.—He then commiffions three demons againft man, under the characters of the World, the Flefh, and Death.

Scene 4. Adam alone.—He laments his fate, and at laft feels his fufferings aggravated, in beholding Eve flying in terror from the hoftile animals.

Scene 5. Adam and Eve.—She excites her companion to fuicide.

Scene 6. Famine, Thirft, Laffitude, Defpair, Adam and Eve. — Famine explains her own nature, and that of her affociates.

Scene 7. Death, Adam and Eve. — Death, reproaches Eve with the horrors fhe has occafioned—Adam clofes the act by exhorting Eve to take refuge in the mountains.

ACT V. Scene 1. The Flefh, in the fhape of a woman, and Adam. — He refifts her temptation.

SCENE 2. Lucifer, the Flesh, and Adam.—Lucifer pretends to be a man, and the elder brother of Adam.

SCENE 3. A Cherub, Adam, the Flesh, and Lucifer.—The Cherub secretly warns Adam against his foes; and at last defends him with manifest power.

SCENE 4. The world, in the shape of a man, exulting in his own finery.

SCENE 5. Eve and the World.—He calls forth a rich palace from the ground, and tempts Eve with splendor.

SCENE 6. Chorus of Nymphs, Eve, the World, and Adam.—He exhorts Eve to resist these allurements—the World calls the demons from hell to enchain his victims—Eve prays for mercy: Adam encourages her.

SCENE 7. Lucifer, Death, Chorus of Demons.—They prepare to seize Adam and Eve.

SCENE 8. The archangel Michael, with a chorus of good Angels.—After a spirited altercation, Michael subdues and triumphs over Lucifer.

SCENE 9. Adam, Eve, chorus of Angels.—They rejoice in the victory of Michael: he animates the offenders with a promise of favor from God, and future residence in heaven:—they express their hope and gratitude.—The Angels close the drama, by singing the praise of the Redeemer.

After this minute account of Andreini's plan, the reader may be curious to see some specimens

of his poetry in an English version. I shall select three : First, the chorus of angels, which
serves as a prologue to the drama, and has been
so ludicrously described by Voltaire; secondly,
the soliloquy of Lucifer on his first appearance;
and thirdly, the scene in which Eve induces
Adam to taste the fruit. I shall prefix to them
the preface of Andreini; but as these specimens
of his composition might seem tedious here, and
too much interrupt the course of this essay, I
shall detach them from it, and insert them as an
Appendix.

The majesty of Milton appears to the utmost
advantage when he is fully compared with every
writer, whose poetical powers have been exercised on the subject, to which only his genius was
equal.

Let me observe, however, for the credit of
Andreini, that although he has been contemp-
tuously called a stroller, he had some tincture of
classical learning, and considerable piety. He
occasionally imitates Virgil, and quotes the fathers. He was born in Florence, 1578; his mother
was an actress, highly celebrated for the excellence of her talents, and the purity of her life;
she appeared also as an authoress, and printed
a volume of letters and essays, to which two
great poets of her country, Tasso and Marini,
contributed each a sonnet. Her memory was
celebrated by her son, who published at her death,
a collection of poems in her praise. Having

distinguished himself as a comedian at Milan, he travelled into France, in the train of the famous Mary de Medici, and obtained, as an actor, the favor of Lewis the XIIIth. The biographical work of Count Mazzuchelli on the writers of Italy, includes an account of Andreini, with a list of his various productions; they amount to the number of thirty, and form a singular medley of comedies and devout poems. His Adamo alone seems likely to preserve his name from oblivion; and that indeed can never ceafe to be regarded as a literary curiosity, while it is believed to have given a fortunate impulse to the fancy of Milton.

If it is highly probable, as I think it will appear to every poetical reader, who perufes the Adamo, that Andreini turned the thoughts of Milton from Alfred to Adam, and led him to sketch the first outlines of Paradise Loft in various plans of allegorical dramas, it is possible that an Italian writer, lefs known than Andreini, first threw into the mind of Milton the idea of converting Adam into an epic perfonage. I have now before me a literary curiosity, which my accomplished friend, Mr. Walker, to whom the literature of Ireland has many obligations, very kindly sent me, on his return from an excursion to Italy, where it happened to strike a traveller, whose mind is peculiarly awakened to elegant pursuits. The book I am speaking of is entitled La Scena Tragica d'Adamo ed Eva, Eftratta dai primi tre capi della Sacra Genesi, e ridotta

a fignificato Morale da Troilo Lancetta, Benacenfe.
Venetia 1644. This little work is dedicated to
Maria Gonzaga, Dutchefs of Mantua, and is nothing more than a drama in profe of the ancient
form, entitled a morality, on the expulfion of
our firft parents from Paradife. The author does
not mention Andreini, nor has he any mixture
of verfe in his compofition; but, in his addrefs
to the reader, he has the following very remarkable paffage : after fuggelting that the Mofaic
hiftory of Adam and Eve is purely allegorical,
and defigned as an incentive to virtue, he fays,
" Una notte fognai, che Moifè mi porfe graziofa
" efpofizione, e mifteriofo fignificato con parole
" tali appunto:

    " Dio fa parte all' huom di fe fteffo con l' in-
" tervento della ragione, e difpone con infalli-
" bile fentenza, che fignoreggiando in lui la me-
" defima fopra le fenfuali voglie, prefervato il pomo
" del proprio core dagli appetiti difordinati, per
" guiderdone di giufta obbedienza gli trasforma il
" mondo in Paradifo.—Di quefto s' io parlafli,
" al ficuro formerei heroico poema convenevole
" a femidei."

    " One night I dreamt that Mofes explained
" to me the miftery, almoft in thefe words:

    " God reveals himfelf to man by the inter-
" vention of reafon, and thus infallibly ordains
" that reafon, while fhe fupports her fovereignty
" over the fenfual inclinations in man, and pre-
" ferves the apple of his heart from licentious

" appetites, in reward of his juft obedience trans-
" forms the world into Paradife—Of this were
" I to fpeak, affuredly I might form an heroic
" poem worthy of demi-gods. "

It ftrikes me as poffible that thefe laft words, affigned to Mofes in his vifion by Troilo Lancetta, might operate on the mind of Milton like the queftion of Ellwood, and prove, in his prolific fancy, a kind of rich graft on the idea he derived from Andreini, and the germ of his greateft production.

A fceptical critic, inclined to difcountenance this conjecture, might indeed obferve, it is more probable that Milton never faw a little volume not publifhed until after his return from Italy, and written by an author fo obfcure, that his name does not occur in Tirabofchi's elaborate hiftory of Italian literature; nor in the patient Italian chronicler of poets, Quadrio, though he beftows a chapter on early dramatic compofitions in profe.—But the mind, that has once ftarted a conjecture of this nature, muft be weak indeed; if it cannot produce new fhadows of argument in aid of a favorite hypothefis.—Let me therefore be allowed to advance, as a prefumptive proof of Milton's having feen the work of Lancetta, that he makes *a fimilar ufe of Mofes*, and introduces him to fpeak a prologuè in the fketch of his various plans for an allegorical drama. It is indeed poffible that Milton might never fee the performances either of Lancetta or Andreini —

yet conjecture has ground enough to conclude very fairly, that he was acquainted with both, for Andreini wrote a long allegorical drama on Paradife, and we know that the fancy of Milton firft began to play with the fubject according to that peculiar form of compofition. — Lancetta treated it alfo in the fhape of a dramatic allegory; but faid, at the fame time, under the character of Mofes, that the fubject might form an incomparable epic poem; and Milton, quitting his own hafty fketches of allegorical dramas, accomplifhed a work which anfwers to that intimation.

After all, I allow that the province of conjecture is the region of fhadows; and as I offer my ideas on this topic rather as phantoms that may amufe a lover of poetical fpeculation, than as folid proofs to determine a caufe of great moment, I am perfuaded every good-natured reader will treat them with indulgence: affuredly I fhall feel neither anger, nor inclination to contend in their defence, if any feverer critic,

" Irruat, & fruftra ferro diverberet umbras. "

In mentioning the imperfect rudiments of Paradife Loft, Johnfon fays, very juftly, " It is " pleafant to fee great works in their feminal " ftate, pregnant with latent poffibilities of ex- " cellence; nor could there be any more de- " lightful entertainment than to trace their gra- " dual growth and expanfion, and to obferve

" how they are fometimes fuddenly advanced by
" accidental hints, and fometimes flowly impro-
" ved by fteady meditation." Such entertainment
would indeed be peculiarly delightful in refpect
to Milton. It is in fome meafure beyond our
reach, becaufe, if we except his fketches of plans
for an allegorical drama, no real evidence is left
concerning the origin and progrefs of his magnificent conception: but fuppofition is often a pleafant fubftitute for abfolute knowledge; and in
the hope that it may prove fo in the prefent
cafe, let me advance in this fhadowy refearch,
and after accounting for the firft flafhes of Milton's fubject on his fancy, purfue the vein of conjecture, in confidering various ideas that might
influence him in the profecution of his work.

When Adam engaged the fancy of Milton,
however that perfonage might firft be impreffed
upon it as a fubject of verfe, many circumftances
might confpire to confirm his afcendency. The
works of different arts, which the poet furveyed
in his travels, had, perhaps, a confiderable influence in attaching his imagination to our firft
parents. — He had moft probably contemplated
them not only in the colors of Michael Angelo,
who decorated Rome with his picture of the creation, but in the marble of Bandinelli, who had
executed two large ftatues of Adam and Eve,
which, though they were far from fatisfying the
tafte of connoiffeurs, might ftimulate even by
their imperfections the genius of a poet. In

recollecting how painting and sculpture had both exercised their respective powers on these hallowed and interesting characters, the muse of Milton might be tempted to contend with the sister arts. I must confess, however, that Richardson, a fond idolater of these arts and of Milton, is rather inclined to believe that they did not much occupy the attention of the poet, even during his residence in Italy: yet I am persuaded he must have been greatly struck by the works of Michael Angelo, a genius whom he resembled so much in his grand characteristic, mental magnificence! and to whom he was infinitely superior in the attractive excellencies of delicacy and grace. In touching on a point of resemblance between the poet and this pre-eminent artist, we cannot fail to observe the abundance and variety of charms in the poetry of Milton. All the different perfections, which are assigned as characteristics to the most celebrated painters, are united in this marvellous poet. He has the sublime grandeur of Michael Angelo, the chaste simplicity of Raphael, the sweetness of Correggio, and the richness of Rubens. In his Samson we may admire the force of Rembrandt, and in his Comus the grace and gaiety of Albano and Poussin : in short, there is no charm exhibited by painting, which his poetry has failed to equal, as far as analogy between the different arts can extend. If Milton did not pay much attention in his travels to those works of the great painters that he had opportunities of furveying (which I cannot think probable) it is certain that his own works afford a moſt excellent field to exercife and animate the powers of the pencil *. The article in which I apprehend a painter muſt find it moſt difficult to equal the felicity of the poet is, the delineation of his apoſtate angels. Here, perhaps, poetry has fome important advantage over her fiſter art; and even poetry herfelf is confidered by auſterer critics as unequal to the taſk. Johnfon regarded the book of Paradife Loſt, which defcribes the war of Heaven, as fit to be " the favorite of children." — Imagination itfelf may be depreciated, by the auſterity of logic, as a childiſh faculty, but thofe who love even its

* The learned, ingenious, enthufiaſtic Winkelman has advanced, in his moſt celebrated work, a very different opinion; but the ardor with which this extraordinary man had ſtudied and idolized the ancients, rendered him deplorably prefumptuous and precipitate in feveral of his ideas relating to modern genius; and particularly in what he has afferted of Milton. Some paffionate admirers of antiquity feem to lament the fall of paganifm, as fatal to poetry, to painting, and to fculpture; but a more liberal and enlightened fpirit of criticifm may rather believe, what it is very poffible, I apprehend, to demonſtrate, that chriſtianity can hardly be more favorable to the purity of morals, than it might be rendered to the perfection of thefe delightful arts. Milton himfelf may be regarded as an obvious and complete proof that the pofition is true as far as poetry is concerned. In what degrees the influence of the Chriſtian religion can affect the other two, it may be pleafing, and perhaps ufeful, to confider in fome future compofition devoted to their advancement.

exceffes may be allowed to exult in its delights.
No reader truly poetical ever perufed the fixth
book of Milton without enjoying a kind of trans-
port, which a ftern logician might indeed condemn, but which he might alfo think it more
defirable to fhare.   I doubt not but while Milton was revolving his fubject in his mind, he
often heard from critical acquaintance fuch remarks
as might have induced him, had his imagination
been lefs energetic, to relinquifh the angels as
intractable beings, ill fuited to the fphere of poetry.   But if his glowing fpirit was ever damped
for a moment by fuggeftions of this nature, he
was probably re-animated and encouraged by recollecting his refpectable old acquaintance, the
poets of Italy. He had not only feen the infernal powers occafionally delineated with great majefty and effect in the Jerufalem of Taffo, and
Marini's " Slaughter of the Innocents," but he was
probably acquainted with an Italian poem, little
known in England, and formed exprefsly on the
conflict of the apoftate fpirits.   The work I allude
to is, the Angeleida of Erafmo Valvafone, printed at Venife, in 1590.   This poet was of a noble
family in the Venetian republic; as his health was
delicate, he devoted himfelf to retired ftudy, and
cultivated the Mufes in his caftle of Valvafone.
His works are various, and one of his early
compofitions was honored by the applaufe o
Taffo.   His Angeleida confifts of three cantos on
the War of Heaven, and is fingularly terminated

by a fonnet, addreffed to the triumphant Archangel Michael. Several paffages in Valvafone
induce me to think that Milton was familiar with
his work.—I will only tranfcribe the verfes, in
which the Italian poet affigns to the infernal
powers the invention of artillery:

> Di falnitro, e di zolfo ofcura polve
> Chiude altro in ferro cavo; e poi la tocca
> Dietro col foco, e in foco la rifolve:
> Onde fragofo tuon fubito fcocca:
> Scocca e lampeggia, e una palla volve,
> Al cui fcontro ogni duro arde e trabocca:
> Crud' è 'l faetta, ch' imitar s' attenta
> L' arme che 'l fommo Dio dal Cielo aventa.
>
> L' Angelo rio, quando a concorrer forfe
> Di faper, di bellezza, e di poffanza
> Con l' eterno fattor, perchè s' accorfe
> Quell' arme non aver, ch' ogni arme avanza,
> L' empio ordigno a compor l' animo torfe,
> Che ferir puo del folgore a fembianza:
> E con quefto a' dì noftri horrido in terra
> Tiranno, arma di folgori ogni guerra.

Valvafone acknowledges, in his preface, that
he had been cenfured for having *fpoken fo materially* (ragionato così materialmente) of angels,
who are only fpirit. But he defends himfelf very
ably on this point, and mentions with gratitude
two excellent critical difcourfes, written in his

vindication by Giovanni Ralli and Ottavio Menini;—there is a third alfo, according to Quadrio, by Scipione di Manzano, under the name of Olimpo Marcucci, printed at Venice, in 4to, 1594. They all beftow great praife on the author whom they vindicate, who appears to have been a very amiable man, and a poet of confiderable powers, though he poffeffed not the fublimity and the refinement of Milton or Taffo. In his general ideas of poetry he refembled them both; and in his mode of expreffing himfelf, in the preface to his Angeleida, he reminds me very ftrongly of thofe paffages in the profe works of Milton, where he fpeaks on the hallowed magnificence of the art. They both confidered facred fubjects as peculiarly proper for verfe; an idea condemned by Johnfon, who fympathized as little with Milton in his poetic as in his political principles. It was by entertaining ideas of poetry, directly contrary to thofe of his critic, that Milton rendered himfelf, in true dignity, the firft poet of the world. Nor can we think that dignity in any degree impaired, by difcovering that many hints might be fuggefted to him by various poets, in different languages, who had feized either a part or the whole of his fubject before him. On the contrary, the more of thefe we can difcover, and the more we compare them with the Englifh bard, the more reafon we fhall find to exult in the pre-eminence of his poetical powers. Taffo, in his critical difcourfes, inculcates

a very juft maxim concerning the originality of
epic poets, which is very applicable to Milton.—
" Nuovo farà il poema, in cui nuova farà la
" teftura de' nodi, nuove le foluzioni, nuovi gli
" epifodi, che per entro vi fono trapofti, quan-
" tunque la materia foffe notiffima, e dagli altri
" prima trattata : perchè la novità del poema fi
" confidera piuttofto alla forma, che alla ma-
" teria."

This great writer illuftrates his pofition, that
the novelty of a poem is to be eftimated more
from its form than its fubject, by the example
of Alamanni, an epic poet of Italy, who loft the
praife he might otherwife have acquired, by copying too fondly, under modern names, the incidents of Homer.—Milton is of all authors undoubtedly one of the moft original, both in
thought and expreffion : the language of his greater
works is evidently borrowed from no model, but
it feems to have great conformity with the precepts which Taffo has delivered in the difcourfes
I have juft cited, for the formation of an epic
ftyle. Yet in criticifm, as in politics, Milton was
undoubtedly

" Nullius addictus jurare in verba magiftri."

He thought on every topic for himfelf; juftly
remarking, that " to neglect rules and follow
" nature, in them that know art and ufe judge-
" ment, is no tranfgreffion, but an enriching of art."

This excellent maxim infured to him the exercife and the independence of his own elevated
mind. There is frequent allufion to the works
of antiquity in Milton, yet no poet, perhaps,
who revered the ancients with fuch affectionate
enthufiafm, has copied them fo little. This was
partly owing to the creative opulence of his own
genius, and partly to his having fixed on a fubject fo different from thofe of Homer and Virgil,
that he may be faid to have accomplifhed a revolution in poetry, and to have purified and extended the empire of the epic mufe. One of the
chief motives that induced his imagination to defert its early favorite Arthur, and attach itfelf
to our firft parents, is partly explained in thofe
admirable verfes of the ninth book, where the
poet mentions the choice of his own fubject,
contrafted with thofe of his illuftrious predeceffors:

Argument

Not lefs, but more heroic, than the wrath
Of ftern Achilles on his foe purfued
Thrice fugitive about Troy wall, or rage
Of Turnus for Lavinia difefpous'd,
Or Neptune's ire, or Juno's, that fo long
Perplex'd the Greek, and Cytherea's fon.

—   —   —   —   —   —

—   — This fubject for heroic fong
Pleas'd me long chufing, and beginning late;
Not fedulous by nature to indite
Wars, hitherto the only argument

Heroic deem'd, chief maſt'ry to diſſect,
With long and tedious havoc, fabled knights
In battles feign'd; the better fortitude
Of patience and heroic martyrdom
Unſung; or to deſcribe races and games,
Or tilting furniture, emblazon'd ſhields,
Impreſſes quaint, capariſons and ſteeds,
Baſes and tinſel trappings, gorgeous knights
At jouſt and torneament; then marſhal'd feaſt
Serv'd up in hall with ſewers and ſeneſchals;
The ſkill of artifice or office mean,
Not that which juſtly gives heroic name
To perſon or to poem : me of theſe
Nor ſkill'd, nor ſtudious, higher argument
Remains, ſufficient of itſelf to raiſe
That name.

Milton ſeems to have given a purer ſignification, than we commonly give to the word hero, and to have thought it might be aſſigned to any perſon eminent and attractive enough to form a principal figure in a great picture.   In truth, when we recollect the etymology which a philoſopher and a ſaint have left us of the term, we cannot admire the propriety of devoting it to illuſtrious homicides.   Plato derives the Greek word from others, that imply either eloquence or love; and St. Auguſtine, from the Grecian name of Juno, or the air, becauſe original heroes were pure departed ſpirits ſuppoſed to reſide in that element.   In Milton's idea, the ancient

heroes

heroes of epic poetry feem to have too much refembled the modern great man, according to the
delineation of that character in Fielding's exquifite hiftory of Jonathan Wild the Great. Much as
the Englifh poet delighted in the poetry of Homer,
he appears to have thought, like an American writer of the prefent age, whofe fervent paffion for
the Mufes is only inferior to his philantropy, that
the Grecian bard, though celebrated as the prince
of moralifts by Horace, and efteemed a teacher of
virtue by St. Bafil, has too great a tendency to
nourifh that fanguinary madnefs in mankind,
which has continually made the earth a theatre
of carnage. I am afraid that fome poets and hiftorians may have been a little acceffary to the innumerable maffacres with which men, ambitious of
obtaining the title of hero, have defolated the
world; and it is certain, that a fevere judge of Homer may, with fome plaufibility apply to him the
reproach that his Agamemnon utters to Achilles:

Αιει γαρ τοι ερις τε φιλη, πολεμοι τε μαχαι τε.

For all thy pleafure is in ftrife and blood.

Yet a lover of the Grecian bard may obferve, in
his defence, that in affigning thefe words to the
leader of his hoft, he fhows the pacific propriety
of his own fentiments; and that, however his verfes may have inftigated an Alexander to carnage,
or prompted the calamitous frequency of war,
even this pagan poet, fo famous as the defcriber
of battles, detefted the objects of his defcription.

But whatever may be thought of the heathen bard, Milton, to whom a purer religion had given greater purity, and I think greater force of imagination, Milton, from a long furvey of human nature, had contracted fuch an abhorrence for the atrocious abfurdity of ordinary war, that his feelings in this point feem to have influenced his epic fancy. He appears to have relinquifhed common heroes, that he might not cherifh the too common characteriftic of man—a fanguinary fpirit. He afpired to delight the imagination, like Homer, and to produce, at the fame time, a much happier effect on the mind. Has he fucceeded in this glorious idea? Affuredly he has :—to pleafe is the end of poetry. Homer pleafes perhaps more univerfally than Milton; but the pleafure that the Englifh poet excites, is more exquifite in its nature, and fuperior in its effect. An eminent painter of France ufed to fay, that in reading Homer he felt his nerves dilated, and he feemed to increafe in ftature. Such an ideal effect as Homer, in this example, produced on the body, Milton produces in the fpirit. To a reader who thoroughly relifhes the two poems on Paradife, his heart appears to be purified, in proportion to the pleafure he derives from the poet, and his mind to become angelic. Such a tafte for Milton is rare, and the reafon why it is fo is this :— To form it completely, a reader muft poffefs, in fome degree, what was fuperlatively poffeffed by the poet, a mixture of two different fpecies of enthufiafm, the poetical and the religious. To relifh Homer, it is fufficient to have a paffion for excellent verfe; but the reader of Milton, who is only a lover of the Mufes, lofes half, and certainly the beft half, of that tranfcendent delight which the poems of this divine enthufiaft are capable of imparting. A devotional tafte is as requifite for the full enjoyment of Milton as a tafte for poetry; and this remark will fufficiently explain the inconfiftency fo ftriking in the fentiments of many diftinguifhed writers, who have repeatedly fpoken on the great English poet—particularly that inconfiftency, which I partly promifed to explain in the judgments of Dryden and Voltaire. Thefe very different men had both a paffion for verfe, and both ftrongly felt the poetical powers of Milton : but Dryden perhaps had not much, and Voltaire had certainly not a particle, of Milton's religious enthufiafm; hence, inftead of being impreffed with the fanctity of his fubject, they fometimes glanced upon it in a ludicrous point of view.

Hence they fometimes fpeak of him as the very prince of poets, and fometimes as a mifguided genius, who has failed to obtain the rank he afpired to in the poetical world. But neither the caprices of conceit, nor the cold aufterity of reafon, can reduce the glory of this pre-eminent bard. —It was in an hour propitious to his renown, that he relinquifhed Arthur and Merlin for Adam and the Angels; and he might fay on the occafion, in the words of his admired Petrarch.

Io benedico il luogo, il tempo, e l' hora
Che sì alto miraro gli occhi miei.

I bless the spot, the season, and the hour,
When my presumptuous eyes were fix'd so high.

✝ To say that his poem wants human interest,
is only to prove, that he who finds that defect
wants the proper sensibility of man. A work that
displays at full length, and in the strongest light,
the delicious tranquillity of innocence, the tor-
menting turbulence of guilt, and the consolatory
satisfaction of repentance, has surely abundance of
attraction to awaken sympathy. The images and
sentiments that belong to these varying situations
are so suited to our mortal existence, that they
cannot cease to interest, while human nature
endures. The human heart, indeed, may be
too much depraved, and the human mind may
be too licentious, or too gloomy, to have a perfect relish for Milton; but, in honor of his poetry, we may observe, that it has a peculiar tendency to delight and to meliorate those characters; in which the seeds of taste and piety have
been happily sown by nature. In proportion as
the admiration of mankind shall grow more and
more valuable from the progressive increase of
intelligence, of virtue, and of religion, this incomparable poet will be more affectionately
studied, and more universally admired.

APPENDIX,

CONTAINING

EXTRACTS

FROM THE

ADAMO OF ANDREINI:

WITH AN

ANALYSIS OF ANOTHER ITALIAN DRAMA
ON THE SAME SUBJECT.

Al benigno LETTORE.

Sazio e stanco (lettor discreto) d 'aver con l'occhio della fronte troppo fiso rimirate queste terrene cose; quel della mente una volta inzanaldo a più belle considerazioni, ed alle tante maraviglie sparse dal sommo Dio a benefizio dell' uomo per l'universo; sentj passarmi il cuore da certo stimolo, e da, non so che, cristiano compungimento, vedendo come offesa in ogni tempo da noi gravemente, quella ineffabile bontà, benigna ad ogni modo ci si mostrasse, quelle in un continuo stato di benificenza ad uso nostro conser vando; e come una sol volta provocata a vendetta, oltre i suoi vasti confini non allargasse il mare, al sole non oscurasse la luce, sterile non facesse la terra, per abissarci, per acciecarci, e per distruggerci finalmente. E tutto internato in questi divini affetti, mi sentj rapire a me stesso, e traportare da dolce violenza là nel terrestre paradiso, ove pur di veder mi parea l' uomo primiero Adamo, fattura cara di Dio, amico degli angeli, erede del cielo, familiar delle stelle, compendio delle cose create, ornamento del tutto,

To the courteous READER.

Satiated and fatigued (gentle reader) by having looked on thefe earthly objects with eyes too
intent, and raifing therefore the eye of my mind
to higher contemplations, to the wonders diffufed
by the fupreme Being, for the benefit of man,
through the univerfe, I felt my heart penetrated
by a certain chriftian compunction in reflecting
how his inexpreffible goodnefs, though perpetually and grievoufly offended by us, ftill fhows
itfelf in the higheft degree indulgent towards us,
in preferving thofe wonders with a continued influence to our advantage; and how, on the firft provocation to vengeance, Almighty power, does not
enlarge the ocean to pafs its immenfe boundary,
does not obfcure the light of the fun, does not imprefs fterility on the earth, to ingulf us, to blind us,
and finally to deftroy us. Softened and abforbed
in thefe divine emotions, I felt myfelf tranfported
and hurried, by a delightful violence, into a terreftrial paradife, where I feemed to behold the
firft man, Adam, a creature dear to God, the
friend of angels, the heir of heaven, familiar with
the ftars, a compendium of all created things,
the ornament of all, the miracle of nature, lord

miracolo della natura, imperador degli animali, unico albergatore dell' univerſo, e fruitore di tante maraviglie e grandezze. Quindi invaghito ancora più che mai, riſolvei col favor di Dio benedetto de dare alla luce del mondo, quel che io portava nelle tenebre della mia mente; sì per dare in qualche modo, a conoſcere ch' io conoſceva me ſteſſo, e gli obblighi infiniti; ch' io tengo a Dio; come perchè altri, che non conoſcono, ſapeſſero chi fu, chi ſia, e chi ſarà, queſt' uomo; e dalla baſſa conſiderazione di queſte coſe terrene, alzaſſero la mente alle celeſte e divine. Stetti però gran pezza in forſe, s' io doveva e poteva tentare compoſizione a me, per molti capi, difficiliſſima, poichè cominciando la ſacra tela della creazione dell' uomo ſin la dov' è ſcacciato dal paradiſo terreſtre (che ſei hore vi corſero come ben narra Sant Agoſtino nel libro della Città di Dio) non ben lo vedeva come in cinque atti ſoli, ſi brieve fatto raccontar ſi poteſſe, tanto più diſegnando per ogni atto il numero almeno di ſei, o ſette ſcene. Difficile per la diſputa, che fece il demonio con Eva, prima che l' induceſſe a mangiare il pomo, poichè altro non abbiamo, ſe non il teſto, che ne faccia menzione, dicendo, " Nequaquam moriemini, & eritis ſicut Dii, ſcientes bonum & malum." Difficile per le parole d' Eva in perſuadere Adamo (che pur aveva il dono della ſcienza infuſa) a guſtar del pomo : ma difficiliſſima ſopra tutto per

of the animals, the only inhabitant of the univerfe, and enjoyer of a fcene fo wonderfully
grand. Whence, charmed more than ever, I
refolved, with the favor of the bleffed God, to
ufher into the light of the world what I bore in
the darknefs of my imagination, both to render
it known in fome meafure that I know myfelf,
and the infinite obligations that I have to God ;
and that others, who do not know, may learn
the true nature of man, and from the low contemplation of earthly things may raife their mind
to things celeftial and divine.

I remained, however, a confiderable time in
doubt, if I ought, or if I were able, to undertake
a compofition moft difficult to me on many ac-
counts, fince in beginning the facred fubject from
man's-creation to the point where he is driven
from the terreftrial paradife (a period of fix hours,
as Saint Auguftine relates in his book on the
city of God) I did not clearly perceive how an
action fo brief could be formed into five acts,
efpecially allowing to every act the number of at
leaft fix or feven fcenes; difficult from the difpute
that the Devil maintained with Eve, before he
could induce her to eat the apple, fince we have
only the text that mentions it, in faying " Nequaquam moriemini, & eritis ficut Dii, fcientes bonum & malum;" difficult from the words of
Eve, in perfuading Adam (who had indeed the
gift of knowledge infufed) to tafte the apple; but
difficult above all from my own infirmity, fince

la mia debolezza, poichè doveva la composizione rimaner priva di quegli ornamenti poetici, così cari alle muse : priva di poter trarre le comparazioni di cose fabrili, introdotte col volger degli anni, poichè al tempo del primo uomo, non v' era cosa. Priva pur di nominar (mentre però parla Adamo e con lui si ragiona) per esempio archi, strali, bipenni, urne, coltelli, spade, aste, trombe, tamburri, trofei, vessilli, aringhi, martelli, faci, mantici, roghi, teatri, erarj, e somiglianti cose, ed infinite, avendole tutte introdotte la necessità del peccato commesso; e però come afflittive e di pena, non dovevan passar per la mente, nè per la bocca d'Adamo, benchè avesse la scienza infusa, come quegli che nell' innocenza felicissimo si vivea. E priva eziandío del portare in campo, fatti d' istorie sacre o profane; del raccontare menzogne di favolosi dei; di narrare, amori, furori, armi, caccie, pescagioni, trionfi, naufragi, incendj, incanti, e simili cose, che sono in vero l' ornamento, e lo spirito della poesía. Difficile per non sapere in che stile dovesse parlare Adamo, perchè risguardando al saper suo, meritava i versi intieri, grandi, sostenuti, numerosi : ma considerandolo poi pastore ed albergatore de' boschi, pare che puro e dolce esser dovesse nel suo parlare e m' accostai perciò a questo di renderlo tale più, ch' io potessi con versi interi, e spezzati, e desinenze. E qui preso animo nel maggior mio dubbio, diedi, non

the compofition muft remain deprived of thofe
poetic ornaments fo dear to the mufes; deprived
of the power to draw comparifons from imple-
ments of art, introduced in the courfe of years,
fince in the time of the firft man there was no
fuch thing; deprived alfo of naming (at leaft while
Adam fpeaks, or difcourfe is held with him) for
example, bows, arrows, hatchets, urns, knives,
fwords, fpears, trumpets, drums, trophies, ban-
ners, lifts, hammers, torches bellows, funeral
piles, theatres, exchequers, and infinite things|of
a like nature, introduced by the neceffities of fin;
they ought not to pafs 'through the mind, or
through the lips of Adam, although he had
knowledge infufed into him, as one who lived
moft happy in a ftate of innocence; deprived,
moreover, of introducing points of hiftory, facred or profane, of relating fictions of fabulous
deities, of rehearfing loves, furies, arms, fports
of hunting or fifhing, triumphs, fhipwrecks, con-
flagrations, inchantments, and things of a like
nature, that are in truth the ornament and the
foul of poetry; difficult from not knowing in what
ftyle Adam ought to fpeak, fince, in refpect to
his knowledge, it might be proper to affign to
him verfes of a high, majeftic, and flowing ftyle;
but confidering him as a fhepherd, and an inhabitant of the woods, it appears that he fhould
be fimple and fweet in his difcourfe, and I endeavoured, on that account, to render it fuch,
as much as I could, by variety of verfification;

fo come, principio; andai, per così dire, senza mezzo seguendo : e giunfi al fine nè me ne avvidi. Onde ho da credere che la bontà di Dio, rifguardando più tofto l' affetto buono che i miei diffetti, (sì come retira fpeffo il cuor dell' uomo dall' opre male, così l' induce infenfibilmente ancora alle buone) foffe quella che mi moveffe la mano, e che l' opera mia terminaffe. Dunque a lei fola debbo le grazie di quella poca che peravventura fi trova nella prefente fatica : fapendo che l'onnipotenza fua, avvezza a trarre maraviglie dal rozzo ed informe caos , così da quello molto più rozzo ed informe della mia mente, abbia anche tratto quefto parto, fe non per altro, per effer facro, e perchè, per così dire, parlaffe un mutolo in perfona mia, per la povertà dell' ingegno come fuole all'incontro far amutire le più felici lingue quando s' impiegano in cofe brutte e profane. Vedafi dunque con l' occhio della difcrezione, nè fi biafimi peravventura la povertà dello ftile, la poca gravità nel portar delle cofe, la fterilità de' concetti, la debolezza degli fpiriti, gli infipidi fali, gli ftravaganti epifodj, come a dire (per lafciare una infinità d' altre cofe) che il mondo, la carne, e 'l diavolo per tentare Adamo, in forma umana gli s' apprefentino, poich' altro uomo nè altra donna non v' era al mondo, poichè il ferpente

and here, taking courage in my greateſt doubt,
I formed, I know not how, a beginning; I advanced, if I may ſay ſo, without any determinate
plan, and arrived at the end before I was aware.
Whence I am inclined to believe, that the favor
of God, regarding rather my good intentions
than my defeĉts (for as he often withdraws the
heart of man from evil, ſo he conduĉts it infen-
ſibly to good) gave direĉlion to my hand, and
completed my work.　Wherefore to that alone
I am indebted for the little grace that may perhaps be found in the preſent labor; knowing
that as omnipotence is accuſtomed to produce
wonders from the rude and unformed chaos, ſo
from the ſtill ruder chaos of my mind it may
have called forth this produĉlion, if not for any
other purpoſe, yet to be ſacred, and to make,
as it were, a mute ſpeak in my perſon, in de-
ſpite of poverty of. genius, as on the other hand
it is accuſtomed to ſtrike mute the moſt eloquent
tongues, when they employ themſelves on ſub-
jeĉts low and profane.　Let it be ſurveyed, therefore, with an eye of indulgence, and blame
not the poverty of ſtyle, the want of dignity in
the conduĉl of the circumſtances, ſterility of con-
ceits, weakneſs of ſpirit, inſipid pleaſantries, and
extravagant epiſodes; to mention, without ſpeaking of an infinitude of other things, that the world,
the fleſh, and the devil, preſent themſelves in human ſhapes to tempt Adam, ſince there was then
In the univerſe no other man or woman, and the

fi moftrò pure ad Eva con parte umana ; oltre che fi fa quefto, perchè le cofe fienò più intefe dall' intelletto con que' mezzi, che a' fenfi s' afpettano : pofciachè in altra guifa come le tante tentazioni che in un punto foftennero Adamo ed Eva, furono nell' interno della lor mente, così non ben capir lo fpettator le poteva. Nè fi de' credere che paffaffe il ferpente con Eva difputa lunga poichè la tentò in un punto più nella mente che con la lingua, dicendo quelle parole; " Nequaquam moriemini, & eritis ficut Dii, " &c. e pur farà di meftieri, per efprimere quegli interni contrafti, meditar qualche cofe per di fuori rapprefentarli. Ma fe al pittor poeta muto, è permeffo con caratteri di colore l' efprimer l' antichità di Dio in perfona d' uomo tutto canuto, e dimoftrare in bianca colomba la purità dello fpirito, e figurare i divini meffaggi che fono gli angeli in perfona di giovani alati; perchè non è permeffo al poeta, pittor parlante, portar nella tela del teatro altro uomo, altra donna, ch' Adamo ed Eva? e rapprefentare quegli interni contrafti per mezzo d'immagini, e voci pur tutte umane? Oltre che par più tolerabile l'introdurre in queft' opera il demonio in umana figura, di quel che fia l'introdur nell' ifteffa il Padre eterno e l' angelo fteffo; e pur fe quefto è

ferpent difcovered himfelf to Eve with a human
fimilitude; moreover, this is done that the fubject may be better comprehended by the underftanding, through the medium of the fenfes;
fince the great temptations that Adam and Eve
at once fuftained, were indeed in the interior of
their own mind, but could not be fo comprehended by the fpectator; nor is it to be believed
that the ferpent held a long difpute with Eve,
fince he tempted her rather by a fuggeftion to
her mind, than by conference, faying thefe words,
" Nequaquam moriemini, & eritis ficut Dii,
fcientes bonum & malum; and yet it will be neceffary, in order to exprefs thofe internal contentions, to find fome expedient to give them an
outward reprefentation; but if it is permitted to
the painter, who is a dumb poet, to exprefs by
colors God the Father, under the perfon of a
man filvered by age; to defcribe, under the image of
a white dove, the purity of the fpirit; and to figure
the divine meffengers, or angels, under the fhape
of winged youths, why is it not permitted to the
poet, who is a fpeaking painter, to reprefent, in
his theatrical production, another man and another woman befides Adam and Eve, and to reprefent their internal conflicts through the medium of images and voices entirely human, not
to mention that it appears more allowable to
introduce in this work the devil under a human
fhape, than it is to introduce into it the eternal
Father and an angel; and if this is permitted,
                                             and

permeſſo, e ſi vede tutto giorno eſpreſſo nelle rap-
preſen tazioni ſacre, perchè non ſi ha da permettere
nella preſente dove ſe il maggior ſi concede, ſi de'
conceder parimente il minor male; rimira dunque
lettor benigno più la ſoſtanza, che l' accidente,
per così dire, contemplando nell' opera il fine di
portar nel teatro dell' anima la miſeria, ed il
pianto d'Adamo, e farne ſpettatore il tuo cuore
per alzarlo da queſte baſſezze alle grandezze del
ciel, col mezzo della virtù e dell' aiuto di Dio,
il quale ti feliciti.

CHORO D'ANGELI *cantanti la* GLORIA DI DIO.

ALLA lira del Ciel Iri ſia l' arco,
    Corde le sfere fien, note le ſtelle,
    Sien le pauſe e i ſoſpir l' aure novelle,
    E 'l tempo i tempi a miſurar non parco.
Quindi alle cetre eterne, al novo canto
    S' aggiunga melodia, e lode a lode
    Per colui, ch' oggi ai mondi, ai cieli, gode
    Gran facitor moſtrarſi eterno, e ſanto.
O tu, che pria che foſſe il cielo e 'l mondo,
    In te ſteſſo godendo e mondi e cieli,
    Come punt' or da ſacroſanti teli,
    Verſi di grazie un ocean profondo.
Deh tu, che 'l ſai, grande amator ſovrano,
    Com' han lingua d' amor, l' opre cotante,

Tu

and feen every day exhibited in facred repre-
fentations, why fhould it not be allowed in the
prefent, where, if the greater evil is allowable,
furely the lefs fhould be allowed.: attend therefore, gentle reader, more to the fubftance than
to the accident, confidering in the work the great
end of introducing into the theatre of the foul
the mifery and lamentation of Adam, to make
your heart a fpectator of them, in order to raife
it from thefe dregs of earth to the magnificence
of heaven, through the medium of virtue and the
affiftance of God, by whom may you be bleffed.

CHORUS of Angels *finging the* Glory of God.

To Heav'n's bright lyre let Iris be the bow,
　Adapt the fpheres for chords, for notes the ftars,
　Let new-born gales difcriminate the bars,
　Nor let old time to meafure times be flow.
Hence to new mufic of the eternal lyre
　Add richer harmony, and praife to praife,
　For him, who now his wond'rous might difplays,
　And fhows the univerfe its awful fire.
O thou, who ere the world, or heav'n, was made,
　Didft in thyfelf that world, that heav'n enjoy,
　How does thy bounty all its powers employ,
　What inexpreffive good haft thou difplayed.
O thou, of fov'reign love almighty fource,
　Who know'ft to make thy works thy love exprefs,

Tu infpira ancor lode canore e fante.
Fa, ch' allo ftil s' accordi il cor, la mano.
Ch' all'or n' udrai l' alt' opre tue lodando
    Dir; che fefti di nulla Angeli e sfere,
    Ciel, mondo, pefci, augelli, moftri, e fere,
    Aquile al fol de' tuoi gran rai fembrando.

ATTO PRIMO.

SCENA SECONDA.

LUCIFERO.

Chi dal mio centro ofcuro,
Mi chiama a rimirar cotanta luce?
Quai maraviglie nove,
Oggi mi fcopri O Dio?
Forfe fei ftanco d' albergar nel cielo?
Perchè creafti in terra,
Quel vago paradifo?
Perchè reporvi poi
D' umana carne duo terreni dei?
Dimmi architetto vile,
Che di fango opre fefti,
Ch' avverrà di queft' uom povero, ignudo,
Di bofchi habitator folo, e di felve?
Forfe premer col pie crede le ftelle,
Impoverito è 'l ciel, cagione io folo
Fui di tanta ruina, ond' or ne godo.
Teffa pur ftella a ftella,

Let pure devotion's fire the foul poffefs,
And give the heart and hand a kindred force.
Then fhalt thou hear, how, when the world begun,
Thy life-producing voice gave myriads birth,
Call'd forth from nothing all in heav'n and earth,
Blefs'd in thy light as eagles in the fun.

ACT THE FIRST.

SCENE THE SECOND.

LUCIFER.

Who from my dark abyfs
Calls me to gaze on this excefs of light?
What miracles unfeen
Show'ft thou to me, O God?
Art thou then tired of refidence in Heav'n?
Why haft thou raifed on earth
This lovely Paradife,
And wherefore placed in it
Two earthly demi-gods of human mould?
Say, thou vile architect,
Forming thy works of duft,
What will befal this naked helplefs man,
The fole inhabitant of glens and woods?
Does he then dream of treading on the ftars?
Heav'n is impoverifh'd, and I, alone
The caufe, enjoy the ruin I produced:
Let him unite above

V' aggiunga e luna, e fole,
S' affatichi pur Dio,
Per far di novo il ciel lucido adorno,
Ch' al fin, con biafmo e fcorno,
Vana l' opra farà, vano il fudore,
Fu Lucifero fol quell' ampia luce,
Per cui fplendeva in mille raggi il cielo;
Ma quefte faci or fue fon ombre e fumi,
O de' gran lumi miei, baftardi lumi,
Il ciel che che fi fia faper non voglio,
Che che fi fia queft uom' faper non curo,
Troppo oftinato e duro,
E 'l mio forte penfiero,
In moftrarmi implacabile, e fevero,
Contra il ciel, contra l' uom, l' angelo, e Dio.

ATTO TERZO.

SCENA PRIMA.

ADAMO, EVA.

O MIA compagna amata,
O di quefta mia vita
Vero cor, cara vita;
Si frettolofa adunque ali vibrando
Peregrina inceffante
Per ritrovar Adamo,
Solinga andavi errando?
Eccolo; che l'imponi? Parla omai
Tanto indugi? deh chiede; O Dio, che fai?

Star upon ſtar, moon, ſun,
And let his Godhead toil
To re-adorn and re-illume his heav'n;
Since in the end deriſion
Shall prove his works, and all his efforts, vain;
For Lucifer alone was that full light,
Which ſcatter'd radiance o'er the plains of Heav'n.
But theſe his preſent fires are ſhade and ſmoke,
Baſe counterfeits of my more potent beams;
I reck not what he means to make his heav'n;
Nor care I what this creature man may be,
Too obſtinate and firm
Is my undaunted thought
In proving that I am implacable,
'Gainſt heav'n, 'gainſt man, the angels, and their God.

ACT THIRD.

SCENE I.

ADAM and EVE.

O my belov'd companion,
O thou of my exiſtence
The very heart and ſoul,
Haſt thou, with ſuch exceſs of tender haſte,
With ceaſeleſs pilgrimage,
To find again thy Adam
Thus ſolitary wandered?
Behold him, ſpeak, what are thy gentle orders?
Why doſt thou pauſe? O God, what art thou doing?

E V A.

O carissimo Adamo,
O mia scorta, o mio duce
Ch' a rallegrar ch' a solazzar m' induce;
Sol' io te desiava,
E tra sì grati orrori,
Solo te ricercava.

A D A M O.

Poichè ti lice Adamo
(Bellissima compagna)
Del tuo gioir nomar radice, e fonte,
Eva, se 'l venir meco,
Or t' aggrada, mostrarti amica, intendo
Cosa non più veduta;
Cosa sì vaga, che per maraviglia
Inarcherai le ciglia;
Mira, sposa gentile, in quella parte
Di così folta, e verdeggiante selva
Dov' ogni augel s' infelva
La dove appunto quelle due sì bianche
Colombe vanno con aperto volo;
Ivi appunto vedrai (o maraviglia)
Sorger tra molli fiori
Un vivo umore, il qual con torto passo
Sì frettoloso fugge
E fuggendo t' alletta,
Ch' è forza dir; ferma bel rivo, aspetta:
Quindi vago in seguirlo
Tu pur il segui, ed ei come s' avesse

E V E.

Adam, my beft beloved,
My guardian and my guide,
Thou fource of all my comfort, all my joy,
Thee, thee alone I wifh,
And in thefe pleafing horrors
Thee only have I fought.

A D A M.

Since thou may'ft call thy Adam
(Moft beautiful companion)
The fource and happy fountain of thy joy,
Eve; if to walk with me
It now may pleafe thee, I will fhow thee, love,
A fight thou haft not feen,
A fight fo lovely, that in wonder thou
Wilt arch thy graceful brow;
Look thou, my gentle bride, towards that path
Of this fo intricate and verdant grove,
Where fit the birds embower'd;
Juft there, where now, with foft and fnowy
    plumes,
Two focial doves have fpread their wings for flight;
Juft there thou fhalt behold (O pleafing wonder)
Springing amid the flow'rs,
A living ftream, that with a winding courfe
Flies rapidly away,
And as it flies allures,
And tempts you to exclaim, fweet river ftay;
Hence, eager in purfuit,
You follow, and the ftream, as if it had

Brama di fcherzar teco,
Fra mille occulte vie dipinte, erbofe
Anzi note a lui fol celato fugge:
Pofcia quand' egli afcolta,
Che tu t'affliggi, perchè l'hai fmarrito
Alza la chioma àcquofa, e par che dica
A gorgogliar d' un rifo,
Segui pur fegui, il molle paffo mio,
Che fe godi di me, con te fcherz' io;
Così con dolce inganno alfin ti guida
Sin all' eftrema cima
D'un praticel fiorito; ed egli allora,
Con veloce dimora,
Dice : rimanti; addio, già, già, ti lafcio
Poi fi dirupa al baffo
Nè feguirlo potendo umane piante
Forz' è che l'occhio il fegua; e là tu miri
Come gran copia d' acqua in cerchio angufto
Accoglie in cupa, e fruttuofa valle
D' allor cinta, e d'ulive,
Di ciprefli; d' aranci, e d' alti pini;
Il qual limpido umore, ai rai del fole,
Sembra un puro criftallo:
Quind' è che nel bel fondo
Nel criftallin dell' onda
Tralucer miri ricca arena d' oro
Ed un mobile argento
Di cento pefci, e cento:
Quì con note canore,
Candidi cigni alla bell' onda intorno;
Fanno dolce foggiorno,

Defire to fport with you,
Thro' many a florid, many a graffy way,
Well known to him, in foft concealment flies;
But when at length he hears
You are afflicted to have loft his fight
He rears his watry locks, and feems to fay,
Gay with a gurgling fmile,
Follow, ah follow ftill my placid courfe,
If thou art pleafed with me, with thee I fport;
And thus, with fweet deceit, he leads you on
To the extremeft bound
Of a fair flow'ry meadow, then at once,
With quick impediment,
Says, ftop, adieu, for now, yes, now I leave you,
Then down a rock defcends;
There, as no human foot can follow farther,
The eye alone muft follow him, and there,
In little fpace, you fee a mafs of water
Collected in a deep and fruitful vale,
With laurel crowned and olive,
With cyprefs, oranges, and lofty pines;
The limpid water in the fun's bright ray
A perfect cryftal feems;
Hence in its deep recefs,
In the tranflucent wave,
You fee a precious glittering fand of gold,
And bright as moving filver
Innumerable fifh;
Here with melodious notes
The fnowy fwans upon the fhining ftreams
Form their fweet refidence,

E fembran gorgheggiando all' aura dire
Quì fermi il piè chi brama a pien gioire.
Sicchè cara compagna
Meco venir ti caglia.

E V A.

Cosi ben la tua lingua mi fcoperfe
Quel, che moftrarmi afpiri,
Che 'l fugitivo rivo miro fcherzante,
E l' odo mormorante;
Ben anco è vaga quefta parte ov' ora
Facciam grato foggiorno, e qui fors' anco,
Più ch' altrove, biancheggia il vago giglio
E s' invermiglia la nafcente rofa;
Quinci anco rugiadofe,
Son l'erbette minute,
Colorite da' fiori;
Quì le piante frondute
Stendono a gara l' ombre,
S' ergono al ciel pompofe.

A D A M O.

Or al frefco dell' ombre,
Al bel di quefte piante,
Al vezzofo de' prati,
Al dipinto de' fiori,
Al mormorar dell' acque e degli augelli,
Affediamoci lieti.

E V A.

Eccomi affifa,
O come godo in rimirar non folo,

And feem in warbling to the wind to fay,
Here let thofe reft who wifh for perfect joy.
So that, my dear companion,
To walk with me will pleafe thee.

E V E.

So well thy language to my fight has brought
What thou defiredft to fhow me,
I fee thy flying river as it fports,
And hear it as it murmurs :
And beauteous alfo is this fcene where now
Pleas'd we fojourn; and here, perhaps e'en here
The lily whitens with the pureft luftre,
And the rofe reddens with the richeft hue;
Here alfo bath'd in dew,
Plants of minuteft growth
Are painted all with flowers;
Here trees of ampleft leaf
Extend their rival fhades,
And ftately rife to heav'n.

A D A M.

Now by thefe cooling fhades,
The beauty of thefe plants,
By thefe delightful meadows,
Thefe variegated flow'rs,
By the foft mufic of the rills and birds,
Let us fit down in joy.

E V E.

Behold then I am feated;
How I rejoice in viewing, not alone,

Questi fior, queste erbette, e quante piante
Ma l' Adamo, l' Amante.
Tu tu sei quel per cui vezzosi i prati
Più mi sembrano, e cari,
Più coloriti i frutti, e i fonti cari.

A D A M O.

Non pon tanti arrecarmi
Leggiadri fior questi be' campi adorni,
Che vie più vaghi fiori io non rimiri
Nel bel giardin del tuo leggiadro volto;
Datevi pace o fiori,
Non son mendaci i detti,
Voi da rugiade aeree asperse siete,
Voi lieto fate umil' terreno erboso,
Ad un sol fiammeggiar d' acceso sole,
Ma col cader del sol voi pur cadrete.
Ma gli animati fiori,
D' Eva mia cara e bella,
Vansi ogn' ora irrigando,
Dalle calde rugiade,
Ch' ella sparse per gioia,
Il suo fattor lodando,
Ed al rotar di duo' terreni soli,
Nel ciel della sua fronte
S'ergon per non cadere,
Il vago Paradiso
Ornando d'un bel viso.

Thefe flow'rs, thefe herbs, thefe high and grace-
    ful plants.
But Adam, more my lover,
Thou, thou art he by whom the meadows feem
More beautiful to me,
The fruit more blooming, and the ftreams more
    clear.

A D A M.

Thefe decorated fields,
With all their flow'ry tribute, cannot equal
Thofe lovelier flowers that with delight I view
In the fair garden of your beauteous face;
Be pacified, ye flow'rs,
My words are not untrue;
You fhine befprinkl'd with ethereal dew,
You give the humble earth to grow with joy
At one bright fparkle of the blazing fun;
But with the falling fun ye alfo fall :
But thefe more living flow'rs
Of my dear beauteous Eve
Seem frefhen'd every hour
By foft devotion's dew,
That fhe with pleafure fheds,
Praifing her mighty Maker;
And by the rays of two terreftrial funs,
In that pure Heav'n her face,
They rife, and not to fall,
Decking the Paradife
Of an enchanting vifage.

EVA.

Deh non voler Adamo,
Con facondia fonora.
L' orecchio armonizzar, dir Eva, io t' amo;
Troppo s' affida il core
Che sfavilli di puro e fanto ardore;
Or tu ricevi in cambio, o caro amico,
Quefto vermiglio dòn; ben lo conofci,
Queft' è 'l pomo vietato,
Queft' è 'l frutto beato.

ADAMO.

Laffo me, che rimiro? oimè, che fefti,
Rapitrice del pomo,
Da gran fignor vietato?

EVA,

Lunga fora il narrarti
La cagion, che m' induffe
A far preda del pomo. Or bafti ch'io
D' ali impennati al ciel l' acquifto feci.

ADAMO.

Ah non fia vèr, non fia
Ch' a te per effer grato
Mi moftri al cielo ribellante, ingrato,
E' n ubbidire a donna
Difubbidifca al mio Fattore, a Dio.
Dunque pena di morte
Non ti fe per terror le guance fmorte.

E V E.

Dear Adam, do not feek
With tuneful eloquence
To footh my ear by fpeaking of thy love;
The heart is confident
That fondly flames with pure and hallow'd ardor;
In fweet exchange accept, my gentle love,
This vermeil tinctur'd gift; you know it well;
This is the fruit forbidden;
This is the bleffed apple.

A D A M.

Alas! what fee I ! Ah! what haft thou done?
Invader of the fruit
Forbidden by thy God!

E V E.

It would be long to tell
The reafon that induced me
To make this fruit my prey; let it fuffice,
I've gained thee wings to raife thy flight to heav'n.

A D A M.

Ne'er be it true, ah! never,
That to obtain thy favor
I prove to Heav'n rebellious and ungrateful
And to obey a woman
So difobey my Maker and my God.
Then did not death denounc'd
With terror's icy palenefs blanch thy cheek?

EVE.

EVA.

E tu credi fe 'l pomo
Efca foffe di morte,
Che l' aveffe inalzato il gran cultore
Dov' eterna è la vita?
Stimi tu fe d' errore
Cagione foffe il pomo,
Ch' alle luci dell' uomo,
Si pomifero e vago,
Fertileggiar l' aveffe fatto all' aure?
Ah fe cio foffe, ben n' avrebb' ei dato
Cagion d' alto peccato,
Poichè natura impone, ·
(Precettrice fagace)
Che per viver queft' uomo fi pafca e cibi,
E che conforme il bello, il buòno ei creda.

ADAMO.

Se 'l celefte cultore,
Che i bei campi del cielo,
Seminati ha di ftelle,
Fra tante piante fruttofe, e belle
Pofe il vietato pomo;
Il più bello, il più dolce;
Fe per conofcer l' uomo
Sagace offervator di voglia eccelfa,
E del gran meritar per dargli il modo;
Che fol nome di forte avien che acquifti,
Chi fupera fe fteffo, e i proprj affetti:
Ben avria di peccar ragion queft' uomo,
Quando di pochi frutti,

Foffe

EVE.

And think'st thou, if the apple
Were but the fruit of death,
The great Producer would have raised it there,
Where being is eternal;
Think'st thou, that if of error
This fruit - tree were the cause,
In man's delighted eye
So fertile and so fair
He would have form'd it flourishing in air?
Ah! were it so, he would indeed have giv'n
A cause of high offence,
Since nature has ordain'd
(A monitress sagacious)
That to support his being man must eat,
And trust in what looks fair as just and good.

ADAM.

If the celestial tiller,
Who the fair face of heav'n
Has thickly sown with stars,
Amidst so many plants, fruitful and fair,
Placed the forbidden apple,
The fairest and most sweet,
'T was to make proof of man
As a wise keeper of his heav'nly law,
And to afford him scope for high desert;
For he alone may gain the name of brave
Who rules himself, and all his own desires;
Man might, indeed, find some excuse for sin,
If scantily with fruits

Fosse il giardin ricetto,
Ma di tanti e sì dolci egli abondando
Non dovrà l' uomo in bando,
Por celesti commandi.

E V A.

Così dunque tu m' ami?
Ah non sia ver, non sia,
Ch' io ti chiami il mio cor, la vita mia
Da te vuo errar solinga,
Piangendo, e sospirando
E me stessa odiando,
Celarmi ancor dal sole.

A D A M O.

Eva mio dolce amore,
Eva mio spirito, e core,
Deh rasciuga le luci,
Ch' è tutto mio quel pianto,
Che t' irriga la guancia, e innonda il seno.

E V A.

Ahi dolente mio stato,
Io, che cotanto dissi, e feci cotanto,
Ad innalzar quest' uomo,
Sovra d' ogni alto Cielo, or così poco
Egli mi crede ed ama?

A D A M O.

Non ti doler, mia vita,
Troppo quest' alma annoia
Il rimirarti mesta.

This garden were fupplied;
But this abounding in fo many fweets,
Man ought not to renounce
The clear command of heav'n.

E V E.

And is it thus you love me?
Ne'er be it true, ah never,
That I addrefs you as my heart, my life;
From you, alone, I'll wander;
Bath'd in my tears and fighing,
And hating e'en myfelf,
I'll hide me from the fun.

A D A M.

Dear Eve, my fweeteft love,
My fpirit and my heart,
O hafte to dry thine eyes,
For mine are all thefe tears
That bathe thy cheek and ftream upon thy bofom.

E V E.

Ah my unhappy ftate,
I that fo much have faid, fo much have done
To elevate this man
Above the higheft heav'n, and now fo little
Can he or truft or love me.

A D A M.

Ah do not grieve, my life;
Too much it wounds my foul
To fee thee in affliction.

E V A.

So ch' altro non defiri,
Che le lagrime mie, che i miei fofpiri,
Ond' or a' venti, a' mari,
Porgo tributi amari.

A D A M O.

Ahi mi fpezza il core,
Che far deggia non fo; s' io miro il cielo
Sento vagarmi un gielo,
Per l' offe che mi ftrugge,
Vago fol d' offervar precetti eterni:
Se la compagna miro
Piango al fuo pianto, a' fuoi fofpir fofpiro,
E mi ftruggo e m' accoro,
S' ubbidirla rifiuto: il cor amante
Fa ch' al pomo veloce apra la mano.
L' alma nel fen dubbiante
La rifpinge e la chiude;
Mifero Adamo, o quanti
Accampano il tuo cor varii defiri,
Quî per l' un tu fofpiri,
Per l' altro godi, nè faper t' è dato
Se tu farai piegato,
Da fofpiri o da gioia
Dalla donna o da Dio.

E V A.

E pur penfa, e penfando,
Vuol ch' Eva fola in bando,
Ponga d' effer felice,
Nel fublimar queft' uomo,
E pur oimè ho d' ogni altezza il pomo.

E V E.

I know your fole defire
Is to be witnefs to my fighs and tears;
Hence to the winds and feas
I pay this bitter tribute.

A D A M.

Alas, my heart is fplitting!
What can I do? When I look up to heav'n
I feel an icy tremor,
E'en thro' my bones, opprefs me;
Anxious alone to guard the heav'nly precept,
If I furvey my partner,
I fhare her tears and echo back her fighs;
'T is torture and diftraction
To wound her with refufal : my kind heart
Would teach my op'ning hand to feize the apple,
But in my doubtful breaft
My fpirit bids it clofe :
Adam, thou wretch, how many
Various defires befiege thy trembling heart;
One prompts thee now to figh,
Another to rejoice, nor canft thou know
Which fhall incline thee moft,
Or fighs or joyous favor
From woman or from God.

E V E.

Yet he reflects and wifhes
That Eve fhould now forfake
Her hope of being happy
In elevating man,
E'en while I hold the fruit of exaltation.

A D A M O.

Muti sì, ma eloquenti,
Sono i tuo' sguardi amica,
Oimè quanto chiedete,
Quanto, quanto ottenete,
Pria, che parli la lingua, il cor conceda,
Occhi soli dell' alma,
Più il bel ciel della fronte
Non sia che tenebrate;
Tornate oimè tornate;
A fugar a irraggiar guancia nembosa;
Alza, alza, la fronte,
Da quella massa d' or, che 'l volto inchioma
Da que' raggi di sole
Bei legami del cor, lampo degli occhi
Fa che la chioma bella,
Oggi leve e vagante
La portin l' aure, e si discopra il viso
Della gloria d' un cor bel paradiso
Mi dispongo ubbidirti,
Sono imperi i tuoi preghi,
Sù, sù, negli occhi e nelle labbra intanto,
Fa balenar il riso, asciuga il pianto.

E V A.

Deh miscredente Adamo,
Ricevitor cortese
Fati omai di bel frutto,
Corri, corri oggimai, tocchi la mano,
D' esca beante il fortunato segno.

A D A M.

Tho' mute yet eloquent
Are all your looks, my love;
Alas, whate'er you afk
You 're certain to obtain,
And my heart grants before your tongue can fpeak:
Eyes that to me are funs,
The heav'n of that fweet face,
No more, no more obfcure,
Return, alas, return
To fcatter radiance o'er that cloudy cheek:
Lift up, O lift thy brow
From that foft mafs of gold that curls around it,
Locks like the folar rays,
Chains to my heart, and lightning to my eyes,
O let thy lovely treffes,
Now light and unconfined,
Sport in the air, and all thy face difclofe
That paradife that fpeaks a heart divine.
I yield thee full obedience;
Thy prayers are all commands;
Dry, dry thy ftreaming eyes, and on thy lips
Let tender fmiles like harmlefs light'ning play.

E V E.

Ah mifbelieving Adam,
Be now a kind receiver
Of this delightful fruit;
Haften, now haften to extend thy hand
To prefs this banquet of beatitude.

A D A M O.

Dolcissima compagna
Mira il caro amatore
Scacciali omai dal core
Le sirti d' aspro duolo, a lui volgendo
Di caro polo desiderate stelle:
Scoprimi il vago pomo
Che tra fior, che tra frondi
(Accorta involatrice) a me nascondi.

E V A.

Eccoti Adamo il pomo:
Che sai dir? lo gustai, nè son già morta,
Ah che viver dovrassi
Anzi farci nel ciel simili a Dio;
Ma pria convien, che 'l pomo
Tutto fra noi si gusti,
Indi poscia gustato
A bel trono di rai, trono stellato,
Ne condurran gli angeli lieti a volo.

A D A M O.

Dammi il frutto rapito
Rapitrice cortese,
Dammi il frutto gradito;
S' ubbidisca a chi tanto,
Per farmi un Dio ha faticato e pianto
Oimè lasso, che, feci?
Quale mi scende al cor acuta spina
Di subitano duolo?

A D A M.

O my moſt ſweet companion,
Behold thy ardent lover
Now baniſh from his heart
The whirlpool of affliction, turn'd to him
His deareſt guide, his radiant polar ſtar:
Show me that lovely apple,
Which, 'midſt thy flow'rs and fruits,
Ingenious plunderer, thou hid'ſt from me.

E V E.

Adam, behold the apple:
What ſay'ſt thou? I have taſted, and yet live.
Ah, 't will enſure our lives,
And make us equal to our God in heav'n;
But firſt the fruit entire
We muſt between us eat,
And when we have enjoyed it,
Then to a radiant throne, a throne of ſtars,
Exulting angels will direct our flight.

A D A M.

Give me the pilfer'd fruit,
Thou courteous pilferer,
Give me the fruit that charms thee,
And let me yield to her,
Who to make me a god, has toiled and wept.
Alas! what have I done!
How ſharp a thorn is piercing in my heart
With inſtantaneous anguiſh;

Oimè qual mi fommerge
Vafto ocean di pianto?

E V A.

Laffo me, che rimiro?
O conofcenza acerba, o vifta nova,
Il tutto s'arma al precipizio umano.

A D A M O.

Ahi cara libertade ove fe' gita?

E V A.

O cara libertade, o fier fervaggio.

A D A M O.

E quefto è 'l dolce frutto,
Cagion di tanto amaro?
Dimmi, perchè tradirmi?
Perchè del ciel privarmi?
Deh pirchè mi traefti
Dallo ftato innocente
Dove lieto i' godea vita felice?
Perchè foggetto farmi,
Di morte alle crud' armi
   u pur, ch' eri mia vita.

E V A.

Fui cieca talpa al bene,
Fui troppo occhiuta al male,
Fui d' Adamo nemica,
Fui contro Dio rubella;

How am I overwhelm'd
In a vaſt flood of tears.

E V E.

Alas ! what do I ſee?
Oh bitter knowledge, unexpeĉed ſight !
All is prepared ſor human·miſery.

A D A M.

O precious liberty, where art thou fled?

E V E.

O precious liberty ! O dire enthralment !

A D A M.

Is this the fruit ſo ſweet,
The ſource of ſo much bitter ?
Say, why would'ſt thou betray me?
Ah why of heav'n deprive me ?
Why make me forfeit thus
My ſtate of innocence,
Where cheerful I enjoy a blifsful life?
Why make me thus a ſlave
To the fierce arms of death,
Thou whom I deemed my life ?

E V E.

I have been blind to good,
Quick-ſighted but to evil,
An enemy to Adam,
A rebel to my God;

E per oſar d'alzarmi,
Alle porte del cielo,
Alle ſoglie cadei del baſſo inferno.

A D A M O.

Ahi qual dardo divin mi ſembra il cielo,
Rotar di fiamme acceſo?

E V A.

Ahi qual flagello
Laſſa mene ſovraſta? Oimè ſon nuda,
E con Adamo i' parlo?

A D A M O.

Nudo ſon? Chi mi cela? io parto.

E V A.

Io fuggo.　　　　　　　　　　　　*Exeunt.*

For daring to exalt me
To the high gates of heav'n,
I fall prefumptuous to the depths of hell.

A D A M.

Alas, what dart divine appears in heav'n,
Blazing with circling flame?

E V E.

What punifhment,
Wretch that I am, hangs o'er me? Am I naked,
And fpeaking ftill to Adam?

A D A M.

Am I too naked? Shelter, hence.

E V E,

I fly.   *Exeunt.*

ANALYSIS of the DRAMA

ENTITLED,

La Scena Tragica d' ADAMO ed EVA.

DA TROILO LANCETTA BENACENSE.

ACT THE FIRST.

SCENE 1.

GOD

COMMEMORATES his creation of the heavens, the earth, and the water—determines to make man—gives him vital spirit, and admonishes him to revere his maker, and live innocent.

SCENE 2.

RAPHAEL, MICHAEL, GABRIEL, and ANGELS.

Raphael praises the works of God—the other angels follow his example, particularly in regard to man.

SCENE 3.

GOD and ADAM.

God gives paradise to Adam to hold as a fief —forbids him to touch the apple—Adam promises obedience.

S C E N E 4.

A D A M

Acknowledges the beneficence of God, and retires to repose in the shade.

End of the First Act.

A C T the S E C O N D.

S C E N E 1.

G O D and A D A M.

G OD resolves to form a companion for Adam, and does so while Adam is sleeping—he then awakes Adam, and presenting to him his new associate, blesses them both; then leaves them, recommending obedience to his commands.

S C E N E 2.

A D A M and E V E.

Adam receives Eve as his wife—praises her, and entreats her to join with him in revering and obeying God—she promises submission to his will, and entreats his instruction—he tells her the prohibition, and enlarges on the beauties of Paradise —on his speaking of flocks, she desires to see them, and he departs to show her the various animals.

S C E N E 3.

L U C I F E R, B E L I A L, S A T A N.

Lucifer laments his expulsion from heaven, and meditates revenge against man—the other demons relate the caufe of their expulfion, and ftimulate Lucifer to the revenge he meditates— he refolves to employ the Serpent.

S C E N E 4.

The Serpent, Eve, Lucifer.

The Serpent queftions Eve—derides her fear and her obedience—tempts her to tafte the apple —fhe expreffes her eagernefs to do fo—the Serpent exults in the profpect of her perdition— Lucifer (who feems to remain as a feparate perfon from the Serpent) expreffes alfo his exultation, and fteps afide to liften to a dialogue between Adam and Eve.

S C E N E 5.

Eve, Adam.

Eve declares her refolution to tafte the apple, and prefent it to her hufband—fhe taftes it, and expreffes unufual hope and animation—fhe fays the Serpent has not deceived her—fhe feels no fign of death, and prefents the fruit to her hufband —he reproves her—fhe perfifts in preffing him to eat—he complies—declares the fruit fweet, but begins to tremble at his own nakednefs—he repents, and expreffes his remorfe and terror— Eve propofes to form a covering of leaves—they retire to hide themfelves in foliage.

End of the Second Act.

ACT

ACT the THIRD.

SCENE 1.

LUCIFER, BELIAL, SATAN.

LUCIFER exults in his fuccefs, and the other demons applaud him.

SCENE 2.

RAPHAEL, MICHAEL, GABRIEL.

Thefe good fpirits lament the fall, and retire with awe on the appearance of God.

SCENE 3.

GOD, EVE, ADAM.

God calls on Adam—he appears and laments his nakednefs—God interrogates him concerning the tree—he confeffes his offence, and accufes Eve—fhe blames the Serpent—God pronounces his malediction, and fends them from his préfence.

SCENE 4.

RAPHAEL, EVE, and ADAM.

Raphael bids them depart from Paradife—Adam laments his deftiny—Raphael perfifts in driving them rather harfhly from the garden—Adam begs that his innocent children may not fuffer for the fault of their mother — Raphael replies, that not only his children, but all his

race, muft fuffer, and continues to drive them
from the garden —Adam obeys—Eve laments,
but foon comforts Adam—he at length departs,
animating himfelf with the idea, that to an intrepid heart every region is a home.

S C E N E 5.

A Cherub,

Moralizing on the creation and fall of Adam,
concludes the third and laft act.

F I N I S.